Prieta
Is
Dreaming

Praise for *Prieta Is Dreaming*

"With *Prieta Is Dreaming*, Gloria Anzaldúa, whose words guided a generation of girls into womanhood, reminds us of what cemented her into the Latino Canon in the first place. Here she's given us a Chicana Odyssey—an epic of Prieta's adventures into nepantla and coming back asserting a more powerful version of herself. Rich, immersive, and profound, this collection records the voices of Prieta's childhood, of her growth into queer womanhood, of her dreams and her nightmares, helping us all feel less alone. Reaching out with a gentle ancestral hand across space and time, Anzaldúa posthumously mothers us with her guiding intelligence."

— Xochitl Gonzalez, author of *Olga Dies Dreaming*

"There is a particular kind of pain in reading *Prieta Is Dreaming*—knowing that Gloria Anzaldúa did not live long enough to finalize these stories. Anzaldúa's voice is as fearlessly honest and vulnerable here as it has ever been. 'The sky and the night and the stars come into my body,' she writes, inviting the perception of other worlds to begin the transformative work of 'reorienting her mind, rearranging the cells of her body, remapping the nerves and synapses.' These are stories from the borderlands, achingly familiar to all of us who take our borders everywhere we go."

— ire'ne lara silva, author of
flesh to bone and *the light of your body*

"In *Prieta Is Dreaming*, Prieta, in all of her facets, guides readers through nepantla and ontological shifts, magnificently displaying life on the borderlands. Through these formidable cuentos/testimonios/autohistorias we (time) travel with them to the montes, ranchitos, and beaches of el valle de tejas as Anzaldúa's Prieta reveals previously suppressed epistemologies under the astute, loving curation by Anzaldúa scholars Zaytoun, Keating, and Bost. This significant collection is required reading for all who dwell en los mundos zurdos."

— Sonia Saldívar-Hull, author of *Feminism on the Border:
Chicana Gender Politics and Literature*

"Even science fiction has elements of autobiography. That is putting it mildly. Here is a collection of writings that shape-shift our banal distinctions between imagination and reality. Here are fusions of fact and fiction, of experience and experiment, works of autohistoria, as Gloria Anzaldúa so beautifully crafted them. Be prepared to be changed by an encounter with these stories, which are not just stories."

— Jeffrey J. Kripal, author of *How to Think Impossibly:
About Souls, UFOs, Time, Belief, and Everything Else*

Prieta Is *Dreaming*

a cuentos-novela

Gloria E. Anzaldúa

EDITED BY **Kelli D. Zaytoun,**
AnaLouise Keating,
AND **Suzanne Bost**

SUNY
PRESS

Published by State University of New York Press, Albany

EU GPSR Authorised Representative:
Logos Europe, 9 rue Nicolas Poussin, 17000, La Rochelle, France
contact@logoseurope.eu

For information, contact State University of New York Press, Albany, NY
www.sunypress.edu

Library of Congress Cataloging-in-Publication Data

Names: Anzaldúa, Gloria, author. | Zaytoun, Kelli D., 1964– editor. | Keating, AnaLouise, 1961– editor. | Bost, Suzanne, editor.
Title: Prieta is dreaming : a cuentos-novela / Gloria Anzaldúa ; edited by Kelli D. Zaytoun, AnaLouise Keating, Suzanne Bost.
Description: Albany : State University of New York Press, [2025]. | Includes bibliographical references.
Identifiers: LCCN 2025013336 | ISBN 9798855804546 (hardcover : alk. paper) | ISBN 9798855804560 (ebook) | ISBN 9798855804553 (pbk. : alk. paper)
Subjects: LCGFT: Linked stories
Classification: LCC PS3551.N95 P75 2025 | DDC 813/.54—dc23/eng/20250505
LC record available at https://lccn.loc.gov/2025013336

I dedicate this book a la memoria de mis mamagrandes,

Eloisa Flórez Anzaldúa y Ramona Dávila García.

Estas historias are for you mis muertos, beloved dead.

Contents

Part Three: University Life

Part Four: Becoming Chamana

Editors' Introduction to
Prieta Is Dreaming: A Cuentos-novela

Kelli D. Zaytoun, AnaLouise Keating,
and Suzanne Bost

I'm very fond of this little girl "Prietita," because that was
my nickname when I was growing up. I'm trying to build a
case on what I call autohistoria, which is a combination of
actual lived personal experience, actual live historical events of
a culture, but using a kind of narrative frame (fictionalizing).
The group of stories I'm working on now are combining
theory and experience. I decided to name at least one of the
characters in every story "Prieta," so that I would be basically
telling the reader that when a writer writes, regardless of
whether it's fiction or an autobiography, they're all the same.
Even science fiction and detective stories have elements of
an autobiography. That is why it's not possible to distinguish
between the two styles of writing. The fictional and the factual
exist in gradations.

—Gloria E. Anzaldúa, interview with
Kate McCafferty (1989)

A versatile, award-winning writer, Gloria Evangelina Anzaldúa
(1942–2004) is best known for *Borderlands / La Frontera: The New
Mestiza* (1987), a genre-breaking, code-switching hybrid of poetry
and prose that put Anzaldúa at the forefront of many significant
theoretical developments, including queer theory, border theory,

1

and theories of hybridity. As suggested by the above epigraph, she was fascinated by questions of genre. Anzaldúa's published works include essays, short stories, two bilingual children's books, and poetry, as well as the following edited works: *This Bridge Called My Back: Writings by Radical Women of Color* (1981), a groundbreaking collection of essays, poetry, and letters coedited with Cherríe Moraga and widely recognized by scholars as a premier feminist text; *Making Face, Making Soul / Haciendo Caras: Creative and Critical Perspectives by Feminists of Color* (1990), a multi-genre edited collection of feminist theorizing by self-identified women of color; *Interviews / Entrevistas* (2000), a memoir-like volume of her interviews; and *this bridge we call home: radical visions for transformation* (2002), a multi-genre coedited transcultural collection that calls for and enacts new modes of feminist/womanist theorizing, social justice movements, and spiritual activism. Her posthumous publications include *The Gloria Anzaldúa Reader* and *Light in the Dark / Luz en lo oscuro: Rewriting Identity, Spirituality, Reality*.

Born in the Rio Grande Valley of South Texas to Urbano and Amelia Anzaldúa, sixth-generation Mexican American rancher-farmers, Gloria Anzaldúa was the oldest of four children. Although her family did not have a lot of money and, even as a child, Anzaldúa took on many responsibilities at home, she enjoyed a rich childhood, filled with loving parents and extended family. The young Anzaldúa was immersed in a magical world of words, and she loved stories—both listening to familial stories and making up stories of her own to share with her sister at night, as they lay in their shared bed. Spending time with her curandera grandmother and the South Tejas land—or what Anzaldúa lovingly referred to as "el monte"—deeply influenced her worldview and taught her that reality extended beyond the human-centered, three-dimensional concrete reality. As she writes in an unpublished autobiographical essay, "I also belong to a landscape essential to my survival, one that is carved into my very bones. I was a thin sun-baked child playing in the monte who believed in the magic power of words. A word once spoken affected the world, could change things." These joyful childhood dimensions coexisted with hardships beyond

Anzaldúa's control, beginning with a rare hormonal condition that led to early puberty at the age of six, when she shot up to her adult height of four feet eleven inches. Marked as physically different from her peers, Anzaldúa's sense of difference was exacerbated by her experiences as a young Mexican American, Spanish-speaking girl in a racist public school system, where she was punished in prekindergarten for not knowing English. A voracious learner, Anzaldúa defied the low expectations of her Anglo teachers and excelled in school, obtaining a bachelor's degree, a master's degree, and a posthumously awarded doctoral degree. Anzaldúa weaves these personal experiences into her Prieta stories—complicating, expanding, and, in additional ways, rewriting her biographical experiences.

While Anzaldúa is most recognized as a nonfiction writer, theorist, and poet, she had a long-standing interest in fiction and was writing short stories and novels from the 1970s until her death. She drafted and revised dozens of short stories but published relatively few during her lifetime. She was, however, in the final stages of preparing what she fondly called her "Prieta stories," a manuscript that interweaves autobiography with history, theory, and fiction. During the decades she spent drafting and revising, the stories underwent many organizational changes and the manuscript had several titles, including "Los Ensueños de La Prieta," "La Prieta Caught/Suspended in Between Realities," "La Prieta on the Dreamside," "La Prieta is Dreaming," and finally, "Prieta Is Dreaming." Anzaldúa's relentless revision practices were complicated and eventually cut short by personal issues, ranging from financial pressures to the health crises that, ultimately, led to her untimely death.

Prieta Is Dreaming is an edited manuscript of Anzaldúa's Prieta stories; it includes nineteen interconnected chapters, divided into four parts, that follow Prieta from childhood to adulthood. Five of the stories were previously published and then revised *after* publication, consistent with the fluidity of Anzaldúa's writing process. Perhaps not surprisingly, this project, like so much of Anzaldúa's other work, blurs genres and languages. As Anzaldúa tells Kate

McCafferty, she put some of herself into each story she wrote, even the science fiction. The fragmented novela en cuentos method she uses in *Prieta* defies linear development and allows the collection to be more open-ended, inclusive, and sometimes contradictory. In *Interviews / Entrevistas*, she tells AnaLouise Keating, "I have to have a central metaphor like la Llorona or la Prieta. Within that central metaphor are these concepts, like working with the interface between different realities—nepantla space." *Prieta* embodies this principle: Each cuento interfaces with the others and, at the same time, emerges from its own distinct reality. Likewise, Prieta herself is somewhat different across the stories, as is reflected in the protagonist's many name changes: Andrea, Paloma, Quelite, Analise, LP, and many others. As Anzaldúa writes in her 1995 notas, "Las Prietas consist of multiple persons and voices occupying different bodies. The interiors and exteriors of all the Prietas are blurred. They challenge the notions of personal experience by complicating self and fantasy. Las Prietas go through different stages of identity formation. They enact certain central myths of their lives" (Papers, 107.8). Another important character, Prieta's primo Teté, evolves from being a cousin to a close friend and lover.

Although Anzaldúa did not see this book through to publication, she was passionate about completing it. Indeed, from the late 1970s until shortly before her death in 2004, she often prioritized the stories over her dissertation and other time-constrained projects. Her journals and writing notas are filled with ideas and comments about the stories, and she talked about them frequently with her writing comadres and others. In a 1994 interview with Carmen Abrego, Anzaldúa described *Prieta* as a book in progress that expands upon her essay "La Prieta," published thirteen years earlier in *This Bridge Called My Back*. She explains, "In *La Prieta*, I'm problematizing lived reality and represented reality. The boundaries between what really happened and how I represent what's happening in a story are blurred. I'm saying that fiction is selective. Fiction is constructed and fiction is invented. So are some of these experiences" (*Interviews* 224).

As this statement suggests, Anzaldúa's interest in these stories was ontological, epistemological, and aesthetic. "Problematizing" reality makes way for imagination, creativity, and the transformation of reality itself, and *Prieta Is Dreaming* is her most revealing and, perhaps, ingenious work. Anzaldúa aspired to reshape the world through her writing. She invented the genre autohistoria-teoría to capture the blending of reality with story, autobiography with fiction, "raw" material with theoretical frameworks, and literal three-dimensional reality with imaginal and daemonic realities. This original approach to creative work, then, calls on readers to consider Anzaldúa's ontological assumptions, assumptions that frequently challenge consensus reality.

Anzaldúa's commitment to imaginative expression extended to other forms of art: painting, sketching, doodling; images and visions were central to her innovative, multi-layered understanding of the world. Since she was a child, Anzaldúa had a keen sense of her body's expansiveness and porous interconnectedness with the external world, or what she calls "yoga of the body." In a 1983 interview with Christine Weiland, Anzaldúa recalls an early instance of this awareness: "I was maybe three: I was on the floor, reaching to get apples or oranges or something, and I was extending to get them; my body was extending. I had the feeling that I was two or three people. It's an image I use in the novel.[1] It was like looking in a three-way mirror or seeing three parts of myself but all con- nected. But it wasn't me, it was almost like I could see sheaths. It was all the same body, but not in one place" (*Interviews* 97). She goes on to explain that this proprioceptive sense was with her from an early age. These apparently impossible acts, such as "walking through the wall," taught her that body and spirit were one, that leaving the physical body, like during sleep, wasn't really *leaving* the body at all but, rather, was an expansion of it, a "return of the spirit" (*Interviews* 99). Adding to the acute sense of expansiveness

---

1. She is probably referring to *Prieta Is Dreaming* here.

that had been with her since a child, Anzaldúa briefly experimented with hallucinogens and regularly used meditation exercises to stretch her own perceptive frameworks. She writes quite a bit about her own shifting consciousness and her changing sense of selfhood.

Throughout *Prieta*, Anzaldúa generously imbues her protagonist(s) with supernatural powers to expand their bodies in ways that most would deem fantasy. Yet these feats were no less real for Anzaldúa than what others define as ordinary "reality." We see this embodied fluidity throughout the Prieta stories: in Prieta's bilocation, her ability to sit, simultaneously, on a fence and in a tree; in LP's experience reading the mysterious book that transports her through walls and moves her from one spatial location to another; and in Prieta's shapeshifting encounters with the jaguar in "La Werejaguar." These radical understandings of shared matter, shapeshifting, and "yoga of the body" resonate with recent studies of quantum realities, nonlocality, bilocation, and supernatural modes of existence. Anzaldúa's experiences point to crucial investigations for the future, changing how we think about not just Anzaldúa's writing but also ourselves and our world(s). But reader beware: *Prieta Is Dreaming* is neither a comprehensive guidebook into the paranormal nor instructions into becoming a curandera; it is, rather, an invitation to step out of consensus reality and begin our own explorations into the uncanny.

In Chapter Six of *Borderlands*, "Tlilli Tlapalli: The Path of Red and Black Ink," Anzaldúa describes the book as having "a mind of its own": "It is a rebellious, willful entity, a precocious girl-child forced to grow up too quickly, rough, unyielding, with pieces of feather sticking out here and there, fur, twigs, clay" (66–67). And indeed, her writing was in many ways beyond her control, a compulsion and synergistic act of transformation. Prieta, imperfect and bold, sometimes fragmented and sometimes full—of herself and the life all around her—fits this description of her writing as well. Sometimes these narratives seem truncated and at other times lush. Given that Anzaldúa was a meticulous, thoughtful writer who spent years revising these cuentos and curating her table of contents, readers must consider the purposefulness of her prose style and chapter organization. We have honored her personal style and authorial decisions, despite the intense vulnerability of her choices.

Anzaldúa's storytelling begins with the protagonist(s) themselves, Prieta, who both is and is not a singular individual throughout the text. Not only does Prieta literally shape-change, but her various encounters reflect different (sometimes even incoherent) aspects of her complex self/selves. The Prietas in Part Two, for instance, are more assertive and graphic in displays of sexuality than most of the cuento-novela's Prietas and other characters in Anzaldúa's work. (There are few overt depictions of sexuality in Anzaldúa's published works, as critics have observed.) The Prietas in Part Four are more metaphysically inventive: shapeshifting, time-crossing, and polysexual. Anzaldúa's animism and intense physical awareness of interrelatedness ring clearly throughout these later stories, exemplifying the ontological possibilities that pervaded her life and work, possibilities that she invites her readers to explore.

So what are the (dis)connections between Anzaldúa and Prieta? Can we assume that Prieta in these stories *is* Anzaldúa herself? To do so ignores both Anzaldúa's emphasis on the roles of fictionalizing experience and the imaginal force more generally at play in her work. In what ways, if any, are Prieta's experiences and desires identical with those of Anzaldúa; and in what ways, if any, do they diverge? Perhaps Anzaldúa/Prieta is challenging us to read with different eyes, to critically evaluate our conventional perceptions of reality and our ontological truths. When Anzaldúa says, "My job as an artist is to bear witness to what haunts us" (*Light* 10), she refers to the "personal" as well as "societal," and in these stories we see Anzaldúa taking the most risks, exposing some of our deepest, darkest, most vulnerable aspects of being human.

The Prieta stories are heterogeneous, generative, and, at times, shamanistic—inviting writer, readers, and the characters themselves on a healing journey. As Anzaldúa frequently observed, writing served, in part, as a process of survival and self-invention. The Prieta stories allowed Anzaldúa to investigate some of the deepest aspects of her psyche, animating, for instance, theories like the "Coyolxauhqui imperative," a means "to heal and achieve integration" (*Light* 19). In her interview with Carmen Abrego, Anzaldúa explains that she works through traumatic autobiographical events through the vehicle of a third person, la Prieta: "I've written about being mugged, I've had several near deaths, and I can't get to them because when you're working on the personal it's very hard to dive into the writing. It's painful. You're reliving the pain. So one method I use is to give it to la Prieta/Prietita, an alter ego. I give her this autobiographical experience, I write it out and then later I can change it to the 'I' if I want to" (*Interviews* 223). We might consider that Prieta, Anzaldúa's constant companion, inspired her to lean into the hard, inner work she needed to do to achieve her writing goals. For the first time—with the publication of these stories—Prieta is honored for her crucial role in Anzaldúa's creative process, one that necessitates change, recovery, and transformation of self and world.

Healing, for Anzaldúa, involves a deep dive into her psyche as well as a projection outward to other aspects of herself. She views third-person characters, like the protagonist from the story "El Paisano Is a Bird of Good Omen," as a particular Prieta with an ability to regulate her own perceptions (*Interviews* 285). In the process of writing, as she lends her pain to Prieta, Anzaldúa channels the strength to rewrite and remake her realities and potentially the realities of others who have also experienced rejection, trauma, and other forms of violence. In so doing, she enacts the Coyolxauhqui imperative—an "ongoing process" with no final conclusion: "There is never any resolution, just the process of healing" (*Light* 20). Perhaps, then, it's no surprise that Anzaldúa was able to complete other works she started much later while *Prieta Is Dreaming* remained in progress until her death. Anzaldúa returned to Prieta, as a creative methodology and experimental muse, again and again to tell her personal story and remake reality. With this complex, recursive process in mind, we carefully examined Anzaldúa's drafts to offer the most recent versions of the stories (at the time of her death) but with the caveat that, as with all Anzaldúa's work, none were "finished" or even meant to be so. Certainly, their powers are endless and ongoing, unbounded by the period of their creation, not unlike Prieta herself.

Prieta experiences a sense of self that both is and is not tied to time, space, or society. Though the stories are, for the most part, grounded solidly in South Texas, where Prieta is born and raised, she also experiences non-ordinary events—shamanistic or paranormal—in which different realities converge. These ontological shifts are epistemological, and Prieta undergoes radical changes in the way she sees the world, accessing hidden and forbidden knowledges. A coming-to-consciousness results in changes in identity, and changes in identity correspond with ontological shifts. Walking in the cracks between the worlds exposes the tears in the weavings of conventional reality. As la Prieta experiences the slippage between society's boundaries and her own boundlessness, a rupture, departure, and passage desde un mundo al otro occurs. As Anzaldúa writes in a draft of her (unpublished) introduction to *Prieta*: "This book is about transformation and metamorphosis, about the relation between nature and culture, between humans and animals. The stories interweave the surreal, unconscious subreality of the inner world of thought, fantasy, and dream and the world of the spirit with the everyday life. All converge at the liminal space I call nepantla, the interface space between all the worlds." As la Prieta grows from childhood to adulthood, we witness her development as a writer, her shifting sexuality, and her metaphysical transformations as she falls into cracks between realities. Anzaldúa's writing style—not just shifting between languages and genres but also her performative use of blank space and section divisions—highlights these different realities.

Anzaldúa developed these stories with a broad and inclusive audience in mind. She wanted the stories to be accessible and enjoyable to a wide range of readers, but the stories she tells are not always comforting or affirming. This book expands norms and expectations, going beyond the literary experiments of other contemporary writers. More than a coming-of-age narrative, these stories present multiple kinds of becoming.

Scholars will discover that *Prieta* can be approached using a variety of interpretative lenses. There are many possible frameworks to apply—from the works of Karl Marx, Carl Jung, and James Hillman to contemporary theories of gender and sexuality;

queer studies; trans studies; ethnic studies; feminism; woman-ism; new materialisms; ecocriticism; postcolonial, decolonial, and Indigenous studies; interspecies relations; speculative worlds, and more. Perhaps, in conversation with the stories and as they come to know Anzaldúa as a fiction writer, readers will develop additional interpretive approaches. Anzaldúa's work calls for new ways of reading and thinking. For this reason, we invite readers to make their own way through these fascinating tales of selfhood, identity, love, loss, and more.

Not only is it remarkable to have a nearly completed unpub-lished fiction manuscript authored by Gloria Anzaldúa—arguably the best-known Chicana writer of all time—but the stories are also genuinely compelling to read. They return to familiar subjects in her obra and foresee current trends in literary criticism and literary writing. As cuentos-novela and autohistoria-teoría, *Prieta* resonates with the genres of both the novel-in-stories and auto-theory. Not surprisingly, given Anzaldúa's concerns in her other writings with complex relationships to difference, the Prieta stories attend thoughtfully to differences in class, color, language, and nationality. While her best-known works, particularly the essays in *Borderlands / La Frontera*, focus largely on race and culture (her land-based Chicana identity is never questioned from the begin-ning), sexuality is more central in the Prieta stories, which focus on intimate scenes and places Anzaldúa called home (especially el Valle del Rio Grande).

Prieta Is Dreaming also offers important insights into Anzaldúa's theories of identity. While her published writings from the 1980s revolve around the figure of, and her identification as, "Chicana lesbian," her later writings move away from conventional identity politics toward more metaphysical and planetary connections. Working with myth and story, with image and imagination, gave her an opportunity to do things she hadn't done in her more overtly political writings. Even as she was creating and conform-ing to a Chicana lesbian identity in her published work, she was challenging and expanding these same categories in and through her stories. This text is, in many ways, the culmination of her life's work. Unfortunately, due to extensive health problems in the last few years of her life, she was unable to see it through to publication. Readers in turn have had only a partial picture of her creative and theoretical vision.

To the extent that Prieta's life resonates with Anzaldúa's own, we can see these stories following a generally chronological and autobiographical order. However, in the later stories she adopts a recursive approach. In a January 1983 letter to her close friend Randy Conner, Anzaldúa shares her vision for the stories' chronology: "I want to start say in 1983 and then dip back and forth to the past or future and return to the present, to the past . . . , past-present, future-present, future-future. That would allow me to explore that idea that all time (past and future) exists now rather than in linear chronology." Though Anzaldúa did not fully adhere to this vision, the stories have much resonance and repetition—a dipping back and forth among landscapes, themes, issues—across them, suggesting a radical connectedness across time periods.

Each story in *Prieta* includes its own glossary, in which Anzaldúa translated Spanish terms into English, but this was not always her practice. As *Borderlands* makes clear, she resisted the implication that *she* had to accommodate the dominant culture's language and often invites non-Spanish readers to perform acts of translation. The fact that she created these glossaries underscores her desire that *Prieta Is Dreaming* be accessible to a broad audience.

Story Overviews

Arguably the most autobiographical section, Part One focuses on Prieta's childhood in South Texas. Each piece offers a turning point of sorts as Prieta tests various boundaries and experiences life-changing threshold events. In Chapter One, "The Second Heart / El segundo corazón," we meet the young Prietita and see, through her five-year-old eyes, an early sexual awakening as she experiences an orgasm while riding a merry-go-round. In Chapter Two, "Out of the Corner of the Eye / De reojo," Prietita boldly confronts a fierce, supernatural animal (possibly her nagual, or spirit guide) while playing in the woods and is transformed through the encounter. In Chapter Three, "In the Mouth of the Sea / En el hocico del mar," Prieta experiences a near-drowning as she defies her parents and wades out too deeply into the ocean. And in Chapter Four, "People Should Not Die in June in South Texas," Prieta grapples with the unexpected, violent death of her father as she relives his death and assists in funeral preparations. In this section, readers watch Prieta grow from a young child to a teen, experiencing her first sexual and spiritual awakenings, as well as her first encounters with death. The stories vividly depict the landscape and characters, offering intimate details about Prieta's relationship to her parents and her self-reflective growth. Readers familiar with Anzaldúa's work will find similarities between these stories and Anzaldúa's narration of personal experiences.

The stories in Part Two offer the most overt representations of sexuality in all of Anzaldúa's obra, and through these stories we see her expanding her explorations of gender identities and desire. In "Como Quelite" Prieta hangs out with her "vatos," and together they gaze at the legs of the beautiful Marielena when she walks by. These stories depict Prieta as a macha: she gets her hair styled like the vatos' crew cuts, and she feels good about her muscles and wide shoulders. Prieta persuades Marielena that she is a better lover than her cousin Teté, but Marielena's internalized homophobia keeps her from engaging in a reciprocal sexual relationship with Prieta. Is Anzaldúa problematizing gender roles, or is she participating in and thereby reinforcing binaries? The answer might be "both." In contemporary terms, we might view Prieta as transgender, but Anzaldúa blurs the distinction between sex and gender by making corporeality itself fluid. "Mita' y mita'," a theory of corporeal multiplicity that Anzaldúa later expanded in *Borderlands*, suggests that "half and halfs" fluidly embody both maleness and femaleness. Prieta's developing sexuality in these stories is also intertwined with the more-than-human world: the ranches and fields she works in, the plants she tends to, and the landscape she's grown up with. (The orange grove in "Eating the Fruit / Comiendo del árbol como Xochiquetzal" is a particularly erotic space.) At the end of this section, in "El Paisano Is a Bird of Good Omen," Anzaldúa experiments with la facultad (a theory of heightened sense perception she developed in *Borderlands* and expanded in *Light in the Dark*), shapeshifting, and cracks between worlds as, in part, a way to evade heteronormative marriage and domesticity.

The stories in Part Three take place at least partially beyond South Texas—in northern and central regions of the state—and introduce readers to Prieta's experiences as a university student, emphasizing her sexual growth and the barriers she faces as she comes into her young adult identity. These stories focus on pivotal moments like Prieta's first sexual experience with a male partner, her first mugging and violent assault, and her interactions with queer comrades and potential lovers. Although Prieta experiences isolation, confusion, disappointment, and pain, she also recognizes that "[s]he couldn't keep leading with her wounds" and stubbornly finds ways to push against the violations and her fears, most importantly by writing ("The Crack Between the Worlds"). "In the Shadow of la Chingada [or Smoking Mirror]" takes readers to la Prieta's dorm room, where she experiences heterosexual intercourse for the first time with her college boyfriend, a scene of intense, raw physical closeness yet emotional distance, which foreshadows the relationship between the two that follows. In "The Crack Between the Worlds" Prieta shares a terrifying experience of being attacked on a routine walk from campus, one in which she fights back, escapes, sees her attacker's arrest for the crime, and comes face-to-face with her attacker as she rides in the police car with him. As the story closes the reader gets a sense of the post-traumatic stress that follows. In "Becoming luciérnaga / Swallowing fireflies / Tragando luciérnagas" Prieta meets and develops a friendship with a woman who is twelve years her senior. However, when Prieta names the erotic feelings between them, the woman cuts her off. Prieta learns to let go yet keeps the light that burns within aglow. "Night of the Lizard / Noche de la lagartija"—originally published in different form as "Puddles" in 1992 in *New Chicana/Chicano Writing*, but substantially more developed here—experiments with the shapeshifter trope that Anzaldúa introduces earlier in this volume and develops throughout her career. Prieta, now a waitress, connects with a customer who leaves two-dollar bills and a puddle behind from his teacup that, when Prieta touches it, turns her finger green. This physical transformation is only the beginning, and Prieta, as "Prieta la lagartija" or "lizard woman," becomes increasingly aware of the world around her.

The stories in Part Four highlight complicated adult relationships that cross sexualities, species, and ontological boundaries, taking Prieta from a heteronormative marriage with a man in "Ghost Trap / Trampa de espanto" to a complex relationship with her male cousin Teté and a mystical shapeshifting jaguar woman in "La Werejaguar in the Woods of the Dream." This section's stories prefigure contemporary currents like trans identities, interspecies relations, timeline jumping, and sacred Indigenous ontologies and epistemologies. In the first story, "She Ate Horses," originally published in *Lesbian Philosophies and Cultures* (1990) and subsequently expanded and revised, Prieta is torn between her commitment to her now female lover and her commitment to her writing (her other lover). Half-immersed in the ocean, Prieta imagines a powerful half-woman, half-mare charging toward her—a symbol of interspecies connection as well as shapeshifting and la Llorona. First published in *The Gloria Anzaldúa Reader* (2009), "Reading LP" blurs ontological realities, calling attention to the physical power of story, the ontological potential in the act of reading, and the expansiveness of the self and body. LP's reading activity facilitates a shapeshifting journey to other three-dimensional worlds that are just as real as her ordinary reality. Revealing Prieta's shadow side, "Like a Crow on the Wing / Como urraca en vuelo" shows readers a broken-hearted Prieta betrayed by a female lover, who left their marriage for another woman. Likening herself to an ugly black crow, Urraca Prieta retells the story of betrayal to an unnamed comadre. "Ghost Trap / Trampa de espanto," first published as "Ghost Trap" in 1990 in Charles Tatum's edited collection *New Chicana/Chicano Writing*, shows Úrsula la Prieta in a heterosexual marriage, trapped there, even after her husband's death. Anzaldúa exhibits her humorous side here as Prieta attempts to get rid of his ghost. "La Werejaguar in the Woods of the Dream" follows Prieta as she explores the cracks between the "real" world and a more expansive metaphysical reality, a world offering cross-species eroticism and new kinds of family. The final story, "Song of the Rattlesnake / Canción de cascabel," is the most overtly autobiographical in this section, giving us an account of Anzaldúa's second near-death experience, triggered by the emergency hysterectomy due to tumors in her fallopian tubes. In the final paragraphs of the story and of the book, Prieta ritualizes this death and rebirth, viewing it as the opening into a new chapter of her life.

We have also included three appendices that offer additional information and insight into *Prieta Is Dreaming*, Anzaldúa's writing process, and the meticulous attention she put into this project: Appendix I, "Instrucciones a la autora," is the draft of a short piece Anzaldúa planned to include at the end of *Prieta*. Appendix 2, "A History of the Stories," offers brief summaries of each cuento's origins and development. Appendix 3, "Anzaldúa's Writing Process," includes portions of several drafts of Chapter Eleven, "The Crack Between the Worlds," to give readers a small taste of her complex, dialogic creative process. We hope these appendices provide additional insights into Prieta, the cuentos, and Anzaldúa's complicated creative process.

It's been an honor to work with Anzaldúa's words. We were as light-handed as we could be in our editing, following Anzaldúa's desires and editorial practices to the best of our ability. Anzaldúa left many versions of each of these stories, and we used the most recent ones we could locate as the basis for final decisions. We struggled with details like the order and placement of translations, the stories that had multiple endings, and notes or questions that Anzaldúa had left unresolved in her most recent drafts. In all cases, our mantra became "What Would Gloria Do?" We included her fragments, her unresolved questions, and her potentially inflammatory content. She was passionate about Prieta; she wanted Prieta's novel-in-stories to be published, and we tried to follow her wishes. We're thrilled that, after all these years, Anzaldúa's Prieta is making her way out in the world, sharing her remarkable journeys with readers. We hope that you enjoy, and are transformed by, the ride.

La Prieta Is Dreaming
genius loci, the Spirit of the Place

The spirits en el aire swirl in the mist
and swoop in through the meshed screen window
The words begin to pulse
from their secret dwelling
and the small inner she
swarms out like a bat to lick the sky
The words slowly unravel like birch bark
curling to the ground
close to the tree she fell from,
Images mark the surfaces of her body
making more scars

She walks down the path through los montes
burrows into that seam
between the worlds that her abuelos called nepantla

alone
suspended between realities
torn this way and that
struggling against the chains of custom
and consensus contrary to the world
without map or guideposts
in times of stress
seeking emotional ballast

She wants to turn her back
on the past, temporarily
find a new way to live in the world

The answer lies in the dark wet woods
The trees sway towards her and whisper
but she's forgotten their language
and their soft sighs disappear into the wind
she can't
can't cross over the boundary
between humans and plants
to hear the story of their own nature
can't talk to the rain

She stands alone,
escaping herself en el monte
only to meet herself
on the path out

They fine-tune her senses
into a different way of knowing
a conocimiento. La Prieta is dreaming
childhood back into being
su pueblo natal, the wind howling alongside los coyotes
las venadas en el monte
and her internal exile from it and other things
her dreams open onto an interior
that converges with an exterior space
her dreams track the line in history
between tradition and transformation
between routine and change
one arm reaching back to the past
the other stretching across the lake
into the horizon
slowly the trees and the lake
move in and live inside her
the urge to connect the discontinuities
to reconcile and integrate
is stronger than her struggle to break out and separate

The monstrous
poised in the shadows
ready to spring out
the demons inside she shuts her eyes to
Possessed by memories and voices
a compulsion of memory
to take the pain and recast it
in the telling
in forms that enhance life
a mass of roles and personal
a vast geography of selves
sliding and grinding one upon the other
like slabs of rock deep under
the crust of the earth insisting
that she herself will construct her identity
never mind society's notions
that she will be
La Prieta the protagonist of
her own cultural narrative
at times the antagonist
the self that she is
formed and unformed
inside and between different realities

Metamorphose
morph into something else
Conocimiento of the uncanny,
of the sacred moments when she experiences
a hidden meaning
in the vision
a watching intelligence all around her,
a guiding intelligence

Part One

Familia

1

The Second Heart / El segundo corazón

Prietita's gaze locked onto the revolving still-life of her parents. Then her black horse took her round the bend and she lost sight of them in the circle of faces. There, among the throng, gray Stetson on his head, hands on his hips, Papi stood slightly behind her mother. Mami's floral skirt flapped around her knees; as the merry-go-round swung by, her eyes tracked Prieta. Then those familiar landmarks, Stetson and floral skirt, disappeared in the sea of South Texas farmers and ranchers.

She wanted to show off to them that she could ride a wooden horse as well as she could uno de veras. El caballo de palo reared, neck arched up into the air. Though she was scared of falling she didn't hold onto the pole or the horse's ears tightly like the other first-grade kids. Up and down, pa' arriba y pa' bajo and around. Her flour sack dress billowed up, baring her legs. She was proud that the black horse held its head high up in the air, its mouth forever opened. Maybe some vaquero had pulled too hard on the reins and the bit had cut into the sides of the horse's mouth.

Unlike the other kids, her family had real horses. They snorted, stamped, and swished their tails and were made of rippling flesh instead of stiff wood. And, unlike wooden horses, they could not be controlled. Keeping a wary eye on them, she stroked and brushed them and sketched them. As she went round and around, she dreamed up a story to tell Dolores, her younger sister, tonight when they went to bed. Había una vez un caballito. One day it broke out of its pen and escaped to freedom, only it got lost.

As el caballito de palo went up and down y alrededor, Prietita rocked back and forth, pressing against the hard saddle with her pelvis. The carousel music played on and on. After a while she lost her papi's Stetson and her mami's floral skirt. She felt her stomach muscles constrict into a ball and drop away. At first she was scared. Then she lost herself in the pulse moving up and down her spine. She heard her mother's voice saying, "No hagas eso." But instead of stopping she rocked harder. She thought she was falling, then she was going up and her body grew feathers and wings and she touched the sky and her body and the sky were one heart y ella descubrió que tenía otro corazón and it too was beating softly, softly between her legs. Tears welled up in her eyes. Slowly her two hearts, like palomas blancas cooing softly, folded their wings and quieted. She wiped the tears from her eyes with the back of her hand.

In her head she heard her mother's voice saying, "Don't! No te atoques allá eso es malo." She answered, "No, Mami, it can't be so bad if it feels so good."

The merry-go-round stopped and she looked around her. Clinging to the horse's neck, she refused to let the attendant unseat her. Maybe he wanted another quarter. Her papi had lots of quarters. When she turned to search for him, Prietita saw her mother eyeing her. She'd been here too long. She got off el caballito and stood on the revolving platform. The carousel music seemed louder and the smell of buttered popcorn made her mouth water.

As she held onto a pole, Prietita again searched for her parents, but again she had lost them in the crowd. Se sentía abandonada, she felt abandoned like an orphan, like when her sister was born and Mami didn't have time to hold and rock her in her arms. There was no one to hold her, but she would hold el caballito negro.

She looked into the open mouth of the black horse. She knew she shouldn't but she wanted to go around and around and let it happen again. She mounted the black horse. And when her other heart started to beat fast, she closed her eyes. When she opened them she looked for her papi y mami. They had vanished again in the crowd. Ahora tenía un secreto. She couldn't tell Mami. She couldn't tell anyone. She felt strangely grown-up, and sad.

Prietita remembered touching allá abajo years ago while her mother had been bathing her.

"Don't touch yourself down there. ¡Niña! No te toques allí . . . ¿M'entiendes? And don't let any pelado touch you down there."

At the time she had been puzzled by her mother's words. Hora ya sabía, now she understood. It made her feel both weak and helpless and strong. She had a sweet secret and it was all hers. From astride her caballo Prietita spotted her mother watching her with Mamagrande's eagle eyes, eyes that she too had inherited, eyes that saw too much. She wanted to tell her, I'm not crying out of fear. But she was afraid. Sí, tenía miedo. Sabía que se había portado mal.

When the dove hearts quieted, Prietita began to rock back and forth. Suddenly Mamí pulled her off. Prietita cast down her eyes.

Her mother said, "Ahora sé por qué te gustan tanto los caballitos."

As they walked away from the carnival, Prietita turned back and looked at the merry-go-round. She caught one last glimpse of the arched neck and the head held high.

That night she turned over and lay on her stomach. Under the covers she saw the horse rear and neigh, heard the doves cooing. They called to her but she was afraid. She felt shame. Maybe if she didn't use her hands it wouldn't be so bad.

She bunched up the covers, rubbed her crotch against the edge of a fold, then stretched out her legs and tightened the muscles as hard as she could until she got her other heart to beat. Lo hizo otra y otra vez. She did it again and again.

That night she told her sister the story of a girl who rode a black horse to the sky.

Translations

como uno de adeveras: like a real one

pa' arriba y pa' bajo: up and down

vaquero: cowboy or wrangler

Había una vez un caballito.: Once there was a little horse.

el caballito de palo: the little wooden horse

y alrededor: and around

No hagas eso.: Don't do that.

descubrio que ella tenía otro corazón: and she discovered that she
    had another heart

palomas blancas: white-wing doves

No te atoques allá, eso es malo.: Don't touch yourself there, that's
    bad.

Se sentía abandonada.: She felt abandoned.

Ahora tenía un secreto.: Now she had a secret.

allá abajo: down below

¡Niña! No te toques allí . . . ¿M'entiendes? No hagas eso, mijita.:
    Child, don't touch yourself there . . . Do you understand?

pelado: some guy

Ahora ya sabía.: And now she knew.

Sí tenía miedo. Sabía que se había portado mal.: She was afraid.
    She knew that she had behaved badly.

Ahora sé por qué te gustan tanto los caballitos.: Now I know why
    you like horses so much.

Lo hizo otra y otra vez.: She did it again and again.

2

Out of the Corner of the Eye /
De reojo

Prietita hears the call of an animal, a deep husky cough ending in a low rumble. The sound resonates through her body like a heartbeat; if night had a heart this is how it would beat. She lies still in her bed staring out the window into the night sky and dark woods, straining toward the sound. But all she hears is the howling of coyotes en el monte. She curls to her side, tucking her fist over her chest and rubbing to ease the ache.

Next morning Prietita walks to the corrals and looks at the woods. Her younger sister, Dolores, asks her why she doesn't hurry up and go with them to play en el montecito.

"I heard this weird sound last night. Some big animal was out there," she tells Dolores.

"You're just making up stories again," Dolores says.

Though she's afraid to go into the woods, she's curious about what made that sound. She hesitates, then charges across the fields, the dogs baying ahead, her cousin Teté and her brother and sister close behind.

They jump over the irrigation ditch parallel to the fence her father built to keep the cattle from wandering into the fields and nibbling on the corn and cotton. El monte de chaparral is inside the fenced circle; outside, the fields radiate like spokes in a wheel.

Just as the dogs are about to scramble under the fence, they yelp, then, tails between their legs, scurry back into the fields.

Prietita looks into the woods. What could have scared them? Her brother y el primo Teté overtake her and step over the barbwire fence. Dolores crawls under it, dirtying her flour sack dress. Prietita places her hands between the barbs and, pulling apart the middle strands, swings over one jean-clad leg then the other, while undulating her upper body across.

She walks through the maze of foot-trails in the thick chaparral, her feet crunching the dry grass. Con ojos de águila she watches the ground for cueros de víbora. She senses some thing watching from deep in the thick granjeno and cactus. A covey of quail rises out of the thicket in a whirring of wings, and her breath hitches. A lizard skitters under a bush. De reojo, out of the corner of her left eye, she sees un correcaminos streak out of sight. A jackrabbit leaps over the brush and disappears.

Feet burning in the powdered dust, she runs from shadow to shadow. A rattlesnake moves lightning fast, leaving a winding track on the sand. Sweat beads on her forehead. As she weaves around the mesquite and prickly pear, peering into the underbrush, she plucks moras from the bushes and plops them into her mouth. The knot in her throat eases. Blackberry juice leaks down her chin. She stops to catch her breath and to stare at the vulture circling slowly above. Algo o alguien se está muriendo. Zapopiles can smell death a hundred miles off.

Like her papi, she searches the sky. ¿Lloverá, lloverá? ¿Quién sabe? Dios dirá. Papi's voice echoes in her ear. El ganado, the cattle, are dropping on the parched earth and not getting up again. In a few weeks their bones will gleam stark white in the sun. They need water now. Oh, please bring the green to the grass.

Prietita walks deeper into the woods until she comes to the lagoon surrounded by mesquite, huizache, y nopales—shriveled now because of the drought. Here, too, in the middle of the woods, is her secret place, a small vaulted room created by a canopy of branches and leaves where she likes to lie on her back and stare through the opening between the trees to the sky, where she watches the shapes of the shadows moving on the ground, the place where she daydreams. No one knows about this place except her grandmother.

She hears Teté call to her and starts back in the direction she has come, walks past her secret place without looking at it in case Teté's watching. She veers off to her left until she comes to the space she and her sister Dolores clear and sweep every day for their juegos. *Alredor de San Miguel, pipiripi de don Pinguel. Mátalo, mátalo que yo no fui, fué Teté. Pegale, pegale, que ella fué . . .*

No sounds, no birds singing, no whirring of wings, no animals scurrying in the underbrush. Not even a tiny breath of wind. Just her heart hammering in her eardrums. Even the trees seem to hold their breath and listen. A smell como azufre drifts in the air, and a different mood, a listening mood, has swept into el monte. A sound she can't identify stops the others who have finally reached her. They crowd behind her, trying to still their labored breathings. Prietita puts her hand over her left ear. The humming sound tightens somewhere in her head.

Out of the corner of her eye Prietita sees the other three break away, turn and run for the fence. Dolores looks back and, seeing her still standing, screams, "Vente."

"Move, Prieta. Run!" yells el primo Teté.

All disappear. Prietita hears them running headlong through the cornfield, hears the dogs way off in the fields.

The humming thickens, falls like a blanket over her. Yet her hearing has never been keener, nor her eyesight as sharp.

Petrified, she stares into the shrubbery and nopales, her eyes probing the edges and tree trunks, seeking out the thing haunting the woods. She is rooted there. Only her eyes move. Ah, so this is how a mouse feels when the shadow of a hawk swoops across the field.

She'll wait the thing out here in the thick bushes and sweltering heat. She looks around, sees a small branch lying on the ground left of her and grabs it. Then she looks for an escape route. The fastest way out of the woods is the way she came in. She waits.

El tiempo pasa.

Something is moving in the chaparral. Ahí, to her left. A light. She tries to swallow, but the saliva dries in her mouth. Blood rushes to her feet. Something shimmers and pulses through her body like a live animal.

A flash of light. She twists around, expecting to see sunlight shining off broken glass. Twin lights are coming toward her. Enormous yellow eyes. But the eyes of an animal reflect light only at night. It is three in the afternoon. The clear South Texas light illuminates every bush. A huge yellowish animal is coming toward her. It sucks the moisture out of her mouth. Even if she makes it up into one of the trees, the thing looks capable of leaping great heights, plucking her out of the tallest branch with its claws.

¿Será el diablo? Only she doesn't believe in the devil. Or does she? Run. Run. Run. The words pulse like a heartbeat in her head.

Su papá's words sound in her head, saying, "The worst thing a person can do when confronted by a wild animal is run." Oh, but she wants to. She imagines her legs churning, trying to escape her fear.

She stands, feet spread, hands gripping the dead branch in front of her, eyes locked with it.

Minutes pass but neither one of them blinks. It knows her. La conoce. ¿Pero cómo? To be near it is like being in the eye of a hurricane—everything still, only her body sending ripples of fear through the woods.

She's felt this paralyzing fear before, but she can't think when.

De repente el chillido de las chicharras breaks the silence, her body jerks and then she's running como un chicote, her legs lean, wily, fast as a whip. She falls, stumbling into a huizache, needles scoring her arms, she scrambles on all fours over rotting tree branches. Her breath saws in and out, cutting a gash in her side. Branch twigs pluck out hunks of hair. Falling again and pulling herself up.

Ducking through the strands of barbwire, she hears the sound of cloth tearing. The barbs bite into her stomach, stopping her. A weakness washes over her. She turns to look behind her. The huge beast inching toward her. Its feet don't seem to be moving. Ojos de lumbre bore straight into hers, its intelligence pulling her into its eyes. Nothing else exists.

She turns to face la tigra, then closes her eyes. She'll make it tiny, she'll make it disappear, she knows she can if she thinks it hard enough. When she opens her eyes the animal vanishes and in its place spins un remolino. When two winds converge, Papi had told them, the hot and the cold, they create a dust devil. The vortex of dust whirls around and around in a tiny tornado. It races through the grass, gathering speed, picking up dirt and grit and leaving faint tracks on the sand. Then it veers into the thicket and disappears in midair.

Her shirt sleeve and some skin from her shoulder hang on the barbwire. She jumps over the irrigation ditch—something she has never once in her eight years been able to do.

Arms thrashing, she plows through the green stalks of corn trying to outrun the hole opening under her feet. The corn whispers, chants, "Run faster, get away, get away. Corre Prietita, corre."

Her brother, Teté, and Dolores leap up from the corn where they've been waiting for her. She runs into Teté, almost knocking him down.

"Why didn't you come away with us, sonsa?" he asks, catching his balance.

They crowd around her, all talking at once. She looks over her shoulder wondering if it's safe to stop. But there is nothing in the woods now. Relieved she begins to sob, hands on her face trying to staunch the tears and mucus. The others are all crying too.

When they get to the house, she calls her grandmother into the bathroom and bars the door.

"Mamagrande, guess what happened to me. You'll never believe it."

"¿Qué te pasó, mijita?"

After her grandmother examines her scratches, Prietita fills the tub with cold water and sits in it. She begins to tremble. She cups her hands and splashes water on her face until the tremors stop. But el miedo is still in her waiting for something to awaken it. The jaguar did not bring the fear—it was already in her—the jaguar only drew it out of her.

She gets out of the tub, dries her body, and puts on clean jeans and shirt.

Her mother is washing dishes in the kitchen and her grandmother sits in a chair sewing. Prietita picks up a towel and starts drying. She tells her mother about the animal en el monte.

Her mother makes a snorting sound.

Prietita turns to her grandmother and asks, "What kind of animal was it, Mamagrande?"

"An apparition," her grandmother replies, threading a needle.

"Not with eyes like that—a fire burned in them," Prieta tells her. She senses that her mother does not believe she'd really seen anything.

"But Mami, I didn't just sense something—I saw it."

"It could have been a dog possessed by a spirit," says Mami, throwing soap in the air as she gestures. "Un perro endiablado."

"No, no era un perrote negro like those in the stories Papi tells, like the ghost dogs that chase his pick-up."

"Or it could have been a nagual, mijita," says her grandmother bent over the mending.

"What's a nagual, Mamagrande?"

"They come in two types, mijita. One is the animal companion. Our antepasados los indios believed that each person has an animal companion, a nagual. Whatever happens to the person happens to the animal and what befalls the animal also befalls the person. El otro tipo de nagual is a person who can transform himself into an animal. A kind of hechizero or brujo."

"Don't encourage her, doña Locha," her mother says. "I'm trying to break her of the habit of making up stories."

"Telling cuentos is a talent, hija," she says looking at Prietita's mother. Then she turns to Prietita, "Maybe you were lucky and what you encountered was your animal nagual and not the other kind."

When Prietita puts away the last dish, her mother tells her, "Anda cuidar a tu hermanito. Don't you hear him crying?"

The cradle hangs from the rafters, la cuna cuelga del techo. Prietita swings it back and forth. Rechina. The leather thongs creak. Carito, el coyotito, stirs, pink fingers uncurl, open, curl up tight.

She listens to the shrill song of the cicadas. The sounds are the same, but something is different. Outside, tumbleweeds crash into empty pails. The sand whips the walls of their cabin. Belly up or rooting, hogs grunt under the house in the crawl space where she usually plays with her sister and brothers. Prietita rocks the cradle. The leather thongs creak. Prietita is dreaming.

"Prieta, come help me with the corn," her mother tells her.

Leaning into the wind Prietita and her mother walk to the shed where they separate grain from chaff. Granitos de maíz ping as they hit the buckets, sounding like sand whipping the sides of tin washtubs.

Después de que ellas acabaron de apartar el grano de la paja, Prietita runs outside and flings cracked corn on the ground. The chickens come running. En el metate su mamá grinds corn. There will be enough masa to make tortillas for breakfast, lunch, and dinner.

From the clothesline above her head, las sábanas blancas flap in the dry wind. Sweat beads down her chest. Spotting a mound nest of fire ants, Prietita walks up to it and eases her bare feet in the soft powder. Giant red ants scurry around her ankles. Not a single one gets on her. She stares into the woods beyond the fence.

The buzz of mosquitos brings evening. Mamagrande lights the hurricane lanterns. Smoke from la chimenea curls into the sky. Her brother and cousin rush in with red welts on their arms and neck and swollen faces from mosquito bites. Mosquitos don't bite her. It's something in her blood, tiene sangre dulce her grandmother tells her, or maybe it's the way mijita smells.

"O tiene sangre mala," her mother adds.

All she knows es que los animalitos don't bite her.

Su mami cards cotton, then sits on the floor hunched over the quilt, arms moving up and down. As she hangs la colcha del techo her giant shadow dances on the walls and over Prietita.

Los aullidos de coyote make Prietita's hair stand on end. The dogs are still howling, still smelling of skunk. La taza de café con leche burns her cupped hands. She is so hungry she stuffs her mouth with a too hot tortilla.

Later she rests her head on her mother's lap. Her mother's fingers comb her hair for lice. Once a week this ritual that she likes. Both know they'll never find any lice in her hair. Se duerme al cantar de chicharras. In her dream her limbs twitch as she swallows the coppery taste of fear.

The thunder wakes her next morning. She stands in the open doorway. Culebrías shoot their bolts of serpent lightning across the sky. A few seconds later a drum tears loose. She looks toward the woods and shivers. She thinks she sees the jaguar. Le dan ganas de hacer algo. Un hambre que no puede nombrar makes her restless. She runs outside and stands with her face to the sky. She wants the rain to fill the hollow in her body that the nagual en el monte opened up.

Suddenly, rain, like grace, falls on everything.[1]

Prietita gasps. Long drops like jewels plop down making craters in the sand.

She stands holding out her thin arms and cupping her hands to catch the rain. She sings, making up a song: *Llovisna grís, zácate verde, yellow maíz, cielo azul, the chickens con los conejos, los beceritos y las vacas flacas will all get wet. . . .*

De repente the rain stops, la manguita de agua se desaparece leaving the sweet smell of wet earth. The hot arms of the sun enfold her. She feels as light as a ball of cotton. The wind, if there was one, could carry her up to the sky.

Next day Prietita goes outside and skips from puddle to puddle. The mother frog sale de la tierra. Prietita squats to watch her mate con el sapo macho in the water. She will lay her eggs en el charco. In a few days tadpoles will stir in the puddles. Before the pools dry up, las ranitas will turn into frogs.

---

1. Anzaldúa included a bracketed question: "[End story here?]."

She plays near the house, occasionally looking toward the woods where su papi burns prickly pear with a torch. Chamusca las pencas de nopal for the cattle.

Anda por las veredas del montecito. She stops before the lagoon; a furred creature scurries off. Out of the corner of her eye the streak of some animal, and Prietita's heart da un brinquote to lodge in her throat. When she comes to the thick strand of mesquite and cactus, she crawls under the branches to her secret dwelling. She lays on her back and stares up at the sky through the canopy of leaves. Prietita oye el chillido de las chicharras. She should be home rocking the cradle. A wind howling like la Llorona rustles through the woods, breathes through her, lifting her hair. The woods call her name. Prietita winds her way through the mazes in the dense scrub brush. Sus ojos de águila see a shadow darker than the others, over there by the clump of prickly pear—is it watching her?

She squeezes her eyes shut and reaches out to the house, to where la cuna hangs from the rafters. She pushes it. It swings itself back and forth. The leather thongs creak. Rechinan. Her baby brother, el coyotito, pink fingers unfurling and curling, holds his arms out to her.

Translations

el montecito: a small wooded area

el monte de chaparral: scrub brush

y el primo: and her cousin

con ojos de águila: with eagle eyes

cueros de víbora: snake skins

granjeno: blackberry bush

de reojo: out of the corner of the eye

un correcaminos: a roadrunner

moras: berries

Algo o alguien se está muriendo.: Something or someone is dying.

zapopiles: vultures

¿Lloverá, lloverá? ¿Quién sabe? Dios dirá.: Will it rain, will it
   rain? God only knows.

el ganado: the livestock

huizache: a tree found in South Texas

nopales: prickly pear cactus

juegos, alredor de San Miguel, pipiripi de don . . . : local game

como azufre: like sulphur

Vente: Come on

El tiempo pasa.: Time goes by.

ahí: there

¿Será el diablo?: Could it be the devil?

Su papá's: Her father's

La conoce. ¿Pero cómo?: It knows her. But how?

como un chicote: like a whip

ojos de lumbre: fiery eyes

un remolino: a dust devil

corre: run

sonsa: dummy

Mamagrande: grandmother, literally big mama

¿Qué te pasó, mijita?: What happened to you, my little daughter?

el miedo: the fear

un perro endiablado: a dog possessed by the devil

no era un perrote negro: it was not a huge black dog

nagual: a person who shapeshifts or an animal companion

mijita: term of endearment, "my little daughter"

antepasados los indios: Indian ancestors

el otro tipo de: the other type of

hechizero: sorcerer

brujo: male witch

doña: respected woman

cuentos: stories

hija: daughter

Anda cuidar a tu hermanito.: Go take care of your little brother.

La cuna cuelga del techo.: The cradle hangs from the rafters.

rechina: it creaks

el coyotito: the youngest born, literally "the little coyote"

granitos de maíz: grains of corn

después de que ellas acabaron de apartar el grano de la paja: after she and her mother are done separating the grain from the chaff

en el metate: in the corn grinder

su mamá: her mother

masa: tortilla dough

las sábanas blancas: the white sheets

la chimenea: the chimney

tiene sangre dulce: she has sweet blood

o tiene sangre mala: or she has bad blood

es que los animalitos: it's that the little animals

la colcha del techo: the quilt from the rafters

los aullidos de coyote: the howls of the coyotes

la taza de café con leche: the cup of hot coffee and milk

Se duerme al cantar de chicharras.: She goes to sleep to the song of cicadas.

culebrías: serpent lightning

le dan ganas de hacer algo: a strong urge to do something

un hambre que no puede nombrar: a hunger or desire she can't name

llovisna grís, zácate verde, yellow maíz, cielo azul: dark rain, green hay, yellow corn, blue sky

con los conejos, los beceritos y las vacas flacas: with the little rabbits, the little calves and the skinny cows

la manguita de agua se desaparece: all of a sudden the rain disappears

sale de la tierra: emerges from the earth

con el sapo macho: with the male toad

en el charco: in the puddle

las ranitas: the tadpoles

chamusca las pencas de nopal: roasts prickly pear

Anda por las veredas: Walks on the paths

da un brinquote: gives a great jump

Prieta oye el chillido de las chicharras.: She hears the cry of the cicadas.

sus ojos de águila: her eagle eyes

3

In the Mouth of the Sea /
En el hocico del mar

Prietita and her brothers scrambled into the back of el troque colorado and her sister into the cab with her parents. As the truck picked up speed the wind plastered her shirt against her chest, whipped her long hair from side to side, and buffeted her back and forth. The wind wailed through the truck's hollow rails sounding like la Llorona. Prietita turned to face the rear. The receding landscape pulled something from her belly. She felt part of herself emptying out into the ribbon of road and back-rush rows of corn.

Her brothers sat on the blanket spread on the hard bed of the farm truck that su papi had just that morning swept and hosed down. As they sped past small towns flanked by green fields, her brothers straddled the inflated inner tube and bounced up and down. Prietita kept an eye on them, ready to separate them if they started fighting.

She smelled it first—the brackish waters where the salt water flowed into the marsh. And then, as they drove onto the causeway, the tires ringing hollow on the bridge, she smelled the saline. As they drove onto the deserted stretches of South Padre Island, a long, narrow strip separated from the mainland by a lagoon, she felt the balmy sea breeze on her face. Soft mounds of dunes, incessantly beaten by wind, sat against the sea. The glistening white sand reflected the intense light of the sun. On the wide expanse of ocean, sparks from the sun struck the surface. The sky was limitless. On the horizon it merged with the ocean in an invisible line. If only she could swim to that thin line, she would reach the sky. Tonight when she told Dolores a story, she'd make one up about a girl who swam all the way to the sky.

Everything was moving to the rushing song of the waves. Dunes, birds, grasses, sand. Prietita stared at a string of seaweed on the beach. It looked like an umbilical cord.

When Papi parked el troque along the southernmost beach where the sand was whitest, Prietita jumped out of the truck into the warm arena. She closed her eyes against the blazing sol, and red dots of light appeared behind her eyelids.

Her papi rigged the canvas awning along the side of the truck. Her mami placed a crate under the tarp, and on top of it laid cheese and bologna sandwiches, potato chips, and the fried chicken she had gotten up early to cook. (*Prietita was already awake and eager to get to the island when her mother had called out, "Ándale, levanta a tus hermanos." Prietita turned toward Dolores curled up asleep beside her and shook her gently. Dolores groused that it was too early to get up and besides it was Sunday. By the time Prietita roused her brothers her mother was banging pots on the stove and the smell of chicken popping in grease permeated the whole house.*)

Prietita dragged the two sand chairs under the shade. Her mother sat on one of the chairs and talked with her papi, one ear tuned to her children's voices. Her father took off his Stetson, plucked out a Big Red from the portable freezer, and reclined in the other chair. Straining against the leash of her parents' voices, Prietita gazed longingly at the cresting waves and the crystalline water, wanting only to run and dip her skin in the cool verdemar.

"Si se pierde la cosecha, I'll have to come back here and fish for shrimp." Papi scrunched his face as he looked up as though looking for the answer in the sky. He rolled the sleeves of his khaki shirt up to his elbows.

"Ojalá que no. You'll work yourself to death," her mother said.

"Ya mero se llega crismas. Can't disappoint the kids," he said.

Prietita shaded her eyes with her hand and looked out into the Gulf of Mexico where the water separated earth from sky. She edged closer and asked, "Papi, why did la isla separate from the mainland?"

"It was never part of all that." He pointed beyond Laguna Madre to Port Isabel on the mainland.

"Well, then how was this island formed?"

"No sé mija, but I think it was first un barro de arena, tú sabes, a thin sandbar. Probably made by a storm. After that as the years went by, the waves deposited more and more sand and shells. It must have taken millions of años to form an island."

Prietita watched the waves, hoping to see them depositing sand on the beach. Seaweed buoyed by air bladders drifted across the surface of the water. "What kind of seaweed is that?" She pointed to a brown algae with a gelatinous sheath.

"Los gringos call it gulf weed, but its real name is sargassum." Papi tilted the chair back a few notches and adjusted his body.

Su papi liked to pick up brochures at the entrances to parks and read about the area's natural history. She wondered if he would have liked being a park ranger instead of a farmer and rancher who worked all the time. If his father hadn't died and he hadn't quit school to be head of the family, he would have gotten more education.

Prietita pried the lid off the foam freezer.

Her mother said, "Don't ask so many questions. And leave the food alone, it's not time to eat yet." Then she started her usual lecture: "You kids are not to fight, you are not to go far and don't go in too deep, no further than your waist. And, no, you can't use the inner tube unless Papi's with you. Maybe later." Again she gave Prietita a piercing look and repeated the words Prietita had heard cien veces: "You think you know everything and can do everything but you don't know how to swim."

Prietita listened for the "You can go play now." Released, she and her sister and brothers ran along the shoreline, feet splashing on the surf. Theirs were not the only footprints. Pin-prick tracks of birds, gull tracks that looked like tiny umbrellas and the delicate tapestry of crab tracks covered the beach. Frothy waves rolled in, leaving mosaics of iridescent foam. The tide etched its image as it lapped against the sand. As she watched, the water filled her footprints and the ebb of the waves erased them as though she had never walked on the smooth sand.

Prietita ran past the waterline. At last her special moment, the one she always looked forward to the most. She stood before the vast flowing olas, watched the sea tower over her, watched its waves folding in on themselves as it rushed toward her.

She sucked in the drenching verdemar and laughed. Again she felt the shock rippling through her body, opening something inside her.

The sea was a rock that rippled. Under her feet the beach swayed, the earth buckled. La mar blew un buche de agua en su cara, almost knocking her off her feet.

Squealing and shoving each other, Prietita and her sister splashed in the shallows. Soda froth lapped Prietita's ankles as she squished the wet sand between her toes.

"Lookit those fat pajaritos," said Dolores.

"Plovers," said Prietita. She watched them scamper about, picking up worms and mollusks. "Their bills look like dove beaks, don't they, Dolores? Those are sand pipers," she said pointing to birds probing the sand with long bills, neck plumes in disarray. "And those are terns," she told Dolores.

They stopped to look at the birds scampering along the water's edge. "Don't their bills look like pointed daggers? Watch them dive headfirst into the water. See? That's how they catch small fish," Prietita said.

Leaving Dolores behind, she plunged headfirst into the water, then rose up and stood to watch a wave rising, rising, then breaking as it moved toward her, depositing foam and shell fragments against her calves.

"Prietita, ven aquí, come here right now." Her mother had left the shade of truck and tarp and stood near the water's edge.

"Mother. I'm nine years old. I can swim a little," Prietita yelled back.

"You're a skinny little girl. You should be afraid of the water. People drown in it, you know, even those who swim real good."

As Prietita approached, her mother, hands on her hips, stared her down. Her shadow fell on Prietita holding her in place.

"Muchacha cabezuda, don't you dare disobey me." Her mother's voice swept over her like the waves, persistent, relentless.

"Bueno, Mami," said Prietita.

As she moved toward the dunes, she marveled at the long curve of beach, bordered by dunes high as windmills where the sands shifted and moved and settled down again. The small ridges and troughs made by the wind looked like water ripples.

She scrambled up and slid down steep slopes, causing small avalanches. Her feet sank into the hot sand as she pulled herself up the dunes by the sea oats sticking up like stiff whiskers.

The sun beat down on her, and the sweat and sand fleas made her itchy. The sibilant voice of the sea surged in her bones, whispering, "Ven aquí, ven aquí. Come here, come here." She pulled off the t-shirt and shorts she wore over her bathing suit and dropped them on top of a horseshoe-shaped dune. She walked toward la playa, heat waves shimmering before her. She watched clams hurriedly burrow into the sand after the backwash of each wave.

"¡No te metas en lo hondo, india ladina!" le grito su mama.

The loud whoosh de las olas, the uprush and backwash of waves, and the hissing sound of the water vied with her mother's voice.

Prietita, poised to dive in, heard her mother call out, "Time to eat. Vengan a comer."

She ran dragging her feet, gouging twin lines on the sand, and joined the others under the awning. She stuffed an empanada de calabaza into her mouth, then pulled out a cream soda from the ice chest. Cold beads of sweat slid down the can and onto her fingers. The slice of chilled watermelon she bit into was crunchy with sand. She wiped her chin with the back of her hand and watched sand fill the air as high as the truck. When she put her napkin on the makeshift table, the wind lifted it.

It soared away. And she chased after it along the water's edge until it disappeared from sight. She wondered if it would sail over Laguna Madre and drift down on the mainland, maybe get snagged on a tree or telephone pole.

When she was out of sight of her mother's eagle eyes, she veered off and ran into the water.

The swells crashed against her thighs; the receding waves sucked the sand from under her feet. Her toes gripped the wet dirt, anchoring her to the earth. She waded in deeper, shuddering at the delicious coolness on her thighs, waist, chest, neck. Wiping the salt spray from her eyes, she watched a wave towering toward her. It swelled about her, buoying her up off her feet, up up toward the sky.

Again, a breaker crashed over her head, knocking her off balance. She tried to regain her feet, but another wave sideswiped her. She gasped; salt stung her eyes and water went up her nose and into her throat. Her heart leaped. Fear dried her mouth. She tried to scream, "Mami, help me," but the sea filled her mouth.

She went under again, striking out at the water. When her head rose above the surface another wave rose in front of her and swept her along. Something grabbed her by the ankles, rolled her body over and over and pulled her down. Her legs scraped against the sand, the grit rough on her knees. Las olas la arrastraron de la orilla, pulling her under, sweeping her out to sea. She thrashed with her arms and legs.

She opened her eyes and saw sargassum seaweed all around her. She was in a shady emerald place, her body rolling over and over, wrapped in the green arms and legs of the gulf weed, an umbilical cord tethering her to the deep.

She struggled to disentangle herself. She flailed, not knowing which direction was up and which down. If only she could turn into una sirenita and, with a flip of her tail, rise up out of the deep and swim to the surface. Or mount un caballito de mar and ride it back to el troque colorado.

Where was the sky? All she could see was the churning verdemar. Pain shot through her chest and throat—un dolor como
cuchillo. Behind her eyelids lightning flashed. Her lungs were on
fire. She couldn't hold her breath much longer.

She floated. La mar verdemar. Don't breathe, verdemar,
don't breathe. She chanted verdemar in her head verdemar. She
gulped verdemar, her lungs emptied and filled   la mar wailed
in her ears   Mami   verdemar   Mami mar   come get
me   please come get me

She was no match against la mar verdemar with her powerful
mouth and seaweed tentacles. Her arms stopped their flailing and
surrendered to la mar verdemar. The knife left her chest y la mar
washed away her pain.

Drifting   between sleep and wakefulness   la mar verdemar humming   la mar crooning   her body rocked   her
face touched and settled on the ocean's bed   la mar verdemar
nudged her   warm and soothing   her bones   pliant as
seaweed   the ocean inside her merged with the ocean outside   between the two waters   she lay cradled   in the in-
between place called nepantla   she had no skin   mar verdemar

She heard someone calling her name. With eyes closed, she
turned toward it. No, no, la mar crooned verdemar, stay stay.
Mother, she said, nestled in the lap of the sea, which one are you?

Something bumped her shins, her feet raked mud and sand.
A sandbar. The jarring uncurled her body, the chains of seaweed
slipped off. She convulsed, spewing acrid water out of her mouth
and nose. Through stinging eyes she saw the ocean bed shift. She
tried to slow the pulse quickening inside her, fought the awakening, said no to the force pulling her up out of the sea. But her
hands sculled, her feet found a toehold on the sandbar, su cuerpo
se enderezó, and her arms shot up. She was rising, rising, a diver
exploding through to the surface.

Her nose cleared the surface; she sucked in air, then vomited.
She opened her eyes and saw a round orange haze. Through her
wet eyelashes saw miniature rainbows. Light sucked her up; luz
filled her with joy. Buoyant, chest heaving, ears ringing, she bobbed.

A wave slapped her face, dragged her under once more. Her feet scraped the bottom. Straightening her knees, thrusting upward, she jumped, arms breaking the surface, reaching for the sky. She blinked, clearing her eyes, and she sobbed, relieved to see the sky again y la luz. Gasping, she snatched mouthfuls of light.

Again the weight of her body pulled her down. Again the waves buoyed her up. She whipped her head to one side flipping the hair off her face, then slowly turned to face the beach. The surface shimmered—espíritus del agua hid themselves in those sparks. Sí, eran luces de los espíritus.

She looked back at the Gulf, eyes measuring the height between the crest and the troughs of the swells moving slowly toward her. Tumbling over and over, the undertow that had taken her had brought her back. It wasn't going to take her again. Between the deep and the shallow water, entre dos aguas, she clung to sky and sun. There were things she wanted to do. With the first gulp of air she'd gotten a glimpse of something. Then it was gone. She couldn't hold on to it, didn't want to hold on to it.

She was afraid a wave would smack her, drive her off the bar into deeper inshore water. She couldn't keep bobbing up and down en el barro de arena forever. Maybe if she held her breath she could crawl to the beach. No, best to wait for the tide to recede.

She watched the clouds moving across the sky. One looked like the woman in white, la Llorona, searching for her lost children. Partially hidden in the middle of otra nube, she thought she saw the spirits of the air gazing down at her.

She pretended she was a bit of cotton fluff, wafting up to the sky and becoming a plume, a tiny cipher under the immense sky. Looking down she saw the thin strip of land, the wide sheet of verdemar, the glint of sunlight on the slant of water.

It felt like she was on a swing in the sky. Up she swung, then down, stomach sinking. A sweet sensation raced down her arms and legs. She slipped from the swing, fell through the sky and plunged back into the depth of the sea. Her nerves became seaweeds and formed new routes through her body.

She heard a keening sound coming from the dune ridge parallel to the shoreline. Her heart jumped. Someone was out there, or something. It saw her. She cocked her head toward the wailing but could hear nothing more. That didn't mean it was gone. Just because she didn't see them didn't mean there weren't creatures all around her.

She waited, willed the tide to pull back from the lip of the shore. The sun was low in the sky. Soon her mother would start packing up. Every once in a while Prietita left the three-foot-wide shoal to see if she could stand with her head above water. Esperaba.

Taking a deep breath, she forced herself to dive off the sand bank. She was caught in the surf moving relentlessly toward land, her face above the crest of the waves. Half dog paddling, she lurched toward the beach. She collapsed on her face en la arena, head tucked to the side, and clung to the hot earth.

Cuando volvió en sus sentidos, she spit out the sand in her mouth. Her body was dry, she was thirsty. She opened her eyes, stared at the tiny grains of sand and cupped a fistful. She too had been a tiny dot in the great maw of the ocean. How had she survived in the water so long? Did her body remember how to breathe in the water like her non-human ancestors did millions of years ago before they turned into land creatures? Only she didn't have gills. Maybe her mother's call had pulled her up, or the call of the earth. Maybe los espíritus del agua had pushed her up.

She shook her head, but the buzz persisted. Legs and arms stiff, she rose to her knees and raised her face to the light, then lifted her hands up to the sun. Her middle opened, expanded. She whooped and swung around faster and faster.

On the sand was the outline of her body, a trough for belly, arms, and legs. Prieta scooped wet sand, shaped it until she had a sculpture of a girl lying on the beach on her stomach. With a piece of broken shell she wrote: I know you are here, there, everywhere. Then she signed her name. She stood back to look at the sand sculpture. Soon the sea would wash over its body and suck the sand grain by grain.

Her legs buckled and she saw by the length of her shadow that several hours had passed. Her mother would be so angry. She clutched her stomach, squinted and looked down the length of the beach. El troque colorado looked like a toy; specks moved around it like ants.

She worried that she wouldn't find the horseshoe-shaped dune, that the wind had changed its shape, that Mami would scold her for losing her clothes. She trudged toward the dunes. Beneath her feet the sand shifted, the dunes flowed like water. The ripples and swirls of sifted sand in the lengthening shadows were marks in a language she was just learning to read. The sands turned into gold, the sea oats into silhouettes against the darkening sky. When she found her t-shirt and shorts, she shook out the sand and stiffness and pulled them on over her bathing suit.

Legs trembling, she trotted toward el troque colorado, fluffing her matted hair and combing her fingers through the tangles. Sweat beaded her face and arms. It was taking her too long. They'd already be looking for her. She heard the wailing again and looked around for la Llorona.

She was in the middle of a blowout where the wind had scooped up the sand and dropped it somewhere else on the island to form another dune. In the middle of the hollow, Prietita saw a bottle with a long neck. She picked it up and blew into the opening. It caught the wind and returned its call.

She reached the truck as they were loading the crate, chairs, leftovers and the tarp. All five stood staring at her.

"Where were you, I've been looking everywhere." Her mother jerked her by the arm and shook her hard.

Prietita felt scorched by the heat of her mamá's eyes, sensed the fear beneath her anger. She looked at her father, who turned away. He always left the disciplining to her mother.

"¿Qué te pasó?" le preguntó su mamá. "Did you go into the deep?"

"Mami, I was just now in the dunes hunting for treasure." Everyone knew pirates had buried treasure on the island where they holed up and waylaid the Spanish ships carrying Aztec gold from Mexico to Spain. People were always digging.

"That's your treasure?" Mami pointed at the bottle.

Prieta held it up to her mouth and blew into it. Her mother looked startled by the woeful sound.

"Yes, Mami, it speaks for the wind."

"Sonsa, only people speak. ¿Te asoliaste mucho? The sun must have cooked your brains."

Prieta looked down so her eyes wouldn't give her away. But it didn't do any good.

"You did go in the deep. Pos oyes que tú 'tás bien tonta. ¿No sabes que te puedes perder?"

¡Jíjole! What if Mami kept them from coming back?

"¡Vámonos!" Papi called out, saving her from having to answer.

She climbed into the back of the truck with her brothers and stared at the lip of the sea nibbling the sand line, listened to the rushing in and rushing back of waves. When they left the island she lay down on the blanket spread on the hard bed. Sunlight came in through the wooden slats streaking her face. She curled her body around the bottle. Safe now, the truck rocked her from side to side. She closed her eyes. The engine sounds faded. La mar hovered over her all the way home. She felt its breath in her mouth, felt its heart beating—a lullaby pulsing in her veins. La mar estaba viva. She shivered. The wind wailed in her ears whispering: One day la mar verdemar will claim you.

Translations

en el hocico del mar: in the mouth of the sea

el troque colorado: the red truck

su papi: her father

sol: sun

arena: sand

Ándale, levanta a tus hermanos.: Come on, wake up your brothers.

verdemar: sea green

Si se pierde la cosecha: If the crop is lost

Ojala que no: Let's hope not

Ya mero se llega crismas.: It's almost time for Christmas.

la isla: the island

No sé mija.: I don't know, my daughter.

un barro de arena: a sandbar

tú sabes: you know

años: years

los gringos: the whites

cien veces: one hundred times

olas: waves

la mar: the sea

un buche de agua en su cara: a mouthful of water in her face

pajaritos: little birds

ven aquí: come here

muchacha cabezuda: hard-headed girl, as in one who does not mind

bueno: OK

la playa: the beach

¡No te metas en lo hondo, india ladina!: Don't go in the deep,
   you wild Indian!

le grito su mama: her mama yelled

de las olas: of the waves

vengan a comer: come and eat

empanada de calabaza: pumpkin turnover

Las olas la arrastraron de la orilla.: The waves dragged her from the shore.

una sirenita: a little mermaid

un caballito de mar: a seahorse

un dolor como cuchillo: a pain like a knife

nepantla: a Nahuatl word meaning the place in-between

su cuerpo se enderezó: her body straightened

luz: light

los espíritus del agua: the spirits of the water

Sí, eran luces de los espíritus.: Yes, they were the lights of the spirits.

entre dos aguas: between two waters (nepantla)

otra nube: another cloud

esperaba: she waited

cuando volvió en sus sentidos: when she returned to her senses

"¿Qué te pasó?" le preguntó su mama.: "What happened to you?" asked her mother.

sonsa: dumb, foolish, or stupid

¿Te asoliaste mucho?: Did you get too much sun?

Pos oyes que tú 'tás bien tonta. ¿No sabes que te puedes perder?: Hey, you're such an idiot. Don't you know you can get lost?

¡Jíjole!: Jesus, damn, etc.

¡Vámonos!: Let's go!

La mar estaba viva.: The ocean was alive.

4

People Should Not Die in June in South Texas

La Prieta sweats in her black dress. The heat is unbearable. After the second day su papi has begun to smell like a cow whose carcass has been gutted by vultures. People should not die in June in South Texas.

Prietita slips through the crowd of mourners en la sala and finds a place near the casket. A slant of light from the half-raised venetian blind falls diagonally across her father's face. One after the other, relatives and friends approach el cuerpo tendido with lowered heads, kneel beside it, and make the sign of the cross. After a couple of minutes they rise, bow, and slowly back away. Even a few Anglo acquaintances have come to pay their respects to el difunto.

Yesterday morning Prieta and her mother had gone to the funeral home. Inside the sprawling Spanish-style building with the well-groomed carpet grass and gushing fountain the light is too bright, garish, the smell of air freshener sickly sweet. She imagined how someone in some hidden room made a two-inch incision in her father's throat. Someone inserted a tube in his jugular vein. In some hidden room una envenenada abuja filled his venas with embalming fluid. Someone stitched his broken face.

They were the only customers. The gringo undertaker with the soft sonorous voice put his palm on her mother's back and propelled her toward the more expensive coffins. She held a hand-kerchief to her eyes like a blindfold, knotting and unraveling it between sobs. Prieta was forced to be the more practical of the two. That's why Mami calls her Urraca Prieta—crows are tough little birds.

"Let's take that one." Prieta pointed to a coffin of mid-range price. Though they'd be in debt for three years, they chose un cajón de quinientos dólares. Then the undertaker escorted them to the clothes section and showed them the backless $70 to $300 suits. Her mami wanted her papi to look nice, his one and only suit was too worn.

"Why are we buying such an expensive suit? Ni siquiera tiene espalda. It's not a real suit. And besides todo se va a podrir," she told her mother softly. Her mother looked at her y empezo a llorar de nuevo. Prieta put her arms around her mother whose sobs slightly shook her from head to foot. She wondered when her mami would abruptly pull away.

Prieta stared at the glossy polished caskets with their plush velvet linings. Memories of her father welled up. She swallowed her own tears. Compraron un traje negro y una camisa blanca con encaje color de rosa.

They returned home in the hearse with the coffin and a body they said was her father. The house overflowed with relatives and friends, y las mesas laden with comida. People held paper plates filled with enchiladas, arroz con pollo y frijoles with one hand and wiped sweat or tears or both with the other. Already the men had started drinking.

"Te acompaño en el pesar," le dice una tía, embracing her, her perfume and body smell pinning Prieta against the wall.

Male relatives pay their condolences. She pulls slightly away and takes short shallow breaths to evade the stench of alcohol. After thirty or forty people hug her she feels helada y asfixiada.

"Qué guapa, la Prieta, so clever. Es la mayor y se parece mucho a su papá," she hears a woman say, bursting into tears and clutching Prieta in a desperate embrace. Whiffs of perfume escape from the women's hair hidden by their thick black mantillas. The smells of roses and carnations, carne guisada, and body heat mingling with the sweet putrid smell of death make Prieta want to run.

Through the throng of people, Prieta makes her way to Mamagrande Locha. Aullando a la virgen, her grandmother falls to her knees en frente del cajón en medio del cuarto. She looks up at Prieta, sus ojos azules stricken with sorrow. Su pelo se mira más blanco under the black shawl. Persignándose, Prieta kneels down beside her. All three, mother, wife, and daughter surround the dead man.

Prieta is the only one at the velorio who is dry-eyed. Why can't she cry? Le dan ganas, no de llorar, pero de reír a carcajadas. She feels like laughing instead. It feels like a show—everyone is acting out a role.

She clamps down her jaws. How dare he die? How could he leave su mamá all alone? Her mother is only twenty-eight. Her mother has not moved from her place by the casket. She will be all alone once they bury Papi. Someone touches her on the shoulder, offers her condolence and a soda. She sips the soda y su cuerpo tiembla.

She remembers when he first abandoned her. He stopped hugging her, although he kept hugging the others. He would gently rap his knuckles on top of her head—the one gesture of intimacy he allowed himself. She wondered what she had done wrong. Why it felt wrong to want him to hold her. Was it because hair had begun to grow between her legs? Now she would never know what had been behind the sad and hungry look in his eyes. Now the quiet man who never had to raise his voice to anyone was lost to her forever.

The room shrinks. Everyone looks ridiculous in black, cackling like black crows, hovering over su papi. The house feels like an alien place with the smell of death and alcohol, el llanto de las mujeres, and a corpse that pretends to be her father.

Running out of the house, Prieta sale corriendo. She crosses the street, tropezándose con las piedras. Cuando llega a la casa de Mamagrande Ramona, she searches for her little brother, el coyotito, and finds him huddled at one end of the sofa. He wants to know when Papi is going to wake up. His bewildered face reflects her own questions, preguntas she cannot answer. She wipes his nose and fixes him un taquito and a glass of milk. Taking care of him makes her feel older.

At nightfall Prietita walks back across the road and slips into the house. The people are quieter. Her father's corpse draws her to the coffin. Standing on her toes, she touches the beige satin lining with one finger. She wants to stroke his face but the flesh-colored putty sealing the cracks stills her hand.

He can't be dead. Someone else's face had lain broken, smashed beyond recognition under the overturned troque colorado. It was someone else's blood that pooled on the highway.

For three days her father sleeps in his coffin. Her mother sits at his side todas las noches and never sleeps. Oliendo al muerto, Prietita duerme en su cama, breathing the sweet smell of death mixed with the perfume of flowers. Su padre abre los ojos y la mira, her father opens his eyes.

"You have to come back, Papi. I need to know. Why did you stop loving me?"

Abre su boca a contestarle, he opens his mouth to answer her, but no words emerge. Se levanta del cajón, he rises out of the coffin. What she's been waiting for is finally happening—he puts his arms around her thin body. The sound of voices wakes her.

On the third day Prieta, too, rises from her bed, eyes vacant. She puts on her black blouse and skirt and covers her head with a black scarf. Though it is early the heat and heavy clothes chafe her skin. She wakes her sister and brothers, makes sure they put on their mourning clothes, checks that their hair is combed neatly. They go to the living room, stand by her mother who sits by the coffin. They wait for the hearse.

On the way to the church, Prietita sits snug between her mother and sister, her brothers hunched together at one end. She clutches her hands on her lap to still their trembling. No one says a word. Tío David drives through the dirt roads of the neighborhood dejando polvo por atrás. As they follow the hearse, Prieta hears the shrill voices of children getting louder then fading. Aging station wagons and cars rusting on cement blocks appear and disappear.

Finally the car stops. Stiff-legged, she gets out and walks toward the hearse. The church yard is filled with people talking quietly. The pall bearers, tío David, Rafael, Goyo, el compadre Juan, and others lift the coffin out of the hearse. They carry it into la iglesia.

She looks at her sister's stricken face and reaches out to take her hand. Tugging el coyotito with the other, she follows her mother into the church.

The small church is packed. El cuerpo de su padre está tendido in the middle of the aisle near the pulpit. They walk past the casket and slip into the first row on the right. Mamagrande Locha and Tió David squeeze in. Prieta shushes her brothers. They stop fidgeting. She watches one woman after another kneel before la Virgen de Guadalupe. Each lights a votive candle. Soon the smell of burning tallow fills la iglesia. What can la Virgencita or anyone else do for her father now?

"Et misericordia ejus a progenis timentibus eum," intones the priest in Latin. How young and smooth-faced he looks, the Oblate father, missionary catechist to the poor pueblito, a Spaniard who lisps the c's. He is flanked by altar boys on both sides. His purple gown rustles as he swings his pewter censers over el cuerpo tendido de su padre, clouds of frankincense billow over the length of the dark shiny coffin.

All rise up as one body, all kneel as one body, voices rising up in response to the priest's as he takes them through the different stages of the Mass. Up, down, Prieta feels like a puppet.

Finally, after the Mass is over, the pall bearers con bigotes y corbatas negras return to the coffin and stand stiffly in their somber suits. She has never seen these ranchers, farmers, and field workers in suits before. In unison they take a deep breath, bend their knees, and in a smooth motion, heave up the coffin. Her mother follows the coffin holding Carito's hands. Prieta and her sister and brother follow.

Outside near the parked Chevys and Fords, Prieta watches the church slowly emptying, become a hollowed-out thing. It had only been alive with el muerto y la gente. When the people left they took their grief with them.

Faces hidden under fine-woven mantillas, the women like black crows in their black cotton and rayon dresses. But she is Urraca Prieta, the black crow. And she'd gotten no premonition. She had not seen las urracas gather on the ébano in the backyard the night before that bright day in June. If the urracas had not announced his death then he couldn't be dead.

Prieta rides with Tió David to the cemetery. On her lap she clutches a bunch of orange zempasuchitl flowers. The shiny black hearse glides in front of them, dust roiling in its wake. As she squints in the fierce light, Prieta is back to el último día que vió a su padre vivo. She sees the wreckage as though she is watching a film. She stands out in the yard watching su papi drive away en su troque colorado. The truck, rail buckling with cotton bales, disappears down the dirt road heading for the cotton gin. One hand leaves the wheel to clutch his chest. His body arches, then his head and chest slump over the wheel, blood streaming out through his nose and mouth, his foot heavy on the gas pedal.

"Wake up, Papi, despierta, turn the wheel," Prieta whispers but the truck keeps going off the highway. Se voltea. The truck turns over and over, the doors flapping open then closing. Her father is thrown out. The edge of the railing crushes his face, wheels spin in the air, white cotton bales are strewn around him.

Her tió Rafael arrived first at the scene. There was nothing he could do. Someone came to tell her mother. And the wailing started. Every woman in the family turned into la Llorona. Only Prieta couldn't cry.

The image plays itself over and over.

Prieta gets out of the hearse clutching the zempasuchitl and walks toward the hole in the ground flanked by a mound of dirt along one side. The smell of dry clay. The portable awning with two small rows of chairs under it, and under the chairs, fake grass, almost a fluorescent green. Dozens and dozens of crows cawing from ebony tree to ebony tree.

Unos hombres push a metal apparatus over the hole. Los padrinos lift the coffin, walk toward the hole under the lone tree. Muscles straining, they lower it over the hole. The chain unwinds from the winch's drum making a screeching sound.

Prieta shuffles over to the open casket. Sus ojos trace the jagged lines en la cara that the undertaker stitched together. The broken nose, the chalky skin with the tinge of green underneath is not her father's face, no es la cara de su papi.

On that bright day, June 22, someone else had been driving his truck. Someone else had been wearing his khaki pants, his gold wire-rimmed glasses. Someone else had his gold front tooth. The blood on the highway was someone else's. Prieta looks away.

¡Qué no quiero verla!
Dile a la luna que venga,
que no quiero ver la sangre

—Federico García Lorca

I don't want to see it
Tell the next moon
that I don't want to see the blood[1]

As she watches su papi, she sees death creep into her father's unconscious body; it kicks out his soul and makes his body stiff. She sees la muerte's long pale fingers take possession of her father—sees death place its hands over what had been her father's corazón. La muerte lo habita. A fly buzzes by her face. She sees la mosca crawl over one of her father's hands, then land on his cheek. She wants him to raise his hand and fan la mosca away. She raises her hand to crush the fly then lets it fall back to her side. Swatting the fly would mean striking her papi. Death, too, lets the fly crawl over

---

1. The lines of Frederico García Lorca are from the poem "Llanto por Ignacio Sánchez Mejías," translated by the author.

itself. Sí, the fly and death are carnales. Ella es esa mosca trying to rouse her father.

She stands by the coffin looking at her own small hands. When her hands are no longer red or pulsating she will lie like him, utterly still. Maggots will find her hands and seek out su corazón. And the world will continue as usual. That is what shocks her the most about her father's muerte—that people still laugh, la gente sigue riéndose, the wind continues to blow, el viento sopla, the sun rises in the east and sets in the west, el sol amanece.

Prieta walks away from the coffin and stands at the edge of the gaping wound under the ebony tree. The hole, el pozo tan hondo, the red clay. Her body sways slowly back and forth. Su mamagrande gently tugs her away.

Under el ébano a procession forms to the hole. The small country composanto, with Mexicans buried on one side and a few Anglos on the other and a line of prickly pears separating the two, is now bulging with hundreds of cars y montones de flores. La gente pile flower wreaths at her father's feet. Fresh flowers, plastic flowers, silk flowers, zempasuchitl, and people are quietly weeping or muttering padre nuestros y ave marías under their breath while she stands in her starched dress feeling like it's all a dream.

The coffin lid slams. Hearing the whir of the machine, Prieta shudders and looks up to see it lowering her father into the hole. Someone tosses in a handful of dirt; the next person does the same and the line moves. She listens to the thuds, the slow shuffle of feet as the line unwinds like a giant serpent. Cuando le toca a ella, when it's her turn, she bends to pick up a handful of tierra. She loosens her clenched fist over the hole. Thud. Clumps fall onto the dirt-covered coffin making little craters on its surface. Prieta drops a marigold flower from the bunch cradled in her left arm, then another and another until el cajón está vestido con las flores anaranjadas del zempasuchitl.

Before her the earth parts. Slowly, her father's coffin slips down the gullet. She teeters on the edge. From the depths, an unknown sweetness and a familiar anguish beckon her. She rocks back and forth near the mouth of the abyss. She hears Mamagrande Locha crying, "Mi hijo, mi hijo, tan bueno. ¿Diosito mio, por qué se lo llevó? Ay mi hijo."

The anguish in her grandmother's voice pulls her back. Prieta goes to her grandmother and the two cling to each other. After everyone leaves, the family gets in the car. As they drive off, Prietita looks back, thinking composantitos son jardines donde plantan a los muertos.

On Sunday the whole family goes to Mass, but Prieta doesn't want to go. How will this bring her papi back, she wonders. Mujeres enlutadas, heavily veiled women, kneel on the cement floor of the small church and recite the rosary in sing-song monotones. Llorosas, hands moving slowly over the beads. "Santa María, madre de Dios, ruega por nosotros. . . ."

On the second Sunday they attend Mass dedicated to her father in the nearby town of Elsa. Flanked by two acolytes, the Bishop makes his entrance wearing su cachuchita roja. Los muchachos sitting in the back snicker at his dress and red cap.

Her mother pays a small fee every Sunday for a year, all for the sake of the soul of the man who never entered church except for the funeral mass of friend or relative, and his own. Her father's attitude had been: better leave religion and church to the women who knew more of spiritual matters. What her father had believed in was the land and what grew in it. And it had killed him.

Her mother wears luto, vowing before a statue of la Virgen de Guadalupe that she and her daughters would wear black for two years and gray for two more. Prieta resents the fact that her brothers and male relatives can wear whatever they want—men don't have to show their grief or devotion.

She misses her father. Something inside her waits.

In September school resumes. Prieta feels all eyes focusing on her and her homemade black dress with its high neckline and long sleeves. As one day passes into another, the curiosity and fascination in her classmates' eyes slowly turn to pity and then disdain. She wants to be invisible to the world.

After school and on weekends her mother shushes them when they speak loudly or laugh, forbids them to listen to música norteña in the radio and covers the TV with a blanket. Prieta remembers when her father bought that TV. The other kids had been envious because hers had been the first Mexican family to have such a luxury. They watch *The Hit Parade*, *The Ed Sullivan Show*, *Amos and Andy*, *The Little Rascals*.

She remembers her papi saying, "Compré este televisión para ustedes, para que aprendan inglés." If they knew English they could get good jobs and not have to work themselves to death being sharecroppers and farmworkers like him. He had worked himself to death at the age of thirty-eight so that his children would not have to. Though he knew English he rarely spoke it. But when he spoke everyone listened.

Pasa mucho tiempo. Days and weeks and years pass. Prieta espera al muerto. Every evening she waits for her father to walk into the house tired after a day of hard work in the fields. She waits for him to gaze at her with his green eyes. She waits for him to take off his shirt and sit bare-chested on the floor, back against the sofa watching TV, the black curly head silhouetted by the glare of the TV.

Now she thinks she hears his footsteps on the front porch, and turns eagerly and fearfully toward the door.[2]

En el día de los muertos, on the Day of the Dead, el segundo de noviembre, ella lo espera todavía. She lights a candle for him, goes to el camposanto with her mother and grandmother, weeds his grave and places fresh flowers. Aunque no más viniera a visitarlos por un ratito. Even if he didn't stay—she wants to see him.

Overhead from atop the ebony tree, a crow caws. She realizes there will be no second coming—neither the One-God nor her father will ever walk through her door again. She is abandoned like all mujeres, son abandonadas. And like her ancestors and all people born on earth and of earth, she too, will return to earth, for the Earth swallows its dead.

---

2. Anzaldúa included a bracketed question, "[End it here?]."

Translations

su papi: her father

en la sala: in the living room

El cuerpo está tendido.: The body lies in wake.

el difunto: the deceased, the dead man

una envenenada abuja: a poisoned needle

venas: veins

gringo: a (sometimes derogatory) term for a white man

Urraca Prieta: Black Crow

un cajón de quinientos dólares: a casket costing $500

Ni siquiera tiene espalda.: It doesn't even have a back.

todo se va a podir: it's all going to rot

y empezo a llorar de nuevo: and she began to cry anew

Compraron un traje negro y una camisa blanca con encaje color de rosa.: They bought a black suit and a white shirt with a pink ruffle.

y las mesas: and the tables

comida: food

arroz con pollo y frijoles: rice with chicken and beans

"Te acompaño en el pesar," le dice una tía.: "I'm with you in your time of sorrow," said one of the aunts.

Se siente helada y asfixiada: Prieta feels frozen and suffocated

Qué guapa la Prieta. Es la mayor y se parece mucho a su papá.: Prieta is so pretty. She's the oldest and looks so much like her father.

carne guisada: seasonal fried meat

Mamagrande: grandmother, literally big mama

aullando a la virgen: howling at the virgin

en frente del cajón en medio del cuarto: in front of the casket in
    the middle of the room

sus ojos azules: her blue eyes

su pelo se mira más blanco: her hair looks whiter

persignándose: making the sign of the cross

velorio: wake

Le dan ganas, no de llorar, pero de reír a carcajadas.: She's tempted,
    not to cry, but to roar with laughter.

y su cuerpo tiembla: and her body trembles

el llanto de las mujeres: the weeping of the women

sale corriendo: running out of the house

tropezándose con las piedras: stumbling on the rocks

cuando llega a la casa de Mamagrande Ramona: when she reaches
    her grandmother Ramona's house

el coyotito: the youngest born, literally "the little coyote"

preguntas: questions

troque colorado: red truck

todas las noches: every night

Oliendo al muerto, Prietita duerme en su cama: Smelling the dead,
    Prietita sleeps in her bed

Su padre abre los ojos y la mira: Her father opens his eyes and
    looks at her

Abre su boca a contestarle: He opens his mouth to answer her

Se levanta del cajón: He rises out of the coffin

tío: uncle

dejando polvo por atrás: leaving dust behind

el compadre: a male coparent or very good friend

la iglesia: the church

el cuerpo de su padre está tendido: her father's body lies

pueblito: small town

con bigotes y corbatas negra: with mustaches and black ties

el muerto y la gente: the deceased and the people

las urracas: the crows

ébano: ebony tree

zempasuchitl: Nahuatl word for flowers for the dead

el último día que vió a su padre vivo: the last day she saw her
    father alive

en su troque colorada: in his red truck

despierta: wake up

Se voltea.: He/it turns over. (the truck flips)

unos hombres: some men

padrinos: in this case, pallbearers

sus ojos: her eyes

en la cara: on his face

no es la cara de su papi: it is not her father's face

la muerte: death

corazón: heart

La muerte lo habita.: Death inhabits him.

la mosca: the fly

sí: yes

carnales: blood kin or very good friends

ella es esa mosca: she is that fly

su corazón: her heart

la gente sigue riéndose: the people continue laughing

el viento sopla: the wind blows

el sol amanece: the sun comes out in the morning

el poza tan hondo: the hole so deep

composanto: cemetery

y montones de flores: and piles of flowers

la gente: the people

padre nuestros y ave marias: Our Fathers and Hail Marys

cuando le toca a ella: when her turn comes

tierra: earth, dirt

el cajón está vestido con las flores anaranjadas del zempasuchitl:
   the coffin is dressed with the orange flowers of the dead

Mi hijo, mi hijo, tan bueno. ¿Diosito mio, por qué se lo llevó?
   Ay mi hijo.: My son, my good son. Dear God, why did you
   take him? Oh, my son.

composantitos son jardines donde plantan a los muertos: cemeteries
   are places where we plant the dead

mujeres enlutadas: women dressed in mourning

llorosas: tearful

Santa María, madre de Dios, ruega por nosotros . . . : Holy Mary, mother of God, pray for us.

su cachuchita roja: red cap

los muchachos: the boys

luto: mourning

musica norteña: north Mexican border music

Compré este televisión para ustedes, para que aprendan inglés.: I bought this television for you, to help you learn English.

Pasa mucho tiempo: Much time goes by.

espera al muerto: waits for the dead

en el día de los muertos . . . , ella lo espera todavía en la segunda de noviembre: on the day of the dead, she waits for him still on the second of November

aunque no más viniera a visitarlos por un ratito: even if he only comes to visit them for a short while

mujeres, son abandonadas: women, they are abandoned

Part Two

Patlache

5

Como Quelite

Él que no cae tropeza.

—Mexican dicho

Who doesn't fall, stumbles.

—Mexican saying

I lean against the whitewashed wall of the pool hall with the vatos. Teté, Yunior, and the other mensos are pushing at each other. They stop zonciando to watch Marielena walk toward us with her ganga of girls. One by one we squat. Tú sabes, to be on eye level with their legs—maybe get a glimpse of their chones. Marielena's walk is like water rippling on the lagoon. That girl has poise.

She looks straight at me with soft brown eyes outlined in kohl, the lashes so long they leave spiky shadows on her cheeks. Her red cupid lips form a tiny smile. Wow, esa sonrisita is for me. Don't let me do something dorky, Virgencita, I pray. I swallow the spit collecting in my mouth and look over at Teté. His face gets real red and he almost keels over when he sees Marielena give me that special smile. Me frunce la cara. I'm afraid he's going to blurt out some pedo to the vatos. He's raked back his hair and the strands look like rat's tails, been too liberal with the mousse again. He's trying to look like a cool cholo but sweat glistens on his face.

71

Marielena walks past us in her tight minifalda, long hair rippling down to her nalgas. Teté's going to blab, me va hechar por la cabeza, I just know it. Should I tough it out or leave? What I really want to do is push his face in it. And to be near Marielena. My calf begins to cramp. I get up and follow her.

When I get home, I follow the smell of chorizo into the kitchen. Amá is stooped over el comal flipping tortillas. A garlic braid hangs on the wall between the pictures of la Virgen de San Juan and John F. Kennedy. The radio plays at low volume to the Harlingen station. "Tu Opines" is all she listens to besides her beloved boleros románticos. I switch to a Tex-Mex station.

"¡A buena hora vas llegando!" Amá eyes me. "Run down to la tiendita and get me a loaf of bread, mi prieta."

I light out of there chisqueada. Run the two blocks to Rodríguez Mart, my feet kicking up polvo. I bump into Alita Chueca buying milk. We trade off insults like good carnalas. She grabs me by the hair y me da un tirón de greñas.

Putting her owl face near my ear she whispers, "¿Sabes qué? Lela se fue a Dallas y ahora está gorda. Some pelado la abujero."

"¡Chale!" I say, walking out of el tendajo con la raba de pan.

"She just started bleeding," says Alita.

"¿Y diay qué? Remember Chavela, she got pregnant when she was twelve. Cheech, I'd never let some pelado stick his palo in me." I spit on the ground.

"Yeah, well, everybody knows you're strange—not liking boys, tú sabes," says Alita Chueca. "If I don't let mi novio picheonearme, he'll dump me and hit on some other ruca."

"Well, if not giving my nalgas to some mocoso pendejo makes me strange, then I'll be strange," I tell her.

I think about my being "strange" as I walk back. A neighborhood dog butts his nose into my hands. A couple of vatos polishing the chrome on their car. One calls out "Ey, Wild Weed, whatchu doing, vato." Sometimes se les olvida, they forget I'm a girl.

When I get home all the papas con chorizo are gone and so are Teté y mis hermanos. I poke my head out the back. Amá is bent over under the orange tree, pruning shears and trowel at her feet. She pounds dried cow pods into the soil, sinewy arms flexing. She's wearing my cast-off white tennis shoes.

"Get over here, ven a ayudarme a embonar estos naranjos, Prieta, tus hermanos se pelaron."

"No vamos a verles las caras hasta la cena a esos huevones." I look at the mustard-colored powder oozing from between the thick swollen joints of her fingers. "Como dice el dicho, a huevo, ni los zapatos entran."

Mi pinche primo acts as if he's my father. When he was real little, Amá's sister got messed up and couldn't take care of him. Amá raised us all together.

"¿Ay, Diosito, con qué fregados les voy a comprar ropa a ustedes cinco?" says Amá. School starts after Labor Day, only a couple of weeks away.

"No te apures, Amá, I'll drop out of school and work in the fields full time and not just after school and weekends." I pulverize cow pod after cow pod. I really don't want to quit school. For what, to get married and work en los files for the rest of my life? I have other plans for my future. Pero ni tampoco quiero ver a mi madre wearing herself out in the fields, the sun sucking away at her. She's as skinny as a stick as it is.

"No mijita, you do so well in school," says Amá.

"Ey, Amá, la Lela está padelante."

"¿Preñada? ¡Qué caray! Ba, girls nowaday, se les van las patas, no sé que les ha pasado. Se han hecho tan dejadas. Gracias a Díos que tú no eres como ellas."

"¿Qué dices? How am I not like other girls?" I wait for her to say que soy hija buena, viva y guapa.

Amá gives me one of her eagle eye looks, like lightning's flashing behind her irises. "Pos a tí no te gustan los hombres pa nada. You've never liked machos no how. No los dejas que se te arrimen."

"No es verda', Amá. Don't I go to the horse races with los vatos and hang out in their cars over at that empty lot. I'm pals with most of them." Yeah, but what I don't say is that when I'm with them I wish I was con las rucas or at home with my books.

"¿Y te hacen las movidas? ¿Tratan de tocarte o besarte?"

"Esos vatos, no way. If one made a move on me, I'd give 'em unos chingazos and rearrange his face."

"See what I mean?" she says.

I pick up the shovel, shove hard into the dried manure. One of the blisters I got from mowing bursts. I ignore the sting. Chingao. Does Amá want me to be like the other girls, chismeando and giggling all day long? I don't think so. Maybe she's resigned herself to having una hija rara. There's that look in her eye. I bet she's secretly pleased I'm not interested in boys.

Amá goes back inside the house. The screen door bangs. I hear her rattling pans in the kitchen. Woodsmoke from the neighbors' backyard curls around the orange trees. Doña Feliza's stirring the clothes boiling in the black olla round and round with a flat board bleached white. La vecina on the other side, Rosita García, wets down the dirt path to her backdoor with a hose. She looks like a round barefoot beetle.

Amá cranes her head out the door and says in a low voice, "Creo que tú eres una de las otras."

In her eyes, miro algo que no me gusta. Sadness or resignation? My stomach muscles contract. I continue to hose down the chips of manure and work them into the soil. What is "una de las otras"? No te hagas, I tell myself, you already know the answer. While otras rucas make cow eyes at the guys, you're busy getting an eye full of them. Yeah, so I like rucas, ¿y qué? I've always known that I'm not like anyone en mi familia. Or in the entire pueblo for that matter. Sometimes I feel like todo el mundo is looking at me, holding their breath and waiting for me to do something escandoloso. I tilt my chin up and look folks straight in the eye. Sometimes I look through them. Boy do they get shit-faced at that.

"What's *de las otras*, Amá?"

She looks at me real serious. "Cada uno es como Dios lo hizo," she says. She searches for words. "Esas mujeres son half and half. Pos, por seis meses they have the men's thing y los otros seis they have vaginas and they bleed."

I lower the hose and face her. "You're saying I'm half and half? Half what, Amá?" I'm afraid she'll say half animal or half evil. Maybe she thinks I'm one of those were-people, half-human, half-jaguar.

"Eres mita' y mita'." she says. "Mita hombre y mita hembra."

Chingao. I drop the hose.

"Cuidado con esa agua, huerca," she says.

My heart flaps in my chest like a chicken with a broken head.

"Dice la gente que por seis meses tienen la cosa del hombre y por seis meses la cosa de mujer—mita' y mita'."

"I've never heard such a thing," I say softly. "¿Dónde sacas esas ideas, Amá?"

"Es lo que dice la gente. Hay señas. One sign is liking girls."

The way she pronounces "liking" tells me that Teté must have told her I liked looking at girls' breasts. I could tell her that he puts a tiny mirror on the top of his shoe to look up the girls' dresses. But I'll not stoop that low. Cómo quiera, le voy a dar una chinga for giving me away.

I stare at her. Amá has always been hard to read. Is she disapproving on the surface, but smug and satisfied por dentro?

"How do you know, Amá?"

"When you were in my stomach, you'd kick and move around so, I thought for sure you were a boy. You never played with dolls. You had crushes on other girls. You've always liked outdoor work, eres muy hombrada, you hate housework."

I stand there real quiet until the door bangs shut. I try to picture my body changing, chest and buttocks flattening, a beard sprouting on my face. The thought of having a penis between my legs for six months makes my skin crawl. I'm afraid. I remember Nastassja Kinski slowly turning into a panther in the movie *Cat People*. When I finish fertilizing the naranjos I walk down to el billar a zonciar with the guys. Teté and Yunior look pissed at my being there. I squat down en la banqueta. The other vatos eye me suspiciously. Why had I ignored the undercurrents? I guess I want to be accepted as just another one of the guys. Only I'm not a vato. They tolerate me 'cause they want to impress me. I hit harder, spit further, and out-smart them any day of the week—and they know it. Yet they still act superior as though having huevos makes them better. To them only males can be queer. They've never heard of a female maricón. But Teté has his suspicions. He's told Amá, but he won't tell the vatos. I'm kin, maybe they'd think that being queer's in the blood.

Though I feel real aguitada, I try to muster up some enthusiasm over our usual spitting contest. I win. As we bandy insults back and forth part of my mind is on what Amá said.

I see Marielena crossing the street. And, jeez, I look at her slender arms and neck and I want to put my face there and breathe in the sun-baked smell of her skin. Marielena and I are in the same grade. I run interference for her, shove the more obnoxious vatos out of her way. If one of them gets too fresh, I kick his fundillo a mile down the road. Oh, man, it's all true. I'm a freak who's neither ruca nor vato. Some sort of off-shoot of a lost tribu? Chingao, what am I going to do?

"Ay los watcho," I tell the vatos and head on home. As I pass Marielena's house, I see her jumping rope with her little sisters. Marielena's chi chis bobbing up and down. As the one rope loops down and the other arches I jump in, bump chest to chest with Marielena. Something inside me loosens, then tightens as the ropes slap the ground. Me dan ganas de tocar her breasts. Me pela tamaños ojos. Chinpiote, am I in big trouble. Amá knows, there's a name for people like me. My feet tangle with the rope and I land on my butt in the dirt.

When I get home, Teté pounces on me, trying to swat me on my nalgas. "No me chingues, Teté." I step aside and sneer.

"Your picante attitude is going to land you in caca, chuca," he says. "¿Qué te crees?"

"Bigger and better than you, that's for sure." He's three years older. He and my brothers act like they're my father, always trying to lay down the law.

"Sangrona, you think you're un macho, or what?"

"You're the one who acts macho. Me? I don't have to pretend."

I level him a good one. "Me echaste por la cabeza, desgraciado," I tell him.

"I'm no tattletale," he says. "Besides, you have no right going out. You should be playing con tus comadritas inside."

"That's more your style, isn't it?" I say, grabbing his arm and twisting it behind his back. "Yo te conozco mosco."

"Yeah, Teté's right," my brother Yunior pipes in. "We don't like que tu salgas todas las noches a dar la vuelta."

"Métetelo en el fundillo," I tell Yunior.

"Pélame la verga." Teté jerks out of my arm lock.

"Not if you were the last person on earth," I say, grimacing at the image of me sucking his cock.

"Marielena loves it," he says.

"Wanna bet?" I jeer.

"I'm telling you, lay off Marielena. It's not normal que te guste paloma. I'm the man of the house—you do what I say."

Amá hurries in from the other room. "¡Caray!" she yells. "Váyense a la fregada, go get your haircuts."

We fight in the back seat of Tío's car all the way to Elsa and we're still squabbling when we walk into the barbershop. When we get back from the peluquería, the boys hightail it to el billar and I go into the house.

Amá takes one look at my cropped hair and says, "¡Pos, qué tienes tú, huerca, peinándote como los machos! De a tiro que estás bien tonta."

My eyes sting. "Si soy una de las otras then I'll wear my hair like one of them," I tell her. I turn away and go to the sink and blink away the tears threatening to overflow. "Amá, there's never any pleasing you," I mutter softly.

I head on back to the outhouse, the only place I can be alone. I listen to the distant barks of dogs and then pull down my pants and examine my panocha. Nada, I put my hand over my chocha and feel the soft bone hiding inside the folds. It's too small to be a cuero.

Someone pounds on the door and I hear Teté say, "Apúrate, I gotta go. You've been in there too long."

"Use the indoor one," I yell. I jerk my pants up and shove the door as hard as I can. Teté lets out a squeal, then asks, "Why is your face flushed?"

"It's hard work laying huevos. You ever seen a woman's eggs? Quick, go look down before they sink out of sight. I laid two of them this time."

Yunior comes over to see what the fuss is all about. They pinch their noses with their fingers, squeeze into the outhouse together and poke their faces entre el pozo.

"What was in your taco? Skunk hair?" Teté asks.

"Rotten eggs." I squeeze in behind them and shove their heads down until they gag.

"Metiches. I don't get into your negocios and I don't want you getting into mine."

Appears to me it's time to go about my business.

I pull the mower out of the shed and push it into Don Sebastian's yarda. I contemplate the disturbances in the field—rocks, pits, trees. The wind swells over a patch of quelites, bending the slender stalks laden with sprigs baring seeds. I yank the mower's starter cord several times. The motor catches. I move that máquina hard. I hear a rock or root ping against the blade and I bear down on the handle quickly to raise the front end of the blade. It stalls anyway. I jerk the cord again. Pendejos, always trying to run my life. Pero no los dejo que me traten con la punta del pie. When I finish school me voy a pelar, leave this backwater.

For the next hour I shove and push and pull the machine through the thick tangle of crabgrass runners, through the tall thick Bermuda and Johnson grass, through tumbleweeds, ragweeds, and wild sunflowers. The vibrations of the motor enter the palms of my hands, crawl up my arms and down my body. Simón, I like that. I like the scent of cut grass, and even the smell of my own sudor. Me da gusto in the razor-sharp blade of the hoe slicing through the stalks, the sounds of the hoe creaking. I like swinging my arms, the sharp twist of the spine, right foot pivoting slightly. The noise of the world vanishes like smoke, and silence surrounds me like a glass dome.

The prickly weeds poke me in the face when I bend down; the nettles sting my neck. It's hot and humid and, under my cap, my hair is drenched with sweat. I love how the breeze ruffles my shirt, my shoulders' sweet ache. Sweet, the anticipation of resting in the shade, gulping down an ice-cold soda pop, the breeze cooling my sweating body.

After another hour of sweating, I stop the máquina and begin pulling the weeds along the edge of the fence that escaped the blade. After a while I drop my gloves. Soon my nails clog with dirt, green juice from the weeds pools in the cracks of my hands. That's how I got my nickname. When I touch the stalks with their lavender veins I feel as though my feet have roots all the way to the middle of the earth y que nada y nadie me pueden tumbar.

People see quelites as the worst of pests, cut them down, burn them out, spray them with poisons, anything to get rid of them. They don't like their sting, nor how they crowd out the plants, take up all the nutrients, all the sunlight. Not me; I think quelites ought to have their own plots. Quelites have good qualities, too. Mamagrande says los indios de más antes used to make tea and soups from quelites. They ate it like we eat spinach. Anglos call them lamb's quarters. Maybe I'll try cooking with them. I pick a bunch of tender lavender-stemmed quelites to take home.

I rub the calluses forming on my hands. I stretch my aching back and look at my work; grass is smooth as a shaved cheek. The anger in me lies in little pieces with the cut grass. Now I hear Patruch's dilapidated truck squawking down the road. A flight of birds tittering across to each other flies overhead. Tía's TV is blaring out a telenovela through the walls.

"Aquí está, Quelite de las manitas verdes." Don Sebastian pulls out a five from a worn flat wallet.

"Why so quiet? You usually have as many words as a yard has weeds."

Teté makes fun of me for cutting lawns, but I like watching the weeds growing. I've learned a lot of things mowing. Like not to do things half-assed so I won't have to cover the same ground twice like he does. I've learned to measure the length and width of the lawn with my eyes and figure the time it will take me and the quarts of gasoline I'll need and how much to charge while he's still dithering. I don't work that hard, pero tampoco hago la perra like some people. Y a todo le tiro. I've learned that there's only one way to work—one step at a time, one chop at a time, one row at a time.

I pocket my earnings and strut down the main drag with my thumbs hooked into my jean pockets, the sun warm on my trimmed hair, feeling good about my taut muscles and wide shoulders.

I wash the quelites, cut them up and sauté them in olive oil with a couple of garlic cloves, half an onion, a chopped tomato, and some cooked chorizo. I add a little chicken stock and scramble in three eggs. When the eggs have almost set, I throw in some cilantro and queso fresco. I don't plan on telling my family what they've eaten until they've eaten.

Translations

como quelites: like weeds

vatos: pachuco words for guys

mensos: stupid idiots

zonciando: horsing around

ganga: gang

tú sabes: you know

chones: for calzones, panties

esa sonrisita: that little smile

Virgencita: diminutive for the Virgin of Guadalupe

Me frunce la cara.: He scowls at me.

pedo: fart

cholo: slang for a Mexican American dude or guy

minifalda: miniskirt

nalgas: butt, ass

me va hechar por la cabeza: he's going to tattle

chorizo: Mexican sausage

el comal: the griddle

la Virgen de San Juan: the Virgin of San Juan

"Tu Opines": Your Opinion

boleros románticos: romantic ballads

A buena hora vas llegando: you come at a good time

la tiendita: the corner store

mi prieta: an endearment that refers to a dark-skinned girl

chisqueada: in a hurry

polvo: dust

carnalas: blood kin or very close friends

y me da un tirón de greñas: and she jerks my hair

¿Sábes qué?: You know what?

Lela se fue a Dallas y ahora esta gorda.: Lela went to Dallas and
    now she is fat. ("Ir a Dallas" is a play on words: "dalas" is a
    slang way to say sexual intercourse.)

pelado la abujero: slick talker made a hole in her

¡Chale!: No way!

el tendajo con la raba de pan: the store with the loaf of bread

¿Y diay qué?: So what?

pelado: slick talker

palo: penis, literally a stick

mi novio picheonearme: my boyfriend pinch my nipples

ruca: from pachuca meaning girl

mocoso pendejo: snot-nosed jerk

se les olvida: they forget

papas con chorizo: potatoes with Mexican sausage

mis hermanos: my brothers

Ven a ayudarme a embonar estos narranjos, Prieta, tus hermanos se
   pelaron.: Come here and help me, Prieta, your brothers split.

No vamos a verles las caras hasta la cena a esos huevones.: We're
   not going to see those lazy jerks until dinner.

Como dice el dicho, a huevo, ni los zapatos entran.: As the saying
   goes, you can't force a lazy person.

mi pinche primo: my damn cousin

¿Ay, Diosito, con qué fregados les voy a comprar ropa a ustedes
   cinco?: Dear God, with what am I going to buy clothes for
   these five?

no te apures: don't worry

en los files: in the fields

Pero ni tampoco quiero ver a mi madre: Neither do I want to
   see my mother

mijita: my little daughter, a term of endearment

la Lela está padelante: Lela is pregnant

¿Preñada? ¡Qué caray!: Pregnant? Geez!

Se les van las patas, no sé que les ha pasado. Se han hecho tan
   dejadas. Gracias a Díos que tú no eres como ellas.: The young

girls of today. I don't know what has happened to them. They
have become so loose. Thank God you're not like them.

¿Qué dices?: What are you saying?

que soy hija buena, viva y guapa: that I'm a good daughter, lively
and smart

Pos a tí no te gustan los hombres pa nada.: You don't like men
for nothing.

machos: males

No los dejas que se te arrimen.: You don't even let them come
near you.

no es verda': that's not true

con las rucas: with the girls

¿Y te hacen las movidas? ¿Tratan de tocarte o besarte?: And do
they put the moves on you, try to touch or kiss you?

esos vatos: those guys

unos chingazos: some blows

chingao: Chicano vernacular for chingado, or fucked

chismeando: gossiping

una hija rara: a strange daughter

Doña: Mrs.

olla: big black kettle

la vecina: the neighbor

Creo que tú eres una de las otras.: I think you're one of the others
(as in queer).

miro algo que no me gusta: I see something that I don't like

no te hagas: don't pretend

otras rucas: other girls

¿y qué?: so what?

en mi familia: in my family

pueblo: town

todo el mundo: everyone

escandaloso: scandalous

Cada uno es como Dios lo hizo: Each one of us is as God made us

esas mujeres son: those women are

Pos, por seis meses: for six months

y los otros seis: and the other six

Eres mita' y mita'.: You're half and half.

mita' hombre y mita' hembra: half man and half woman

Cuidado con esa agua, huerca: Be careful with that water, girl

Dice la gente que por seis meses tienen la cosa del hombre y por seis meses la cosa de mujer.: People say that for six months they have the man's thing and for six months the woman's thing.

¿Dónde sacas esas ideas?: Where do you get such ideas?

Es lo que dice la gente. Hay señas.: That's what people say. There are signs.

Cómo quiera, le voy a dar una chinga: Whatever you want, I'm going to give him a beating

por dentro: in the inside

eres muy hombrada: you are very masculine

naranjos: oranges

el billar a zonciar: the billiards to fool around

en la banqueta: on the sidewalk

huevos: balls

maricón: gay

aguitada: wilted, tired, depressed

fundillo: ass

tribu: tribe

Ay los watcho: We'll see you later

chi chis: breasts

me dan ganas de tocar: I want to touch

Me pela tamaños ojos.: She eyes me.

chinpiote: damn it

No me chingues.: Don't mess with me.

picante: biting, hot

caca: shit

chuca: short for pachuca, zoot-suiter, homegirl

¿Qué te creés?: Who do you think you are?

sangrona: snob

Me echaste por la cabeza, desgraciado: You gave me away, damn you

con tus comadritas: with your little girlfriends

Yo te conozco mosco.: I see through you.

que tu salgas todas las noches a dar la vuelta: that you go out
     every night and make the rounds

Métetelo en el fundillo: Stick it up your butt.

Pélame la verga.: Suck my dick. (vulgar slang)

que te guste paloma: that you like pussy

caray: geez!

váyense a la fregada: go to hell

peluquería: barbershop

¡Pos, qué tienes tú, huerca, peinándote como los machos! De a tiro que estás bien tonta.: Well, what's wrong with you, girl, combing your hair like men. Really, you're pretty stupid.

si soy una de las otras: if I am one of the others

panocha: pussy or cunt

nada: nothing

chocha: pussy or cunt

cuero: penis, literally skin

apúrate: hurry up

huevos: eggs (in the literal sense)

entre el pozo: into the outhouse hole

metiches: buttinskies, gossips

negocios: business

Don: Mr.

yarda: yard

quelites: weeds

máquina: machine

pendejos: jerks

Pero no los dejo que me traten con la punta del pie.: But I don't let them walk all over me.

me voy a pelar: I'm splitting

simón: yes, of course

sudor: sweat

me da gusto: it gives me pleasure

y que nada y nadie me pueden tumbar: and that nothing and no one can shake me

mamagrande: grandmother

los indios de más antes: the Indians a long time ago

telenovela: Spanish soap opera

Aquí está, Quelite de las manitas verdes.: There you go, Quelite of the green hands.

pero tampoco hago la perra: but I don't slack off (literally "make the dog")

Y a todo le tiro.: And I'll work at anything.

queso fresco: fresh white cheese

6

Mita' y mita'

Alita Chueca and I sit out back on the tire swings and sip cream sodas. The heady smell of orange tree blossoms goes to my head.

I see Marielena walking down the street. She's wearing a tight shirt that outlines her boobs. She looks like a go-go girl in her miniskirt and cowboy boots. Marielena turns her head real slow and gives me a tiny smile. Wow! What was that about? It's as though she knows what's going through my mind. I feel my face heat up. Does she know I'm one of those half macho-half hembras? She couldn't be one, too, could she?

There it is, staring me in the face. I could look the other way and pretend I wasn't different, haven't seen it, keep running from it. Or I can face what I am and see where it leads me. I think I've always known. When the girls talked about how some vato is going to take them out of the dirt and away from the fields I just couldn't picture it for me. My dreams are different. There's always a ruca there in the dream shadows. She looks at machos straight in the eye, never bows her head, never shuffles her feet.

"You know what, Alita Chueca?"

"No, what?" she says.

"A mi me gustan las rucas."

Man, she doesn't even blink an eyelash. "Yeah, I guessed. It'll be our secret."

"I want to tell everyone," I say.

"You can't. They'll think you're sick. Nobody will talk to you."

"Alita, I think they already know I'm different from the other girls." Alita and all the other rucas in the eighth grade are totally gaga over boys. Lela and Chavela are barely thirteen and now they're pregnant and have dropped out of school.

"They don't know for sure that you're a homo," says Alita.

"I'm a what?"

"You know, eres un queer."

"Do queers go into cantinas?"

"Not if people know they're queer. Oh, wait a minute, you're not thinking of . . . you're too young to get in."

"I could always borrow Tía's I.D. We look sort of alike."

Alita Chueca snorts. "I know what, pretend you like vatos. If you start going with a guy, they'll forget about you being strange."

"That sucks. If la gente says go right and I go left, I'm supposed to feel bad about it, supposed to feel I'm doing something wrong or that there's something wrong with me. Well, fuck that shit."

Maybe I should try it. Then I'd know for sure.

I let one of the high school vatos corner me against the chainlink fence of the community center. Just stand there passively and let him pinchonearme. But while he's grinding his body into mine all I want to do is belt him. Yuck it's gross. Jeez, how do girls stand their clumsy groping hands?

Late one afternoon I decide to try the local cantina. I see myself flirting with las cantineras. The rucas drool when I swagger in whistling so cool. But what actually happens is all the guys stare at me and la cantinera says to get out. When Teté finds out he starts raving at the mouth. "Cantinas are for putas," he yells.

"Tú sabes que te quiero vida mia pero tu sigues viviendo en las cantinas . . . ," I croon in his face and he gets so mad I think he's going to explode.

I slam out of the house and go sit on the swing and talk to la Virgencita in my head. I ask her if it's a bad thing being a woman for six months and a man for the other six. No sé cómo caminaría con esa cosa hanging between my legs. I'd be afraid to get it caught on barbwire or something. The thought of growing a penis suddenly disgusts me. Maybe it would be handier than fingers. But how would las rucas react when they'd see it? I could tell them I'd strapped on a watchamacallit, a dildo. I guess I could get used to having a penis, but only if I didn't have to give up my hole.

I sit on the swing whistling, trying to picture the day I'm going to wake up with a dick between my legs. I'd be tall and strong but womanly. No one would try to ponerme en mal. I'd put la movida on Marielena. Sweep her right off her feet and carry her away to Corpus Christi for our luna de miel. She'd put red polish on her fingers and toes and an off-the-shoulder dress tight as chorizo casing.

I light a cigarette then jump off the swing and practice strutting around with huevos between my legs. ¡Chin! A foot comes out of nowhere tripping me.

"Ay, mi prietita, chiflando como un macho?" dice mi primo. "¿Qué dirá la gente?"

"Baboso, I can whistle better than you." I imagine taking out my pipi and pissing on him. Instead, I blow smoke in his face.

Amá comes out of the kitchen. "Que boquita tienes," says Amá. "You brag like a macho, mijita."

I lower my head. People who boast have the least to brag about.

'Amá looks at me sharply. "Sácate ese cigaro de la boca, muchacha. ¿Se te van a podrir los pulmones antes de que cumplas los veinte años, pos, mira, que tienes, tonta?"

"Oh mom, chill out."

I go back to the swing and talk to la Virgencita some more. It's your call, I tell her. I leave it up to her whether I'm going to be a marimacho or not. Pero, ¿sabes qué? I already know the answer.

Amá calls me to come in and get ready to go shopping. Teté, Yunior, and me get in the car. When we get to the store, I pick my clothes off the boys' racks and buy zapatos at the men's department. I get me a thick black belt with spikes and a smaller one for around my upper arm. I cut the sleeves off my t-shirts. Now I've got to learn the moves, how a marimacho does stuff.

When Tío drives us to Edinburg to get groceries, I leave Amá pushing a cart up and down the aisle and sneak out for a few minutes. Brazenly I get copies of *Penthouse* and *Hustler*. The store clerk winks. When I get home I hide them under my mattress.

Later, I take them out and tuck them under my shirt and go to the escusado. I flip the pages in the half light. Spider webs glistening all around me. Jeez, would you look at that dark mound where see-through panties meet thigh. I put my hand up my shirt and squeeze my pezones, smear them with my saliva, then blow on them. I rub my gusanito. A warmth spreads through my body, and my arms and legs feel heavy. Something tightens in my paloma. After about half an hour I stagger back to the house. I always feel like I've done something right but that I can't let others know I do it.

On my thirteenth birthday I borrow Tío's pink Chevrolet and drive to Harlingen. I don't tell him I'm going out of town. I'm curious. I'd heard one of the vato's older brothers talk about this porno place on Third. I park a block away and sit in the car until I get my nerve up. I walk past the place a couple of times trying to get the pachuco strut just right. I muster up my courage and saunter in before I chicken out. The Adult Bookstore is dark as a bat cave. But instead of bat droppings I smell urine and disinfectant. There's something sticky under my shoes.

The man behind the counter turns a blind eye. Los pelados watching the skinflicks give me knowing looks. On the screen a bare-chested guy wearing a black hood and dressed in black leather is whirling a whip, while a woman dressed in red bra and garter belt, stockings and heels stares at him, her tongue peeking out of her mouth. She pretends to look vulnerable. Behind her, skinny whips and silver chains hang on the walls.

Videos of cocks of all colors and sizes, come shots in slow motion, repeated sequences of fucking like two dogs doing it. No touching, no tenderness—not exactly what I'd come to see. After half an hour I walk away. I like the movies in my head better.

Esa noche I lie on the lawn and look at the stars. I close my eyes and ease into the sky. When I open my eyes something in my middle opens up too. The sky and the night and the stars come into my body. My heart beats to a slower rhythm, my breath slows.

I go back inside the house and get into bed. I go through my repertoire of fantasies. In one of them I'm standing at the corner and she walks by, mamacita, and my body gets real caliente. Me da calentura. I'd ask her, "Wanna be my novia? I wanna go all the way with you." I take her to the lake, start real slow so as not to spook her. And after kissing her y acariciándola, what?

I practice the words and the moves for weeks. Finally, I make the movida. I go up to Marielena at the ball game when she's away from her friends and call her out. She hesitates and then nods her head shyly.

We stop at the burger place for take-out then drive to the lake. With the screech of tires I brake the car at the edge of the lake. Hot breeze blows in through the window. As we get out of the car, sweat starts pooling in my armpits.

I spread out the towel on top of the clumps of grass along the edge of the water. Just staring at her makes my crotch wet. My heart lurches. I feel squishy and faint. I take my eyes off Marielena and stare at the calm surface of the lake. I feel mesmerized by the glimmer of water. After we eat she wades in the water. "Want me to swim across the lake and back?" I ask her.

"In the dark?" She's incredulous.

I'm not any better than the vatos who try to impress her except I can swim across and back and none of them does that—too scared.

She comes out of the water. I dry her legs with my hands, coax her into the backseat. I stroke her neck. I put my hand down her top. She has small erect breasts. Soft but they soon get hard. I tug her bathing top off her shoulders, baring her breasts. I wet her nipples with my tongue. She tastes like warm sun on skin. My nose flares as I smell her wet cunt.

When I start to tug off her bikini, Marielena pulls my hands away.

"OK, OK," I whisper, returning my mouth to her breast. I wait a few beats then cup her panocha, rub it back and forth.

Marielena bursts into tears. I draw away. Shit. When I see she's really upset, I hold her, rock her back and forth until she stops crying.

For days all I can think about is Marielena. What if she tells Teté? What if she tells the whole town. Then I remember her smell, her taste. I tremble just thinking about our next date. Two more days. What if Marielena says no when I ask her to be my novia? Should I tell her about being half and half and the change my body will go through? Will she be repulsed?

On our second date we hang out at her folks' place. We sit on the couch and I put my hands on her bare skin. I start kissing her and squeezing her breasts. I fumble around her front, then ease one finger into her blouse and sneakily begin to unbutton it. Before she notices her breasts are bare. I yank off my shirt and pull her body against mine. I rock us closer, feel the warmth and softness. She giggles and tries to wiggle away but I can tell she likes it. We tickle each other, wrestle and roll around on the sofa. Her giggles set me off. I nip tiny sucking kisses on her face and neck, inhaling deeply all that sweetness. I can feel my lips getting swollen. She'll probably end up with a hickey on her neck. I turn her on her back and nibble on her soft inner arms. I put the palms of my hands on her breasts and squeeze firm like mangoes. I run my tongue over her pezones then close my mouth over it and suck hard. She's sweeter than mangoes. She moans. I keep on sucking while I stroke her stomach and hips.

"Do you like that, babe-ita?"

"Yes," she gasps, "not rough like Teté."

I cup her crotch and move my palm back and forth. I know what she wants, my stroking here, 'cause I like to touch myself there. Then I put my thumb on her gusanito and press in firmly. I spread her pussy lips; they're wet and swollen. Tiene el burro hinchado. I draw her clit into my mouth and then suck her pussy. Me la como, leche quemada, thick y sabrosita. Her legs begin to tremble.

"Ay, Prieta, Prieta, Prieta," she cries.

Her hips jerk up, her gasps turn into little breathless screams. Su panochita contracts around my finger. I come up for air, spitting cunt hairs out of my mouth. I'm so dizzy I think I might faint.

Marielena bursts into tears. The shock of coming and by my hand not Teté's or some other vato's. I hold her in my arms and rock her until she stops crying.

"Wow," she says, "I've never let Teté go that far."

I sprawl back against the couch. After a few minutes I say, "Your turn now, baby. Ahora va la mia." I think about letting go like that, screaming out her name like she did mine.

Marielena just lays there. I shake her arm.

"I can't," she says. "You should go now."

Shee-it, I can't believe she wants me to leave. "Why'd you let me do it?" I ask her.

"Well, it's not like doing it with a guy. I mean, with you I don't lose my virginity," she says.

"Baby, I got news for you. You just lost yours and I was your first, not Teté or some other vato." I jerk on my clothes and rip out of her house. I feel so stupid thinking she'd want to be my novia. Que pendeja soy. The little shit, I'll never speak to her again.

But after five days I'm back at her house. Como dice la gente, amor de lejos, amor de pendejos. I didn't want her to forget me. And I want another chance. Let's go to my room, she says. I lock the door. I watch Marielena, listen with one ear to the sounds in the next room where su papá y mamá are watching Pedro Infante on TV. When she gives me that little secret smile, I go to her and kiss her mouth, deeply.

We sit on the bed and I take off her blouse. A deep rose flushes up her chest.

"Take off your panties," I whisper. "I want to see. No, don't turn off the light."

She leaves the lamp alone and just sits there. But she doesn't stop me when I pull her underwear off. Her pubic hair is lighter than mine and softer.

I stroke Marielena's vaginal lips. They're velvety sleek, soft as a baby's cheek. They turn a deep purple, swell. I suck her clit, hold it between my teeth, roll my tongue around it while I stroke inside her with my forefinger.

I cream her cherry, but again she won't return the favor. When I ask her to be my novia she says she's afraid of what la gente will say. I'm so mad at her I almost tell her either you be my novia or I'll tell everyone you got caught shoplifting. But I want her to want me without my forcing her. Finally I leave, furious again.

I walk to the empty lot. Ando vuelta y vuelta. I can't stand that mierda, what will people say. For all my bravado I at least put my hand in. But Marielena no vale cuacha, se queda con los brazos cruzados. She doesn't have much to say either. Or maybe I talk too much. Dice 'Amá que me brotan palabras de la lengua como quelites. Maybe I'm full of shit too, thinking some day I'm going to make use of all those words that sprout out of my mouth.

Next day at the ball game I see Marielena with Teté. Marielena glances at me sheepishly, then quickly looks away. Later she comes up to me when I'm alone at the water fountain. She says she's sorry for having torcido su cara and snubbing me. She tells me she just wants to hang out, you know, and me do her. Period. Says I've ruined her for Teté, that he's ignorant about girls' bodies.

I don't like it much, but I want to be with her so bad I'll put up with her not touching me the way I want. But for now, I'm not talking to her. Maybe in a while. Give her a chance to think about us. I do have some pride. Ya lo verá. Now she's in for it. I'll wait a few days. Maybe by then she'll feel what I feel for her and she'll touch me. It's real hard, but I walk away from her.

I see a girl with close-cropped hair, the macho stance, the searching glance. I go up to her. We eye each other and nod. We recognize each other right off the bat. I stand by her, want the others to notice that we're similar. I want Marielena and the whole world to know I'm not ashamed of what I am.

We eye each other and nod. She's the starting pitcher for the San Juan team. Chingao, she can throw those balls. You don't even see the ball when a thud hits the catcher's mitt. Taller than most of the tejanitas in these parts, not built close to the ground like most of la raza. Está guapísima, esa muchachona.

She brings her girlfriend over to me. Her ruca has hair down to her ass. She wears livid purple lipstick and has pencil-thin eyebrows. We lean against Tío's pick-up and talk. La marimacho says they know a whole lot more volteadas como nosotras.

"If you want to meet some, come to the gay bar in McAllen Saturday night," she says. "We'll be waiting for you."

When I get home I do my chores. I feed the chickens and while they're eating I clean out el gallinero. La gallina culeca sits on her eggs. Ignoring the sharp pecks on the back of my hand, I ease one hand under her. The eggs are warm. One of them is cracked. I take it out and I hold it in my hand. I feel something inside, moving tenuously at first then more vigorously until the tiny beak appears through the crack. With three more shoves the head emerges then its entire body. Pink trembly body, white feathery wisps, then out staggers the newly hatched chick leaving la cáscara behind. That's how I feel, alive and newly born.

Translations

mita' y mita': half and half

hembras: females

vato: pachuco word for guy

ruca: chick

A mi me gustan las rucas.: I like girls.

eres un queer: you're a queer

tía: aunt

la gente: people

pichonear: pinching

las cantineras: the barmaids or loose women

putas: whores

Tú sabes que te quiero vida mia pero tu sigues viviendo en las
    cantinas . . . : You know that I love you my life but you
    continue to live in the cantinas

no sé cómo caminaría con esa cosa: I don't know how I'd move
    with that thing

ponerme en mal: put me in wrong, put me in danger

la movida: the move

la luna de miel: honeymoon

chorizo: Mexican sausage

chin: short for chingado

"¿Ay, mi prietita, chiflando como un macho?" dice mi primo. "¿Que
    dirá la gente?": "My little prieta, whistling like a man," my
    cousin tells me. "What will people say?"

baboso: idiot

Que boquita tienes.: What a little mouth you have.

mijita: diminutive for "my daughter"

Sácate ese cigaro de la boca, muchacha. ¿Se te van a podrir los
    pulmones antes de que cumplas los veinte años, pos, mira, que
    tienes, tonta?: Take that cigar from your mouth, girl. You are
    going to rot out your lungs before you finish your twentieth
    year. Well, look what's the matter with you, dummy?

marimacho: mannish dyke, stone butch

Pero, ¿sabes qué?: But, you know what?

zapatos: shoes

tío: uncle

escusado: refers to the bathroom in general, in this case outhouse

pezones: nipples

gusanito: clit

paloma: pussy or cunt

pachuco: Mexican American man who is part of an urbanized youth subculture

los pelados: the perverts

esa noche: that night

caliente: hot

me da calentura: it gives me a fever (calentura means passion)

novia: girlfriend or lover

y acariciándola: and caressing it

panocha: pussy or cunt

Tiene el burro hinchado.: Her pussy is swollen.

Me la como, leche quemada, thick y sabrosita.: I eat her, boiling milk, thick and tasty.

su panochita: her little pussy

Ahora va la mia.: Now comes mine.

Qué pendeja soy.: What a dummy I am.

Como dice la gente, amor de lejos, amor de pendejos: Like people say, out of sight out of mind.

su papá y mamá: her father and mother

ando vuelta y vuelta: roaming in circles

mierda: shit

no vale cuacha: is not worth shit

se queda con los brazos cruzados: just lays there with her arms
   crossed

Dice Amá que me brotan palabras de la lengua como quelites.:
   Mom says that words bloom in my tongue like weeds.

torcio su cara: contorted her face

Ya lo verá.: She will see.

chingao: fuck

tejanitas: Chicanas from Texas

Está guapísima, esa muchachona.: She is very handsome and clever,
   this big girl.

volteadas como nosotras: queer (literally turned) like us

el gallinero: the coop

la gallina culeca: the brooding hen

la cáscara: the shell

7

Movidas of a Baby Butch

On Saturday night I drive to McAllen in Tío's pick-up, mine now. When I turned fifteen last week, I forked over the $200 I'd saved for months. As I zip along 281, I fantasize about what could take place at the bar. I'd find people like me—I wouldn't be the only ruca who likes other rucas. My friendship with Marielena isn't really real. I'm only half of myself with her, and she's only half of herself with me. The pretend half. I never know what she's really feeling or thinking. With her I'm sort of like I am with the vatos, but more me.

I park at the back of the gay bar so folks wouldn't see me. When I enter the bar I almost choke on the smoke. My body droops with the sinking feeling of letdown when I see guys there. Now why did I think there'd be only rucas?

The young maricón behind the counter smiles and winks as he plops down a Dos Equis in front of me. I start getting my blood up when the bottle is half empty. I raise my head and look around me. On my right two pirujas holding each other by the hips, mouth glued to mouth. Many more flores are slow dancing in a small space in the back. I unclench my jaw and watch two women looking dreamily into each other's eyes, barely chancleando on the dance floor, oblivious to those around them.

I lock eyes with una chavalita wearing tight blue jeans and a white halter top. Me da ganas de tumbárselas. Anda sola. The blood in my veins surges up like water in an irrigation pipe. My legs and arms feel so weak I think I'm going to ooze off the stool. I would've sat there drooling all night if I hadn't had to close my mouth to swallow. Couples whirl past me, the percussion thumps become my heartbeat.

People start leaving. All night I've had my eye on this cha-parrita in jeans and white halter. Anda sola. Though others come up to her and chat briefly, she's not with anyone. She tosses her hair back whenever she catches me looking. The way she moves her body, hips swelling out from a slender waist. ¡Ay! ¡Que cuer-pázo tiene esa chula! I look at the curve of her throat, let my eyes slide down to the swollen, slightly drooping chi chis. I'm about to chicken out. My bladder is full and I am tired of standing in line for the bathroom. The maripó is looking at me and I'm starting to say olvídate and split when I see him slowly, without moving his head, point with his eyes toward the end of the bar. And there she is, sitting alone.

I rev up my nervio. Estoy pisteada but I manage a waddle through the smoky dimness, my legs spread out like a sailor try-ing to balance on a rocking ship. I ease into the stool next to her. My fingers tighten around the beer can. I can't think of anything original to say to her, so I say, "Can I buy you a drink?" She smiles at me and I feel heat flush my face. My hand trembles against the sweating on the cerveza. I want to put my hands on her so bad my stomach hurts.

"What's your name, baby?" I ask.

"Carmela. What's yours?"

"They call me la Prieta, a sus órdenes," I say with a slight bow. Chingao, butches bow not femmes. We talk until the maricón comes over and says he's closing.

"You need a ride?" I ask.

"Sure, why not," she says.

We get in the car. The radio blares y le doy más quedito. My hands are slippery on the steering wheel. I cup first one hand then the other on my jeans, but my hands remain damp.

I ease the car into her street and park it in front of her house instead of the driveway. Don't want to risk waking her folks. We slip in through the dark kitchen. I cringe when the floorboards creak loudly.

"Mis padres can't hear. Not even a hailstorm can rouse them," she says. "Do you want some café con leche?" she asks.

I don't want any coffee, but I also don't want her to know how eager I am to find her bed, so I say yes. I don't want to ruin anything. She reheats the coffee, then hands me a cup. I take a deep gulp and burn my throat. An air bubble hurts my chest. El café is awful. Finally, I put down the empty cup. I can feel my muscles vibrate against my bones.

When I start kissing her Carmela pulls me by the hand into her bedroom and we fall on the bed. "Shit," I whisper. I unhook her halter as I kiss her and tug down the zipper of her jeans. I slide my mouth down her throat, across her collarbone and down to her tetas and move my hand toward the dark mound where calzones meet thighs. The trembling in my thighs and legs turns into shaking.

While I suck hard on her nipple, I manage to pull her jeans along with her panties down her hips and free her feet. I move my hand down her stomach to her pubic hair. It feels so soft and springy. I cup her panchona then press down firmly. Her pelvis jerks up into my hand and she moans. I slide two fingers between her thighs and into the moist folds, stroke in and out and around, and then smear her pezona with her cunt cream. She whimpers, sighs and ahs so loud I think she'll wake the neighborhood. I bring my mouth to her breast and tug her chi chis with my lips tucked over my teeth before trailing my open mouth down her belly, over her thicket. I anchor my mouth into her crevice and move my fingers up near her clit. I suck her juices like a thirst-crazed orphan in the desert. Silky coolness at first, her skin, but now some inner sun has sent its rays through her and slowly, like an ear of corn, she thrusts up toward the heat. The light slowly opening her until she lies there, silky liquid como la flor del elote. She clutches my hair and her body heaves up almost unsitting me. She lets out a long low scream, then flops back into the mattress and just lies there.

I listen for her parents' footsteps, for the banging on the door. Nothing.

I hold her and I wait, thinking in a few minutes she'll get herself together. Finally, a woman is going to do me. This is it. I've always been the one que mete la mano primero. For the first time in my life I am going to get laid. Forget that shit about a marimacho never allowing la mujercita to do her.

I rock her soft weight along my side. She sighs and her warm breath stirs the hair on my forehead. She kisses me firmly and just as my tongue begins to search for hers, her mouth disappears, leaving mine open like a fish gasping for water and floundering on dry land.

"You gotta leave now," she says.

"¡Jijo de su!" I say. "It's your turn to fuck me."

"'Tás loca, I'd never do a thing like that. It's dirty, man. I mean, I'm not queer like you all."

"You were at the bar, you let me bring you home, you let me do it. ¿Por qué Carmelita?"

"Marimachos como tú are better than the guys. You know where to touch a woman. But I'm not like you. You'd better go."

"Chingao, I can't fucking believe this. You led me on."

"Yeah, well now you have to go. What if my padres catch you here. It isn't natural," she says.

I jerk on my jeans and give the table a good whack with my foot.

"Shush," she says. I kick the chair.

"Wake up, everyone, wake up." I sort of go crazy knocking down everything I can reach. Then I throw myself against the walls.

"Carmela?"

When I hear su mamá's voice, I sober up fast. I jump through her open window, knocking down the screen and trampling plants.

Driving home I turn up KRIO full blast and blink back the tears. Freddy Fender is singing, "Ábrenme paso que vengo herido con esta vieja. . . ."

I keep seeing her push me away like I had the mange and she'd catch it if she touched me. ¡Qué gacho! How could I have wanted that mierdita so much? She was just like Marielena, couldn't find the fucking fuse box if her life depended on it. Pretending helplessness with that passivity that sours into real weakness if kept up long enough. What could I possibly see in straight chavalas like her? I'm supposed to have the most feria, the chick with the dick. So why do they get to call the shots? Ni modo.

What had that pájaro called me? Buchita? Buchona? Yeah, las buchonas make all the moves, do all the work. It's up to us to spot a potential, make la movida, lead the way, decide what movie to see, where to stop for burgers, the one who counts her money, borrows the car, puts gas in it. The one who decides whether to put her hand down her blouse or up her skirt.

Las mujercitas get restless around me and give me coquettish looks from behind lowered lashes. Maybe they've heard that I know my way around a woman's body. I don't know that much, but next to those randy vatos who are all cock, I'm a virtuoso. I've learned how to rev up las rucas—much more fun than trying to get the lawn mower going. It's a challenge to try to figure out exactly what rucas want.

When I get home I go straight to my room. I stick Freddy Fender in the cassette player and turn the sound all the way up. I have it plugged into a couple of speakers I found in the dump. After I re-wired them, they were as good as new.

"Since I met you baby, my whole life has changed." Freddy's rough brassy voice brings pieces of my life into the room.

"Prieta, dale más quedito," Amá yells from the other room. I grab the headset and jam it on my head, turn it up until my eardrums ache.

Well, I've had it up to here with initiating the kissing and the pigeoniada, with creaming cherries. No more. I am going to switch over, see how being a passive muñequita cuts it.

'Amá looks up as I walk in wearing una falda y blusa that I borrowed from Chucha. The look on her face is priceless.

"Ay, mija, ¿qué te hiciste?" she screams when she sees the blood running down my leg.

"It's OK, I cut myself shaving," I tell her. Tío scrunches his face. You would have thought I was a man who had shaved his legs.

"Look, I shaved my underarms too." I raise them to show blood caked along one of the folds.

'Amá gives another little shriek and Tío says, "Pos, ¿qué te dio hacer eso, niña?"

I stand before the mirror, twist around to see how my rear end looks. I stick out my boobs, try to walk with mincing steps like the rucas. I feel encased in a sausage skin and my legs feel wobbly in the narrow patent leather shoes with two-inch heels.

"How do women walk in these things?" I ask 'Amá who is still staring at me with her hands on her hips. "Don't give me that look. You've always wanted me to stop acting como un macho and start acting like a vieja. Well, you got your wish."

"Huh! The day you do what I tell you will be the day they lay me down in my grave. ¿Quieres fooliar a alguien? Don't you?"

"¡Újale, 'Amá! No matter what I do you're never satisfied."

"Well, now that you're a girl—look at that red fingernail polish. Alejandra, do you see that?" Tío says, lifting my hand up. "¿Que hiciste con tus greñas? You look like a cantinera with that flower in your hair. Where'd you get those chapetas?" says Tío, touching the long earrings that dangle down to my shoulder.

"But you've got a macho haircut, large earrings don't go with it," says Amá.

"That's OK, it'll grow and I'll be just another femme."

"¿Femme? ¿Qué es eso, femme?"

"Tú sabes, it's short for feminine."

"Pos, qué cosas se te ocurren a ti, mijita. Ave María Purísima. Ándale, quítate esa ropa y ven ayúdame a desgranar las mazorcas," Amá tells me.

After that my fantasies change. Instead of the tall handsome vato, I'm the ruca with the bright-red fingernail polish and an off-the-shoulder dress, skintight, walking in black spike heels. I am now the other half of the mita' y mita'.

When my hair grows a bit, I get Tía Queta to give me a permanent, one of those soft curl perms. At Woolworth's, I get some fabric and a pattern that is the closest I can find to the off-the-shoulder dress of my fantasies. I ruin the neckline so I go and get more material and this time I get it to look just right, although Amá says it is fruncido on one side.

On Saturday I get all dolled up and drive to the mixed bar in McAllen. I check out las buchonas but my eyes keep coming back to a femme sitting at the bar. Alone. I move up to a bar stool closer to her and watch las rucas flock around her, sniffing, tongues hanging out. I smile when she ignores them.

She is wearing black hose and a burgundy dress that looks like a slip. The color of her dress would look like wet shine if she spilled any water on it. It rides halfway up her thighs. A wide, red belt hangs low on her hips. Her hair tumbles in wild curls all the way down her back. Between the hem of her dress and the garter belt, I catch a glimpse of soft mounds of flesh, tinged blue-ish white by the bar lights. I can't seem to take my eyes from that stretch of flesh. With a black gloved hand she slowly brings the glass to her mouth. I hear the clink of ice against her teeth and think, she's the one.

Sensing someone staring at her, she turns around in her stool with a slight motion of her bare shoulder. We make eye contact. Pink lace outlines and falls from under her high-nippled breasts. A thin black cloth nestles between them. As my eyes rise, I see that it is a man's tie hanging loosely around her neck.

Ay mamacita, I can almost feel the rough texture of her blouse against my breasts. And the sight of her peaked brown titties makes my nipples harder.

"Hey, mamá," I say. My palms are sweating, my heart is pounding and I'm wearing the wrong costume. What a time to try to switch. All I can think of is this raunchy woman, sweet shy woman, scandalously, wickedly sexy woman, chaste pure innocent woman en la cama conmigo and how tart her pussy juice would be.

"What you looking at?" she asks in a sultry voice, looking at me out of eyes so big and round with what looks like soot from lid to brow. She lowers her eyes once and I see her long thick lashes. But her arched eyebrows are so thin I can hardly see them in the semi-darkness of the bar. Two spots the same color as the highlights in her dress dot each cheek. She has the wide nose of mestizos with African blood. Her mouth is full and round but no bigger than one of her eyes.

Ahora sí chispas, quémenme. Make your move, I tell myself. I feel sweat breaking out under my armpits. Se me baja la sangre hasta los talones.

"Can I buy you a drink?" I say, trying to keep my voice cool and impersonal like Sergio Guerrera in the movie *Tierra caliente*.

"Why not, you look pretty thirsty yourself," she says as I sit down on the stool next to her. I can sense a wave of astonishment cresting into mild shock in the vatos with elbows leaning on the tables and counter near us. Me miran como perro en barrio ajeno. How come I had gotten in, when they had been axed before they could rise from their chairs and begin their movidas.

"Wanna go for a ride?" Damn, there I go, I'm already making the first movida. It's hard for me to just sit there and wait for her to pick me up. Can't sit on my hiney and just wait. Not me.

I take the femme home. Even if she doesn't fuck me.

What is that shit, these rucas who fantasize of being seduced and conquered by the macho, and they wait all trembly, waiting for some pelado to discover them and pounce. Aunque la mona se vista de seda, mona se queda. A perro huevero aunque le quemen.

Para acabarla de amolar, la caca hit the fan cuando Teté me echo por la cabeza. If he thought that would stop me going to the gay bar, se quedo picado.

It shouldn't shock la gente so much. Everybody has seen male dogs do it with other male dogs. I've seen cows mount other cows. Yeah, queer folks are like picante salsa, we spice up an otherwise boring act.

Simón, I've heard the story that when the first human was born it was two sexes in one, hombre y hembra. Only she got split. La leyenda dice that forever after cada persona looks for su otra mita'. But mita' y mita' does not always equal one.

Translations

movidas: moves, as in "make the first move"

tío's: uncle's

ruca: from pachuca meaning girl

vatos: pachuco word for guys

maricón: queer male who's effeminate

pirujas: sluts

flores: queers

chancleando: dancing, from chancla (shoe)

una chavalita: a young chick (girl)

Me da ganas de tumbarselas.: I get the urge to take them off.

Anda sola.: She's on her own.

chaparrita: short woman

¡Ay! ¡Que cuerpázo tiene esa chula!: Wow, what a body that girl has!

chi chis: breasts

maripó: short for mariposa, a gay man

olvídate: forget it

nervio: nerve

estoy pisteada: I'm drunk

cerveza: beer

a sus órdenes: at your service

y le doy más quedito: I turn down the volume

mis padres: my parents

café con leche: coffee with milk

tetas: tits, breasts

calzones: underwear

panchona: pussy

pezona: nipple

como la flor del elote: like flower on an ear of corn

que meta la mano primero: who finger fucks first

marimacho: mannish dyke, stone butch

la mujercita: the little woman

¡Jijo de su!: Jesus! or Holy cow!

'tás loca: you're crazy

¿Por qué?: Why?

marimachos como tú: macho dykes like you

su mamá's: her mother's

Ábrenme paso que vengo herido con esta vieja.: Make way for me as I've been wounded by this woman.

¡Qué gacho!: What a bummer!

mierdita: little shit

chavalas: girls

feria: money or change, meaning the one who has the most power

Ni modo.: It doesn't matter.

pájaro: literally bird, also slang for queer

buchita: little butch

buchona: big butch

dale más quedito: turn it down

'Amá: mom

pigeoniada: taking the initiative with another women

muñequita: little doll

una falda y blusa: a skirt and blouse

Ay, mijá ¿que te hiciste?: Oh, my daughter, what have you done to yourself?

Pos, ¿qué te dio hacer eso, niña?: What possessed you to do that, child?

como un macho: like a male

vieja: old lady

¿Quieres fooliar a alguien?: Do you want to fool someone?

Újule, 'Amá: similar to "Geez, Ma."

¿Qué hiciste con tus greñas?: What did you do with your hair?

cantinera: barmaid or loose woman

chapetas: earrings

¿Qué es eso?: What is that?

Tú sabes: You know

Pos, qué cosas se te ocurren a ti, mijita. Ave María Purísima.: The things that you come up with, child. Mary, Mother of God.

Ándale, quítate esa ropa y ven ayúdame a desgranar las mazorcas: Come on, take off those clothes and come help me shell the corn husks

mita' y mita': half and half

tía: aunt

fruncido: puckered

en la cama conmigo: in bed with me

Ahora sí chispas, quémenme.: If she sparks, she'll burn me.

Se me baja la sangre hasta los talons.: I get nervous. (literally, my blood sank down to my heels)

Tierra caliente: Hot land (a film)

Me miran como perro en barrio ajeno.: They're looking at me like a dog in the wrong neighborhood.

pelado: pervert

Aúnque la mona se vista de seda, mona se queda.: Clothes do not make the person.

A perro huevero aunque le quemen.: A dog will persist even if it gets burned.

para acabarla de amolar: to top it all off

la caca: the shit

cuando Teté me echo por la cabeza: when he threw it at my head

se quedo picado: it remained hot

la gente: the people

picante: biting, hot

simón: pachuco word meaning yes

hombre y hembra: male and female

la leyenda dice: the legend says

cada persona: each person

su otra mita': her other half

8

Eating the Fruit /
Comiendo del árbol como Xochiquetzal

As she scuttled from tree to tree, la Prieta listened to the wind whistling through the orange leaves. She stopped and stood still, peered in all directions trying to pierce the darkness. Clouds drifted across the sky baring una luna hinchada y anaranjada. The moon illuminated the occasional skeletal tree, turning the grove into an alien landscape. As she had last night and all the other nights she had sneaked into the orchard, she felt herself becoming a spectral shadow. A castaway walking deeper into the forest of stark silhouettes, she felt as though she was the only person to ever set foot en el naranjal.

She heard a slight sound to her right and froze. Even the shadows stopped breathing. She scanned the terrain, smelled the damp earth and the smoke. Smoke from the smudge pots swirled up to the moon, disappearing into the nightsky. The trees, too, seemed to lift their arms up to the moon. Her breath whooshed out softly.

She fell to her knees on the soft ground, and, crouching under a tree, reached for a golden sphere. With one hand she righted the cap dragged askew by the branches and with the other she snapped off la naranja with a precise twist of the wrist. The limb sprung back into place with a slapping sound. She winced and looked around. The heft of the orange was a comforting weight on

her palm. Again she reached, twisted, and snapped. Here she was
stealing don Benito's oranges and all because of a dare. She should
be mortified for giving in to her macha side, but the thought of el
patrón ripping off su gente stropped the sharp edge of anger and
her body burned again. She couldn't go to the authorities. Her?
A mocosa of a girl from the wrong side. And if evening things a
bit meant stealing, pues, then she'd keep doing it.

Prieta looked from one side of the orchard to the other.
Where was he? El viejo had been there every night for the past
two weeks trying to nail la ratera, but she'd eluded him. Would
her luck hold out, she wondered. She imagined his beady eyes
stalking her, a 30-30 cradled in his arms and the jeep's headlights
pinning her like a paralyzed liebre. Don Benito was a good shot
and he already had a grudge against her. Last year she'd stood up
to him in front of all the farmworkers.

"Debes respetar más a la gente que pisca tus naranjas, viejo,
y pagarles lo que merecen," she'd told him cara a cara.

She'd been thirteen then. Now she had a greater grudge
against him. When they'd gone to collect their earnings expecting
the few more pennies per crate he'd promised them, he claimed
he'd said no such thing, and if they thought they would get
otro pinche centavo más they were even more pendejos than he
thought. If only Papi was still alive, he'd tell him what to do with
his pinche centavos.

Simón, she hated don Benito's guts, but it wasn't like him
to renege on his word. Renege or not, he'd cheated them. Cupping the smooth round orange, she rocked back and forth and
thought of Reyba, el patrón's daughter. She pictured her asleep in
her bed, naked except for a white t-shirt, all toasty under a pile
of soft blankets.

As she emerged from under the tree, la luna Coyolxauhqui
gave her a long shadow. She sensed the muted outer ripple of a
mood descending on the orchard. The close-cropped hair at her
nape stood on end and she stiffened. She swiveled her head right,
then left, feeling like Xochiquetzal trespassing in the underworld.
Raising her head, she looked up al cielo and sniffed the air. A

change in the weather. Though gray clouds were gathering speed in the south, it wouldn't rain any time soon. The fragrance of orange blossoms mixed with the smell of newly turned soil filled her senses. The fibers of her denim shirt scraped against her skin; cool air puckered her nipples.

As she watched las nubes overtake the pale luna again, she took deep breaths, letting her mouth and jaw drop, and rolled her left shoulder to ease the ache where the straps of her rattan bag cut into her collarbone. In the distance, she saw the flicker of fireflies. Just half a dozen more naranjas and she would go home, collect her twenty-five-dollar bet from her primo Teté. She swallowed, anticipating the victory and the sweet taste of forbidden fruit.

She turned back to the green shadows. Shoving a branch aside she cleared a path through the glossy leaves. ¡Chinpiotes! A stinging pain shot through her left hand. She plucked the thorn free and sucked the pierced flesh between thumb and forefinger. She scrambled out from under the foliage thinking about el patrón's daughter encerrada en su castillo lying snugly in her bed when suddenly she collided with a soft body.

¡Jíjole! It was her, Reyba.

They leaped away from each other. Then, stunned, they stared at each other. A gust of wind rattled las ojas de naranja. Prieta held out her hand and stepped toward Reyba.

"Hey, don't be scared, Reyba, soy yo."

"La Prieta. What are you doing here skulking around in the middle of the night? You scared me half to death."

"Shh, not so loud, tu 'apá's around here somewhere. What are you doing here?"

"I couldn't sleep, OK? When I can't sleep I come out here. The orchard, the smell of orange blossoms, something here always calms me."

"In the middle of the night?"

"No, not usually. Papa's always out here with his rifle. Tonight I got real restless. So I came out here. And then I heard someone rustling the branches. What have you got in the bag?" Reyba asked.

"Something that belongs to your father."

As Prieta slung the strap over her head to put down the bag, she heard a ripping sound and thud, thud, one by one all the oranges spilled out at their feet. They looked at the hole in the bottom of the bag, stiff fibers sticking out like porcupine needles.

Reyba giggled. "If Papa should see you now, he'd come after you. He turns absolutely murderous when people try to steal from him."

"Yeah, maybe that's 'cause he steals from others," Prieta said. If anyone sneaked into his domain and touched his precious fruit, he'd get lead up his ass. Don Benito always claimed that he shot into the air as a warning, but Prieta had her doubts. If the ratero didn't get a hole through his hide for sure he'd get a tongue-lashing from don Benito. And a $200 fine. And maybe a jail sentence. And if the transgressor was a female, he'd be más listo to punish her.

"What do you mean he steals from others? You're the one stealing his oranges."

"For short-changing us." Only now that she said the words, it didn't feel like the real reason she was here.

"Oh, that. He'll eventually pay you what he promised. He just wants to show your family what you've cost them by alegando con él."

"Yeah! Well, tell him that in my family we stick up for each other."

"So how did you get past him?"

"His blind side. I crossed over the canal."

"The canal? Wow. He'd never figure it out. People always sneak in from the road. Or at least they used to before he started taking shots at the least little noise."

"Yeah, tell me about it."

"You swam? Naked? Your clothes are dry."

"I put a plank across and walked over."

"Que viva eres. No one's ever tried that before," said Reyba.

Prieta looked into Reyba's eyes, and then looked down, not wanting Reyba to catch her looking at her tits.

A cloud floated under la luna dimming the light. Feeling that she was acting muy tímida, Prieta said, "Ay mijita, las naranjas de don Benito son las más dulces." Her eyes focused on Reyba's pert breasts. She'd bet Reyba wasn't wearing a bra under her shirt and denim jacket. She gazed back up into Reyba's hazel eyes. They had become enormous and flared golden como una braza. Feeling she was being too bold, Prieta added, "La fruta más sabrosa en Tejas!"

The moon slipped clear of the clouds and illuminated the two figures. Prieta heard the cooing throat-call of a mourning dove, saw awareness flash in Reyba's eyes. The silence thickened between them. When Prieta heard the glitch in Reyba's breath, her own quickened. Reyba's lips reddened. She'd noticed the same reaction one day last year. Astride her quarter horse, Reyba had galloped through the field where Prieta and her bunch were working. Her long light-brown hair was luminous and flowing behind her. She kept watching Prieta. Prieta joked even more and sang along with her friends, pretending to ignore Reyba, but all the while sneaking peeks. She knew Reyba couldn't see that she was watching her just as avidly—the sun was behind Prieta, silhouetting her figure and obscuring her features.

Her best friend, Ofelia, laughed saying, "Vaya, she's making eyes at you, Prieta."

"Come on, tú que te crees tan macho, I dare you to show her que eres hembra," her primo Teté called out. "Ay, anda empelotada." She didn't know if Teté was referring to her or to Reyba.

When Reyba reined her horse close to her, Prieta looked into her moist eyes. The voices of her amigos hocicones fell away. Prieta opened her mouth, but a sudden shyness snapped it shut. The image of una güera rica riding double con una prieta campesina had her thinking. What's wrong with this picture? No way, their worlds were too different. Sensing that Reyba was about to leave, Prieta looked up in time to see her press her heels against the horse's flanks and spring toward the big house where she lived alone except for her father and the servants.

"Aren't you sick of oranges by now?"

Prieta stared at the ground. Caught red-handed by the last person in the world she'd expected to see. Or had she somehow hoped to see her? Naw, not in the middle of the night in the middle of the orchard.

But the bet wasn't so much with her primo Teté as it was with herself. Era una prueba she had made up and tricked Teté into proposing it. Prieta scraped the mud off the sole of her right boot against a protruding root. She had to face up to each fear one by one, si no, no valía pa' nada. The trick tonight was to avoid getting caught by el patrón—nobody had ever gotten past his guard—and pay him back a little for all the sweat money he made off others.

"Oh, come on Prieta, la puesta's not the only reason you're here."

"Isn't it?"

"Uh uh," Reyba giggled. "Only machos pull stunts like this."

Chingao, she's just like the rest who think guts come with cojones.

A loud drone soon drowned out the sounds of the wind rustling through the leaves. A pair of headlights cut a swath through the night giving the orchard a spooky look. The lights shone fully on first one tree then another, turning each into a ghost tree. The engine's whine got louder; the jeep inched toward them. It stopped four rows across from where they crouched, Prieta holding Reyba's arm.

"Oh wow, he's seen us," Reyba said, getting in front of Prieta and pushing her back. "Go. Run before he sees you."

Prieta said, "No time now. Quick, let's get out of here before he starts shooting."

"He won't shoot while I'm with you."

"Sonsita, you think he's going to ask who it is before he starts popping. Ven pa' ca." Prieta grabbed Reyba's hand and, crouching, pulled her through into the next row and kept going. When she thought they were far enough away, she urged Reyba to run. The thumping of their feet and the sound of their panting seemed extra loud. Even Reyba's twin trenzas slapping against first one shoulder then the other sounded like thunder. Bullets making holes in their backs would sound even louder. Legs churning, heart roaring in her ears, she felt like she could run forever.

The sharp crack stopped them in their tracks. They pivoted on their heels, saw a light puncture a hole in the night. Then thunder split the sky. Another white flash sent them hurtling, arms flailing, legs pumping, mouths and eyes opened wide. The night bucked and wallowed. Their feet sank up to their ankles in the freshly plowed soil and their momentum tumbled them to the soft ground.

"Prieta, is that you in there with your good-for-nothing cousin? I know you're there," el viejo shouted.

How could he know it was her? She'd eluded detection the past two weeks. All he knew was that there was a thief in his orchard.

"Come out of there. I won't hurt you. This is my land. I've worked too hard to let some fool huerca malcriada and a two-bit pachuco take what's mine!" don Benito shouted.

Prieta crawled under the nearest tree tugging Reyba with her. She heard the spat of the second bullet like a whip snapping, then the thunk in the trunk of their tree. Glossy leaves from the walls of their cave feathered down around them. The pulse of the world changed. The night gasped, the leaves quivered. Prieta felt Reyba's body trembling against hers and she put her arms around her. Two hearts knocked against each other.

"I'm going to plug you both full of holes," he shouted.

Prieta shivered, catching Reyba's arm.

"No, let me go to him. He'll think it's just me here."

"No, it's too dark, he might not recognize you and shoot." She hugged Reyba closer and felt her breath sawing against her neck. Sensing the full-blown fear in Reyba, she said, "It's all right, mihija. No nos hace nada."

Prieta pulled Reyba up and led her away from the moonlit area into deeper shadow. The blinking lights of a plane traveled across the nightsky. The tiny lights made Prieta feel even more of an exile in the dark huerta.

"Listen," Prieta said, "he's coming this way." The thrum of the motor seemed to make the whole huerta throb. The engine changed gears.

"Ven aquí, mija. Let's get under that tree." Prieta scurried under the low-hanging ramas, pulling Reyba with her. The branches clawed at her. A twig cracked. They both shot up, then realized it was not a bullet.

"Let me call out to him—ouch!" Reyba clutched her neck.

"Ssshh, cállate." Prieta hugged her closer. "If we don't move or make a sound, he'll pass by us."

"There's a thorn in my neck."

"All right, all right, let me see." Prieta skimmed her hands over Reyba's body until she found a twig clinging to her back. She could feel Reyba's heartbeat through her shoulder blades.

"Don't make a sound. I'll try to pull it out quick. OK?"

"OK."

Maybe Reyba was not la soflamera she appeared to be. With exquisite care Prieta got a firm grasp on the twig and in one quick tug pulled it out.

"Ouch!"

Prieta soothed the spot, stroking slowly.

"I know my dad treats you like trash."

Prieta looked at her sharply.

"I'm so sorry. Maybe he knows," says Reyba.

"Knows what?" Prieta said, acting as though she didn't know. "Get down," she said. The leaves resting along her back were quivering. Had Reyba noticed her tremors? Her heart was rearing back and the trees were rearing back with it.

The engine's roar two rows over was getting louder. Suddenly it idled. Through a gap in the leaves Prieta saw don Benito rise up from inside the jeep, his upper body clearing the window, his head rotating slowly like that of a giant insect. Then he jumped down and stepped through the trees, lord of all he beheld.

A whizzing sound in the top branches and then the ear-splitting shot. Prieta flinched and clenched her teeth, biting into her tongue. She wanted to laugh when she realized that it was an orange that had hit her and not a bullet. She swallowed, tasting blood. She remembered Teté telling her that the sound of a bullet aimed at you sounded different from all the others.

Under the canopy of branches and leaves, Prieta lay still, the weight of the ripening oranges along her back. Reyba squirmed and Prieta wound her arms around her, her hand coming to rest under Reyba's breasts. Part of her watched and waited for the bullets, part of her was aware of Reyba's body.

Prieta rose to her knees, eyes searching for the man with the gun. Realizing that her movements would give her away, she froze.

The minutes stretched.

Under the giant wings of the tree, the two girls kneeled, embracing each other. Fear and a sweet aching tension drew them closer until breasts pressed against breasts and belly against belly. Prieta's body hummed until it drowned out her fear. After what seemed an eternity, Prieta heard the jeep snarl into gear. Her breath whooshed out in a cloud of steam. She sagged against Reyba. They waited, unmoving, arms still around each other until they no longer heard the jeep. Prieta resented its departure; now there was no reason for Reyba's body to lie heavy against her, no reason to cling to her like the roots of trees cling to the deep earth.

The smell of Reyba's sun-toasted skin made Prieta dizzy and warm. She shrugged out of her jacket and laid it on the ground. "Ven aquí, mija," she whispered, easing Reyba down on top of the jacket. Surrounded by the dark green walls of their cave, the leaves stirring around them, they lay facing each other. Like palomas blancas roosting for the night, they settled in their nest. The earth cold beneath them with its heavy dirt smell, the lush green curtain, the moon looking in through a gap in the branches.

Prieta groped Reyba's chest with one hand and curled the other around her neck. Reyba giggled. Pulling her closer, Prieta gently pressed her lips against Reyba's. She rubbed them up and down Reyba's lips, with tongue traced her upper lip. Reyba jerked away.

"Ya, mija, ya." Prieta whispered stroking her face, then probed the entrance with the tip of her tongue. Reyba sucked in her breath and parted her lips. Prieta's tongue delved in and Reyba opened her mouth wider. A strand of Reyba's hair and a stray leaf got in her mouth and Prieta blew it out in a soft puff.

"Bésame. Let me feel your tongue," Prieta told her, the darkness making her bold. She felt Reyba's warm breath blowing on her face, heard her muffled giggle, then the tentative touch of Reyba's tongue. Prieta's heart swelled and her chest hurt. She felt something loosen in her muscles and escape out through her ragged breath. She unbuttoned Reyba's jacket, tugged her shirt out of the waistband and pulled it up and over her breasts. She put her mouth on Reyba's stomach and licked. Dragged her tongue up her breast to her nipple. Heart beating, chest rising and sinking—she wanted to become the heartbeat, become the chest rising. She took Reyba's whole breast into her mouth. Small green orange, firm yet incredibly soft. She sucked hard. Reyba buckled.

"That feels strange, strange but good," Reyba whispered. "Do it again."

Prieta laughed, fumbled around Reyba's waist, unsnapped her jeans and pulled down the zipper. When her hand brushed the soft sparse pubic hair Reyba moaned. They rocked together. Prieta felt the tree rock, the earth rock, felt the roots of the tree uncurl and stretch out tautly.

"Come on come on come on baby, ven aquí," Prieta crooned. She felt the roots of the tree clench and then go limp. As she lay back, she saw the moon between the leaves, saw the sky rushing past.

"Oh, my god. If my father could see us now," Reyba gasped.

A sadness swept through Prieta. If the penalty for stealing oranges was getting shot, what would it be for stealing el patrón's daughter.

A loud sound. She jerked her head up. Chingao, the wily old bastard had left the jeep behind and snuck up on them. Somehow he'd seen or sensed where they were. She heard the crunch of his boots on the ground. He could be on top of them any second. She pulled away from Reyba and buttoned her up as fast as she could in the dark. She couldn't see Reyba's face but imagined it pinched with fear.

The footsteps were getting closer. They stopped near their tree. He couldn't possibly see them; the clouds had again hidden the moon, the leaves of their cave were thick. Suddenly she saw a light moving up and down—he had a flashlight. He was looking for tracks. He shone the light at their tree, up and down and around.

She could feel Reyba's tremors. Shsh, don't rattle the leaves. That's what he wants, just a small sound to give us away.

His feet moved. She held her breath. He moved on to another tree, shone the light over it then moved on.

They sat still for a long time, propped against one another. Prieta heard the jeep start up on the other side of the grove, listened until the engine sounds faded to nothing. Weak-kneed, she crawled out of their green cave. Reyba followed behind her, shaking her hair and buttoning her jacket. She reached under the tree and dragged out Prieta's coat.

"Are you OK?" Prieta asked.

Reyba nodded, then said, "Yeah."

Prieta heard the surprise in her voice. Or was it relief?

"It was great. No more pretending to like vatos."

Prieta was startled; she thought Reyba had been responding to her father's threat, not to their making out. Prieta reached up and snapped off a twig bearing orange flower buds and twined it into Reyba's hair.

"Tu 'apá couldn't have seen my boot tracks where I crossed the irrigation ditch." Prieta said, her voice low and thick. "I smoothed the soil but . . . "

"You could have been killed. We both could have been killed," whispered Reyba. "And all because of a bet."

"Not just a bet. I have my reasons. And mija, you're one of them."

"Couldn't you have come to the house during the day?"

"Yeah, sure with your father and the whole world watching."

"And you're afraid? Of my father?"

"Yes. Of people with guns, of people finding out how we look at each other. And I came because I'm afraid of the dark."

Reyba raised her brow. After a moment she said, "I didn't think you were scared of anything."

"Ha! Didn't you feel me trembling?" said Prieta. "I'd better go."

"No, don't go yet."

"I don't guess you're going to tell your 'apá?" Prieta asked. She wondered if Reyba felt disloyal to her father for not giving her away. And for the other. She wondered what she'd do if she were in Reyba's place.

"Tell him what? That you're stealing his oranges or for doing what we did in his grove?"

Prieta felt her chest go hollow. She was surprised. Reyba wasn't taking anything back. She wasn't like Marielena who always acted like Prieta had never touched her.

Plucking a ripe orange from the tree that had sheltered them, Prieta took out her pocket-knife and began to peel back the leathery rind of the baja orange, as the winter variety was called. She liked its tart sweetness better than the mild sweetness of the Valencia, the summer orange. The Spaniards had at least done one good thing by bringing oranges to this continent.

La cáscara spiraled down, dangling almost to the ground. Prieta felt Reyba's eyes on her. She tried to see herself as Reyba must see her—Levi's faded to a dull blue, worn shirt with the two top buttons missing while Reyba could wear real leather and silk whenever she chose. She was dirt poor, grubbed in the dirt, while Reyba lived in the great house, each board bought and paid for with the sweat of the pickers. One day Reyba would inherit all her father's wealth and the land that the Spanish colonizers had granted her ancestors.

She placed her hand, oily from the rind, on Reyba's stomach, felt the palpitations. A part of her was still under the orange tree covering Reyba's body with her own.

"What's going to happen to us?" said Reyba, putting her hand over Prieta's and pressing both hands into her stomach.

"Don't you know?" she muttered recalling the mixture of fear and pleasure. "Always having to meet in secret. Hiding from everyone. Always scared of being caught. Can you live like that?"

Prieta kept her gaze on Reyba's eyes. She pulled her hand from under Reyba's and shoved the knife back in her left pocket. Again she felt Reyba's eyes on her. Prieta divided the naranja and put one of the halves in her mouth. She sucked it, then bit into the juicy inner flesh all the while looking into Reyba's eyes.

"Here, mija." She handed Reyba the other half. Reyba separated a wedge, put it in her mouth and choked on a seed. With the flat of her hand, Prieta thumped her between the shoulder blades. The seed flew out. Reyba's eyes watered and she blinked away the tears.

There was her answer, Prieta sighed, then straightened her back.

"Does that mean you're not going to get pregnant and give birth to un naranjito?" asked Prieta, forcing herself to grin.

"Eat the fruit and your eyes will open and you will be as a god," Reyba half recited, then blushed. "Guess I've been reading too much."

"Yeah, well I read signs."

"What kind of signs?" asked Reyba.

"Not the ones that are printed," Prieta told her.

She had had to learn not to give in to her mother's dominating ways. Since her father's death her mother depended on Prieta to do everything. Prieta had already lost so much schooling. And Teté and her brothers would run her into the earth, make her their slave if she didn't stand up for herself.

"I guess you can't ever get too much knowledge, living en un jardín and all that," said Prieta.

"That's what I mean. I want to experience things, too, and not just read about them." She looked sideways at Prieta. "Do you know what I like most about you, Prieta?"

"No, ¿qué?"

"You move so loose, so easy, you are so sure of yourself." She gestured smoothly with her wrist and fingers. "You know who you really are. And you always look straight-on at people."

"Pos, gracias," said Prieta squirming. "Right now I'm not liking much who I am."

"Well, I do, I . . ."

"What?"

"I've been watching you for a long time." Reyba stumbled on her words, looking away and then back into Prieta's eyes.

"I know. And I've been watching you," said Prieta.

"I wish I could be out in the fields cantando and chiflando with you and your friends."

"In the fields?" Prieta snorted. "Doing stoop labor como un animal? 'Tas loca, mijita."

"Maybe, but I'd still like to work alongside you. I want my father to treat you and the other workers better, but if I say anything he'll guess that it's something to do with you. If 'apa finds out, he'll kill us both. He hates your marimacho hair. Calls you an arrogant little bitch. If he caught us like this I, well, I can hardly wait till I'm old enough to leave."

"Ven aquí." Prieta put her arms around Reyba and held her. "Yo sé, mijita. But don't sit around waiting for someone to rescue you from your castillo. Someday you'll have to stand up for yourself. Guts don't come just with cojones."

Prieta gazed steadily into Reyba's eyes. She wanted to pull Reyba under the orange tree again. After a long time, she pecked Reyba's mouth.

"See those lights?" she asked, turning Reyba to face the row of trees. "And that bunch of stars? Keep those before you as you walk and you'll be safe en tu camita in ten minutes. Tu 'apá's gone down to the road hoping to catch me coming out of the grove." Taking off her cap, she bowed to Reyba and walked toward the yellow pool of oranges lying on the ground.

She looked up at the clouds speeding past la luna. Then she turned back to look at Reyba who stood watching her, hand covering her mouth. A blankness settled over Reyba's face. Already she looked lost and enchanted, already looking like an apparition.

"When you get near your house, you'd best skirt around and approach it from the other side. He may have one of his workers patrolling the area," she told Reyba.

She reached into her Levi jacket for the watch, no watch. She'd lost it but when? Yesterday. Oh, no. That's how he knew it was her. She'd lost it last night while she was stealing oranges. He must have found it. Cagada. She'd carved her name on the thick band. Dead giveaway.

She walked back to where she'd dropped her bag, picked it up, pulled the strings and knotted the mouth closed. Turning the bag upside down, she quickly stuffed the oranges through the hole. She picked up the bag and walked away. As she picked her way out, she thought of the oranges. They were always at the mercy of the spray of insecticides, at the mercy of pecking birds and insects, the prey of fungus, and the prey of human pickers. Y la gente como ella were always at the mercy of los don Benitos of the world.

The clouds freed the moon. Glancing back over her shoulder, Prieta saw Reyba move back into the green cave where they'd hid, saw Reyba crouch and move her hands over the dry leaves and twigs, saw her fingers follow the coiled roots of el naranjo. Searching for what? Did it lay there in the soil—the moment the orchard had been flooded by a sweet tasting stream?

Clouds swept over the moon again and Reyba receded completely into the shadows. Feeling goosebumps on the back of her neck, Prieta turned up her collar and, flanked on both sides by the dark green trees, she resumed her walk. Again her steps faltered. Had she been playing with Reyba, and was she now playing it safe with don Benito? Oh yeah, such a tough macha—her and her soft inner parts.

She came to the irrigation canal and peered into the water trying to pierce its dark skin where la luna rocked in the water. She heard owls hooting and the distant barking of dogs. She picked up the board from its hiding place, raised it up in the air and let it fall across the canal. As she walked across the canal the gap between her world and Reyba's seemed to widen with each step.

The patrón's daughter. The reflection of the moon in the water was a giant eye. That was it. How much had this lark had to do with don Benito and how much with Reyba? She spit into the canal, but the sour taste clung to her mouth. Cagada.

It seemed she walked forever on the narrow plank, following her own inner moonlight, teetering, then catching herself to keep from plunging, trying to catch a truth too painful to know. When she jumped off on the other side, she pulled the board after her and stowed it back in the culvert.

Prieta walked onto the road. She stopped and rubbed her hands on her jeans to wipe off the citrus oil. She raised her fingers to her mouth and sucked at the yellow sheen. Her body went still. There would be no more nocturnal raids into the green shadows, no more nights of slipping past his outpost and tramping through his huerta and its long empty rows.

It wasn't just the fruit that was forbidden. She rubbed the wound in her palm, saw again the white slash cracking open the night.

Translations

Comiendo del árbol como Xochiquetzal: eating from the tree like
    Xochiquetzal (an Aztec fertility goddess)

una luna hinchada y anaranjada: a swollen and orange moon

en el naranjal: in the orange grove

la naranja: the orange

macha: mannish female

el patrón: the boss

su gente: her people

mocosa: brat

pues: then

el viejo: the old man

la ratera: the thief

liebre: rabbit

Debes respetar más a la gente que pisca tus naranjas, viejo, y pagar-
    les lo que merecen.: You should respect the people who pick
    your fruit more, old man, and pay them what they deserve.

cara a cara: face-to-face, or eye-to-eye

otro pinche centavo más: another damn penny more

pendejos: dummies

simón: yes (in Chicano slang)

Coyolxauhqui: Aztec moon deity

Xochiquetzal: Toltec/Aztec goddess of love, both illicit and accept-
able, who ate of the fruit of the sacred tree (which I interpret
as awakening passion) in Tomoanchan, one of the eight heavens
in Aztec mythology, and was exiled for violating the taboo

al cielo: to the sky

las nubes: the clouds

primo: cousin

chinpiotes: damn it

encerrada en su castillo: shut in her castle

jíjole: holy shit, damn

las ojas de naranja: the orange leaves

soy yo: it's me

tu 'apá: your father

ratero: thief

más listo: eager

alegando con él: arguing with him

Que viva eres.: How cunning you are.

muy tímida: very timid

Las naranjas de don Benito son más dulces.: Don Benito's oranges
are sweeter.

como una braza: like a live coal

la fruta más sabrosa en Tejas: the sweetest fruit of Texas

vaya: go on

tú que te crees tan macho: you who thinks of yourself so macho

que eres hembra: that you are a girl

Ay, anda empelotada.: She's in love.

amigos hocicones: foul-mouthed friends

una güera rica: a light-skinned rich girl

con una prieta campesina: with a dark-skinned field hand (female)

era una prueba: it was a test

si no: if not

no valía pa' nada: she wasn't worth beans

la puesta: the bet

machos: males

chingao: fuck

cojones: balls

sonsita: silly

Ven pa' ca.: Come here.

trenzas: braids

huerca malcriada: ill-bred girl

pachuco: guy (in Chicano slang)

mihija: my daughter

No nos hace nada.: He can't do anything to us.

huerta: orchard

ven aquí: come here

ramas: branches

cállate: be quiet

la soflamera: the babyish one

palomas blancas: white doves

bésame: kiss me

vatos: pachuco word for guys

La cascara: The peel

un naranjito: a little orange

en un jardín: in a garden

no, qué: no, what?

pos, gracias: well, thanks

cantando: singing

chiflando: whistling

como un animal: like an animal

'tas loca, mijita: you're crazy

marimacho: butch

Yo sé, mijita.: I know, my dear.

en tu camita: in your little bed

cagada: shit

y la gente como ella: and the people like her

9

El Paisano Is a Bird of Good Omen

La Prieta climbs the corral. Straddling the thick mesquite post, she searches for signs in the sky. The sky is a flat plate dwarfing chaparral, mesquite thickets, clumps of prickly pear, the cattle grazing. The vast and empty sky sucks her up the long stretch of el rancho la Tigra. El sol dominates the land. Always. Su tierra. The air feels heavy, muggy. She smells the dust that precedes rain. Twisting her upper body around she looks at la casa grande, an oasis in the middle of the brushland, a refuge flanked by mesquite trees on one side and el portal on the other with its round knot of los invitados. El portal she and her younger brothers built shelters the guests and tables of food from the fierce sun.

El mesquite with its gnarled limbs reigns over the portal, the house, and the yard. Its fifty- or sixty-foot-deep roots tap the same underground water source as the windmill. When she stays still long enough her feet worm themselves like roots into the moist core. The branches of el mesquite remind her of once catching Belinda twirling on one leg, tossing arms and head to the sky.

The mesquite, la casa, y el portal shimmer under the sun's white glare like clothes rippling on a clothesline. Only the compact shadows give them y la gente moving under el portal the solidity of reality. Los invitados to the prewedding fiesta, madrinas y padrinos and neighboring ranchers all dressed in their church clothes. Amidst the clinking of knives on plates they talk about the lack of rain or the possibility of rain. Pale as a ghost su abuela sits alone outside the circle of people. Prieta scans the crowd looking for her uncle Efraín, but his balding head is nowhere to be seen. Tarde como siempre. Under the quickening hum of the guests' conversation, the hens cluck over dry grass seeds.

Under her buttocks the posts become appendages growing out of her body. She's part of the corral anchored to the land. Los corrales built by los vaqueros de su mamagrande, caretakers of the land, leaving domesticating imprints, marking where civilization begins and ends.

She smells her blood. Anda en la garra—she's on the rag. During her menses she feels fragile, expansive; the limits of her body stretch beyond her skin. Her fingertips tingle and heat courses up from her feet. She billows out like a sheet, encompassing trees, people, and everything around her. As the familiar tingle travels up her arms, she feels su cuerpo flowing from one post to another until she, too, encircles what the corral encircles. But the gates are wide open. The circle will be incomplete until dusk when the newly calved cows are rounded in for the night. No, not complete until la casita being built for her and Zenobio is finished. She turns to look at the partially finished casita behind la casa grande. It looks like the gutted side of a cow: two walls up, a skeleton roof. Mañana es la boda. There is still time. Todavía hay tiempo.

She shifts her nalgas. The post is now on the left side of her cunt. Gently, she rocks back and forth. If she presses just right and can stay with the rhythm she can bring herself off. Not as good as during a fast run, the wind whipping the mare's mane, her own hair across her face, strands caught in her mouth with only the wind hearing her keening.

"Andrea, mi prieta."

'Amá walks toward her. She's dressed in a pinstriped jacket and skirt, white blouse, black hat, veiled at the back, white open-toed pumps. The best-dressed señora de los ranchos alrededor and her nose up.

"Sí, 'Amá, ¿qué quieres?" she asks.

"¿Pues, qué tienes, niña? What's wrong with you? I don't want you embarrassing me today. You've got that look again, hot and hollow-eyed."

"The knowing, 'Amá. It's come back."

"No hables tonterias, hija. I've told you and told you not to spend so much time con tu abuela. You're starting to sound like her."

"Don't blame mamagrande for what I am," Prieta tells her, looking at her abuela sitting all alone under el cedro. Her grandmother turns, locks eyes with her.

Noticing the exchange, her mother says, "Between you, Zenobio, and her, I don't know what I'm going to do. Caprichosa, hazme caso. I want you to get out of those pantalones de macho and go mingle with the guests. Zenobio is there, enverijado, hiding in the house with your sisters draped around him. I can't understand why you're mooning out here like a lost calf."

"OK, 'Amá, no te aguites. I'm getting ready." Prieta fingers the bone pendant around her neck.

His family owns el terreno adjacent to hers; they've known each other their whole lives. She's sensed that he's been staying away from her all day watching her from the corner of his eye, waiting for her to decide. She knows that he thinks that if he's not around to remind her, she may never give him the signal.

"Go and change, greñuda, ¡véte! Chase your sisters out of the house. Tell them to bring out more tortillas de masa y la carne."

"No," Prieta says, hugging herself.

Her mother opens her mouth then closes it again.

"I'm making allowances for you, mija. I know you're under a strain. That's understandable on the eve of your boda, but why do you have to be tan malcriada?"

"What if there's no boda, Amá?"

"What do you mean?"

"What if I decide to go, far away, to school maybe."

"You have to go through with it. You don't want to end up a solterona like your tía Mana. No one to care about you, no sons and daughters to look after you? You will go through this ceremony, cabezona, if you know what's good for you."

"Cálmate. Why don't you go talk to Doña Inés," Prieta says more gently. "Todos la hacen menos." She looks at Zenobio's mother standing alone in the middle of the portal, wringing a pair of black gloves. Her face looks emaciated and sullen under the crownless parachute hat. She looks funny in her 1930s and 40s style clothes. Her beige jacket hangs loosely from her thin shoulders and her black wide-hemmed skirt skims the dirt.

"All she talks about is how well her bebé, Zenobio, can cook. I suppose if he wanted to she would let him take up sewing," says her mother under her breath as she walks away.

"If he enjoys cooking, why shouldn't he cook?" Prieta calls after her, wishing she'd kept her mouth shut, regretting her habit of contradicting her mother. Though her mother is partially to blame, Prieta knows that on top of the stored-up grievances, she will heap future griefs on her mother's back. Her mother has enough to deal with, with la boda.

Prieta searches the mesquite trunk for a sign. It looks like a black wrung-out piece of cloth whose whorls and twists point toward some revelation. In its center a thin-lipped vaginal mouth oozes a black gummy secretion.

As the wind stirs the tree's branches la Prieta sways como el papalote, her hair rustling like leaves. This tree is not just a tree. She is now part of it.

Laughter sputters the men sitting on bales of sorghum that lie sprawled in a semi-circle under the portal. She is not part of that half circle.

Directly west of the house are the corrals. Next to them, towering over the ranch house and corrals, is the windmill whose roots plumb the rivers under the earth. Prieta twists around. El papalote, the beacon that guides los vaqueros home from a sea of brush and cactus, is moving. The wind pushes the arrow shaft. Now it points south. Hay algo en el aire. Something is in the wind. El papalote's sails rotate faster and faster as the south wind blows stronger. The words LA TIGRA on the shaft shine brightly in the afternoon sun. Prieta's hand tingles. She feels the heat travel up from the soles of her feet. Though she sits motionless down below, la Prieta, too, rotates with the sails. Prieta hears los hombres talking. She cocks an ear and instantly she's right there where they're talking.

Hearing a burst of laughter behind her, Prieta looks down the length of the corral. She looks back at the younger men congregating at one end of the corral. Astride posts, legs dangling, bottoms squirming, they pummel each other's arms as they trade witty nonsenses. She might as well be sitting right next to them. Secretive whispers, boasts of macho prowess at roping, at riding, at fucking the cantineras. They ogle las muchachas, most often the López girl. A few eye the sleek flesh of the horses snorting water from the trough or standing stiff-legged, tails swishing off flies. Clear across the yard she feels the older men's sly glances like brushes over her skin. Feels them rest on her hennaed hair.

Prieta feels the inner streaming and she's no longer atop the corral, but down with the men sitting on the bales of hay eating roasted grilled corn. Their felt Stetsons lay on the ground beside them or hang from the mesquite branches. In their stiff dark cotton suits, some drink while they discuss the drought.

"El gobierno puso mi ganado en quarantine," says one.

"Did you hear about la movida que la viuda made on el compadre Juan?" interrupts another.

"Las viejas, todas son putas, traidoras, every one of them," says one of the men.

"What do you know about las viejas? The closest you've been to one is that cow you keep in your kitchen and in your bed." There is a roar of laughter.

"Well, the ones to watch out for son las que hacen chisos, las que embrujan," interrupts another, glancing around.

"¿A quién buscas, Bigotón? ¿A la Prieta? Allá está. Ándale, te apuesto que no te atrevas a hacerle la movida."

"Watch yourself. Look at her wrong and she'll put una hechiza on you and your cojones will shrivel up like turds and drop off," says another.

When they all laugh Bigotón gets up and strolls up to the corral.

"Psst, psst," he signals to Prieta, but she pretends not to notice. Angry at herself for the pretense. Wiping the grin off his face with her fist would just encourage all of them. Something happens a los hombres when they bunch up in herds. Alone not one of them would stare her in the eye.

She focuses intently and hears his thoughts, "Esa Prieta, she's willful and impulsive, terca la cabrona. I'd like to throw a saddle on her, dig my espuelas into her sides, pull hard on the bridle until her mouth runs red. That would stop her chingaderas."

He's got nothing on her primo Teté. Prieta shifts her buttocks on the post and pushes their voices away.

Well, today she's not going to laugh or smile at their snide jokes. La fiesta's just barely started and already her jaw is tense. She touches her throat, no pearls around her neck like a noose. She smooths her thighs with her hands, denim instead of the silk of her dress she's supposed to be wearing. Sweat drenches the hair in her armpits. She takes a deep breath. Another.

After a while the no's rattling in her head become quiet. She touches the grainy flat cow bone hanging between her breasts. She pulls into herself and waits for the everydayness to fold its wings around her again. Warm and safe. Home. If only the wind would turn. Now, that would be a sure sign.

She jumps off the corral, walks to el papalote. As she climbs up, the rough wooden tiles under her hands and feet feel immensely thick and deep. She reaches the platform and she sits under the blade, careful of wind changes—she doesn't want to get rapped on the head by the sails. She allows the quiet to seep into her body, waits for the flash of knowing to rush through. The image of Teté putting a cage in the back of his truck comes to her. He's planning something. Just to annoy her. She remembers finding Teté and Zenobio in the corn shed, Zenobio's jeans down to his knees. Zenobio's too smart not to know that Teté is toying with him.

She looks toward the winding road. A Ford pickup drives up, leaving a tail of dust in its wake. It pulls up alongside half a dozen vehicles parked under the three lone cedars—quiet sentinels watching over the land. It disgorges the whole Flores family: muchachos, mamas, papas, niños, abuelos, and Teté spill out. Familia, the things a person will do to have one. Like getting married. But if she does that no va a poder hacer lo que le de la gana.

Don Efraín drives in. He gets out of his Lincoln Continental Coupe. He looks it over, and spotting a bit of dirt on his left fender, spits on it then wipes the spot off with his shirt tail. Slowly, he wades through the crowd, greeting his compadres, stopping briefly to talk to her mother, then slowly makes his way to her.

The platform trembles. Su tío Efraín is climbing, his arm muscles taut. Her own muscles tighten, the fingers grasping the ladder become her fingers.

"Tío, take my hand and I'll pull you up. You shouldn't pretend to be a young man."

"You're not supposed to know that," he says, ignoring her hand. He gives a little hop and lands his scrawny buttocks on the platform. "Your brand of frankness frightens people, mija. Besides, men will always try to impress you, tú sabes."

"Why?" she asks.

"Sepa Dios, maybe to prove they're better. ¿Qué te pasa? Tu mamá said you were being difficult."

"Difficult is the only way I can be with her." Prieta looks at him, hesitates, then says softly, "I can't decide."

"There's nothing to decide; it's all been decided for you. Like it was for me. I wouldn't go through a marriage a second time, though. Not for all the land in the Valley."

Prieta gazes at her terreno. The land—some people married for it; others were married to it. She could understand that. When she gazed at la Tigra she felt connected to something larger, felt she was part of that larger something.

"It's peaceful up here, like being in another world, a tiny island floating above everything. A person can dream up here."

"You're right, mija. It's . . . freer up here. Up here one is another person."

Tío plucks a carved animal from his shirt pocket and hands it to Prieta.

"A roadrunner," Prieta turns it over in her hand, runs her fingers over it. "What a nice gift, Tío. Must have taken you weeks to carve it."

"Si mijita, este paisanito was a long time coming. I sure loved working on it! Couldn't get it right until I got the idea of carving a base for it. For balance. Had to send my chamacos out into the brush. They came back with enough cow horns to make a dozen roadrunners, and enough bones for mija to paint on for months."

Prieta puts her hand between her breasts. She touches the pelvic bone, her finger pushing into the hole. She fingers the thin strip of cowhide around her neck. The bone is warm. Tío's daughter had carved and painted el mesquite with el papalote in the background on the bone.

Sensing that he's looking at her, she raises an eyebrow at him.

"You've got that I'm-not-really-here look in your eye, my girl. What you need is some cerveza, only you're too young to drink. Y una muchacha mocosa besides."

They climb down and stand off to one side to watch the la gente carousing. Her tías frown at the beer in her hand. The male guests give her a questioning look.

Again Prieta feels the tingle begin at her fingertips and the heat travel up her body. She takes her beer to the corral and places the bottle on a post where it rocks a bit but doesn't topple. She climbs on the fence and looks at the women. The bridesmaids are dressed identically. Wide pink skirts swirl around their calves as they traffic among the tables. They cast flirtatious looks at the men as they ladle out chunks of carne asada, arroz con pollo y papas con frijoles, and serve chocolate, limonada, or beer. She hasn't eaten since noon yesterday, but the hollow feeling and the tingling in her hands is not due to lack of food.

She turns to look at the women, hears one say, "Sí comadre, tiene razón. Esa Belinda se cree grande, anda pa' qui y pa' ca'. Se porta como una cantinera. Si no se watcha se va quedar una soltera."

"Pos, la Prieta también se porta muy mal," says another. "Su pobre mama no sabe que hacer con ella. Imagínate, esa huerca quiere pelarse. Quiere irse pal norte, a un colegio como si fuera macho."

They rush through their words. Funerals and weddings are the only events that bring them all together. Always, they talk of their men and children. Prieta wants to run away. She wants to run to her grandmother and, kneeling before her, bury her face in her lap, breathing in her old woman smell, salt and sweat comingling with lavender. A world lies in her grandmother's smell. Her mamagrande would know what to do.

Her grandmother is sitting on the Windsor chair that Prieta has taken out of the house for her. Her abuela, head cupped with short curls, sits near but not with the other women. She seems impervious to the bodies milling around her, to the food and laughter. Prieta knows she is there, but not there, her inner eye on some distant place. Prieta walks over to her and places her hand on her shoulder. Their eyes lock, Prieta's dark brown and Abuela's light amber with the fierce look of an eagle's. Prieta is deaf to the chuckles that follow the jokes, the tittering of the young in the backyard. Motionless, not even seeming to breathe, feeling nothing, thinking nothing. Prieta is rooted to the ground, Abuela to the chair.

"Mamagrande, Zenobio is not like the others, he accepts what I am. Other worlds exist out there, maybe even one where I can be myself."

"You may never find a place where people such as we are accepted . . . Soon you will know what to do, Prieta," her grandmother says.

Prieta looks at the women and overhears la comadre Tencha say, "Fue un escándalo. Sleeping naked con una serpiente. A huge rattler Prieta calls Víbora. A diamondback. She had her hennaed hair spread all over her body. Y esa víbora, it was wrapped around her waist. Ay comadres, if you'd have seen it you would have fainted. Why the snake's head was lying on her pubic patch. Its body rubbing all over her."

"Esa Prieta, I'll bet she'll lavish more care over her snake than she will over Zenobio," says another.

She'd had the snake since it was a baby, no more than a foot long and thin as a tapeworm. Now the snake was over eight feet long and as thick as her arm. She has to keep it outside in the nopal thicket—everyone in the house is terrified of it. La Víbora, the most venomous of all snakes, loved for her to rub the depression between the eye and nostril on each side of its snout. She would take the tail between her hands and study its hollow ring-like bulb at the base. Several times a year, it would shed its skin and a new one would emerge under the old one. Then the old one would slough off except for the old tail sheath, which would remain loosely fitting over the new one to form a new joint. With each molting another joint would be added to the tail. If only she could shed her old skin and grow a new one as easily.

Prieta walks to one of the tables. The head of steer, pit barbecued, is spiraling steam out of its gaping eyes toward the branches of el mesquite. Her mother had gotten up at three in the morning to spice the head, wrap it in burlap, bury it in the ground, and cover it with live coals; it has simmered slowly. For ten hours. She smells the rich odor . . . too rich. It's as if her nose were buried in the head. No, it can't be one of her pets, she thinks to herself. Revulsion pinches her gut. The wild ones sometimes get caught, too. Don Sebastián, it was said, had taken the entrails of one of his dead cows into his kitchen and laying the bowels over a gridiron had lit the stove murmuring, "That will burn la bruja real bad. Then we'll know who la naguala is."

Someone puts a hand on her shoulder. Without looking she knows it's Zenobio. Su carnal, the only one besides mamagrande that she can really talk with. With downcast eyes, he places a plate of food on her lap, and she grabs his arm before he slinks away. His small slender build making him appear younger than twenty-one years.

"Are you scared, too, Zenobio?"

"No. Yes. Look at you, you don't look scared. I can't hide what I'm feeling." He shrugs his shoulders. "I feel exposed, tú sabes."

"So, what's Teté trying to get you to do?"

Zenobio just shakes his head.

"This marriage will save us from having to marry. Just like it did mamagrande. Like her I won't cook for a man, nor bear his dark moods. I'll not bolster his spirits when the cattle die off like flies, nor when his balls dry up," she says.

He nods and, putting a pomegranate in her hand, goes back inside the house.

Prieta climbs back up and sits on the top post of the corral. She looks up at the sky, searching for clouds. She will have to burn prickly pear and mesquite pods to feed her cattle this summer if the rains don't come. Los hombres will be upset, not so much at her doing a man's work but for doing it better. Teté had better not come around smirking.

She hears the thud of knives that a couple of huercos are throwing at a tree stump in the backyard.

"Bullseye!" shouts one of the muchachos, drowning out the laughter of the older guests. A young boy chased by a gobbling tom turkey tears across the backyard. He runs into the rope that some girls are jumping and falls amid skirts, soft bodies, squeals, and slaps. A group of screeching children surround a boy in a yellow shirt dangling a horned toad over a heap of swarming red ants. The horned toad squirms, body convulsing. Her fingers tingle and her body heats! The sudden piercing pain in her arms and hands almost shock a cry out of her. She rolls up her sleeves. The red spots on her arms were made from climbing the windmill, she tells herself. But those on the back of her hands? She watches a boy in a purple shirt break up the children and release the horned toad. The toad scuttles out of sight under some nopales.

"¡Hijita! Get off of there. A fine hostess you are." Prieta looks down. Her mother again, arms crossed, a scowl on her face.

"I want to be alone, 'Amá."

"Prieta de la Cruz, get down, anda a saludar a los Flores." The pearls around her neck jiggle up and down. "They've just arrived—late as usual."

"They shouldn't have bothered."

"Pórtate bien, mi prietita. You have to stop this bickering with your cousin."

"All right, as long as he behaves himself." Prieta leaps off the corral, raising a cloud of dust. Her mother backs off, a scowl on her face.

"No se mira bien que una mujer alega and quarrel with a man," her mother tells her, "especially about . . . well, it's just not done."

"You mean it's not good for women to have opinions on anything." The Flores approach, and she jumps off the fence to greet them. She ignores Teté's sneer and outstretched arms.

"Here's your wedding gift. I'm sure Zenobio will love it," he says, pushing his hat back with his middle finger. She snorts. He holds the cage out to her, crowding her, then drops it at her feet. She stands her ground.

"The paisano will bring you good fortune," he says.

She remembers the dream that woke her up. She is standing at the bank of a river holding a bucket. She drops it into the water and then draws it up. With a big paisano, a rare one. She throws it back into the river and it metamorphoses into a serpent. The snake glides on top of the water, then, with a flick of its tail, it turns and slithers to shore.

"I've already received my good fortune," she says. What had ever possessed Zenobio to let Teté touch him? It's not like Teté is the only one around. Pete and Mando son del ambiente.

"No one can have too much of a good thing," says Teté, mustache twitching. "Fried paisano is a remedio for the itch, or so they say." Someone snickers.

"A caged animal never brings luck, least of all to the one who trapped it."

"How do you like that for thanks," says Teté, scratching his ears as he searches for sympathetic eyes among the guests looking on. All avoid his beady eyes. It is to Prieta they always come when they're short of money or water or feed for their cattle. At other times, when their cows go dry, they whisper behind her back, say that fulano saw her cast a stone over her left shoulder toward the west.

Prieta looks Teté in the eye. Her eyes absorb the hostility emanating from him. Her body fills itself with it. And he knows. He and Zenobio. Innocent, trusting Zenobio. "The betrayal" as Zenobio dramatically called it when he told her about his last clandestine encounter with Teté. (It makes her angry; she loves Teté but is mad at him for pulling this shit.) Pendejo, she should have warned him. Pobrecito Zenobio. She would never forget the look in his eye when he found out Teté had been toying with him, que lo había chingado pero bien.

"If you even think about making trouble, I'll boot you off of my land."

"Your land? You're a woman. Or are you? You think your mother is going to leave you el rancho?" The Flores edge closer to Teté. More guests are turning toward them.

"No, it's not her land. It's mamagrande's and therefore mine." Teté moves toward her. Again, he crowds her.

"Va a haber pedo. A fight! A fight!" the boy in the yellow shirt chants.

As Teté moves closer Prieta sticks out her hand, pointing her forefinger at him. His hand runs into it. Shocked, he backs off, staring at the blood dripping from his hand.

Don Efraín pushes his way through the group. "Now, now, now," he says putting his arm around Prieta and turning her around. "Ease off, you're both not as bad as you make out to be."

There is complete silence, all eyes riveted on the dripping blood.

"She didn't have no knife," whispers one of the kids.

"Consider Zenobio," Don Efraín whispers into Prieta's ear, guiding her away.

Teté's brother takes his arm and pulls him toward el portal.

"Should have given her la yerba—would have cured the chingadera out of her, would have made her real mansita," he mutters. He swallows the last words, then moves his hand to his throat as if he were gagging. He turns to find her twenty feet away standing very still, her eyes wide, standing glowering at him. Prieta sees the caged animal in his eyes cringe, hears him gagging again. Don Efraín releases her arm and she picks up the cage, holding it at eye level with both hands. It is made of bleached dry twigs and grass stems.

She stares at the paisano, killer of rattlers, alacránes, and tarántulas. It cocks its head to one side, then the other, all the while looking at her. The bird blinks. Its fierce eye clouds then clears. She examines the bare patch of vivid blue and red skin behind the eyes. The eyes clear then cloud. A tingling in her hands and the feeling. Ah, yes. She opens the cage door. It doesn't move. Just the eye. Clouding and unclouding.

De repente el paisano darts out of the cage and takes off down the back road, long legs churning, tail flat in a streak so fast it seems to be skimming the ground. The road branches out to the right and the left. La Prieta silently urges it to cross the road from left to right, a lucky omen, but what does it mean? Squatting, she looks at the track the paisano left, two toes pointing forward, two toes pointing backward—to mislead the evil spirits.

She looks toward the north. A flash of light. She counts slowly and when she gets to seven there is a low rumble. She begins to count again and at seven the wind comes sweeping over the rancho. Prieta turns to find the boy in the purple shirt watching her.

"Will you teach me how to do that?" he asks.

Both smile.

Prieta looks for Zenobio. She focuses on the house. He's not there. She looks toward Teté. Not there either. Ah, he's with his mother on one of the benches that have been set up to accommodate the Flores. The benches, she notices, close off the circle. Zenobio's standing by the wedding cake laughing at something Don Efraín is saying. They stand close together.

The pink, blue, and white frosted cake lies in the middle of the center table. As she looks at the stiff figures of the novia y novio smiling inanely on top, she begins to feel her body becoming plastic. She touches her arm to reassure herself. Pan de polvo, empanadas de calabaza and pitchers of hot chocolate lie by the cake awaiting la merienda. Tall glass vases with huge red and white roses from her grandmother's jardín grace each end of the table. A chocolate stain on the white lace tablecloth. It's not too late, she thinks. Not too late.

"Oh, there you are, Prieta linda," says Don Efraín, putting his arm on Prieta's shoulder. "Oye, paisana, I was just telling your hombre here how lucky you are."

"Ya lo sé." She doesn't want to hear any more about "luck." "I'm cutting him loose. And myself. We're rescuing each other. For now, anyway."

"What are you saying mijita? You sound more and more like your abuela every day. Ten cuidado. La gente won't tolerate those who are different."

"They tolerate Mamagrande," says Prieta.

"Unlike you, she has never played up her difference," he replies.

Prieta is annoyed with herself. Zenobio doesn't seem to be put off by the conversation. He's not flustered nor self-conscious. He always looks . . . beautiful. She looks at Don Efraín. Why, he's chuckling at our situation. And pitying it, she realizes.

A lizard scurries out from between her legs.

"Some more mezcal, Tío?"

"Yes, but I'll get it. I'll leave you alone to fight with your novio," he says. Los músicos feed their music with whiskey, fueling the songs' fire before the dance begins. As she picks up her beer, the tingle in her hands intensifies and heat sweeps up her body. A wind flows like liquid down her throat. Her hands are fluid. The edge of the glass and her mouth fuse. She tries to control the feeling, but it gets away from her. What if she can't return to herself? Then she reassures herself. When she wants to become the other, all she has to do is focus and allow her mind to flow into that person or thing. In an instant se vuelve lo otro. To come back to herself all she has to do is think it.

The music starts. A group of men begin picking up the tables and moving them to one side to make room for the dancing. Everyone turns to look at Prieta and Zenobio. Don Efraín urges them to the center of the portal saying, "Ándeles, the bride and groom always start the first dance."

"I'd rather not," says Prieta. "Nothing personal, Zeno."

"Cagada, let's get it over with," says Zenobio, putting his arm around her. They stand motionless, a smile congealing for the photographer, then waltz smoothly, her hands on his shoulders, his gripping her waist.

She is a hollow body doing the courting, being courted. He is a substanceless body doing the courting, being courted.

"Why are you looking at me that way?"

"I don't think we should go through with it," she says.

"Tás loca. It's too late to call it off."

"It was a bad idea. Just why are we doing this?"

"It was your idea. Pa' no tener que casarnos de verás you said. If we married each other we wouldn't have to marry for real, you said."

"Yeah, I thought I was so smart."

She looks around. Others are dancing the waltz, and in the next beat, a foot-tapping, dust-raising Texas Mexican polka full of ajúas begins. Prieta walks away, Zenobio follows. They stand on the sidelines watching the dancers. The girls left without partners are trying to cajole their young brothers into dancing with them. Two seven-year-old girls dance with each other.

Prieta walks up to the López girl, pushing through the throng of machos surrounding her, tongues falling out like cattle around a salt lick. Belinda López has been flirting con los hombres, then turning down man after man.

"Ven. Baila conmigo."

Belinda smiles at her as Prieta takes her into her arms and whirls her around the circle. Prieta's head is full of music. The strings of the guitar twang inside her skull. The beat emanates from her own pulsing blood, her hips expanding, opening her, widening her diaphragm. Only the tune exists and Belinda López. Throbbing, her pelvis rotates on Belinda's navel. Prieta shakes her head and blinks. Her lips glisten, jaws fall slack. Her spine is undulating. Gradually, she notices that most of the dancing couples have taken root in the middle of the portal and are staring at them, their lips thinning. One spits as they waltz by.

"Stop, let go," says Belinda López, who is no longer smiling. "They're staring at us."

"Aw, come on, you like it," says Prieta, drawing Belinda closer.

"This isn't right, no matter how much I like it."

"I don't care," says Prieta.

"Well, you may be able to get away with stuff, but I don't."

"Ay chulita, I'm sorry, I didn't think about how this would affect you." Prieta stops. She realizes that though she feels estranged from la gente she at least has a strong connection to la tierra y con su mamagrande, pero Belinda is alone.

"They won't do anything to you. They're scared of you. They call you Prieta la bruja behind your back. They make the sign of the cross when they say your name," she says. But they're not scared of me. They'll tear me to pieces." She breaks from Prieta's hold, and breasts rising and falling, runs out of the circle.

Prieta walks back to Zenobio.

"¿Qué pendejada fue ésa, Prieta?" hisses Zenobio.

"I know. I shouldn't of done it. It's just . . . well . . . I know you want to dance with el muchacho in the purple shirt that's staring at you," she says.

"What I want and what I do are two different things."

"Yeah? What about Teté?" says Prieta. "Oh, let's stop squabbling. We're beginning to sound like we're married already."

"Don't even think it, Prieta. Forget about running off and leaving me," he says. "We need each other, Prieta. We understand each other. No one else does. We have to stay together."

When she makes no reply he says, "Take me with you. I don't want to stay here without you."

She puts her arms around him. The image of a tumbleweed wrapped around her while the wind whirls past her is in her mind. Zenobio is that tumbleweed. Over his shoulder Prieta sees her mother glaring at her. She feels a little guilty, feels the tug of loyalty. The warmth and love that is her mother's due, she gives freely to abuela, Zenobio, Víbora, el terreno.

"I wish we hadn't started building our casita yet," she tells him.

"It'll be finished in a month, then we'll have some privacy."

"You don't know my mother."

"Querida, it won't matter. We can put up with her for a month. And she with us."

"Or, we can skip out. It's not just her, Zeno, it's me. And it's you. We don't fit here. So maybe we won't fit anywhere else, but we'll never know if we don't try."

"You mean in the gabacho world?"

"I mean anywhere that's a long way from this ranchito. I don't know. Zenobio, don't look like that—you look like a calf going to the slaughterhouse."

"Stop talking like this. You're scaring me. That's why I've been avoiding you. I'm hungry. Let's go eat."

"I'm not hungry. I'm going to talk to Mamagrande."

Her grandmother is sitting on a bench under the windmill, arms on her lap, quietly rocking. "I was waiting for you, mi prietita." They listen to each other without speaking. She remembers her grandmother telling her, "Yo soy una de esas. Soy naguala. I've passed on la facultad to you same as my abuela passed it on to me."

Knowing the secrets of others, knowing something was going to happen before it happened had been OK with her. She'd only become uncomfortable with her "abilities" when she realized that others didn't have them. All she had to do was imagine it and she could do it. Finally, her grandmother says, "It's a closeness, a connection. The thin cover disappears and you can see the veins, the bones, all that's hidden."

"Yes," says Prieta, "but only with certain people and certain things at certain times. It's scary."

"Sí, because it's new and unfamiliar. The more you use this gift, the more at ease you'll feel, mija."

"But la gente is scared of it—of me. Why do I threaten them?"

"Because you're different. Because you allow yourself to be who you are. Because, mija, they're locked up, prisoners of their upbringing, shaped by the upholders of lo decente," says her grandmother.

"This facultad is terrible! It means always being alone."

"I've lived my whole life alone. Siempre sola. Even when your grandfather was alive. I want more for you. Fighting my powers almost killed me. Finally I gave in and became what I was—a naguala."

"But what about mi querer? Is it linked with mi poder? Do the two go together, Mamagrande?" asks Prieta.

Her abuela resumes her gentle rocking.

"Sí," she says.

Prieta is not surprised that her abuela knows about su "querer."

Su gente. Su terreno. Beyond la laguna está el monte where the cattle shelter, nibbling mesquite pods or what grass they can find. The dark clouds are looming nearer. She can feel a weather pressure building.

Prieta gets up and walks back toward the portal, then turns to go back to the corral instead. A small group has gathered around Teté. Teté covers the bird's head. El paisano runs back, then runs forward. It bangs against a post. Prieta decides. He playfully puts a pair of pants over a heifer's head, one of the ladinas. He opens the gate and hits her sharply on the shanks. Blinded, she whirls around and around trying to shake off the cloth over her eyes. Frightened, she runs straight toward Prieta. There is an audible sucking in of air from the guests. The heifer is almost on top of Prieta. She jerks the pants off her horns. The animal stops dead in her tracks, wild-eyed, spewing rivulets of saliva. Prieta whispers to her and walks into the corral. The wild heifer follows her. Prieta turns and locks the gate. The circle is complete. She ignores the whispered remarks behind her back. She says to herself, "No es cosa mala, this gift. I'll do what's right for me."

Suddenly Prieta is blinded by a white glare.

Then the glare dims to a glow that settles over everything like a fine dust. A white world superimposed over the everyday one. The land, the people, everything takes on a fused quality where figures are carved out of the same white rock. She wonders what it was like before, where the Prieta that left her bed that morning is. It doesn't matter where she or the other is. The land is inside her, etched forever in the very marrow of her bones.

Again the white glare. The family cemetery. An older Prieta watches as they lower the coffin into the ground. She had come back to her grandmother's bedside in time to say goodbye. She will stay this time.

When the vision ends she hurries back to the portal and sits down beside Zenobio. The land. How can she think of leaving the land—it would be like leaving part of herself. Casarse o no casarse. Irse o quedarse. She's got to make up her mind. Before sundown when the guests leave. As she stares at Zenobio he multiplies. Several selves transparently superimpose upon the physical Zenobio. The other Zenobios are Zenobios she has never met. She feels a tightness in her head and a great wind in her bones. She puts her hands on her temples and presses hard. Her facultad is getting stronger.

She looks up at the windmill. The vane is now pointing toward the north.

Zenobio puts his hand on her shoulder. "¿Pa' dónde vas?" he asks when she starts to leave. "No, not me, us," she says, pointing al norte.

"I have something to do." She walks slowly to el portal. She finds a broom and pulls out a sprig. She imagines the sprigs turning into feathers. She walks to the trough and dips it in water. She knows that the feathers of an eagle consume all other feathers if they're mixed together.

Soon a fine rain begins to fall. Leaning against the gnarled mesquite, her hair touching some of its leaves, she begins to bid the guests goodbye.

Translations

el paisano: roadrunner, informally correcaminos

el rancho la Tigra: Tiger Ranch

el sol: the sun

su tierra: her land

la casa grande: the big house

los invitados: the guests

y la gente: and the people

madrinas y padrinos: godmothers and godfathers

su abuela: her grandmother

tarde como siempre: late as always

los corrales: the corrals

los vaqueros de su mamagrande: mamagrande's ranch hands

Anda en la garra.: She's on the rag.

su cuerpo: her body

la casita: the house

Mañana es la boda.: Tomorrow is the wedding.

Todavía hay tiempo.: We still have time.

nalgas: butt, ass

mi prieta: my Prieta, used as a personal endearment in this case

Sí, 'Amá, ¿qué quieres?: Yes, mama, what do you want?

¿Pues, qué tienes, niña?: Well, what is it?

No hables tonterias, hija.: Don't say silly things, daughter.

con tu abuela: with your grandmother

mamagrande: grandmother

el cedro: the cedar

Caprichosa, hazme caso.: Listen to me, capricious one.

pantalones de macho: men's pants

enverijado: excessively dependent

no te aguites: don't worry

el terreno: the land

greñuda: uncombed

¡véte!: go

tortillas de masa y la carne: corn tortillas and meat (Tejanos call corn tortillas tortillas de masa as opposed to flour tortillas)

mija: my daughter

tan malcriada: so poorly raised

solterona: spinster

tía: aunt

cabezona: big-headed, meaning stubborn

cálmate: calm down

Doña: Mrs.

Todos la hacen menos.: Everyone misses her.

bebé: baby

como un papalote: windmill

los vaqueros: the cowboys

Hay algo en el aire.: There's something in the air.

los hombres: the men

cantineras: barmaids

las muchachas: the girls

El gobierno puso mi ganado en quarantine.: The government
    quarantined my cattle.

la viuda: the widow

las viejas: the old ladies, implying that they are gossips

todas son putas: all of them are whores

traidoras: traitors

son las que hacen chisos, las que embrujan: those who curse are
    the ones who bewitch

¿A quién buscas, Bigotón? ¿A la Prieta? Allá está. Ándale, te apuesto
    que no te atrevas a hacerle la movida.: Who are you looking
    for, Big Mustache? For Prieta? She's over there. Go on. You
    won't dare make a move on her.

una hechiza: a spell

esa: that

terca la cabrona: stubborn

espuelas: spurs

chingaderas: fights, tricks (or, literally, fucks)

primo: cousin

la fiesta: the party

muchachos: young boys

mamas: mothers

papas: fathers

niños: children

familia: family

no va a poder hacer lo que le de la gana: she won't be able to do
     what she wants to do

su tío: her uncle

tú sabes: you know

Sepa Dios.: God knows.

¿Qué te pasa?: What's the matter with you?

tu mamá: your mother

este paisanito: this little roadrunner

chamacos: kids

cerveza: beer

y una muchacha mocosa: and a bratty girl

carne asada: roasted beef

arroz con pollo: chicken and rice

papas con frijoles: potatoes with beans

limonada: lemonade

Sí comadre, tiene razón. Esa Belinda se cree grande, anda pa' qui y pa' ca'. Se porta como una cantinera. Si no se watcha se va quedar una soltera.: Yes, comadre, you're right. This Belinda thinks she's big and goes off from here to over here. She acts like a barmaid. If she doesn't watch out, she is going to end up single.

Pos, la Prieta también se porta muy mal.: Well, la Prieta also behaves pretty badly.

Su pobre mama no sabe que hacer con ella. Imagínate, esa huerca quiere pelarse. Quiere irse pal norte, a un colegio como si fuera macho.: Her poor mother doesn't know what to do with her. Imagine, this girl wants to split. She wants to go north to a college far away as if she was a man.

la comadre: close female friend

Fue un escándalo.: It was a scandal.

con una serpiente: with a serpent

y esa víbora: and this snake

nopal: prickly pear

la bruja: the witch

la naguala: the person who shapeshifts

su carnal: her friend

huercos: young kids

hijita: dear daughter

anda a saludar a los Flores: go and greet the Flores

pórtate bien: behave yourself

no se mira bien que una mujer alega: it doesn't look good when a woman argues

son del ambiente: are of the ambience, that is, homosexual

remedio: remedy

fulano: nobody in particular; equivalent to "so and so"

pendejo: stupid

pobrecito: poor little one

que lo había chingado pero bien: that he was fucked up good

Va a haber pedo.: There's gonna be a fight.

la yerba: the herb

mansita: tame

alacránes: scorpions

tarántulas: tarantulas

de repente: suddenly

novia y novio: bride and groom

pan de polvo: cinnamon sugar cookies

empanadas de calabaza: turnovers made with squash

la merienda: late afternoon lunch

jardín: garden

linda: pretty

oye: listen

paisana: countrywoman

Ya lo sé.: I already know that.

ten cuidado: take care

la gente: people (as in what will people think)

mezcal: alcohol distilled from maguey cactus

novio: groom or boyfriend

los músicos: the musicians

se vuelve lo otro: she becomes the other

ándeles: go on

cagada: shit

Tás loca.: You're crazy.

Pa' no tener que casarnos da verás: So we won't get married for real

ajúas: exclamations

machos: males

Ven. Baila conmigo.: Come on. Dance with me.

Ay chulita: Oh, honey, sweetie

pero: but

¿Qué pendejada fue ésa?: What kind of stupid thing was that?

querida: dear

gabacho: white, originally referring to Spaniards

ranchito: little ranch

Yo soy una de esas. Soy naguala.: I am one of those. I shift shapes.

la facultad: the ability to see deeper realities

lo decente: what's decent

siempre sola: always alone

mi poder: my power

mi querer: my desire

la laguna está el monte: el monte is beyond the lake

ladinas: wild

no es cosa mala: it's nothing bad

Casarse o no casarse. Irse o quedarse.: Marry or don't marry. Go or stay.

¿Pa' dónde vas?: Where are you going?

al norte: to the north

Part Three

University Life

10

In the Shadow of la Chingada
(or Smoking Mirror)

I drive past fenced fields covered with tawny grasses, slick as the gold manes of lions. Humo. Black clouds of smoke billowing ahead to the left—a burning car on I-35. Raise window and shut vents to the acrid fumes. Pall of smoke obliterates the sun, turns my windshield into a smoking mirror. What I need is a scrying mirror to read my future. The smoke curls away and the world is bright, clear, with sharp edges once more.

A road sign up ahead: "San Marcos 5." To the right, a field of giant windmills. They seem like a strange species of tree. Should have said good-bye? Uh uh, can't see him till I figure things out. He'd just talk me into doing things his way, and I'd let him. So instead, I'm in my chariot escaping from reality. No quiero saber, haciéndome sonsa. My body's tensing just thinking about it—missed the 123 bypass. Got to make a U-turn and zip back under Interstate 10. But wasn't the cut-off back there? Pay attention, sonsita.

The sun slowly arches across the sky and gradually the world turns dusky y el cielo a dark powdery blue, or so it seems to these half-mast ojos. Stay awake. The occasional flurries of rain washing over the car are hypnotic, monotonous, instead of washing out estos pensamientos pesados.

Not a lot of traffic on 123 South for a Sunday afternoon, 3:30 on the car clock, three days till Christmas. School's behind me; home, winter break and Mami and Dolores for the next two weeks. I zoom past Zorn, Texas. Another road sign: "Seguin 15," and I catch the undulating shadow of my car riding the tall thin-posted fence. I take the curves, y las sombras del carro are slightly behind; on the straight road they're parallel and slightly ahead of me. Inside the shadow car, a lone driver's head, my head.

Poised like ballerinas, the mesquite trees rush toward me. Los árboles, solitary, adopt a stance and, though limbs break off and new ones grow, though their trunks grow knobby and gnarled, they hold that stance for the rest of their lives. My reflection in the rearview mirror, pale. My body feels light, insubstantial. Any minute now I'll float to the ceiling. The wimpiest wind will uproot me.

"¿Qué es ese ruido?" Engine doesn't sound right. Probably nothing. Screech, screech. Windshield wipers scratching glass—gotta get a new set. I switch on the radio. "And coming up, an oldie but goldie, 'Poison Ivy.'"

4:00 pm. Watercolor wisps of pastel nubes on the horizon to the left—pink, mauve, amber. Quaint, like a fairyland in a picture book. Cops have pulled over a ruca in a Volkswagen. I slow to 65, one eye on the pick-up behind crowding me. I pull over to the right shoulder, letting two frat rats pass. Potted plants swaying in the back. Marijuana? They wave, then call out, "Oh you hot mamacita."

"Pinches gringos," give them the finger. Pick-up brake lights flash; it turns left without signaling.

Leafless trees like storks stand gray against straw grass. Fall and winter, all one season in Texas. A clump of bamboo, gold limbs shining in the late afternoon sun. They'd make a good mobile. Sign: "QUILTS FOR SALE." The fence top rail is covered with cow skulls, bottom with smaller ones. Rabbit skulls? On the radio Foreigner is singing "It Feels Like the First Time." Carlos, ¿cómo estará? Don't think about him, tonta. But I see it all again as though it is happening to someone else. . . .

∿

He pulled the mattresses off the twin beds, dragged them onto the floor. He unbuttoned her shirt, then tugged her white slacks down over her hips and buttocks. In the cool breeze se le enchino el cuerpo. He pushed her onto the mattress, his body followed hers and settled on top. How compact and muscular his body was. She rocked from side to side enjoying its weight and warmth. She touched the cool shock of his black hair, rubbed the strands between her fingers. He put his mouth on hers and thrust his tongue into her mouth. After a deep kiss, he slid his mouth down to her chin, neck, chest to her tit. He suckled her breast gently and with his teeth softly le mordío el pezón. She stared at the eye of God on the opposite wall and felt nothing.

When he switched to her other breast her eyes dropped to the paperweight on her desk, a chunk of white crystal that kept her papers from blowing off in all directions. Its stone edges sharp, surfaces unyielding.

He rose up from her body. Le apartó las rodillas y le puso un dedo sobre la vulva. He stroked the folds of her sex, then mounted her again. His erect penis trembled against her stomach. He pushed, but his penis missed the hole. He guided it to her opening and pushed again. El pene no podía penetrar no matter how hard he shoved into her. The more he pushed, the more she tightened. He couldn't get in. He shoved harder. La Prieta felt something break inside her, felt a sharp cutting pain y le entró un miedito. She couldn't keep herself from crying out. He stopped moving, his glittering eyes stared down at her. He pulled out a little then plunged in again.

He plowed her for what seemed like hours. Her back hurt. She wanted to buck him off but said to herself, "give it a chance, let him finish it." She concentrated on letting her pelvic muscles relax, allowing his penis to enter her again and again. She wanted it over with, the experience she'd longed for, for a long time—all the girls in her pueblo had become real mujeres way back in junior high. She'd been determined to lose that precious commodity, that bit of skin that had chafed her nerves like a burr. Pero ya, que se acabé esto. Quítate . . . get off, get off, she wanted to say. But she kept silent.

Finally, she could feel a change in him; his hands tightened around her shoulders. He thrust into her again, then he froze. He came quickly and fell to her side, arms and chest slick with sweat. He fell asleep almost immediately.

That was it? That was what everyone raved about? Yet, nothing had changed. She was still la bella durmiente del bosque, still Sleeping Beauty. Lo que había sacado de este fiasco era un cuerpo roto.

She scooted away and touched her sore genitals. Her thighs were sticky and beginning to cake. Even her long black hair felt sticky with his semen. The sweetish smell of the marijuana they had smoked earlier mixed with the musk of sex. Feeling nauseous, she got up, slipped on her oversize t-shirt, and tiptoed down the hall to the bathroom. She felt a burning sting as she urinated. She wet some paper towels and cleaned her thighs and genitals. She crept back to her dorm room and lay down beside him—there was nowhere else to lie. She remembered the first time she'd seen him.

He'd been sitting with the raucous soccer players at a middle table in the University dining hall. Prieta had smiled to herself, proud of these South Americans for their arrogance, their laughter drawing attention from the surrounding gringos. In their own countries these Latinos had not been second-class citizens with hyphenated identities. If there had been any Chicanos in the dining hall they would have been quiet, polite, timid. But there were few Chicanos in the university. Hungry for the sounds of Spanish, she went to their table. They introduced themselves and talked for a while. She felt warm and protected, though still an outsider, a foreigner to them. Soon, in the typical macho ways, one would cut her away from the herd and claim her. They all left except for one, Carlos, the short one with the wire-rimmed glasses. He moved over and sat next to her. Uh oh, she always attracted the short ones, not being tall herself.

They met next day and he asked her if she wanted to go for a ride on his Harley-Davidson. She looked at the huge shiny machine and swallowed. She hopped on behind him and laced her hands around his waist. They flew up and down the Texas streets black with rain, heart rising to her throat. The wind flailing her long hair over her eyes.

He made a right turn too fast and nearly dumped them. She realized he was showing off, trying to impress her.

"Not so fast," she shouted, hugging his middle, her pulse streaming up her body. Maybe he'd done it on purpose, to get her to hold on tighter. She decided she would date him if he asked, maybe even sleep with him. Latino males, everyone knew, were hot, bold, sure of their masculinity. What impressed her more than his soccer and the Harley was that he was a poet. He must have picked her because he'd guessed what was on her mind. She wanted to fit in, but was he the right guy? Ni modo, she was tired of being the odd girl out and probably the oldest virgin in Texas.

"Es increíble que eres virgen. Why didn't you tell me, eh?" His voice startled her. She'd been lying awake while he snored beside her. They both sat up. She covered her breasts with the edge of the sheet and turned on the lamp. They stared at the diluted burgundy stains on the sheets. She'd have to wash the spots out before the Mexican cleaning lady changed the sheets tomorrow.

"Bueno, si yo hubiera sabido que eras virgen nunca te hubiera tocado, eh. I don't want the responsibility ¿entiendes?" He sounded totally pissed off. "I thought all americanas sleep around, you know. Bueno, I mean they have experience. They are more sexually liberated than our own women, eh," he finished lamely, noticing the look in her eyes.

Strange, this was the first she'd heard Chicanas being called "americanas." "You mean we 'americanas' are all putas?"

He took her hand and put it over his downcast penis. It sprang up.

She snatched her hand back. "You didn't use anything; I don't want to get pregnant."

"¿Eh? You mean you are not on the pill? Do you not know how to take care of yourself?" He pushed her down to the spotted sheets. He squeezed her nipples, touched her vagina and fucked her again.

"Tomorrow you go to the student health center. ¿Entiendes? I do not like rubbers." So much for contraception, she thought, rolling her eyes. Did all guys expect women to deal with it?

Every day he waited behind the locked exit door. She would open it from inside and lead him up the back stairs to the women's floor. She would peer up and down the hall. At her signal he would dash into her room. Huh, some self-proclaimed knight scaling the grim brown fortress.

She did not go to the student health center but that weekend she drove down to the Valley. She told her mother, "I'm not on the pill. He doesn't ever wear a rubber and I don't want a child." Her friend Juani couldn't believe she could be that honest with her mother. When she left home to go to college she decided that the only way she could stay close to her family was not to hide anything from them.

∽

"How could you get involved with un mojado. Los hombres no más quieren una cosa. I thought you were different from the other girls—todas son putas. La gente se va a dar cuenta que andas con ese pelado." She lectured Prieta as they drove the seventeen miles to Raymondville to her mom's doctor.

They fucked every night on the mattress on the floor of her room. "Did you come, eh? Was it good for you?" he would ask.

"Ya mero, ya mero. Almost," she would say. According to her family she'd always been a liar, so why was she being truthful? Ella miraba ese hombre manipular sus genitales y no sentía nada. She got more aroused by the wind flapping her blouse against her nipples. With all the friction she sometimes got a mild arousal, enough to make her wet. But she wanted romance, tenderness. And he just wanted sex.

Penetraba con su lengua, penetraba con los dedos. "Please, please I wanna come," she chanted to herself. She wanted to be a normal woman; she wanted him to get off her. The in-and-out suction made popping, slapping, farting sounds. Beads of sweat slid down his nose and chin onto her face below. He kept strumming her nipples then checking to see if they were hard. Después de hora y media de estar forcejeando con ella y jalando, he got off and shouted, "Frígida, you're frigid, eh. Other women go crazy when I put my mouth on their sex."

His words cut into her skin and she stiffened.

"Let's just be together. We don't have to have sex every time," she told him. He opened one of his books and read poetry to her in soft melodious Castilian.

Afterwards he put his hands on her breasts and his mouth on her throat and they ended up on the mattress again. She willed herself to have an orgasm. Quería darle gusto al cuerpo, but she felt so ignorant about her body. But the more she wanted the less she felt. Her pelvis was an iceberg waiting for him to pull it up into the sun, then draw the light through her whole body. Pobre hombre. She realized it was too big a burden to put on him. The small heat she felt in her genitals after all the rubbing and kneading burned when she urinated, but the heat never reached her heart.

She got up, turned the radio on low and cracked open a window.

❧

The static of the radio jolts me. "This is Robert Ramírez on WOLI, and I've got 'You're No Good, You're No Good, You're No Good, Baby,' by Linda Ronstadt for all you tejanos out there." A windmill. I'm supposed to make a sculpture of a papalote for class. What's it a symbol of? It pulls up water from the depths. Like trees they move con el viento. Like trees they have a rooted stance—unless calamity strikes them. Like trees they stand alone. Something's moving on my leg. I suck in my breath, clinch my stomach. No, it's just the pants clinging—Ah, cold generates static electricity. I hate going home for Christmas. Pass another tree trussed with green lights.

I pull onto a narrow bumpy Rest Area, park and get out of the car, walk around to jar the stiffness out of my body; I wonder what Carlos is doing—watching TV—childishly delighting in it. Guess they don't have many TV programs where he's from in Ecuador. He delighted in driving my Camaro, though not used to power steering or power brakes, jerks the car in fits and starts. Of course, he always insists on driving and I always smile indulgently, though that is getting irritating fast. I said "adios." Shouldn't have left for the holiday so soon after our quarrel, should have stayed and talked it out with him. I wonder if his friends are jeering at him, "pendejo, can't you control your vieja."[1]

If I walk away from him, I fail us both. I finally have a boyfriend just like all my amigas. I'm no longer the odd girl out. Besides he and I do have some things in common: Spanish literature, similar cultures, sort of similar languages, same color skin. He likes to show me off to the other Latinos. He likes that I have a car. Maybe he feels he owns me because he's my first.

I get back in the car, back on the highway. It's over 300 miles to el Valle. Didn't get very much sleep last night; my eyes ache from watching the road and the signs. Damn! Forgot Barthelme's book of stories. Have to make up an incomplete, write a paper on it during the break. Pastures dotted with cattle. ¡Wáchate! Mailbox too close to the highway, almost hit it.

Rain and the squeak of the wipers. 4:30. Almost dark. I pass under Highway 87. A hint of pink on the lower horizon. Stunted leafless mesquites, graceful with their naked limbs. Chingao—I'd better ease up, keep to 65 miles an hour. Las pinches chotas hide in the bushes with their radar, need time to brake. Break. Broke my mother's heart. What did she expect, for me to remain virgin forever or until I married. Pos sí.

With my shoes off my feet are cold. Static on my clothes, static on the radio, static in my life. How can I escape? Ghosts riding sobre mi espalda. The talk on the radio, the talk in my head keep the images at bay. Without the radio and my talking brain, the silence would drown me. Why doesn't that fuchsia car

---

1. In the original manuscript, she includes, in brackets, "put porno here?"

pass me? ¡Wáchate cabrón! Want to rush yourself to death? The sky's azul with streaks of lilac. Really beautiful. It's getting dark. Wonder how much time has passed. Glance at my watch. Click on the car lights.

"Howard Cosell speaking of sports"—I twirl the dial searching for the soccer scores. Nothing. I switch it. Tank's almost empty, remember to gas up at Three Rivers. An ache throbs at the back of my head. Rain pings on the car roof. A stray dog, nose to the ground, lopes along. Nice perrito, don't get splattered on the highway, not an evening for dying. The car behind me has four headlights. Must be an illusion. A gust of wind almost lifts the hood of the car.

It's raining hard now; the sky's turned a slate blue. Watch that pick-up; it might cut in front of you. "Sundown" by Gordon Lightfoot plays on the radio; I sing along. Think of Dulie in Chicago who likes the song. Probably in a mental ward by now. Outsiders, kooks, crazies—wonder why I draw them to me? God, am I a freak, too? A barefoot boy plays in the rain in the front yard with a stick near a gray weather-beaten shack.

The sky clears up suddenly as it can only in Tejas. "Mellow Yellow" on the radio. Striking patches of lime green among yellow fields of corn plowed under on the dark blue slopes, not even hills. They look like eyebrows.

What I like about Carlos are his protruding eyes. My uncle Balme has ojos like that. A tight sexuality, lean lanky body—not chunky like Carlos. I never knew until now that I wanted him. My uncle, not Carlos. "Show Me the Way," on the radio. Why can't I respond to Carlos? Not even sure he really likes me. Maybe he just needs a woman to prove his masculinity.

The sky's a green sea. Chingao. I've wandered into the oncoming lane. Small town, Karnes City. A woman waves, I wave back. Totem pole, a rotting palm with gorgeous paper streamers in rainbow colors. Yeah, he's probably sitting in front of the TV. What was it I forgot? Getting sleepy. Open the vents, crack a window. If only my body would open as easily. Bread singing "I Want to Make It With You."

~

She opened a window of her dorm room while Carlos slept, the breeze drying the sweat on her body. She heard him stirring on the mattress.

"Did you come, eh? Was it good for you?" he asked again. His pride wouldn't let him give up.

"Uh huh." He took that as a yes and she let him so he wouldn't get on her so soon. But soon he reached for her again.

Afterwards, as semen dripped down her thighs, he read "¿Qué es poesía? Poesía eres tú." Bécquer, García Lorca, Parra, Vallejo, Darío. Sometimes he read her his own poetry. Once he read a poem he'd written to her. The first line began with P, the second with R, the third with I then E, T, A. As Prieta felt the words enter her body (something in the poem spoke to her though he didn't really know her), she caught a look of something soft, something in him he kept hidden from her. Maybe he did know her a little. She felt her throat thicken. At least he knew that words got through to her in a way his touch never could. Pobrecitos los dos.

A week later, she handed him a poem she'd written in Spanish. He took his pen and crossed out every other line, substituting a poetic phrase here, a word there. Chicanos were corrupting the Spanish language, he told her, and constantly corrected hers. Mexicans didn't know how to speak it right either, he argued. She stopped speaking Spanish, spoke only English to him, while he spoke mostly Spanish to her. Though his English was bad she never corrected him. And she showed him no more of her writing.

One night he laid his hand on top of her head and pushed it slowly to his crotch. He pressed his penis against her lips. Arrodillada ante él, she pictured herself kneeling before a statue of an erect phallus.

She stared at his penis. It looked like a brown mushroom. There was a tiny slit in the middle of the pink tip. A bead of liquid glistened there. She remembered her dogs, pets she'd acquired, at different times in her life, five male dogs in all. Their erect penises looked like lipsticks with the pink shafts unscrewed all the way.

"Tuck your teeth in like this, eh," he said, sucking in his lips over his teeth. "Squeeze my balls," he said, his hands urging hers to cup his testicles. His huevos felt like two soft peaches in a bag of skin. He loved it when, with her tongue, she stroked the underside of his penis where the thick vein throbbed, when she wrung music out of the musty crevices.

"It hurts my feelings, eh, that you don't swallow my cum," he told her when she ran to the waste basket to spit. Despite el asco que le daba, she felt a small tenderness for the penis when it was soft and vulnerable.

"Bueno, it's the greatest honor a woman could pay a man. Besides, it's full of protein."

"It tastes like snot to me," she told him.

Whenever he rammed his penis too far into her mouth, she would choke almost to the point of vomiting. "Your throat is too shallow," he told her and took her to see *Deep Throat*. Her feelings of tenderness faded. Though she felt like a recalcitrant servant performing a repugnant task, she did want to learn. And she did like seeing him lose control. The sooner he came the sooner he stopped trying to wring an orgasm out of her.

They tried all the positions possible and some that were impossible. One day they fucked in the men's gym showers, her back pressed against the tiles, her legs around his waist, his thighs trembling with the strain. Knowing that any second a bunch of guys could saunter in after a game, cracking jokes and sprinkling the walls and floor with their sweat and urine probably turned him on. Eso era lo que él quería—for his buddies to see him making out con una "Americana." Knowing that they could find her naked and impaled on his palo distracted her. Water was her only lubricant.

It was only when both were facing each other on their sides and he was inside her that she felt tiny inner shivers inside her. During those few times, making love was slightly pleasurable. But side by side was his least favorite position because his penis kept popping out. Quickly she would coax it back in. And just as her pelvis started moving involuntarily and she felt the intensity in her body building up, he'd come and was out of her before she could find her own release.

One night he got her on her knees, face in the pillow, hands clutching the sheets. He spat into his hands and rubbed his penis. He lifted her buttocks into the air and eased his cock into her asshole. She tried to scamper away. He pulled her back, fingers digging into her hips, and plunged in. She bit into her pillow. There must be a better lubricant than saliva, she thought. The slap, slap of his belly against her buttocks and his cock against her cervix. His breath sawing faster and faster.

"Relax your sphincter muscle," he coached her. She thought she was shitting, was afraid she would get caca all over him. She wasn't, but it felt like it. After the first couple of times she started to like it—at least she could feel something, even if it was only pain, a pain that could become pleasurable if only she could open herself to it. What kind of masochist did that make her? Just like all the other Chicanas who tolerated abuse from their hombres. After the second time she refused him her ass.[2]

Back on the road. Red sun hovering over a cemetery. The horizon blushing deep amber with deep rose at the fringes. Like tripping on drugs, only better. A car too close behind me. Don't like it in the ass—hurts too much. Shouldn't ask me to do it. "That's the way uh huh uh huh I like it." Not me, cabrón.

I think of all those trips I've taken with half of the soccer team in the station wagon, trips to Houston, San Antonio, and other Texas towns. The radio full blast, los vatos cracking jokes and filling the car with marijuana smoke while Carlos and I necked in the back seat of the station wagon. Once on the way to the Valley to play Pan American University we almost made out all the way in the back seat. In the front seat, all the guys were laughing. I felt exposed, ashamed, and finally I shoved him away.

---

2. Here Anzaldúa included "[More on her pain here?]."

Shit, only his macho possessiveness prevented him from sharing me with the guys.

But at last I had a man. I'd already told my amigas back home about my "novio." They welcomed me into their ranks. At long last I had escaped that desert with its utter desolation.

I used to wait for him every day at our rendezvous bench near the Latin American Studies building. Sandwich in hand I'd wait for him to get out of class or soccer practice. Lo esperaba y esperaba while he was probably chatting up some professor. I felt a little humiliated. Pinche vato takes me for granted. Yet he doesn't want me to spend time with my friends. He doesn't like my friend Jauni. I had let myself drift away from her.

I remember the day I waited for him in his apartment. I pulled out a half-opened drawer. Jíjole, it was full of "how to" sex manuals—pictures of humongous tits and penises the size of stallions. I left and went back to my place.

❧

Two red serpents peep out from behind a cloud. Then their tails vanish behind the sun. The world is split—light blue sky on the right, lilac-gray on the left.

Take a chug from the soda I picked up back a ways. Tastes funny. Can't find a service station that matches my gas card. Pure and vivid, the yellow horizon makes my breath knot in my throat. High above, silver half-moon nests in a sun-lit sky. Trees behind trees edging the road that looks as if it's lit with fire—bright orange flames with blue centers. Hypnotic green dots everywhere. What to do about Carlos? Can't see on-coming cars.

What would it be like to burn with green fire in a quiet fury, to waste and never to consume myself entirely? A car surrounded in purple light is coming. As it gets closer, I see it's a VW with a huge purple dot on the hood. I stick my head out the window and look up. The problem is all inside my head. "50 ways to leave your lover / just slip out the back Jack, . . . don't need to be coy Roy, . . . just drop off the key Lee / and get yourself free."

Is it habit and inertia that keep me from leaving? Or am I afraid to be left afuera otra vez? Against the vivid blue sky, a windmill looks like a woman standing with legs opened wide to feed the thirsty. Sign: "Fishworms for Sale." The sky is changing to a sea anemone purple. I feel something coming on. Maybe the stubbornness my mother hates, maybe maturity's about to firm up my backbone.

The thin leg of a feather-like cloud, like the leg of a road-runner. Stop ahead a car on the side of the road. Need help? I start to brake. Empty. Oh well, accelerate, keep going. "Why am I living . . . my brother he died in a coal mine . . . sister above sweet jesus . . . singing with the band I blew it bad, unemployment. What am I living for . . . I had me a sweet woman."

George West 10 . . . Alice 50. Yuck—a church cross lit like an Xmas tree. A wooden sign: "Fresh Water Catfish Ice House." Ahead a dark clump like the beak of a prehistoric bird? A patrol car? No, just a tree with a reflector nailed to a short trunk. Should I stop and call him? No, he's out chasing balls. Just a few more towns: Rachel, Falfurias, San Miguel, then turn right onto 186 then left onto 463 and home. I think about when I took the whole soccer team home for my mother to feed.

❧

The soccer team fell on the meal her mother cooked like starving coyotes.

After they left to play against Pan American University, her mother asked, "Pa' qué quieres a ese mojado?"

"He's not a wetback, Mami. He's not even Mexican."

"He's from the south of the border, isn't he?" she snapped.

"'Amá he's from South America. And he's upper middle class." Under her breath she muttered, "Se cree muy chingón."

When they were back in school, she tried to talk to him about her ambivalent feelings.

"Prietita, mi amor, no me hagas esos papeles, eh," he said. "En mi país el amor es cosa seria." Then softening, he added, "How soft your skin is. Me gusta el calor de tu cariño."

After he left, she picked up her white topaz stone, a stone someone had dug out of the entrails of the earth. She looked at the fire frozen inside the rock. She rubbed it, trying to warm it. Was this the way things were for all women—men always having the upper hand? When she complained Carlos told her she was exaggerating and to stop whining.[3]

Like her mother and grandmothers, she had been raised under the old law: mujeres decentes smother their needs and their sense of things. They weren't supposed to have any needs nor a different take on things. How deeply she had learned the old law came as a surprise to her. She'd thought herself free and liberated. But its reality lay like a stone in her cunt. The new sexual freedom chipped away at the rock. The new law claimed that a real woman had orgasms. A real woman had a man, but she had to be "chosen" by that man. No matter how much she kicked against the restraints she was entombed in the frozen tundra between the two laws. She was hung by her titties if she did, hung by her clit if she didn't. Jodida. There had to be a way out.

One morning a week before winter break despúes de que él se fue se levantó en vez de acostarse otra vez. She woke up with a headache and trudged down the hall to the communal bathroom. Barelegged women in terrycloth robes, towels slung over their shoulders, trekked in and out of the bathroom. She locked the door to one of the bathtub cubicles and lay on her back in the tub. Raising her pelvis and moving it back and forth, she let the water from the faucet gush on her clit, then on the opening of her vagina. The water washed away the dried semen. She rested her thighs for a moment on the rim of the tub, her feet gripping, pressed against the cool tile. Niña, no te atoques allí, she remembered her mother's voice telling her when she was a child. Again and again she positioned her genitals to the stream of water.

---

3. At the beginning of this paragraph, Anzaldúa inserted in brackets "move to earlier?"

Jijo de la chingada. A shudder jerked her body up. The whole world was coming into her cunt, or coming out through it. She lay back again, keeping the water jetting on her clit and cunt. More contractions. The muscle from left hip to crotch was pulsing. The sound of water gushing covered her moans and gasps. Prieta wanted more, but she was afraid her body couldn't stand the convulsions. Afraid it would wring itself inside out. The sleeping serpent, her second heart—the cunt had woken up. The beating of its heart became her world. Le tenía miedo a ese animal pulsing between her legs, a esa llama dentro de la roca. La clit es un puente, a bridge, por la vía del cual ella viajaba al otro mundo. As she touched the other world, se convertía en la tierra y el cielo y el aire, se convertía en animal inspiritada.

While the tub gurgled until it emptied, Prieta floundered on the white porcelain, a fish gasping in an alien element. Había descubrido que ella sola podía encender esa llama, se había dado cuenta que tenía pasión hasta en las rodillas. Una pasión grandísima que la asustaba. How had she forgotten it, this fire she herself had lighted many times when she was a child? She would lie in bed boca abajo and cross her legs con fuerza mientras que se mesia. Prendía el fuego sacro, the heat would set her second heart to beating. Su hermana en la misma cama would not awaken. Though a child, sabía que ese placer solitario era un placer condenado. Esa llama nunca debe ser encendida, but if it *was* lit, only the other, el marido, should light it.

Wrapped in her big towel, she shuffled back to her room in her slippers. Stretched out on the bed amazed at her body. After a while, she got up and lit copal incense in the lava-rock bowl by the mirror. As tendrils of smoke spiraled up, she stared at the face in the mirror. Something was different, yet her face was the same. As she stared her face was replaced by another and it, in turn, was replaced by another. A succession of different faces stared back at her. She touched the long nose, wide mouth, receding chin, traces of Coahuiltecan, Azteca, Maya, Basque, Spanish, Moor, Berber Arab, Sephardic Jew, Gypsy. A mix, a mestiza, her body a battle ground where white conquistadores had clubbed the indio, the Black, and the Asian into submission.[4] El doble ritmo de la sangre indígena contra la española batia su cuerpo.

"Pura india, mijita," her grandmother's voice. Again she heard the voices of her mother, aunts, uncles, cousins: "Pura india ladina, mijita. ¡Qué lástima! ¡Pobrecita Prietita!" Regret and love rang in their voices, along with embarrassment for the dark skin, short body, round face, sharp nose, and flat feet. La presencia viva y muda de la india pulsed under her skin. It burned like a live coal. Vivía entre guerras, a civil war raged under her skin.

As she stared into the mirror the face of la Chingada stared back at Prieta. She felt the invader's hard hands spread her thighs and mount her, heard la india scream and kick and scratch, saw la india hold her ground. Then gradually the features began to take on a white cast.

She thought she heard the rumble of thunder. She opened her window wide. A breath of air entered her room. Los espíritus bathed her face. Dejó la toalla caer. She dropped the towel y anduvo desnuda alrededor del cuarto. She lit more copal incense and turned on her stereo. Y brincando en los colchones que todavía estaban tirados en el piso comenzo a bailar. Naked, she danced to the music viéndose en el espejo. In the mirror she watched el humo swirl around sus pechos pequeños, watched her breasts subir y bajar. She watched la piel de la vulva enrojer.

Watching herself in the mirror she touched the inner lips, maroon and burgundy, slid her fingers inside her cunt, raised the wet finger up to her nose and then put it in her mouth and sucked it. Del secreto hueco, de su cuerpo probó el almidón que su útero había batido. Untó las gotas en su frente, su corazón, sus chichis. She touched her body, anointing it. All her life she'd heard that the genitals were ugly and smelled bad.

For the rest of the day, she couldn't focus on the day-to-day activities. All her energy flowed inwardly into those wounds she was trying to close. When he showed up wanting to fuck, she thought of telling him she was having her period, but that had

---

4. In the 1970s and 80s, these problematic, essentialist categories were typical.

never put him off. So she told him she wanted to be alone. Así lo quería. Pero la ternura de su voz de enamorado called to her, the possibility that he would yet ignite the fire in the stone and lead her into the mysteries of being a real woman.

But if she ever let herself go, she would go wild, become uncontrollable, the animal inside her would waken, snap its tether. No, she must kill the spirit of this animal before it could stir and awaken like it once had threatened to awaken with her father, with her brother. That spirit had to be sacrificed before it flared out of control like a wildfire.

∞

At 6:30 I pull into the garage. A door slams. Mamá is hurrying toward me. She helps me with bags and boxes containing gifts. I unpack then shower. We sit on stools eating arroz con pollo off the kitchen counter. "Mami," I say, "he wants me to marry him."

"No con ese mojado," she says.

Dolores tried to get into my journal like she always does, but I kept it hidden. She did find a couple of love letters from Carlos. That was good for a few jokes at my expense.

Six days later, Dec. 28. Driving north back to the university, the tawny golden hues of the grass has turned to gray straw. I wonder what I forgot . . . toothbrush? Again?

At Ben Bolt the highway is under construction. Taquito stand, off to the right, chorizo con huevo, fresh tamales. I stop to pick up two dozen tamales. Maybe I'll give Carlos some, maybe not. Only a quarter of a tank left. Chicago, singing "Beginning" on the radio. Shamrock gas station; I pull in, four cars parked haphazardly on left, two in front of me. "50 ways to leave your lover." Not again!

Twenty-mile stretch to George West. The road going north is a lot like the roads in Indiana, a long gray ribbon of highway, sloping hills, brown loafs of toasted hay in fields.

El chulo I picked up at Three Rivers is still keeping close behind me. Bales of hay piled in pyramids.

Seguin 15. The town, where la chota hides in clumps of oaks on the side of roads. My car casts its dancing shadow against a chainlink fence. At the skyline I see sprawled rusty derricks, fossils and carcasses of tractors. A white-top station wagon with four dry palm leaf husks, two small deer strapped to the hood—red mouths, bloated stomachs, pathetic cold unblinking eyes. A killer behind the wheel.

I catch a glimpse of myself in the mirror. Pelo negro parted down the middle caé sobre mis hombros forming a curtain around my face. Enormes ojos oscuros behind my glasses. I had conveniently forgotten what I'm hiding from others, forgotten the secret that haunts me, like a ghost. Why I don't want to get demasiado cerca del otro. But what am I really afraid of? ¿Rendirme a un pelado? ¿Diretirme? ¿Perder mis paredes? That is what women do. Softened by the two tender words, "te quiero," they surrender. Pendejas.

I do want my mother's passion—Mami and Papi made love a lot. I want Mamagrande's perseverance, her stubborn pride and dignity. But their serfdom to husbands, brothers, sons, grandsons—their martyrdom to marriage? Already he's talking of marriage. How can I turn my body over to him when I'm only now getting to know it myself? No sentía placer porque no tenía cuerpo. I didn't have a body because I couldn't feel anything. De la cintura pa' bajo ningún rompehielos podia quebrar la piedra de hielo. Según él, mi vagina no secreta lo suficiente, ni el clitoris se hincha.

Johnny Nash singing "I can see clearly now." I suspect he wanted his "papers." Marrying an "americana" is the easiest way to become a U.S. citizen. Maybe he does love me, but his idea of love sure is different from mine. But am I worthy of love? If I marry, I'll become like the rest, part of the flock. No vale la pena; it isn't worth it.

¿Qué es ese ruido? The engine doesn't sound right—wouldn't want to end up stalling. I search for signs written in the world, search for glyphs to give meaning to this passage, as if I could find my story and my gods in the smoke, the burnt grass, the solitary tree, the shadow of my car on the fence posts.

On the right, fence posts catch my eye. A shadow car, my car, rides the tall post fence. Shadows slightly behind, slightly ahead, sombras rippling on the thin posts. Mi silueta a través de los árboles. The shadow of a driver's head, my head, the shadow of a man in my backseat. How could he have gotten in my car? When I stopped for gas. My foot slips off the gas pedal. Keep driving, keep driving, don't look back. Blink. He's gone. Feel I'm under water, drowning can't breathe. Have to turn my head. Have to look. No one. No one in back. Stop.

No, go faster. Don't look. But I look again.

Shadow car undulating on the fence. Silhouette of a driver's head, me. Sombra de un hombre in the backseat looming behind me. Foot on gas pedal all the way to the floor.

Translations

humo: smoke

No quiero saber, haciéndome sonsa.: I don't want to know, you're making me crazy.

y el cielo: and the sky

ojos: eyes

estos pensamientos pesados: those heavy thoughts

y las sombras del carro: and the shadows of my car

los árboles: the trees

¿Qué es ese ruido?: What's that noise?

nubes: clouds

ruca: pachuca word for girl or woman

¿Cómo estará?: How could it be?

tonta: dumb

se le enchino el cuerpo: she got goosebumps all over her body

le mordío el pezón: he bit her nipple

Le apartó las rodillas y le puso un dedo sobre la vulva.: He parted her knees and placed his finger over her vulva.

el pene no podía pasar: the penis couldn't go in

y le entró un miedito: she got a little scared

pueblo: community

mujeres: women

Pero ya, que se acabé esto.: That's enough; let this be over.

la bella durmiente del bosque: Sleeping Beauty in the forest

Lo que había sacado de este fiasco era un cuerpo roto.: What she'd gotten out of the fiasco was a torn body.

ni modo: doesn't matter

Es increíble que eres virgen.: It's incredible that you're still a virgin.

Bueno, si yo hubiera sabido que eras virgen nunca te hubiera tocado.: Well, if I had known that you were a virgin I wouldn't have laid a finger on you.

¿entiendes?: Do you understand?

putas: whores

¿Eh?: What?

un mojado: a wetback

Los hombres no más quieren una cosa.: Men only care about one thing.

Todas son putas: They're all whores

La gente se va a dar cuenta que andas con ese pelado.: The people will notice that you are hanging out with that guy.

Ya mero, ya mero: I'm almost there, I'm almost there

Ella miraba ese hombre manipular sus genitales y no sentía nada.: She watched that man manipulate her genitals and felt nothing.

Penetraba con su lengua, penetraba con los dedos.: He penetrated her with his tongue, he penetrated her with his fingers.

manteniendo su pene erecto dentro ella: maintaining an erect penis within her

Después de hora y media de estar forcejeando con ella y jalando: After an hour and a half of heavy petting and intercourse

frígida: frigid woman

Quería darle gusto al cuerpo.: She wanted to give pleasure to her own body.

pobre hombre: poor man

papalote: windmill

con el viento: with the wind

adios: good-bye

pendejo: asshole

vieja: old lady

amigas: female friends

el Valle: the Valley (Lower Rio Grande Valley in South Texas)

¡Wáchate!: Chicano slang for "watch out!"

chingao: fuck

las pinches chotas: the damn cops

pos sí: well, yes

sobre mi espalda: over my spine

cabrón: bastard

azul: blue

perrito: doggie

ojos: eyes

¿Qué es poesía? Poesía eres tú.: What is poetry? You are poetry.
(a line from Rubén Darío)

pobrecitos los dos: sad for the both of them

arrodillada ante él: on her knees in front of him

huevos: literally eggs, in this case, testicles

y le daba asco: it grossed her out, made her nauseous

Eso era lo que él quería: That's what he wanted.

palo: stick

caca: shit

cabrón: asshole

los vatos: the guys

novio: boyfriend

lo esperaba y esperaba: waited and waited for it

jíjole: damn or wow

afuera otra vez: out again

¿Pa' qué quieres a ese mojado?: What do you want with that
wetback?

Se cree muy chingón.: He thinks he's really cool.

mi amor, no me hagas esos papeles: my love, don't give me that line

En mi país el amor es cosa seria.: In my country, love is a serious thing.

Me gusta el calor de tu cariño.: I like the intensity of your love.

mujeres decentes: decent women

jodida: raw deal

después de que él se fue se levantó en vez de acostarse otra vez:
  after he left she got up instead of going back to bed

Niña, no te atoques allí: You filthy thing, don't touch yourself there

jijo de la chingada: son of a bitch

le tenía miedo a ese animal: she was afraid of that animal

a esa llama dentro de la roca: a call from the rock between her legs

la clit es un puente: the clit is a bridge

por la vía del cual ella viajaba al otro mundo: by the way in which
  she traveled to the other world

se convertía en la tierra y el cielo y el aire, se convertía en ánimal
  inspiritada: she became the land, the sky, the air; she became
  an enspirited animal

Había descubrido que ella sola podía encender esa llama, se había
  dado cuenta que tenía pasión hasta en las rodillas.: She discovered that she could light that flame; she had passion even
  on her knees.

una pasión grandísima que le asustaba: passion so huge that it
  scared her

boca abajo: open mouth

con fuerza mientras que se mesia: with force while he messed around

Prendía el fuego sacro: He lit a sacred flame

su hermana en la misma cama: her sister in the same bed

Sabía que ese placer solitario era un placer condenado: She knew
  that this solitary pleasure was not condoned

esa llama nunca debe ser encendida: this call was never lit

el marido: husband

El doble ritmo de la sangre indígena contra la española batia su cuerpo: The double rhythm of Indian and Spanish blood beat in her body

pura india, mijita: pure Indian, my daughter

pura india ladina: pure wild Indian

¡Qué lástima!: What a shame!

pobrecita: poor thing

la presencia viva y muda de la india: the living and mute presence of la india

vivía entre guerras: she lived between wars

Dejó la toalla caer.: Let the towel drop.

y anduvo desnuda alrededor del cuarto: and she walked around the room nude

Y brincando en los colchones que todavía estaban tirados en el piso comenzo a bailar.: Jumping on the mattress that was still lying on the floor, she began to dance.

viéndose en el espejo: seeing herself in the mirror

sus pechos pequeños: her small breasts

subir y bajar: go up and down

la piel de la vulva enrojer: the skin of her vulva turned red

Del secreto hueco, de su cuerpo probó el almidón que su útero había batido.: She tasted the starchy wetness her uterus had churned up.

Untó las gotas en su frente, su corazón, sus chichis.: He smeared the drops on her forehead, her heart, her tits.

Así lo quería.: That's how she wanted it.

pero la ternura de su voz de enamorado: but the tenderness of the voice of her beloved arroz con pollo: chicken with rice

No con ese mojado: not with that wetback

chorizo con huevo: chili-spiced sausage scrambled with eggs

tamales: cornmeal and meat filling steamed in corn husks

el chulo: the cute guy

la chota: the cop

pelo negro: black hair

caé sobre mis hombros: fell over my shoulders

enormes ojos oscuros: big black eyes

demasiado cerca del otro: so close to the other one

rendirme a un pelado: giving myself to some jerk

diretirme: dissolving

perder mis paredes: losing my walls

te quiero: I love you

No sentía placer porque no tenía cuerpo.: I didn't have any sensation of pleasure because I didn't have a body.

De la cintura pa' bajo ningún rompehielos podia quebrar la piedra de hielo.: From the waist down she was a mountain of ice that no icebreaker could crack.

Según él, la vagina no secreta lo suficiente, ni el clitoris se hincha: According to him, the vagina doesn't secrete enough and the clitoris doesn't swell

no vale la pena: it isn't worth it

sombras: shadows

Mi silueta a través de los árboles: My silhouette through the trees

sombra de un hombre: a man's shadow

11

The Crack Between the Worlds

La llama de mi terror al desencanto
hace de mi ventana,
luciérnaga despavorida
iluminando la noche.

— "Flash" from *Alabanza* by Kyra Galván

If thou gaze long into an abyss, the abyss will gaze into thee.
—Friedrich Nietzsche[1]

La Prieta started down the mouth of the ravine, taking her usual shortcut through the university. A muted unease drew her to this place every day on her way home, a sinking feeling like a trace or residue of some dream or a fear long buried ready to be awakened. There was pleasure in the feeling, in her compulsion to repeat. Something in her reached out to that fissure riddled with weeds and potholes, rubble and chunks of cement, and bordered by trees and shrubs on three sides and by the creek on the north side. In the middle of the vacant lot stood a crane that seemed to have a life of its own. Today the mystery that la barranca held for her, and one she wanted to figure out, was buried by the unease, more intense than before. She wished she'd taken the bus home.

---

1. The manuscript ends with a third literary reference, part of a poem by Federico García Lorca, following the glossary. We don't know why she chose to place this where she did.

189

She was part way down the steep narrow footpath, sliding and slipping, when she saw him. At the bottom of la barranca stood a gringo in a white sweatshirt. He was smiling. He blocked the path as though he owned it. Directly behind him towered the silver crane.

She considered going back up the path, but that would mean admitting she was afraid, and for some reason she didn't want him to know she was afraid. Anyway, she had as much right to be there as he had. And contrary to popular belief, assaults were rarely made by strangers. He looked like the innocent güero with his blond, close-cropped hair, so different from the long-haired, long-bearded, sullen-looking college boys. Ignoring her instincts and her heart's little hop, she hurried down.

"Can I help you?" he asked, the smile wider on his face. Cat-like he sprang up to give her a hand down the last leg of the path.

"No, thanks," she said, not making eye contact, adding to herself, You gringos have helped yourselves to too much already. He was standing too close, her eyes level with the bright yellow SMILE button on his sweatshirt. Feeling exposed, she hurried around him. As she brushed past him, his arm snaked around her. He hooked her neck with his elbow and jerked her back. The impact knocked her breath out and she fell backwards, her tailbone hitting a slab of cement, jarring up her spine. He tugged on her bag and she clutched it tighter against her body and struggled to get back on her feet. ¡Chingado! ¡Que atrevido! In broad daylight. How dare you! Fear swelled in her throat. Images of him knocking her down, straddling her body, squeezing her to death while forcing his penis between her legs flashed through her mind.

Their individual breaths seemed to congeal in the autumn air. She felt his heart galloping against her back. She twisted her body, managing to loosen his grip a little. Sucking in air, she belted out a scream. She kicked at his shins when his fingers like pincers found her face. He clamped a sweaty hand over her mouth. She opened it and bit the edge of his palm as hard as she could.

He cuffed her in the face, his thick paw knocking her down again. Pain shot up her thighs when her knees hit the ground. She screamed again. He grabbed her by the throat, fingers gouging into the soft flesh. She could not breathe. The pressure in her lungs became unbearable. La estaba ahorcando. ¡Este gabacho desgraciado la querría matar! Get him off me, someone get him off me! Prieta clawed his blue eyes and smooth-shaven face leaving thin red lines.

Handsome blond anglos with the baby-blue eyes were not supposed to be the enemy. Whites had forgotten all about lynching Mexicans—and so had Chicanos like her mother, who had warned her time and again about mojados and Blacks, that the darker the man the more dangerous; this fair-skinned young man could not be attacking her.

Get up, don't let him keep you on the ground. Don't give him ideas, or your bag will not be all he'll try to take. She pushed herself to her feet. Don't fall. No te caigas. She raised her knee up hard into his groin with the last of her strength and heard him grunt. The hands around her throat loosened and slid to her shoulders. Finally, she was going to escape. But he snagged her long black hair from behind and wrapped it around his fist. He pinned her arms from behind. Half mounting her, he clung to her back, his hot breath sawing in and out along her neck. The only other sound was the thud of her shoes hitting his shins.

She kept kicking. This was her body. It did not belong to this stranger. ¡Desgraciado! Surprised you, sonavabitch. Thought you'd take the money and run. Took one look at me, decided I was easy prey. You're a foot taller and weigh almost twice as much. Ningún pinche pelado's going to take my hard-earned money.

By twisting her arm he turned her around, then kicked her in the stomach. Her breath whooshed out. He dragged her, face down, bag and all, across the broken rocks, her pants tearing at the knees. Jerking her upright, he pulled her onto the bridge across Waller Creek.

When they got to the middle of the small bridge she wrenched away. He caught her and shoved her against the wooden rail, bending her body over the side. Rail digging into the small of her back, she looked over her shoulder down to the trickle of water washing over the stones twenty feet below. The thought, "But my shoes will get wet, my clothes will get torn by the rocks," ran through her head.

Gritó, y gritó. He picked her up by her shirt, shoved. Below her the rocks got bigger. Just when she felt herself losing her grip on the rail, just when she thought, "This is it," and saw herself falling head over heels, the strap of her bag broke. In an instant el asaltante dropped her and, bag in hand, leaped across el puente and ran into la cruzada and the traffic on Lafayette Street, bringing cars screeching to a halt. She saw the white sweatshirt disappearing into the alley behind the 7-Eleven.

Prieta let go of the rail and ran after him. As she crossed Lafayette she almost plowed into the door of a blue Toyota. When the shocked woman stopped, Prieta shouted, "Call the cops. Tell them I live over there," pointing to the apartment complex behind the 7-Eleven. She ran around the Toyota and into the shadow-filled alley. Two hippies with bead necklaces hanging down their bare chests sat on their back steps.

"Did a guy run by here just now?" she asked, panting. "He just tried to kill me. He has my bag. I need to get it back!"

"He ran thatta way," one of them pointed north.

"Want us to come with you?" asked the other.

When she nodded her head, they jumped up and followed her. Unlike the blond con la cara sonriente, they looked like muggers.

She ran up the alley breathing hard, the two hippies behind her. After the three searched up and down several alleys and streets, they gave up and returned to her apartment.

Two cops and the apartment manager were talking in the patio. The tall cop took out his notebook and put his foot on the white metal chair when she began telling her story. Something in the tall cop's eyes made her falter. Disinterest? Was he only going through the motions? Just another victim, a woman and Mexican at that. The other cop met her eyes and asked in a soft voice, "What happened?"

After Prieta finished her account, the tall cop said, "You shouldn't have fought him."

She asked if she could ride along. The cops caught each other's eye. She said, "I know what he looks like. And so do they." She gestured toward the two hippies. There was safety in numbers.

She didn't feel comfortable with Texas cops, especially not with the tall one. The soft-voiced cop nodded, and Prieta and the two hippies scrambled into the backseat of the police car.

They cruised up and down the neighborhood which consisted mostly of small houses and student apartment complexes. After half an hour the tall cop dropped off his partner, whose shift was over.

The driver turned to the backseat and said, "Let's call it a day."

"Just a few more minutes, please," said Prieta.

They continued to search and a few minutes later the dispatcher squawked through. An old lady had just reported seeing a suspicious-looking caucasian crossing her backyard. The cop speeded up and headed north of the campus. They drove around the old lady's neighborhood but saw no suspicious characters. Just as they were about to give up Prieta gasped, "That's him, el pinche gabacho! That's him over there, crossing the golf course. I knew we'd catch him."

With siren blasting, the cop jerked the wheel and the car bumped over the curb and onto the golf course. Startled golfers stared at them. The mugger swiveled his head to look, then took off across a shallow creek, but stopped in the middle of the water—must have realized he couldn't outrun the car. He raised his hands over his head, turned his back, and tucked his head into hunched shoulders.

The cop got out of his car and leisurely walked toward him. At the edge of the water he stopped and motioned the assailant over. He cuffed the guy's hands behind his back, then patted his chest, waist, and thighs. From the mugger's pant pockets he pulled out a small journal with her name and address on it. She saw the cop's jowls fall in surprise. Now he believed her. From another pocket the cop unearthed eighty dollars—her food money—a black fountain pen and a tube of aloe vera lip balm.

By then it was seven or eight and sundown, and the two hippies decided to walk home. The cop put el asaltante in the front seat and, without looking at her, told Prieta, "Get in the back."

In the back Prieta fumbled with her torn blouse. She listened to them talk all the way to the station.

"This your first time?" asked the cop.

"No, my third."

"Where were you at?" the cop asked. "You got the haircut."

"Huntsville."

"Where'd you dump the purse and the rest of her stuff?"

"A couple of streets down, in a clump of bamboo."

Not once had the cop looked at her directly. Neither had the mugger. When he was hitting her, she had been the center of his world. Prieta felt herself becoming smaller and smaller, almost disappearing into the night. She hugged herself to stop the shivers.

"This will put you away for a long time, you know. They throw away the key with third-time offenders," the cop said.

"I know."

"Why'd you do it? It was a stupid move."

"I don't know. I just got out a couple days ago, and I needed the bread," said the blond man. "She looked easy."

The cop checked her out in the rear-view mirror. She felt as if she had committed the crime.

"Well kid, look on the bright side: at least you'll have food and a roof over your head."

In the backseat Prieta felt her body heating up all over again. What's taking so long? The cop's driving like he's on a Sunday drive. Finally the mugger pointed at an alley. The cop drove into it and stopped midway. She and the cop got out. After searching through a clump of bamboo she spotted her purse hanging from one of the shoots. Her wallet lay on the ground along with a pocket stapler, address book, and a sanitary napkin. Her textbooks were missing. Then she remembered them falling at the bottom of the ravine. She would have to go back for them.

At the station Prieta sank into a hard chair, eyes blurring. The cop told her that if she wrote out a full statement she wouldn't have to go to court. The evidence was incontestable, and he would get a fast sentence. After shuffling some papers, the policeman left to go down the hall, leaving her alone with him.

He looked at his handcuffs. Then slowly raised his eyes and holding hers he jerked the handcuffs and hissed, "I'm gonna get you, bitch!" He pushed his face close to hers, his spittle spraying her face. "I'm getting out of here and I'm coming after you, bitch!"

The attack had occurred at five o'clock. It was after midnight when the same policeman drove her home. He didn't say a word. Never once had he asked how she was. He dropped her off and she climbed the outside stairs to her third-floor apartment, hands holding onto the vibrating iron rail. She locked the door, checked to see that all the windows were locked. She opened her refrigerator and took a soda into the bathroom. She plugged in the tub and opened the hot water valve all the way. She pulled off her torn pants, looked at the hamper, then tossed them in the waste basket.

In the mirror the huge welts on her face shocked her. Her bottom lip had swollen to twice its size. She ran her tongue along the inside of her mouth, prodding. The cuts stung like fever blisters. The scraped skin over her knees was stiffening. The cop could at least have offered her a band-aid. She lowered her body into the tub and lay back. Exhaustion hit her, and her legs and arms trembled like fish. For the first time that day she was terrified. She saw her hands flailing at him, sus manos como peces mudos y ciegos golpeando al hombre hecho de piedra.

She couldn't sleep; every bone in her body ached. A slight trembling vibration, a sign of someone walking up the stairs. She got up, checked all the windows again, and put a rod inside the grooves of the sliding glass door. She staggered to the kitchen and took the long knife out of the drawer, got back into bed, placing it on the floor within reach.

How dumb! She should have taken Carito's pistol when he tried to give it to her saying that a woman alone had to protect herself. "Violence is no solution," she'd told him sanctimoniously. Well now she knows; she's got violent tendencies. In that moment when she was kicking and scratching, she'd been so angry she could have torn off his face. So much for being a pacifist.

It happened at five in the afternoon, a las cinco de la tarde. But why to her? What had she done to deserve it? Yeah, sure, she shouldn't have been out in broad daylight. Maybe she should ask a friend to come over, keep her company. But she was ashamed.

She didn't want him to see the cuts and welts on her body. It would be weeks, maybe months before the bruises on her throat disappeared. Her body might bear the scars of that struggle for the rest of her life.

She was freezing. She pulled up the spare blanket at the foot of the bed and huddled under it. Prieta thought about the violent embrace. He'd gotten a hard-on; she'd felt it prodding her belly. But she hadn't thought he would rape her. In his rage she did think he would kill her. She gasped, realizing that she too had been aroused. The danger, the adrenaline, and his sexual energy, the two bodies pressed together, rubbing. What a bizarre kind of intimacy, that between victim and victimizer.

She uncoiled her body from the fetal position and reached for the journal and pen on top of the nightstand, the ones he had touched. Spilling words on paper—if it didn't always make sense of things, it always made her feel better.

Finally, exhaustion caught up with her and she fell asleep—only to be jerked up by the alarm clock two hours later. She was tempted to stay in bed, skip all her classes. Grunting, she forced her sore body into jeans and t-shirt, forced it out the door, across Lafayette, and onto the bridge over Waller Creek.

Heart pounding, mouth dry, she forced herself to walk across the ravine. A atrancas y a barrancas, she picked her way through the rubble, then stood in the cool, shady ravine, alone except for the silver crane and her books scattered on the rocks. The dull roar of traffic faded, and all was quiet. Again, she felt the whack of the solid blow against her spine. She picked up her books y su cuaderno. She had recovered everything—her pen, her money, and now her books. But she'd lost something—the sense of her body being solid, contained. Something had torn open, and now she must mend the tear. But the hole seemed to be widening, and she seemed to be slipping toward it an inch at a time. And the world kept slipping with her. She felt as if she were falling into it, yet at the same time she felt la barranca slipping into her.

The ravine, the empty lot, the crane: all were the same yet different. The spot where el animalote had leaped shimmered. El lugar endemoniado de Matlalcihua, the malevolent spirit of ravines. "Be careful, be careful, cuidado," it whispered to her.

A las cinco de la tarde. At five o'clock. She took the same path on the way back home.

She heard a sound, sensed a sudden movement behind her, thought she saw his white sweatshirt with the SMILE button. Adrenaline rushed through her veins y una barranca opened beneath her feet, threatening to swallow her. Just a kid playing with his dog. The world had always seemed a safe place. She often walked the streets por las noches. She loved the evening air and the night sky, the distant bark of dogs. Now her trust in people was gone. Evil walked in the world, walked on two legs. Hid in unguarded places and pounced on the unwary. A las cinco de la tarde. Eran las cinco en punto de la tarde. Ya luchan la paloma y el leopardo, a las cinco de la tarde. She couldn't get the lines of Lorca's poem out of her mind.

She stayed home on Friday. Didn't leave her apartment for three days—not even out to the balcony. At night when the stairs trembled and she knew someone was coming up the stairs, she'd hear his words once again. "I'm going to get you, bitch. I'm coming after you." The memory intruded when she least expected it. She spent her days writing and her nights trying to not think about it. She'd watch the midnight horror movies on TV hoping they would desensitize her. In order to sleep she began to take Percodan that her next-door neighbor, who dealt drugs to pay tuition, had sold to her.

On the sixth day she was able to drink hot coffee and tea without her mouth hurting too much. As she scuttled across the ravine, the hair on her body stood at attention and her heart rose to her throat. She froze. A concentration of energy, something that breathed, began to unravel like a knot and turn itself loose in the ravine. As she scrabbled up the path it followed her. Why was it showing itself to her?

One night she heard in the news that there'd been a break in the county jail. Prieta was afraid that he had broken out, or that the cops had turned him loose. He was coming to get her like he'd promised. He could be coming right now. "I'm going to get you, bitch, I'm going to get you."

"You shouldn't have fought him," her friends told her. "You shouldn't have fought him," the cops said. You should not have scratched his face nor screamed, they all said. "You should have been passive. To fight back is to die," they said. "To fight back is to survive," she had replied.

For the next two weeks she crossed la barranca every day, the memory of the assault dogging her footsteps. She wanted to hide her slender exposed neck, her sunflower face, the open places in her body. But she knew that she had to keep crossing that barranca until she was no longer afraid. Somehow, she had to see the universe as it had once been—friendly. Or at least neutral. But not as just dangerous. For every act of evil there were a dozen acts of kindness. And if there really wasn't any harmony and balance in the universe, then she'd have to create it in her life or at least act as if there were. She couldn't keep leading with her wounds, couldn't keep making them her badges of identity.

Before going to bed, she took the bottle of wine out of the refrigerator—her neighbor was out of Percodan. The wine would soothe her, the writing would make sense out of her fears.

Se arranca de su sombra
a boca de noche entra el umbral de la barranca.
Con el sabor de miedo entre los dientes
cruza la boca de cráter
rompiendo la opacidad del silencio
y el murmullo del grillo.
Sabe que algo en ella
se había abierto para siempre
y ahora anda sobre arena movediz.
Ya no está intacta.
Con cada paso hay otra quebradura,
con cada paso oye las sombras respirar.
No quiere pescar ese momento de conocimiento

que el camino no es seguro
esos rumores que le es ajeno y no ajeno.
Aquí a este umbral
el silencio rotó lo inesperado.
Algo en ella se abre como una contraventana.
Su mirada como lengua saboriando
el ruido de sus tiernos huesos quebrandose
los cabellos enredados en sus puños
el coraje arrebató su voz
haciendo agujeros en el viento
su cuerpo como papel de china
y las sombras fracturándose detrás de ella.

She tears herself away from her shadow
at the threshold of the ravine at nightfall,
with the taste of fear between her teeth
she crosses the mouth of the crater
breaking the opaque silence
and the shrill sounds of the cicadas.
She knows that something in her
had opened forever
and now she walks on quicksand.
She is no longer intact.
With each step there is another break,
with each step she hears the shadows exhaling.
She does not want to catch that moment of realization
that the path is not safe,
those hints that she is alien and not alien.
here at this threshold at nightfall
silence tore the unexpected.
something in her opens like a shutter
her gaze like a tongue tasting the air
the sound of her tender bones snapping,
her hair wrapped around his fists
the silence snatched her voice

making holes in the wind
her body like crepe paper
as the shadows fragmented behind her.

Translations

la barranca: the ravine

güero: a gringo, literally it means light-skinned person

¡Chingado! ¡Que atrevido!: Fuck, how dare he!

La estaba ahorcando. ¡Este gabacho desgraciado la querría matar!:
    He was strangling her. This damned white man wanted to
    kill her.

mojados: wetbacks

No te caigas.: Don't fall.

desgraciado: shameless

ningún pinche pelado: no damned guy

Gritó, y gritó: She screamed and screamed

el asaltante: the assailant

el puente: the bridge

la cruzada: the crossing or the crossroads

con la cara sonriente: with smiling face

el pinche gabacho: the fucking white guy

sus manos como peces mudos y ciegos golpeando al hombre hecho
    de piedra: her hands like deaf and blind fish hitting the man
    made of iron

a las cinco de la tarde: at five in the afternoon

a atrancas y a barrancas: with many difficulties and obstacles

y su cuaderno: and her notebook

el animalote: the big animal

el lugar endemoniado de Matlalcihua: the bewitched place of Matlalcihua (a spirit of the ravines)

cuidado: careful

por las nochas: at night

A las cinco de la tarde. Eran las cinco en punto de la tarde. Ya luchan la paloma y el leopardo, a las cinco de la tarde.: At five in the afternoon. It was five o'clock in the afternoon on the dot. Now the dove and the leopard struggle at five in the afternoon.[2]

---

2. From Federico García Lorca, translated by the author

12

Becoming luciérnaga /
Swallowing fireflies /
Tragando luciérnagas*

Prieta first saw her at the student union. No make-up, pelo negro pulled back so tightly it gave her eyes an exotic look. Tall, bordering on skinny, she wore a blue cotton dress to mid-calf. Graceful and poised, she seemed to glide when she walked past Prieta on the way to the pizza line. Her look of aloofness and mystery drew Prieta's eye.

Prieta shoved off the wall she was leaning against and sauntered after her. She got in line behind her and "accidentally" bumped her arm. "Oh, disculpe. I'm so sorry."

"That's all right, this place is crowded."

"Hey, you're a Chicana," Prieta said.

"I don't use that term for myself. I'm Mexican American."

They ordered slices of pizza and picked up their trays.

"It's noisy here; why don't we eat out in the patio?" Prieta said.

They walk out and sat at a table in the shade of a tall encino tree. Prieta talked about her art classes and of how frustrated she was with her instructors trying to shove European aesthetics down her throat and discouraging her from expressing her Mexi-

*An earlier version of this story appeared in *Lesbian Love Stories*. I'd like to thank my writing comadres, AnaLouise Keating and Carmen Morones, for reading and commenting on this story.

can Indigenous roots and traditions. Suel talked about trying to get her public school to include Mexican American material in the classes. Suel was twelve years older and doing graduate work. Both were frustrated with being in a gringo university filled with caras güeras in a city where Chicanos lived on the other side of the river and were not encouraged to go to college.

As the fierce summer sun slanted down, they lost the shade. The light shimmered on Suel's skin, turning it into a luminous glow. Prieta watched the movement of Suel's throat as she swallowed and the graceful windmilling of her hands as she talked. Keeping each other afloat with slices of cold watermelon and iced drinks, platicaron de sus familias. Prieta spoke of her close relationship with her mamagrande and her primo hermano, Teté. Suel said her mother was very religious and strict. Suel was a devout catholic whereas Prieta was delving into nagualismo and Indigenous deities.

When Prieta mentioned reading Judy Grahn, a lesbian poet, Suel looked uncomfortable and said, "I don't read those kinds of writers."

Finally, the heat drove them into the air-conditioned Commons where they talked for another three hours. When they tired of the noise and of sitting on wrought iron chairs, they left and walked across the green, well-kept lawns of the Austin campus.

They descended a ravine to Waller Creek which wound around the sprawling campus. The shrill song of cicadas was deafening. Shucking off their sandals, they plopped down on a flat white limestone rock, legs hanging over the creek. Prieta inched closer to Suel and held her breath, but Suel didn't move away. The water gurgled over the sound of their voices. Prieta leaned over and peered into the green pool formed by a dam of round rocks. She stared at their reflection on the water. Inching closer to Suel she "accidentally" brushed her breast, a movida she'd picked up from the vatos. Their eyes locked. Heat seared Prieta's skin. Before Suel dropped her gaze Prieta glimpsed a flash in her eyes. It winked out like the tiny spark of a firefly.

Suel stirred, plunged her feet into the cool water. Their twin reflections rippled, fragmented, and dissolved. Cupping water in her palm, Prieta raised it to her flushed face. She fanned away los mosquitos hovering over them. Self-conscious and shy, they sat in silence listening to the trickling water and the croaking frogs. From upstream the cooing call of palomas blancas serenaded them. The sounds of their breathing seemed inordinately loud. Surrounded by the smell of ferns and moss and decaying leaves, they stared at the shafts of sunlight as afternoon turned into dusk and the fireflies came out and lit the creek like tiny flying Christmas lights.

One summer day turned into another. Prieta wore a secret smile, the corner of her lips at a perpetual lift. She flitted around the edges of Suel's calm presence, eased into her tranquility as though slipping into cool water on a hot day. Every now and then a tremor would flash through, leaving ripples on Prieta's flesh. Like it did the Sunday Prieta asked Suel what she saw in her.

Suel was polishing her nails a bright red. She raised luminous eyes to Prieta, then lowered them and said, "I like it that you surprise me. I never know what you're going to say or do. You have such strong feelings. Sometimes they . . . make me uncomfortable."

"Ay mijita, I think we fit well together. You're quiet and reserved, I'm talkative and crazy about you. See, we complement each other," Prieta grinned.

The corners of Suel's lips lifted; she shrugged and smiled.

It was so hot the asphalt softened and stuck to their sandals. Prieta said, "Qué calor. Why don't we go on a picnic and cool off at Lake Travis, Suel?"

Suel remained silent.

"Ándale, Suel. Let's make a day of it. I'll bring the food. I know a spot that's hidden away. It's very private. The water there is nice and deep."

"I'm scared of getting in over my head," Suel replied.

"I'll get you a life preserver. And I'd be there to give you mouth-to-mouth . . ."

"Uh uh," Suel interrupted. "Besides, I have to go to Mass."

"Bueno," Prieta said, trying to hide her disappointment. She knew that if she suggested going after Mass, Suel would find another excuse. She had to ease off, else Suel would bolt.

Prieta pulled out a roll of Lifesavers and offered one to her.

Suel laughed, shook her head and said, "Too sweet for my taste."

Next day the bright red polish had disappeared from the nails of Suel's tanned slender hands.

The summer session would end en dos semanas. Each would pack up and, in their separate cars, drive 300 miles through the rolling hill country of central Texas to the flat delta del valle near the border. The more Prieta thought about the 69 miles between their two South Texas pueblos, the more she wanted to tether Suel to her wrist and the more she felt Suel slipping away. She needed to talk to Suel about what was happening to them and make plans for seeing each other when they got home. Suel had said that her familia was traditional, conservative, and very religious. Prieta wondered if they'd think it strange for dos mujeres to be so close. And they were close, so close Prieta felt they didn't need words to convey their feelings. Their eyes said it all. But time was running out.

The two had been up all night writing papers in Suel's room. Prieta's head felt hollow. Not just from too much coffee and too little sleep, but from being in Suel's presence. Prieta squirmed in her chair. Suel lifted her ojos luceros and looked at her. Prieta felt like she'd swallowed the light. It surged through her veins, filling all the secret places and making her body vibrate. When away from Suel, Prieta craved the constant euphoria that swamped her when they were together. At night after hours in Suel's company, Prieta would lie awake esperando el amanecer, anticipating meeting Suel for breakfast.

Prieta stretched her hands over her head and arched her spine. Prieta stared at Suel leaning against the headboard of the bed, her long legs crossed at the ankles. She wanted to ask Suel to rub her sore back but was afraid of frightening her away. What she really wanted to ask was if she could spend the night. Now that would really spook her.

Prieta left her books and paper and stretched out on the bed alongside Suel. They lay lado a lado, arms and thighs touching.

Where Suel's skin brushed hers una lumbrita spread through Prieta. She could feel the boundaries of their separate skins dissolving in the heat. The tousled sheets chafed, her skin felt prickly. She scooted closer, barely resisting the urge to place her nose against Suel's neck and breathe in her sweet-smelling skin.

Prieta opened her mouth to speak then hesitated, afraid of how Suel would react if she broached the subject. She remembered the tiny spark she'd seen in Suel's eyes when they'd met at the start of the summer session. Since then, she'd seen esa luzecita de luciérnaga flickering on and off in Suel's midnight eyes.

Prieta stroked the soft skin on the inside of Suel's elbow. Suel gave a little jump and then relaxed. Prieta cradled Suel's hand palm up and slowly traced the lifeline. "Do you . . . ah, want to talk about it?" Prieta asked.

Suel looked up briefly, then lowered her head to the teaching manual.

Prieta searched for words to describe the air that breathed her when she was with Suel, the air that breathed between them like a live animal cuando se sentaban juntitas.

Prieta thought back to the second week after they'd met. She remembered waiting at their usual meeting place for Suel to get out of class. She sat by Littlefield fountain staring at the three bronze horses, rearing on webbed feet, muscles rippling. Suel walked out of Parlin Hall and sat down beside her. She smoothed her blue dress under her legs looking serene and cool. Prieta couldn't take her eyes off the cleavage of her bare toes and the swell of the bluish veins along her calves and feet. Behind Suel water spouted from the nostrils of the middle horse rearing to unseat the rider pulling the reins and jerking the caballo's head back. Being sprayed by the gushing water didn't seem to cool Prieta. Sweat drenched her armpits and damped the crotch of her loose cotton pants.

Thinking back on their conversation, Prieta realized that only she had actually talked about her ex-girlfriends. When she'd pressed Suel about her novio, Suel had dropped her gesturing hands to her lap and had looked behind her at the man astride the horse, mane in his iron fist.

"I want to talk about us, Suel," Prieta said.

"About what?" Suel glanced at her out of the corner of her eye, the same frightened eyeball side-glance the bronze horse at Littlefield fountain gave its rider.

"Don't look away, mija." Prieta steeled herself and asked, "How do you feel about me? I've made it pretty clear how I feel about you."

"What are you talking about?" Suel's voice rose. She pulled her hand out of Prieta's palm and averted her face.

Prieta felt the beginning of a hairline crack between them. "Tú sabes. Don't you feel it every time we look at each other?"

"Feel what?" Suel sat up.

"You know." Prieta propped up on her elbows. "All these erotic feelings, and how we want to touch each other and be with each other all the time. You know I want to see you when we return to the Valley."

Suel snapped her head around and stared at her. She saw Suel's eyes go flat, Medusa eyes freezing her in place. Suel edged off her bed. Not looking at Prieta, she gathered her books and shoved them into her bag. She hurried out of her apartment, gently closing the door behind her.

Prieta's heart fisted in her chest. Throat prickling, she swallowed. She swung off the bed and, on shaky legs, went to the kitchen and gulped down a glass of water. She paced around the room. Stopping before the window, she peered out hoping to see Suel coming back. After a long time she left the window and started pacing again. She stared at el Sagrado Corazón de Jesús hanging on the wall. Holding two fingers over his naked bleeding heart Jesucristo looked down on her.

A small blown-glass figurine de una palomita lay on top of the shelf. She picked up the fragile dove and stroked the tiny wings thinking of all the signals that Suel had given her showing feelings that went beyond mere friendship. She hadn't misread the look in her eyes, those shy touches, had she? Prieta had been blatant about being a marimacha. So why had Suel acted shocked just now?

Prieta barely restrained herself from going out and combing the campus until she found Suel. She'd probably gone to one of the libraries. But which? If she'd gone into the stacks of the graduate library Prieta would never find her. Suel wouldn't like it if she tracked her down. She'd wait. Sooner or later Suel had to come back to her place to sleep. Where else could she sleep? Prieta sat on the bed and picked up Suel's discarded shirt lying on the bed and brought it up to her face and breathed deeply.

The UT tower bell tolled, jerking Prieta from her thoughts. She pushed her hair out of her face and glanced at the bedside clock. Two hours since Suel had walked out. Suel wouldn't appreciate finding her asleep on her bed. She'd call Suel when she got to her dorm.

Next morning, after getting no response to her phone calls, Prieta walked over and knocked on Suel's door. She wasn't home. Shoulders hunched, Prieta turned away. She went to all their usual haunts: the Commons, the fountain, Guadalupe Street, or the drag as it was called. Again she knocked on Suel's door, thumping hard in case Suel was asleep. No answer. Prieta revisited their hangouts, questioned everyone who knew them. No one had seen Suel.

As Prieta trudged down la barranca to Waller Creek and their pool, the mournful calls of las palomas blancas were bittersweet. She sat under the green canopy and watched the light filter through the tree branches and make dancing shadows in the water. She was too agitated to enjoy the beauty. She wondered if Suel had been barricaded in her apartment all this time, refusing to answer her phone.

After calling and knocking on her door for two more days, Prieta went to the Registrar's office. They told her Suel had a family emergency and had left without finishing her course work. Prieta's heart sank and the rest of her body followed it.

Next morning Prieta called Suel. Maybe she'd come back. She got a recording saying the phone was no longer in service. She forced herself to brush her teeth, get dressed, go to classes, eat. Her appetite had completely deserted her; she cinched her belt tighter by another notch. She had no interest in going out or seeing other people. All she wanted to do was stay in bed and brood. The scorching Texas sun chilled her flesh. She lost track of time and did not notice how she moved through the world nor how it moved through her. It was worse during the night. She lay awake in the darkness counting the hours. She'd get up to pee, and while sitting on the john, smoked cigarette after cigarette.

On the afternoon of the last day of the summer session Prieta walked down la barranca to Waller Creek, took off her sandals, and sat on their rock, startling a frog into jumping away. As she stared down at her reflection in the water, Suel's face appeared beside hers. She dipped a foot in the water. The ripples distorted her perception; Suel's face disappeared. A light blinked across her mind. The distortion in the water was a sign of. . . . Before she completed the thought, Prieta picked up a stone and tossed it into the pool. As the ripples radiated out, she pushed the thought with its ray of light down into the water.

She remembered the last time they'd come here. As they'd waded along the creek bed Suel had splashed her, drenching her shirt. The shock of cool water hardened Prieta's nipples. She looked down at them, then looked at Suel to find her ogling them. Suel looked up. Their eyes locked. The smile on Suel's face waned. Una luciérnaga flew into Prieta's hair startling her out of her reverie. She combed her fingers through her hair and captured the lightning bug, cupping it in her hand. It was about half an inch long and had light organs on the underside of the belly and a soft dark brown body marked with orange. It crawled on her hand tickling her palm. She watched as more and more fireflies flitted down the creek. The frog she had chased off their rock whipped out its tongue, snaring a lightning bug. When it ate enough luciérnagas, her father had once told her, a frog would glow in the dark. For the glow she, too, would tolerate the firefly's bitter taste. She wondered if the fireflies' rhythmic flashes were signals to attract a mate or defensive reminders to predators of its acid taste.

Elbows on knees, chin propped on her hand, she sat for hours listening to the wind moaning like la Llorona as it blew through the trees. When it was fully dark she trudged up the ravine, slipping and sliding. Back at her place, she packed, loaded her car and drove out of Austin. Playing classical music Prieta drove through the night. She knew Suel didn't want any contact, but Prieta vowed to see her even if it meant keeping their relationship platonic.

After two days at home Prieta gave in to the urge to speak to Suel. She firmed her jaw, sucked in a deep breath, and dialed. Suel's sister answered and called out, "Suel, Prieta's on the phone."

At the other end Prieta heard Suel say, "Dile que no estoy en casa. Tell her I've moved away."

Time dragged. Prieta longed to hear Suel's voice. On Thanksgiving, after picking up the phone half a dozen times only to put it down, Prieta dialed Suel's number.

An older woman, probably her mother, answered saying, "Please stop calling. Suel doesn't want to talk to you." She hung up before Prieta could get a word in.

Before school resumed in January, Prieta went to an all-Valley teachers' conference. She wandered into the auditorium for the keynote address and stood at the threshold clutching the schedule of events. She saw Suel sitting in the middle of the huge room and her heart stuttered. The sight of Suel's elegant neck with hair caught at the nape flooded her body with tenderness and yearning. She hurried down the aisle, but when she reached Suel's row something stopped her in her tracks—the impulse to protect Suel from the shock of seeing her, or the fear that Suel would spurn her?

Suel turned and saw her. A spark flashed in her eyes, then her eyes went cold—Medusa eyes.

Prieta gulped. Bracing her shoulders, she tried to contain her fear, but it drove her outside herself. Zooming back like the eye of a camera, she saw a speck in the ocean, a cipher longing to connect with the shore. She felt the rows of seats receding; like waves they sucked her back to the sea. Suel got smaller and smaller; the coast disappeared. Light flickered, then darkness se tragó la luz.

Like the strobe of a firefly, a light pulsed through her and she knew that Suel would jump up, rush to the side aisle, and dash out the door. Before Suel could move, turning her to stone, Prieta turned and walked out.[1]

Translations

tragando luciérnagas: swallowing fireflies

pelo negro: black hair

disculpe: excuse me

encino: live oak

caras güeras: white faces

platicaron de sus familias: talking about their families

mamagrande: grandmother

primo hermano: cousin/brother

nagualismo: shapeshifting

movida: move, as in "make a move on"

vatos: a pachuco word meaning dudes

los mosquitos: the gnats

palomas blancas: mourning doves

ay mijita: short term for "mi hijita," my little daughter, a term of endearment for girls

qué calor: how hot it is

Ándale: Come on

---

1. Anzaldúa wrote at the end of the story: "add when Prieta was with her she glowed as though she'd swallowed hundreds of fireflies, she felt their fluttering wings brush her heart.

Prieta followed Suel as though following the light of las luciernagas, their light showed her path, lit her path."

bueno: OK

en dos semanas: in two weeks

del valle: of the Valley, as the Lower Rio Grande Valley is called

pueblos: towns

dos mujeres: two women

ojos luceros: luminous eyes

esperando el amanecer: waiting for dawn

lado a lado: side by side

una lumbrita: a small fire

esa luzecita de luciérnaga: this light of the fireflies

cuando se sentaban juntitas: when they sat close together

caballo: horse

novio: boyfriend, lover

Tú sabes.: You know.

el Sagrado Corazón de Jesus: the Sacred Heart of Jesus

Jesucristo: Jesus Christ

de una palomita: of a mourning dove

marimacha: butch dyke

la barranca: the ravine

la Llorona: the ghost woman who wept in the night for her lost children

Dile que no estoy en casa.: Tell her I'm not home.

se trago la luz: swallowed the light

13

Night of the Lizard /
Noche de la lagartija

Verde que te quiero verde . . .

—Federico García Lorca

The guy's back. How odd he carries his body, contained, folding into itself, with a gawky bird-like grace. He turns his petal face and solemn eyes toward Prieta. As he slips into his regular table in the patio of the restaurant, su mirada verde holds her gaze. After several long beats his lashes descend, veiling the light of recognition she has glimpsed. The olive green poncho he always wears flows down around him, covering him to his knees. Wearing more than t-shirt and shorts is asking for a heat stroke. The sun filtering through the leaves and branches of the tall pecan tree speckle his body creating a flickering camouflage. A lizard scuttles up the wisteria shrub twining purplish flowers up the tree trunk and scurries along a branch over his head.

As she weaves around the patio tables of Les Amis Café she feels his eyes tracking her movements. When she waits on him, he does not speak to her, just points at a menu item. He continues watching her as he hovers over his spinach salad and veggies and rice. He nods when she comes around with the coffee carafe. As always cuando se va he leaves a pale green puddle in the middle of his chair and a two-dollar bill tip on the table.

She stares at the puddle, flexing her shoulders to ease the ache from months of hefting food-laden trays. She looks at a loud group of students, feet sprawled all over the aisles between tables. She hesitates, then wipes up the puddle with a towel and pockets the bill. The tip is always a two-dollar bill. He must have a stash of the rare bills. She now owns ten of them, all safely hidden in the zippered slot of her pocketbook.

During a lull, Prieta tells Amy, the other waitress, that she feels suffocated by the smell of burnt coffee and the fumes from the brazier, the monotony of waiting tables and cleaning up the messes people leave on their tables. She's especially irritated by the obnoxious patron that keeps rubbing the rim of his wine glass with the edge of his finger and making it squeak. She's had it with the snotty cafe owner, the pretentious cook—pardon me, chef—and the equally pretentious musicians. And above all, she's tired of jumping at shadows, tired of being afraid of walking alone in the streets since her mugging. She's even lost her appetite for her literature classes.

"I'm fed up with my life. It's going nowhere and has no purpose," she tells Amy. Boredom, she realizes, is the result of something wrong with her life. She thought college would be different, but the mugging had been a harsh reality check. She felt like a pilgrim in search of something that would change everything for her forever.

The group of four students sitting at one of her tables gestures to her. She says "later" to Amy and strides over to refill their cups, all the while trying to figure out if he just spilled his tea and left a puddle and how he manages to leave it on the chair without her noticing. Yeah, sure, he knocked his tea over on ten different occasions and in the exact same place.

After a week of scrutinizing the trace he leaves behind and waiting for him to tell her what he wants from her, she can't resist the urge to touch the puddle. She dips her left index finger in the liquid and brings it up to her nose and sniffs. Not piss, too green to be agua. Before she can stop herself, she puts the wet finger in her mouth. It tastes like the grass stems she plucks from the side of the road and sucks and chews on the way to the bus stop. With a hint of salt. Could it be lágrimas, saliva? Surely not semen. Rattled, she takes off her apron and tells her boss she's taking off early as business is slow. When she gets to her student apartment in South Austin and is pushing the key in the lock she notices the olive cast on her finger. She scrubs it with harsh Lava soap.

"What's wrong with you," Dolores asks her on the phone. "Why don't I drive up for a visit?"

Her sister must sense something in her voice. "It's too far for you to come when nothing's wrong," Prieta tells her. Dolores and the rest of her family live in the Valley, 300 miles south of Austin. She hasn't told them she was assaulted.

Feeling muddle-headed she curls up in bed early, hiding her head in a coil of arms and bringing her knees up to her forehead. She listens to the dripping faucet that on other nights drives her crazy but that today anchors her to the familiar sounds and things. Se duerme y sueña. In her dreams she scuttles over the ground like a hunted animal. She moves so fast that flames like lizard tongues sprout out of her body.

In the morning it is difficult for her to raise her upper torso. A faint musk odor emanates from her underarms. She finally drags herself out of bed and into the bathroom, lunging to the side as though thrown off her center of gravity like a ship listing in the swells. She gasps. The tip of her finger y la lengua have turned green. She scrubs her tongue with a toothbrush until blood taints the surface. Todavía verde. She gargles with mouthwash. Still green. Jíjole, it's no longer just a little strange.

Panic flutters in her throat as she hurries to catch the shuttle to get to her Women's Studies class. She jogs down the path with arms held stiffly away from her body. Un lagartijo darts out of the oleander bushes y Prieta piensa de aquel hombre y lo verde. Green, the color of fertility and birth, of decay and death. As the bus dips and sways she scratches the itchy skin on her arms and fights down the nausea. There has to be a rational explanation.

The air blowing in through the open window smells fresh in the April heat. She gets off the bus at Guadalupe and looks up and down the drag at the throngs of students walking up and down or crowding around the street vendors with their rugs on the sidewalk full of earrings, bracelets, beaded works. She'd been crossing Guadalupe when his eyes first locked with hers. After that she noticed him hanging around outside, sneaking looks at her and her friend Amy. Then he started coming into the patio and sitting at one of her tables, always the same table. Why not one of Amy's? Both are mestiza dykes. But while Amy cracks jokes with the customers, who are mostly UT students, Prieta bitches about the twenty-five wars being fought on the planet.

When she gets to Les Amis Café, Amy asks, "What's happening to your hand? I thought it was just bruised."

Prieta straps on her apron like a shield, then stares at her finger, "¡Ay no!" It's chartreuse now, and the nail's a bronze sheen. The green has begun to creep up her hand. The skin feels leathery and dry. What if the green creeps up her arm and shoulders? Though the heat is stifling and not a breeze in sight, a cold shiver courses up her body. When aquel hombre comes in she'll pin him down about the rash, ask him why he left the puddles for her.

The floor tilts slightly; she grabs the back of a chair. The tables stretch then squat like slumbering beasts. The customers' voices sound shrill; their faces and gestures border on caricature.

"Houston, Houston, do you read me?" Hands on her hips, Amy waits for Prieta to answer.

"Would you believe I have a way with plants? Tú sabes, a green thumb?" Prieta says, trying to turn her grimace into a smile.

Amy raises a brow. "Imagine you with a sense of humor. Hey, you feeling alright? You look kind of, what's that word for green, verde?"

"Yeah, isn't the mange supposed to look red? ¡Ay 'mamita!" Prieta says. "I feel like a pod in *The Invasion of the Body Snatchers*. No, en serio, I'm on a weird sort of high, only I haven't taken anything."

"That green stuff, is it catching? You're not infected with something, are you?" Amy looks at her suspiciously.

How can she explain what's happening to her when she doesn't have a clue? She'll keep it to herself. Scanning her diners she's reminded of Edward Hopper's painting *Nighthawks*. Like those in the painting, these diners too are alone, separate, not looking at anyone else. She decides to keep what's happening to her from Amy, at least until she talks to the maricón who makes puddles.

As she bustles from table to counter to kitchen, one minute she feels strong, clear, and safe, and the next her stomach clinches and the floor ripples like the linoleum in her childhood home when the Texas winds blew through the floorboards. She is alarmed to find that when she looks into the customers' eyes she catches fleeting snatches of their thoughts. Something dreadful is happening to her. Could it be that she's suffering from susto?

The boss is staring at her and a man gestures for another round of Shiner beer. Prieta ignores them and sneaks into the washroom where the stink of disinfectant vies with the odor of urine. Bracing her hands against the cold enamel, she peers into the cracked, spidery mirror over the sink. In the stuffy four-by-four room, a Gorgon stares back. "¡Jíjole!" Strands of hair hang around her face like cords. Ya no se reconozco. She sticks out her tongue. It's completely olive green, the same shade as the bathroom walls. She pulls down the toilet cover and sits down to think and smoke a cigarette. She massages her feet. What if the green spreads like fungus creeping up a live oak until it suffocates and kills it? She feels like she did when she was eleven and her period started. She thought she was bleeding to death, and she didn't know how to staunch the bleeding.

After work she checks in at the Health Center. The doctor tells her she has jaundice or maybe a rash. Is she allergic to anything? He prescribes an ointment. Faithfully she rubs it on her skin every time she bathes or washes her hands.

A few days later the customers begin eying her hands when she sets their plates down. Like a bug spreading a plague and about to land on them. A girl stares, fascinated as Prieta scratches the thick wrinkled lizard-looking skin covering her left rodilla. She's favored that knee since landing on it after having taken a dive off a horse when she was five.

As she chats with the customers her words come out jumbled. Often a word in an unknown language slips out. She fixates on a fly buzzing on one of her tables. The light seems too bright and red as if she were looking through infra-red goggles.

Llega a su casa without remembering what happened to her after leaving the restaurant. On her way to campus she gets twisted around and finds herself in West Austin. One night after leaving the Dobie theater she gets totally lost and stands in the middle of the street como venada acantilada. It scares her because she knows Austin like she knows her own fingers and hands. Only she no longer recognizes her own hands or eyes. Scales are growing under her fingers and pads on her feet and toes. Her eyes are like lichen growing on two round rocks. She fibs to her friends, says she's wearing tinted contact lenses.

During the night sus ojos relumbran en la oscuridad. She listens to something stirring in the weeds outside her window and the whine of mosquitos, the cockroaches scuttling across her kitchen floor. Escucha el sonido del zacate creciendo. She's up all night. Like Gregor in Kafka's *Metamorphosis*, she's afraid that, if she goes to sleep, she'll wake up one morning to find she's running up the walls like a gecko or upside down on the ceiling. Or maybe worse, the infection could kill her. During her nocturnal wake she tries to take la rienda de esos pensamientos scurrying from one side of her head to the other.

Next morning her skin is unusually dry and covered with multicolored patches, some blotched, pebble-like, others puckered and furrowed, and the knuckles tough and horny. Her scalp itches. When she scratches a spiny ridge is growing over the crest of her head. She's got calluses on her nipples. She slathers ointment on every inch that itches. Textbook opened beside her plate she sits down and eats her breakfast. She pushes the plate away when she realizes that she's tearing and bolting her food instead of chewing it. When she brushes her teeth she sees that her flat-crowned molars have all turned into long conical teeth.

She wears long-sleeved shirts buttoned up to her neck and tucks the serpentine strands of hair into the bandana tied around her head when she goes out. Still, she feels as though she were naked, and everyone is staring at her. The heavy beige make-up can't disguise el cambio.

A week later su piel crustácea begins to flake off like dandruff. Her skin is molting again. At least she won't end up as a belt or lizard-skin boots like some alligator. Underneath it she sees a livid pink skin, otra nueva piel. No more brown skin, prieta no more. There goes her identity. She had an atavistic need for a shell, to encase herself and carry her home with her and defend it. After all, people were descendants of reptiles and sea creatures.

Pero si está para renacer, what kind of creature will she turn into? Are there others of her tribe? The new tender skin, mottled with patches of tough green lizard armor, looks even more gross than the previous stage. Once the green armor falls off completely, how is she to know how to keep herself in and everything else out?

By the third week she knows what each customer is going to order before they open their mouths. She casts her eyes over any one of the men hunched over his lunch or dinner and knows if he's planning to surprise his lover with a gift or if he's sticking it to his daughter. One day she slaps down the check y una servilleta on the table of one of her regulars and hisses at him. The bold green letters on the napkin read:

"We know what you are doing. If you do it again your penis will turn green and fall off and you'll turn into stone."

With hamburger sizzling behind her in the kitchen and the click of forks on plates, she hears air rushing into her lungs and wonders, what's this "we" of her note that she's a part of? The man looks at the napkin, then up at her flicking her tongue. He rears up and slams out of the cafe shouting maldiciones at her. Now that she can see clearly, the fear that one of the men will retaliate by assaulting her on the way home at night vanishes. None of them have the cojones.

People look suspiciously at her gloved hands and layers of clothing. Her muscles contract, the air rushing in and out of her lungs is louder, the pulse beating in her throat is a palpitating trill. The urge to scamper into the undergrowth of the pyracantha and hide among the fire-red berries and lush fronds bordering the patio is almost irresistible.

After work she goes to the library. In the Encyclopedia Britannica, she finds there are 3,000 species of lizard in the world. She wonders what vestigial organs from the evolutionary past are growing in her body. Yes, she had noticed the vertical slit of eyes, the moveable lower eyelids, the nostrils flattening. Cold-blooded creatures take on the temperature of the environment. She goes out to the fountain, sits on a rock, and basks in the sun.

She walks down the drag, not making much progress. The sidewalk undulates like waves, y su cuerpo se estremece como ojas. Every few steps she leans against a storefront until the world stops buckling. There he is, she catches the eye del hombre who left the puddles. He smiles at her and nods. Awareness shimmers like a cool wave down her spine. Something in her shifts and she feels the skin of her former self slip off. What if he's like the alien in the movie *Man Facing Southeast*?

At the end of the fourth week her boss runs her off, la corré, accusing her of scaring the customers. "Ni modo," she shrugs and, dropping her apron on the floor, stalks out of the restaurant leaving him standing con la boca abierta. When Amy phones later that evening she tells Prieta that the boss was surprised she hadn't threatened him with discrimination or dumped her tray on him.

"Convertida en lagartija. Ni modo," says Prieta.

"What, I don't know Spanish, remember. What are you saying?"

"I accept. I accept that I've turned into a lizard woman. At least the small things will not take me by surprise, and I'll always know where I left the keys," Prieta tells Amy.

"You're talking nonsense again. You got to go see somebody."

"You mean a shrink, don't you?"

"Yeah, you need help. Listen, I got to go, or I'll be late." Amy hangs up.

In the middle of the night Prieta wakes from a deep sleep smiling.

Prieta stops at the Asian food cart and buys a fried wonton and lemonade from Hua, the Vietnamese woman who has fed generations of students. She continues walking up Guadalupe, jostling shoulders with jean-and-t-shirt-clad male students and girls in flimsy 30s and 40s muslin dresses. She searches the crowd for the green guy with a pink triangle earring in his left ear, or other gente verde. She locks gazes with certain others. Besides the obvious sign, the green skin, the flickering, knowing look in their eyes marks their difference. Their smile of recognition reminds her of the interest in Amy's eyes.

After five o'clock when the boss has left, she drops by Les Amis, sits at one of Amy's tables under the flapping awning and the pecan tree with wisteria twining up its trunk and waits for her to come with her order pad.

"Ey, Prieta you look—I don't know, just real different. What's been happening to you?" Amy peers into Prieta's face looking worried.

"I seem to have shed my old self," she replies.

"No kidding," says Amy. "Aren't you tired of wearing that green overcoat? You must be roasting in there."

"Amy, I've even taken a new name, Prieta la lagartija. Soon the new skin will be in place and I won't have to cover it up."

"New skin? Jesus, you told me you weren't contagious? Did you go to the Health Center again?"

"No, but I did consider going to una curandera. It's too late now," Prieta says, rubbing the new bronze skin on her arm.

Curiosity is cracking open a tiny sliver in the impenetrable tough dyke veneer Amy wears with her swagger. Yes, Amy is ready.

Prieta eats her New Orleans red beans and rice, leaves a tip of a pair of two-dollar bills and a puddle, and splits before Amy returns. She can't guide Amy; no words can make her understand. She'll have to go through el cambio on her own.

Cuando el árbol retoña and before the semester ends Prieta moves to another town. She gets a temporary job in a restaurant where she catches glances of recognition from gente verde. When she meets a likely candidate, Prieta uncovers her knee in their vicinity, lets slide a puddle of lágrimas, blesses them with a smile. After a few weeks she moves on to the next town.[1]

For Rodrigo Reyes and Jaye Miller, victims of AIDS.

Translations

Verde que te quiero verde.: Green I love you green.

su mirada verde: his green look

cuando se va: when he goes

agua: water

lágrimas: tears

Se duerme y sueña.: She sleeps and dreams.

y la lengua: and her tongue

todavía verde: still green

jíjole: shit

una lagartijo: a lizard

y Prieta piensa de aquel hombre y lo verde: and Prieta thought about this man and green

aquel hombre: that man

tú sabes: you know

---

1. Before this paragraph Anzaldúa had this in brackets: "[Omit or tell Dolores]," and after this paragraph, Anzaldúa included the following notes to herself: "to add: It could be eczema, or a rash she can't get rid of. Maybe she's been hallucinating and just imagines seeing a puddle. When Dolores comes to visit she asks, 'What's with the rash?' Prieta tries to tell her about it, quaffs about it, says she's been busy, that she's been going through changes ever since the mugging. Tells Dolores that she's written about it for class and gives her the story."

Ay 'mamita: Oh, little mama

en serio: seriously

maricón: queer

susto: fright

Ya no se reconozco.: She no longer recognizes herself.

rodilla: kneecap

llega a su casa: arrives at her house

como venada acantilada: like a deer in headlights

sus ojos relumbran en la oscuridad: her eyes glow in the dark

Escucha el sonido del zacate creciendo.: She hears the sound of the grass growing.

la rienda de esos pensamientos: the rein of those thoughts

el cambio: the change

su piel crustácea: her crustacean skin

otra nueva piel: another new skin

pero si está para renacer: but she is ready to be reborn

la peseta: the quarter

la lengua verde: the green tongue

y una servilleta: and a napkin

maldiciones: curses

cojones: balls

y su cuerpo se estremece como ojas: and her body shudders like leaves

la corré: ran her off, fired her

ni modo: whatever

con la boca abierta: with open mouth

convertida en lagartija: changing into a lizard

gente verde: green people

cuando el árbol retoña: when the trees bud

Part Four

Becoming Chamana

14

She Ate Horses*

Before she plunged into the gulf waters la Prieta breathed deeply, pulling the briny tang of the sea into her body. The sea was a giant woman, and she wallowed in her tart breath, swam along her velvet resilient back, arms arcing above the swells. When her arms began to tremble, she swam back to the white beach, floundering, gasping for breath as the waves broke over her head. She allowed her body to relax and let the tide carry her toward the shore.

Prieta stood on the wet sand, water sluicing down her body and the surf sucking at her ankles. Shading her eyes against the glare of the sun, she stared eastward into the Gulf of Mexico and felt as though she were standing at the edge of the world. The pale ghost of the full moon rode low on the water.

The surface of the water mirrored the sun like pieces of mica. Shimmering golden lights undulated with the slow-moving waves rushing onto the sand in an endless, rhythmic motion. As the waves broke water frothed up onto the beach, then rolled back into the sea leaving mosaics of iridescent foam. The surge and wash of the waves with their ceaseless sighs, their incessant shushing, their endless ebbing and waning.

The gulf breeze ruffled Prieta's hair, billowing the strands up over her head. She curled her toes, feet burrowing deeper into la

---

*An earlier version of this story appeared in *Lesbian Cultures*, edited by Jeffner Allen (SUNY Press, 1990).

arena mojada. It seemed the shore, not the sea, was swaying. Her body rocked to its rhythm, her insides listing first to one side and then the other. Bending from the waist, she touched her toes, then dug her fingers into the sand. Her dark cabello skimmed the water like seaweed. Anchored by both hands and feet she was a plant rooting up out of the earth. She dug deeper in the sand. Something sharp pricked her palm. A stab of dread zinged up her body. She jerked out her hands and shot up like a dancer.

Half of a bivalve shell nestled in her palm. It was a sawtooth sea pin, the most common shell on the beach, brittle and thin. She looked around searching for its other half. In her mind's eye she saw the ligament holding the twin halves together sever, saw the waves push them apart to opposite ends of the island, someone pick up a piece, a treasure to take home from the beach.

She stared into the blue haze of distance, then at the curved arm of the shoreline with its broad white beach encrusted with coquina shells. Everything was white: sand, shells, clouds, and most of its birds. The Spanish explorer who had landed on Padre Island called it la Isla Blanca, the White Island. Behind her to the north sand dunes rose up as high as fifty feet. In her mind's eye she saw a hurricane ripping against the shores, pushing a Spanish galleon laden with plundered gold from Mexico and dashing it to pieces. Doubloons (gold coins) spilled from the bowels of the ship. Windblown sand heaped over the wreck to sculpt tall dunes. Even now after four hundred and thirty years people found gold coins buried in the sand. The long thin barrier island had its history and its secrets. What else has lain buried under some of those dunes?

"Where were you?"

"What?" Prieta jerked. She hadn't sensed Llosi approach.

"You seemed a hundred miles away. En tu otro mundo, where you spend most of your time these days."

Prieta gave Llosi a sharp look. "I was just thinking of all those pirate ships with stolen treasure getting wrecked on these shores."

"Yeah, well, why don't you think about what's wrecking our relationship?" Llosi flapped their blanket in the air. It hung in the air and gradually floated down and settled on the sand. She dumped the backpack on it and plopped down and began slapping on sunscreen, lathering up furiously, the smell of coconut mingling with the smell of the sea.

Prieta raised her arm to throw la concha back into the water, but something in the luminous sheen of Llosi's eyes checked her and she dropped her arm.

"I'm going for a walk. We'll talk when you cool down, 'ta bueno?" She knew they had to decide what to do.

"Véte si te da la gana," Llosi said, flouncing away, butch haircut, slick grace, the scraggly fringe of her cutoff jeans.

Prieta shoved on her dark glasses, picked up her sandals and backpack, and headed for the less crowded end of the beach. She felt Llosi's eyes tracking her. Three years ago on this same beach during la luna llena Llosi had carved a circle in the sand with a sea shell, maybe the other half of the shell in her hand. Llosi had stepped in and held out a hand to her. Prieta had hesitated, staring first at the circle and then at Llosi. The urge to join and lose herself in the other was an insistent pulse, but an equally persistent beat urged her to flee. She swallowed her doubts, entered the circle, and took Llosi's hand. They faced east, and while the water lapped around their feet filling the round furrow, they spoke vows of unending love. Un beso y un abrazo and, as one, they walked into the arms of la madre mar.

Though the water was warm that day Prieta felt chilled to the bone, the same deep chill she'd felt when she'd been swallowed by this sea and nearly drowned when she was eight. She looked to the horizon to get her bearings, but she couldn't discern the line of demarcation between sea and sky.

She felt a sense of relief when the sea that had swallowed them spit them out again, relief when the waves washed out their mark. But almost immediately she'd felt guilt for feeling relieved.

In the beginning there had been no fighting, no jealousies, ni pleitos, ni celós. She had been so much in love, staying home and fooling around with Llosi, giggling, a perpetual smile on her face. She'd felt as though she could do anything as long as Llosi was at her side. Prieta felt protected, cherished, needed, wanted, valued, appreciated. Love had opened her to all possibilities.

A wave sloshed against her. It hurt to remember the good times. No se quería acordar de todos esos meses when being in Llosi's presence was like basking in the sun's warmth. She was afraid it had all been a dream world of her own illusion.

It had not all been hot passion and togetherness. Their luna de miel sometimes rose, sometimes sank. Its feast momentarily satisfied Prieta but could not feed her hunger, could not quell her fears. They'd left the Valley to study art at UT Austin. Llosi found it difficult to keep up with the mitote of social life and the work school demanded. She complained of being the token Chicana in her classes, felt undermined by the smug privileged articulation of los gringos, and had dropped out during the first semester. Prieta spent more and more time in the solitary discipline of her art. Her work, exhibited with the more renowned artistas, received accolades from teachers and other artists. She made new friends.

A beating of wings. Prieta looked up. Gulls flapped away then swooped to hover over the water, huge eyes above amber beaks scanning the waves for food. Then they rose high above the shore, their white bodies soaring free and disappearing into the sky.

Now here they were in the middle of their third year and the illusion of true love and happily ever after no longer held Prieta in thrall. But she still had the same fear, that the boundaries between the two, even their skin, were too porous, that she was losing herself. Like sand in a storm, the wind was still shifting her, pulling her from the comfortable and familiar bedrock, stumbling into the hollow place in her soul.

She found a spot at the edge of the high-tide line and sat down. From her backpack she fished out the water bottle, a towel, and her sketch pad. She sat on the towel, pad on her thighs, and waited for an image to come.

A horse neighed.

Prieta's head snapped up and she looked around. No horses on the beach, just in her head.

She took off her sunglasses and started making broad strokes with Cray-Pas. Gradually a horse cantering along the water's edge began to emerge. An image de una yegua flashed in her mind, that of a coyote dun, a yellow-skinned mare with a paler gold mane they'd had on their ranchito when she was a kid. Her father had raised horses. As a child she'd drawn hundreds of pictures of them. As an adolescent she'd painted horses peacefully grazing, horses running with sweat glistening on their slick flanks. Stallions, mares, geldings, potrancas.

She felt she knew the horse, felt inside the horse. Whenever the horse tossed its head Prieta felt that it was her head it tossed. Mamagrande had told her that she had a strong connection to horses, that a horse must be her nagual. In the other world, en el mundo de sueños, an animal is born at the same moment a person is born. Mija, she had said, a nagual is an aspect of your soul. The two share the same spark of life, share the same fate. In the world of night, the world of dreams, your nagual is your eyes, your ears, your feet, your wings. Your nagual shows you things in the darkness.

Prieta remembered. She'd been twelve when she'd gotten on the coyote dun. Straddling the fence, she'd coaxed the mare to come to her, had rubbed her soft black muzzle. Then Prieta vaulted over onto its bare back and clutched the mane, wrapping the rough strands around her two fists. La yegua stood perfectly still testing the air with flaring nostrils, a tremor passing through its body. Prietita felt the rippling of its flesh against her soft inner thighs.

Prieta clucked with her tongue on one side of her mouth, the way her papi did. The horse's ears went back and its massive shoulders twitched in an effort to dislodge the small body straddling her. When Prieta clucked again, it snorted and moved in a sideways hop, hooves dancing on the hard ground, and puffs of dust flew up in clouds. It reared, then leaped into a gallop. Prietita slithered and bounced on the heaving back. She clung to its powerful neck, reveling in the sweet, musky smell of horse flesh, the harsh breathing, the slick muscles rubbing against her legs.

Her body rising and falling, at one with the animal. No bridle, no saddle, now she was a real vaquera, queen of the Río Grande. Everything was bright, the mesquite leaves fluorescent green, every blade of grass in sharp detail and quivering with aliveness. She too quivered with elation. Then she was sailing over the horse's head.

The shuddering jar, then stillness.

"Chingao." Stunned, she lay face in the dirt, lip bleeding, watching the horse's withers disappear, great swath of tail high in the air.

Her papi came running and kneeled beside her. "Are you OK, miha?" he asked, running his hands over her limbs. He picked her up and dusted her off.

"Mesteños, half-wild, are harder to tame," he told her. "Ese animal will kick, fall on its side and roll over on you. Or it'll sink down on its forelegs y zas, send you flying over its head."

She hung her head; she should have controlled the horse.

"Mi hijíta, you have to show it who's boss. Bridle it and keep a tight rein. No le des cabeza."

"Bueno, Papi."

She tipped her water bottle, swallowed thirstily, letting water dribble down her chin. Holding the pad at arm's length, she squinted, then elongated the legs and tried to convey tension in the haunches. There'd once been wildlife on the dunes of Padre Island. Mesteños. Her father had seen them, had followed their unshod hoof prints, had watched them run wild. The voice of her dead father was so clear in her head she could almost hear him.

Her father had been dead a long time and South Padre Island had changed. Now they had tamed horses for tourists. When she'd driven off the Queen Isabella Causeway and onto the long thin barrier island, she'd seen white people on horses moving slowly along the trail. Huge chain hotels and luxury condominiums complete with golf courses littered the landscape. Hundreds of scantily clad bodies frolicked in the azure waters. Some tossed Frisbees or softballs. The island had been tamed, the seashore urbanized.

Sensing someone watching her, Prieta raised her head. Yep, Llosi was stretched out on their red blanket, eyes locked on her. This must be how a wild horse felt upon raising its head to scan el monte for vaqueros and see one bearing down. This must be how a wild horse felt when it heard the whining of the lasso and then felt the lariat tightening around its neck.

Prieta remembered when she had been the one who pursued Llosi with a deep, unquenchable hunger, su boca hambrienta por conocer el cuerpo y alma de la otra. Face burrowing into Llosi's neck, she'd cling, glorying in the smell of her skin, a faint musk with the tang of lemon from her soap, all the while disliking what and who she was becoming, hating depending on Llosi for feeding her hunger, but never filling the hole.

It hurt to remember the times it had been good. She didn't want to remember sus labios brushing down Llosi's collar bone, her lips bajando a los pechos de Llosi, su boca prendida between Llosi's thighs. All those early months of being with Llosi, had it really felt like basking in the sun's warmth or had she revised reality to suit her desire?

Something, maybe passion, awakened the animal inside her, roused it out of its lair. At those times the animal turned on her, sometimes gently nibbled on her innards. Other times its rapacious, insatiable, ravenous appetite turned carnivorous and consumed her from the inside out. She was losing parts of herself; she was becoming someone else.

She tried to contain the animal, to reign in that reflex, but it had run away with her in tow. Though she couldn't get rid of el animal, she was able to hobble it. Sometimes. Other times Llosi's words or her hands and lips unfettered el animal. Whether free or hobbled Prieta felt tied hand and foot, the cinch around her middle pulled tight. Blindfolded, she felt the animal mount her. Its spurs drew blood, the horse grew fangs. It always ended the same, Prieta bucking herself into exhaustion.

Prieta scrutinized her drawing. Not there yet. When anyone looked at this drawing she wanted them to hear the hooves of the wild horse pound the earth, see the clots of dirt flying, imagine water welling up where its hooves had gouged out holes.

She flipped the cover and shoved the pad back in her pack along with her sandals, and leaving the lip of the sea, headed north toward the sand dunes. Feet burning, Prieta ran toward a patch of grass burned brown by the sun. She ran from one clump-of-grass shadow to another, feet sinking into the cooler sand.

At midday the sands were glistening. Her feet sank into the soft hot sand as she scrambled up, pulling herself up by the sparse zacate quemado that grew in clumps. Under her feet slipfaces flowed like rivers down the flank of the dune.

When she reached the top she looked back at the beach. Sand, sea, sky—their edges met, blurred, merged. A sense of boundless space, limitless time enveloped her.

Sweat trickled down her face, beads of sudor ran down the crevice between her breasts. She edged two fingers beneath her bikini and scratched los pelos de elote at her crotch. She lifted her hair from the nape, letting the breeze cool her hot neck.

She sank down into a dune pocket, let the warm hollow embrace her, let it sooth the animal that hungered for she knew not what. It beat like another heart in the hollow place in her body. Grains of sand stuck to the back of her thighs and arms. She unhooked her bikini top and, dampening a white handkerchief with bottled water, spread it over her breasts. She glanced back. The wind blew her hair out of her eyes and she saw the two sets of tracks on the sand. Their huellas almost identical. There was still wildlife on Padre.

Below far away on the beach, on their red blanket, Llosi leaned on an elbow watching her. Prieta looked away and stared at the tawny strands of sea oats. Despite the lack of water and strong winds their fragile stems clung tenaciously to the shoulder of the dune.

Closing her eyes to the speck that was Llosi, Prieta dozed, letting herself bathe in the music made by the sea. She pictured how she would paint sea oats against the pale blond flank of the dune, what colors to mix to capture both the fragility and the strength of the sea oats, what meaning they would carry.

She heard sand slipping and crunching under foot; someone was trudging up. She sensed Llosi behind her, felt her body heat. Prieta rolled up onto her haunches, put on her top and dusted the sand from her arms and neck. She stared at the threads hanging from Llosi's Levi cutoffs, then stared at the tracks on the sand waiting for Llosi to speak.

"Listen, Babe, we gotta' talk. Yo sé que viniste a puro huevo, but you can't pretend I'm not here, in your life."

Prieta raked the sand con la concha that she still had in her hand. Borró las huellas.

"Oh no, it's not going to be that easy, mija—erasing me from your life," said Llosi, a mutinous set of lines bracketing her mouth.

Prieta put the shell in her shirt pocket and draped the shirt across her sunburnt shoulders. She remained silent, then said, "We've gone through a lot. I know that we still love each other, Llosi. It should be enough. But it isn't."

"What would be enough?" asked Llosi.

"That's what I'm trying to figure out. And I can't do it with you always on top of me. All I know is that it's not working."

"We could make it work. If only you tried harder."

"Me? You mean us?"

"Novia, you're the one who's always got her head buried in some book, when you're not up to your fundio in paint. Always wanting more time to yourself," a look of defiance in her eyes.

"What else is new? You don't get what you want, I don't get what I want," Prieta said through set teeth. "I snap, you lose it and we go flying off the edge. What a way to live." She opened her hand and held it palm up to Llosi.

Llosi ran her fingers over the shell and touched the faint blood-etched cut. She held Prieta's eyes, then stalked off.

Prieta stared at her retreating back. Streamers of sand whipped by the wind dusted the fine sheen of sweat on her body like pollen. The salt-laden wind pulled tears from Prieta's eyes. Through blurred eyes she saw molten ripples undulating (swelling) in a sea of sand.

She dropped down into the dune pocket, where she would be protected from the strong winds. Prieta felt _____.[1] She watched a bunch of yellow primroses growing out of the sand, stems under the sand, leaves and flowers quivering in the wind. She closed her

---

1. Anzaldúa left a blank here.

eyes and the world disappeared. She was under the horse's hooves, clots of sand falling on her face. She sucked in her breath but no air reached her lungs.

Someone prodded her out of the dream. Llosi squatted over her, peering into her face. Llosi wanted too much from her, wanted her too much. That's what she had fallen in love with, Llosi's fierce passion bordering on obsession. Now it was sucking the air from her lungs.

"¿Qué tienes? ¿Te soliaste?" Llosi reached down to yank her up out of her shallow cave. Prieta drew back. Llosi let go. Prieta saw the sheen of hurt in her eyes before she whirled and hurried away. Prieta sprang up, grabbed her shirt and pack, and ran after her, sand streaming down the flank of the dune.

"¡Chin!" Prieta stumbled on something half buried in the sand. Arms flailing, she twisted her body trying to regain her balance. Startled, gulls lifted off into the blue with their shrill cries. Llosi looked back and chuckled, then ran toward the crowded part of the beach.

Prieta plunged after her, skirting a group sprawled on a blanket eating their lunch. Drumstick in hand, a guy in a leopard skin thong leered at her tattoo and pierced navel. She wove in and out among kids leaping at beach balls and toned bodies strutting on the beach, and barely evaded an umbrella catapulting down the beach toward her.

At last she reached Llosi's side. "Hey, wait up. Espérate, I thought you wanted to talk."

They stared at each other. When Llosi's shoulders relaxed Prieta put her arm around them and steered her back toward the deserted end of the beach. Heads swiveled toward them, scrutinizing them from head to toe.

"Mensos, haven't you ever seen rucas with hair on their legs and underarms?" yelled Llosi.

"Marimachas," snickered a male voice.

Llosi looked back and threw him the finger.

Prieta's arm tightened around Llosi—being outcasts in the straight world always brought them closer.

They walked a long time, the cool breeze drying the sweat on their bodies. Prieta stopped, let go of Llosi and dropped her backpack on the sand. She stared at the rays beating the surface of the water into sheets of gold. Sargassum seaweed, called gulf weed, buoyed by small air bladders, drifted across the surface of the water. Pelicans and terns skimmed the shallow waters for fish and small crustaceans. The wind whipped her hair across her face. She pushed the image of the horse away, pushed away its blood-colored mane rising and falling, its hooves thundering on the wet sand.

They faced each other. Neither spoke. Prieta felt a sand crab nibble her toe.

"Let's eat," said Llosi, spreading the red blanket.

"That's what we do when we're mad at each other—eat, make love, or fight," said Prieta, plopping down opposite Llosi.

"Well, we can't make love, supposing you'd even want to, and fighting is beneath you." Llosi pulled out a bag of fruit and handed Prieta a mango.

"None of those have ever solved anything." Prieta peeled part of it with her fingernails and bit into the lush fruit. Its sweet tartness was delicious but if her mouth came in contact with the skin she'd get a rash.

"Well, they liven things up, make things bearable. Mira, Prieta, let's settle things now, today. I know you need more space. Haven't I bent over backwards trying to give it to you?"

Prieta raised her brow.

"Well, I do. ¿No te dejó sola? I've stopped chasing after you when you go into those veredas que llenas de nopales so I won't follow you. Heck no, you want to curl up with thorns, baby, you go right ahead. When you sit in front of your damn easel day after day and daydream the rest of the time, don't I let you?"

"That's just it, Llosi. It's not up to you to give me space—it's not yours to give."

"I just want us to do things together like we used to. We never go out dancing anymore. Or go to parties together," said Llosi edging near.

"I'd rather do other things, Llosi. And what you call close feels like you trying to crawl under my skin," said Prieta, inching back.

"¡Por Diosa! I'm tired of you pushing me away como perra sarnosa."

"Oye tú, don't you hear what I'm saying. I need solitude to do my work. Why can't you respect that? I can't work when you're constantly interrupting." Prieta stepped back.

"Don't you ever pull away from me," Llosi said, smacking Prieta on the arm.

"Pos' ora sí, Llosi, that's it, now you've really done it!"

"Sorry. You just make me so mad." Llosi swung around and then back. "I just don't understand you. In the beginning you always wanted to be with me. Y ahora you'd rather go to bed with a book. You don't even want me in the same room with you. We may live in the same fucking house, but even when you're there you aren't really there. Tú ya no vives conmigo, mija. Te fuiste pa' otro lugar donde yo no te puedo seguir."

Prieta just looked at her. "Don't you see, honey? Even when you give me space you crowd me. You're always watching me, always hovering. That's not leaving me alone. You're jealous of the time I spend painting, Llosi," she said gently. "You're even jealous of my fantasies."

"I know painting is important to you, baby, but aren't I as important? No, don't answer that. It's one thing for you to go to your art galleries and political meetings, to those lectures at the college, the library, and bookstores. You have time for that but not for cuddling. But that's OK. If only the rest of the time you weren't in your own private dream world. What do you want, Prieta? You want out of the relationship, don't you?"

Prieta shrugged her shoulders. "Don't know what I want—that's the problem."

"¡Chingao! Prieta, ya no puedo aguantar más. I've had enough."

"You lay it all on me just because I refuse to fit your mold."

"We married each other right here. ¿Te acuerdas, Prieta? Three years ago today, we swore we would always be there for each other."

"How can I forget when you bring it up every three minutes," Prieta said, her voice calm.

"Well, if I didn't you'd probably forget you're in a relationship."

"What you want is total merger. No me and no you, just an us."

"Oh, quit with that psychological crap. Cabrona, why can't you tell me what's really bugging you?" Llosi said, with tears in her voice.

They were silent for a while. Prieta watched the wind trail plumes of sand westward from the biggest dune.

"Let's talk about our other problem, Llosi. You want sex on demand, even when I don't feel like it."

"You never feel like it. ¿Por qué? You used to really like it."

"It scares me—such intense feelings. I always feel . . . shattered afterwards. Don't take this the wrong way. It's not about you, it's about me. When we fuck I forget who I am and the me gets buried in the relationship."

"Yeah, well, there's no me or you, we're a couple, we're an us. And that's the way it should be," said Llosi. "You're getting all these weird ideas from those PC gringa dyke feminists. What a bunch of caca. It's just an excuse for you to cop out of this relationship, Prieta."

"How many times are we going to argue about the same shit. What do you want me to say, Llosi? The problem is not one thing, it's about a lot of things. Like you wanting me to do stuff I don't want when we're fucking."

"Oh, but it was OK when you did it with that pinche gringa jota during that fling?"

"Ajá, so that's it. We'd split, remember—for a whole three months. What I did and with whom was my business. I can't believe it's bothering you that much now."

"I'm your novia! Chingao, don't I have some rights?"

"Not so loud! You want to tell everybody our business?"

Llosi ran past a group of people and flopped into the water, thrashing at the waves. She came out dripping and whispered harshly, "You had to have that fucking gadget."

"Oh no, not the magic wand again. First it was the easel, then the computer, and now the vibrator," said Prieta. "You really want to know why I prefer it? Because it takes a lot to get into rhythm; dry humping is too much work. I hate peeled cucumbers. And I stop at . . . hey wait a minute, we're getting off track, again. Coming back to the island to try to work things out is the last resort."

Prieta wondered who would take the molcajete if they broke up. Llosi could have the floral sheets. Prieta couldn't stand them. The sheets had triggered one of their screaming matches.

When Llosi remained silent, Prieta said, "We're not getting anywhere. Let's take some time out."

Llosi nodded, eyes glistening.

~

Prieta looked around and saw Llosi walking back to her, her face all scrunched up. Llosi was waiting for her to proclaim The End. Why should she be the one to do the breaking up? If they did split up, Prieta wanted to stay friends. Llosi would refuse. Llosi would never forgive her. All or nothing, that would be Llosi's revenge. Prieta felt the hard shell in the pocket of her shirt and wondered why she'd kept it.

"Hey, calm down. OK?" she said putting her arms around Llosi. Madre Diosa, Llosi was so predictable. And her, too. They didn't surprise each other anymore.

"You have to commit yourself to me, to us, once and for all, Prieta." Llosi put her hands on her hips and gave Prieta a piercing look. "No, don't look at me that way."

"What way?"

"Like I got lice or something. The university gabachos sure did a number on your head. They washed your brain in their bolillo ways. You've turned white on me. Ahora te creas grande. You've become a self-centered bitch. We should never have moved from el Valle. At least there we would have. . . ."

"Oh, spare me your trite political crap. I'm tired of you using it to get back at me," said Prieta. She saw annoyance, anger, impatience flicker in and out of Llosi's face, saw Llosi's body tense. Llosi's mouth moved, Prieta heard the words she'd heard a hundred times before. It was all her fault because she'd changed. Llosi wanted her to change back. Prieta shut out Llosi's voice. The wind shifted and she smelled the leftovers baking in the trash bins. She swallowed to keep from throwing up.

They walked to the lip of the sea and watched the emerald waves froth spume over their feet. To maintain the relationship each had to stay near the edge, and not move back from la orilla. Only her edge was not Llosi's edge.

"Fighting makes me feel mean and ugly. Bitching leaves a taste of ashes, la boca llena de ceniza," Prieta said.

Both were silent.

"Can't have a fire on the beach anymore," she told Llosi. "And long ago they caught the last of the wild horses." Hungry, Prieta walked back to the crowded end of the beach where Llosi had left her backpack with the food. Llosi followed her. Kids straddling a black inflated inner tube waved at them, showing off, and yelled out something in Spanish.

"Are you ready for la merienda?"

"So now you're hungry," Llosi looked at her through narrow eyes. "Fuck, you really are in your other world. Well, sabes qué, when you come back to Earth, look for me at the car. Ay te watcho."

Prieta watched a sulking Llosi walk away. Her spirits sinking, she looked east toward the gulf. La luna llena had lost its ghostly paleness, it hung swollen and heavy over the water. Sintió el momento decisivo comes washing up with the waves, slapping her. ¿Qué iba hacer?

The sun set in a glory of orange streaked with red. Prieta watched the dark silhouettes of gulls wheeling across the blood-red sky. She saw la yegua, mane and tail streaming in the wind, come out of the west. It shot down the side of the dune showering sand in all directions. Drumming the wet earth, its hooves opened the ground. The mare plunged into the sea, hitting the water with a hollow thud. Spray jetted up in all directions. Then she surged out of the sea, galloping toward Prieta, drops of saliva or water flew from her open mouth. Prieta held her ground, but the animal inside her wanted to fling itself against the constraints. Whatever that thing was, that hunger that gnawed at her entrails, the emotion, fear, resentment, that predatory beast beat at the walls, seeking out the chinks for toe holes and scaling those walls time after time, trying to escape, to jump free.

La yegua loomed over her, ears pricked, eyes pivoting wildly, muscles tensed. As she halted, casting her shadow over Prieta, the horse seemed to swallow the red sun. The sun's rays shone through her tail, combed her mane, outlined her arched neck in gold. The sleek powerful thighs rippled and brushed against Prieta as she sped past. Prieta trembled, the heat of her body seeping down into the sand, her legs folding as she watched the horse circling and coming back straight at her. La yegua sacudio la cabeza. Prieta stood and faced la yegua ladina fast approaching her. Just as she thought it would plow into her, the mare disappeared. El sordo palpitar de la yegua followed Prieta into the shallow water where she bathed the sweat from her face.

The white clouds darkened, the sea furrowed and then became choppy. La luna llena looked brighter. La gente were leaving la playa. The sun began to drop and shadows stretched across the sand. Though the heat had dropped only a few degrees, ella temblaba de frío. Shorebirds huddled against the wind, wind wailing in her ears. The chilled feathers of the wind hitting her face numbed her nose and cheeks.

She picked up her backpack and, heading north toward the interior, she walked between the dunes. The wind picked up sand and flung it in her face. Thousands of grains of sand swirled around Prieta. She couldn't see anything. Disoriented, she took a few hesitant steps. She blinked the sting away, tasted the salt on her lips. The sands cleared for an instant and Prieta saw the monstrous Llorona with the head of a horse. She curled her lips revealing long pointy teeth. Her neigh beckoned. Prieta wanted to go to her antigua madre and at the same time to flee from her.

She thought of all those times she had laughed with Llosi, shared secrets with her. Se acordó de todas las veces que había gozado de su vida con Llosi. She remembered when their love-making had been so good. Los dedos de Llosi penetrating her mouth, ears, nose; Llosi's tongue leaving a wet track on her inner thighs, Llosi sucking the place that smelled of the sea; su lengua y boca on Prieta's open flesh, su carne abierta, abierta. Why hadn't it been enough?

Finding a low spot between two tall dunes, she dropped to her knees and began digging with her bare hands. She clenched her fists tighter and tighter until in their trembling they resembled two fish jerking in the sand. When she'd dug for about three feet, she touched moisture. Brackish water flowed up into her hands. She knew it wasn't pure enough to drink but put a wet finger into her mouth. She thought about the strong breezes combing back the salt grass and depositing the coastal dropseed. The seeds sprouting. She pictured the meadowlarks in the grasslands, the blue herons and the great horned owls. The island in a constant renewal.

She went back toward the beach. The white caps ruffled the dark velvet sheen of the sea. When she found her dune she clambered up. She lay on the hollow, squirming her lower body into the sand. Like horned lizards at night she dug herself into the warm sandy soil until only her head peered over the rim. La noche se le atrepaba encima, night mounted her. La hundía en la arena. Her body relaxed into the earth. The crash of waves smoothed into a murmur, the world seemed far away.

She lay cradled by the warm sand for hours, eyes closed waiting for an inner voice, the spirit of the horse to tell her what to do.

She heard more people pack up and drive away in their cars and pickups. Now she was the only one on the beach. Llosi had not returned. No doubt she was still pissed at her. Maybe she'd taken the car or gotten a ride back to Port Isabel. No, no matter how awful the fight, Llosi would not leave her stranded. She was probably curled up on the back seat of the car waiting.

Prieta unearthed herself, stood and stretched, watching the lace border of spume edging the shore. Over her head three sea gulls rose and disappeared to the north. She had to pee. She looked around and, seeing no one, squatted down and pulled the crotch of her bikini to one side to meo en la arena.

Her warm urine left a tiny indentation on the sand. Near the spot she saw the hoof mark, vio la pezuña de caballo. Esperaba a la yegua con el cuerpo de mujer, but all she heard was el suave sonido of the sea. No más oyó el suspiro del mar. She lowered her body back into the hollow, lay on her back and let night cover her. She turned on her side, dug a deeper hole and curled up in it with her backpack. It still retained a little of the heat of the sun. She felt the familiar pain low in her belly. Her dreams were always more vivid before her menses. She looked up and found Coyolxauhqui la luna, a gold coin suspended in the sky.

Como Coyolxauhqui era una mujer hecha pedazos, she was a woman in pieces, fragments lapped thin by the tongues of the sea. En su boca algo caliente and salty bled from a wound que apenas había comenzado a conocer. She had never considered herself una rajeta, a quitter. She had always thought that if one of them left, it would be Llosi. She was frustrated with her inability to get swallowed up, but at the same time rejoiced in her grand refusal. Pa' ella entregarse no era imposible, what was impossible was giving herself totally into Llosi's keeping. She wiped the salt from her cheeks with the back of her hand.

She had not intended to sleep.

She woke con un despierto de golpe. In the dream she stood by the mare looking into its face. Ahí amidst the salt-stiffened grass a jolt surged through her body, pegandole cómo ola de agua helada. She saw the horse raising its head, scanning el monte for vaqueros. When she saw that the animal had a horse's head with the body of a woman, the spell she had been under all these years broke.

The horse reared up, head and shoulders sticking out of the sand, and listened to the silence. Prieta waited for the woman with the horse's head to appear, waited for this train of thought to continue. The horse had followed her here, back to where life had first slipped out of the sea, emerging from the moon in the water. Somewhere there were still wild horses. Or maybe there had never been any wild horses. She'd heard her grandmother say that in the old days during times of great hunger starving people killed and ate their horses.

The wind was icy, the stars were patterns of light in the sky as she walked toward the sea. The pure white spume had turned into dirty scuds and the surface of the water a flat black. To the west across Laguna Madre she could see the lights of Port Isabel dotting the seashore. On the horizon dark clouds were brewing.

The wind gusted without warning. Thousands of grains of sand swirled around Prieta. She couldn't see anything. She took a few hesitant steps and then halted. The sands cleared for an instant and Prieta saw the horse. A red orange ribbon extended from its mane to its tail. It was a coyote dun with feathered legs. She saw the long hairs growing on the cannon and the backs of the fetlocks, the monstrous Llorona, a woman with the head of a horse—su antigua madre. La Llorona curled her lips revealing long pointy teeth. Her soft whinny beckoned. Prieta's heart thundered. She didn't know whether to embrace la Llorona or flee from her in terror.

Prieta stopped and looked back. She saw the horse-headed woman following her, slick neck arched, nostrils flaring. Prieta forced herself to hold her ground, to not flee from the breath of the sea and la Llorona. On the edge of thought something was forming deep inside her . . . an image was emerging. The animal was dissolving into another shape, transforming into . . . No, it couldn't be, the horse's head with the body of a woman, her body. No not her. But the recognition was too strong. The moon was riding low on the water. Prieta walked into the waves then turned her back to the sea. The water receded, tugging the sand from around her feet. She felt as if she were in the stern of a boat looking landwards. Under her feet the sea was traveling away. She let go, allowed the motion to uproot her. She took the shell out of her shirt pocket and gently dropped it into the out-going water. Above her she heard the beating of wings.

She dropped on her knees. Se hincó y metió su cara en el mantel de espuma. After dunking her face in the white spume, she walked to her backpack, took out a towel and wiped her face. Tugging the towel around her for warmth, she followed her own tracks back toward the dunes. She waited for the horse-woman to complete her change. When the horse-woman emerged from the sea Prieta mounted her.

Prieta mounted the Llorona-faced mare, rode its smooth and glossy back a la jineta, bareback like the Berber Arabs. She felt the wind on her face, her hair its flaming mane. She felt the power vibrating from the mare into her body. Her legs became those of the horse, together their feet shook the earth. La yegua, una yegua con alas, respiraba en su pecho. As she plunged into the sea algo relámpague adentro de ella. Inside her lightning zigged. She had become the nagual.

Translations

la arena mojada: the wet sand

cabello: hair

en tu otro mundo: in your other world

la concha: the shell

'ta bueno: it's good

Véte si te da la gana: Go if you want to

la luna llena: the full moon

un beso y un abrazo: a kiss and an embrace

la madre mar: the mother sea

ni pleitos, ni celós: no fighting, no jealousies

no se quería acordar de todos esos meses: she didn't want to remember all those months

luna de miel: honeymoon

mitote: fuss

de una yegua: of a mare

ranchito: little ranch

potrancas: colts

mamagrande: grandmother

mija: my daughter

nagual: animal spirit

vaquera: cowgirl

chingao: damn it or fuck it

miha: my daughter

mesteños: mustangs, wild horses

ese animal: that animal

y zas: and bam

mi hijita: my dear little daughter

No le des cabeza.: Don't let it have its head.

bueno: good

el monte: the chaparral

vaqueros: cowboys

su boca hambrienta por conocer el cuerpo y alma de la otra: her
    mouth hungry to know the body and soul of the other

sus labios: her lips

bajando por los pechos de Llosi: her lips moving down Llosi's breasts

su boca prendida: her mouth upon

zacate quemado: sun-burnt grass

sudor: sweat

los pelos de elote: the hair like corn tassels

huellas: tracks, footprints

Yo sé que viniste a puro huevo: I know you came here begrudgingly

con la concha: with the shell

Borró las huellas.: She erased the tracks.

fundio: asshole

novia: girlfriend

¿Qué tienes?: What's the matter with you?

¿Te soliaste?: Did you get sunburned?

chin: shit, damn

espérate: wait

mensos: dummies

rucas: girls

marimachas: dykes

mira: look

¿No te dejo sola?: Don't I leave you alone?

veredas que llenas de nopales: trails full of cactus

¡Por Diosa!: By goddess!

como perra sarnosa: like a mangy bitch

oye tú: listen

Pos' ora sí: Now you've done it

y ahora: and now

Tú ya no vives conmigo.: You don't live with me anymore.

Tú fuiste pa' otro lugar donde yo no te puedo seguir.: You've already gone someplace where I can't follow you.

Ya no puedo agüantar más: I can't take anymore

¿Te acuerdas?: Do you remember?

cabrona: stubborn like a goat

¿Por qué?: Why?

pinche gringa jota: damned white queer

molcajete: mortar and pestle for grinding garlic, pepper, and cumin

Madre Diosa: Mother goddess

gabachos: whites

bolillo: white, as in white bread

Ahora te creas grande: Now you think you're so great

el Valle: the Valley

la orilla: the edge

la boca llena de ceniza: my mouth is full of ashes

la merienda: afternoon snack or tea

sintió el momento decisivo: she felt the decisive moment

¿Qué iba hacer?: What was she going to do?

la yegua: the mare

sacudio la cabeza: shook her head

la yegua ladina: this horse

el sordo palpitar de la yegua: the dull throbbing of the mare

la gente: the people

la playa: the beach

ella temblaba de frió: she was trembling from the cold

la Llorona: a Mexican folk figure, the weeping or wailing woman, a
    ghost who wanders in the night looking for her lost children
    whom it is said she had drowned

antigua madre: ancient mother

Se acordó de todas las veces que se había gozado de su vida con
    Llosi.: She thought of all the times she had enjoyed her life
    with Llosi.

los dedos de Llosi: Llosi's fingers

su lengua y boca: her tongue and mouth

su carne abierta, abierta: her opened flesh, opened

La noche se le atrepaba encima: Night mounted her

La hundía en la arena.: It sunk her into the sand.

meo en la arena: pee in the sand

vio la pezuña de caballo: she saw the hoof mark of a horse

esperaba a la yegua con el cuerpo de mujer: she waited for the
    mare with the body of a woman

el suave sonido: the soft sound

No más oyó el suspiro del mar.: She only heard the sea sighing.

Como Coyolxauhqui era una mujer hecha pedazos: Like Coyolxau-
    hqui she was a woman in pieces

en su boca algo caliente: something hot in her mouth

que apenas había comenzado a conocer: that she had only now
    begun to be aware of

una rajeta: quitter or someone who reneges

pa' ella entregarse no era imposible: for her to give herself wasn't
    impossible

con un despierto de golpe: woke suddenly

ahí: there

pegandole cómo ola de agua helada: hitting her like a wave

Se hincó y metió su cara en el mantel de espuma.: She kneeled and put her head in the blanket of foam.

a la jineta: bareback

La yegua, una yegua con alas, respiraba en su pecho.: The mare, a mare with wings, breathed in her chest.

algo relámpague adentro de ella: something flashed inside her

15

Reading LP

The splash. Her body slicing the water. Water backing up through her nostrils, hitting her throat. Her hands and arms thrashing en el agua. She can't swim. The shock of finding herself at the bottom of the irrigation canal pulses through her. A thump, her right hand hits the cement wall and pain shoots up her arm. She bounces up sputtering, coughing, gasping, and spewing out the putrid water. Through waterlogged lashes she sees the rim, her right hand shoots up to grab it. And misses. Her body slides down the cement, the sting of scraped skin on forearms and elbows.

She sinks back into dead leaves and water. Again she arches, reaching up, grabbing blindly for the rim. Again she misses. As she slides down the grainy side, a fingernail breaks off. Again she hurls her body up. Her fingers grasp the edge and cling, the weight of her body wrenching the muscles in her arm. She hoists her torso out, swings one leg over the rim, pulls her upper body onto it and balances on her stomach, the rim digging into her middle. Then she twists her body and rolls over onto the grass-covered ground.

Standing on shaky legs, she peers down at the ten-foot-deep canal. ¡Cagada! What the hell made her fall? The last thing she remembers is lying on her stomach on the patch of grass by the canal reading the book. She shakes her head and body and swings her arms around, scattering drops of water in the air. The clothes are plastered to her body. Already she feels the hot summer sun beginning to dry them. Groaning, she bends to pick up *the book* lying open on the grass. She thumbs through it, comes to the page she was last reading: ". . . wind ruffles and turns the pages. Like pale gray moths . . ." No answer there.

She gazes at la Tigra, looks around at her patchwork of fields, pastures, lagoon, woods, culverts, ditches, and fences. Everything still here: windmill, barn, garage, corrals, and cows. She sees her work everywhere. La Tigra, the land she's plowed, planted, and mulched. La tierra that mothers her, feeds her, comforts her. The buildings and fences she's pounded, patched, and painted. The cows she milked, fed, and watered.

She turns to the ranch house, the two-hundred-year-old sprawling white frame house with wrap-around porch, surrounded by tall mesquite trees and [birds][1] singing in the trees. La cara de su casa, its size and shape holding the imprint of her forebears. She studies the landscape as she would a painting but she can't maintain the distance necessary to be merely an observer. She is embedded in it. To look at it is to look at herself. She could solve the mystery of what's just happened to her if only she could read the landscape, as if the land could give her a message through its feel, sounds, and smells.

Bo, her German shepherd, comes running up to her and sniffs her wet clothes. Boots swish sucking, and still trailing water, she staggers from the backyard to the house and up the porch steps. She props herself against the kitchen's outside wall. Tremors course through her body chilling her. The sun filtering through las ramas de mesquite, leaves shifting, casting filigree patterns on her body. She sticks her finger in her ear and flicks out water. The strident sound of chicharras rushes into the silence and throbs in her head. She pushes herself off la pared, opens the screen door and enters the kitchen. She drops the book on the table and walks toward the dining room.

The room's doorway frames the living room door, and inside that frame is the full-length mirror on the opposite wall. Something

---

1. The brackets here suggest that Anzaldúa planned to replace "birds" with a more specific species.

about the layout stops her eye. As she walks toward it, she sees a slight dripping shape. It takes her a second to realize it's her own reflection. Though she's looked at these walls hundreds of times, this time algo feels different. She shivers, cold to her huesos.

As she walks toward the bathroom she's surprised at how the doorway de cada cuarto frames another doorway and that el espejo reflects two more doorways—those of the bedroom and bathroom.

She tosses her clothes over the towel rack and, grabbing a used towel from the hamper, mops up the water on the floor. She showers quickly in water hot as she can stand. She rinses off the stagnant smells and gargles out the taste of canal water. In the bathroom mirror, her cheekbones are stark against her washed-out face, her cropped hair sticks up in wet spikes. The white band on her forehead where her hat roosts looks paler. In the mirror she sees el espejo de la sala and all it reflects. Walls within walls and the spaces in between supported by beams and entremados. Putting on her blue comfortable but worn bathrobe, she pads barefoot to the kitchen. How did she fall into the canal?

The last thing she feels like is eating, but Bar-Su will be hungry. Out of the corner of her eye, she sees *the book* on the red-and-white gingham oil cloth. With half shrug, she opens the refrigerator, takes out tortillas, cucumber, tomato, onion, a jar of tahini butter, places them on the counter. Maybe some tea will sooth her nervios. She grabs a fistful of orange leaves from a paper sack and drops them into a pot of water then turns on the burner. She stares at the book, then places the honey bear, a quart of milk, and a cup on the counter by the stove. Her head cocks: tires crunching on gravel, car engine shuts off, a door slams, a shadow falls across the door, and then a tall woman enters, leather sandals squeaking.

"Hi, honey. I know, vengo tarde. What you up to?" says Bar-Su.

"Quiúbo corazón. I was just about to fix you something to eat. ¿Tienes hambre?" la Prieta asks, stretching to give the tall woman a smacking kiss on the lips.

"Sí, pero no por comida. What's this, LP, mi Prietita consentida con los ojos soñadores?" she says cupping LP's breasts, one in each hand, squeezing them, thumbs strumming nipples.

"Ay qué fresca. Those, I'll have you know, are my two best assets. Show some respect, ruca. I wanted to be ready, pa' no gastar tiempo. I'd pounce on you as you walked in, tear your clothes off in one swoop," says la Prieta, making a tearing sound. "And then we'd take a running dive into la cama."

"Oh, yeah? I'd say these are your best assets," the tall woman says, palms stroking then slowly rotating on LP's buttocks. "Your tetas aren't bad either, pero tu panocha y gusanito están a toda madre," she whispers in Prieta's ear, putting her palm over Prieta's pubis and pressing down. "Forget the bed, we could fuchi-fuchi right here . . .

Then looking intently into LP's face she says, "What's wrong?"

"I fell into the canal."

"Whoa, what did you say? You fell?"

"Yeah, it was really weird," says LP.

"Are you OK, honey? Here, let me look at you. Hey, you don't look so good."

LP glances at the book on the table. "Water got into my ear." She bends her head and hits the side of it against the edge of her hand.

"How'd you fall?"

"I don't know. One minute I was reading that book and the next I was at the bottom of the canal."

"But that's crazy," Bar-Su says. "I told you, el trabajo te está matando."

"Yeah, tell me about it."

"How'd you get out?"

"It wasn't easy."

"I wish you'd learn how to swim; dog paddling doesn't cut it, Prieta."

Prieta reaches for the whole wheat tortillas. Bar-Su swats her hands. "Deja eso," she says. "That healthy stuff may be good for you but it tastes awful. Here, I'll fix us some real Tex-Mex taquitos."

Bar-Su begins to clear the table. Picking up the book, she says, "You know, you spend more time with this book than you do with me. Every time I turn around it's in your hand."

"Something about it fascinates me. Besides I've got to write my paper, want to do good in school."

"Yeah, I know. What an eerie-looking cover," Bar-Su says.

They both stare at the black whirlpool disappearing into a light blue background. "Where's the title?" asks Bar-Su. "It's strange for a book cover not to have a title."

"That, querida, is one of the reasons I chose it for my paper. Besides . . . it *does* have a title. This glyph aquí represents words, only you have to know the language. It means 'entremados.' I had a hard time persuading el cabrón English prof to let me write my paper on it."

Bar-Su sits down and pulls LP onto her lap. LP leafs through the book with Bar-Su looking on.

"Who's that author? Never heard of him," says Bar-Su.

"I think the author's a her. The style and other stuff feels like a woman's. Or maybe I think the author is a woman because I'm reading like one."

"You mean you're projecting your stuff into the book?"

"Yeah. John Q . . . you remember him? You met him at Sabas Q's funeral. He lives by this book, says it's the best thing he's ever read and he's read everything. You've seen his house, it's a library; even the bathroom is full of books."

"Sounds familiar, ¿eh? Well, John Q's a queer one. But then they're all locos, your cousins. Does it by any chance run in your family?" she asks jerking the book out of LP's hands and putting it on the window sill. She clasps her arms around Prieta.

"My family's swimming in two-dollar bills. Y tu familia doesn't like that a whole lot," LP says, looking into her novia's eyes. "Can you stay tonight?"

"Why? So I can wait for you to do your chores then read this book yet again and then fall into bed exhausted never noticing if I'm in bed with you?"

"Don't start, Bar-Su. I don't have the energy for it."

"Sorry, babe. I can't stay anyway. Mi pobre madrecita—I couldn't get Joe to stay with her tonight. I can't leave her alone. What if she has another stroke while you and I are here fucking? Or while I'm thinking of fucking and you're reading this book."

LP scrunches her face, then, catching the look in Bar-Su's eyes, says, "Hey, hon, I do want to spend more special time with you. Really. And your brothers should take more responsibility with your mother. I want a live-in lover, not a part-time one."

An hour later after they've eaten, Bar-Su is sitting on the wide back porch swing, one foot pushing it back and forth. LP's head is propped across her middle. LP looks at the western sky, its faint streaks of purple and orange. Then she picks up the book and reads a passage aloud.

"There's something weird about this book. You heard how the main character falls into a lake?"

"So? I wish you'd stop reading that thing."

"Well, words from this book were running in my head when I fell into the canal. I think John Q gave me this book for a reason."

Bar-Su sits up and looks at her. "I don't think I like what I think you're saying."

"You're not the only one! It was creepy, Bar-Su. I lost track of . . . well, me, for a few minutes. It was like I'd stepped out of time. I don't know where I went. I mean I, me, this self that I am sort of got lost. Maybe it was just for a few seconds. No, don't look like that."

"Now where are you going?"

"Gotta fix the fence," says LP. "The cattle will get out and I'll spend all day tomorrow rounding them up."

She goes out to the shed, straps on the staple gun and hammer, puts on her work gloves and picks up the posthole digger. She strings barbwire, stapling it to the posts. When it grows too dark to see she turns on the lights attached to the tall railroad ties encircling the homestead's perimeter and continues working for another hour.

At midnight Barbara-Susana stands up and paces from one end of the wrap-around porch to the other. The chicharras' shrill sounds drown the sound of her footsteps on the creaking wood. "I'm getting pretty tired of how you're always so busy with la siembra and school and now this. When you're with me you're not really with me."

"I know, hon, I really do. I am trying to do better."

"That's what you always say." After a few minutes of silence Bar-Su jumps off the porch and leaves behind a shower of gravel.

LP stands and stares at the plume of dust rising behind the tail lights' reddish tinge, listens to the shushing sounds of leaves as the wind works through them. She flips off the high-powered lights in the yard and corrals. Everything is pitch black.

Book in hand, she walks into the house and to the bedroom where she falls into bed and starts reading. As she reaches the last page, she hears the bantam rooster crowing from the skeletal ebony tree. Stretching and yawning she looks at the clock, 2:31 am. Shit! two hours eaten up by the book. Dos pinches horas and where was she all that time?

La luz de la luna slipping in through Venetian blind slats cuts vertical strips across her body. The rest of the room is dark. She falls asleep. When she wakes, her breathing is shallow. The cool perspiration on her bare body has roused her out of a dream. En el sueño una mujer in a familiar landscape is inside a hollow, gutted, round book. The giant cover flapped open and shut, open and shut. As her right thumb prods her ear, LP becomes aware of the pain in her left side and turns over. She loses the rest of the dream and slips into sleep once more.

She wakes up at about 5:00. The first thing she thinks of es el libro. Time to get her ass out of bed and start her chores.

She walks out to the cotton fields and checks the plants for insects, blights, rusts, smuts, wilts, rots, and fungi. She bends down and palms a handful of dirt. Feels the soil, rubs it between her fingers: Is it too coarse and gritty, too silty and clay-like? Maybe she should test the pH. Maybe in the fall she'll sow some green manuring. Yeah, plant alfalfa or clover right here, then plow it under while still tender and young. Return the crop to the soil for decomposition, give the land back the nutrients she's taken from it. And hope the wind won't blow away the top soil. Uh huh, she'll cultivate a rich layer of humus. She'll borrow a chisel plow, maybe one with straight shanks, go in deep and break up the compacted subsoil. Or maybe she should just stubble mulch.

At lunch, she goes to the family plot and sprawls on a grave under the shade of a copse of mesquite trees. After she eats her papas con chorizo in flour tortillas and drinks her thermos of iced tea, she walks up and down looking at the headstones, reading the names of the people who had left their signature on the land but whose bodies had years since moldered into dust. Weather and erosion had dulled the names and dates carved in stone. Her mother and brother stopped tending the cemetery years ago. When she bought their parcels, the dead became hers, too. She bends down over her mamagrande's grave and straightens the wreath of cempazuchitl flowers, its orange blossoms beginning to fade. Hoof-and-mouth disease and unpaid taxes did her grandmother in, forcing her to sell a big chunk of the land in order to keep a few hundred acres. Her roots, her history. As she walks among the graves she treads a moving current. She is part of a continuum. She doesn't own the land, it owns her. She is its caretaker. She was supposed to marry and leave her home. Not for women their homeland. Andrea, another Prieta, had been forced to leave . . . or had chosen to leave. But not LP. She refuses.

She takes the book out of her lunch bag. She'll read a few minutes then go back to work.

After afternoon chores she returns home to get something to eat and make a few calls. When she hangs up the phone, she picks up the book. Antes de que se de cuenta, she's read the book from cover to cover. Read the whole thing without stopping. Where in the hell does she go when she's reading? She's not here, that's for sure. She looks outside through the window, gauging how low the sun's sunk, then she looks at her watch. ¡Jíjole! This time it took her only an hour and forty-five minutes to finish the book, less time than before. She pokes her ear with her finger then places the same hand on the sheet-rock wall. Its cool solidity reassures her. But it's not that solid, there are the hollow spaces, entremados, between the walls. She could stick her head through it.

Next morning she wakes muttering, "gotta get away from that book." She pushes her fist through the sleeve of her faded denim jacket, the one with the tawny embroidered jaguar on its top left pocket, and shoves bare feet into her scuffed boots. Semi-naked, she strides out into the backyard. Breathing in the cool morning smells, she peers into the rosy sky looking for the rising sun. Mist envelops the top of the mesquites and brings a chill to her bare legs. The fog from the lagoon hovers over the tractor, shed, and shrubs. She watches dawn dissolve the night mist and gradually shroud the tree and rooftops. The sun is a diffused yellow light.

Her eyes track Bo trotting across the field. She whistles. The dog stops, raises his head, cocks his ears, and runs toward her. He leaps up to lick her face and then bounds away, wanting a game of catch. LP runs after him, bare legs pumping, blood surging. Bo turns around and jumps her; she falls and rolls around, hugging him. Cool hard ground, dew-wet dog smell, warm panting breath, rasping tongue on her face. She buries her face in his fur, blocking out the sun. When she comes up for air, the dog shakes his body, dispersing drops of water like pollen in the wind.

"When was the last time I gave you a bath?" she asks, cuffing the dog's head. "Enough, Bo. Time to work, now. Ándale, go, go, go. Vámanos, round up the cows."

The dog lopes quickly across the cowpen. With short, mock-angry barks, he dashes in and out among the cows, nipping at their shanks. A slow-moving, heavy-uddered Guernsey lumbers toward her. Prieta swings the corral door open, the bottom scraping the ground. She spreads silage in the trough and as la vaca lowers her head to it, she picks up the stool, puts it down near the cow's rear, and straddles it. She leans her forehead against the cow's shank and places her right hand on the gaunt hip bone, listens to the intestines gurgling and the tail switching off flies. With a moist rag she wipes the udders clean and begins wringing milk from las chichis. The milk sputters and hisses as it hits the bucket. The smell of warm milk engulfs her. Shoving the stool back, she kneels on the ground, lips and mouth reaching for a tit. Her tongue and palate pull the milk into her mouth and throat. She wonders what it would be like to suck milk from Bar-Su's breasts.

She goes to the feed bins and scatters corn for the chickens. After cleaning out the cowpen with a fork, she shovels the manure into a wheelbarrow and pushes it to the orchard where she spreads it around the trees. She no longer minds the stink of ammonia from the cow pies, but she hates cleaning out the pig pen. She finishes repairing the windmill pump and hurries through the rest of her morning chores. She's done them thousands of times. Daily rituals.

LP drops her gloves on the ground and bends over the sink pump over the trough. She works the handle up and down; when the water gushes out she splashes cold water over her neck and arms.

She gets into her pick-up truck and heads into town, making a list as she drives: feedstore, post office, grocery and hardware stores. Behind her she leaves twin plumes of rising dust and sounds of tire sucking sand and gravel. The fresh breeze coming off the green fields feels good against her short wet hair.

Returning from her errands, LP approaches her ranch from the west entrance. She stops, jumps out of the pick-up and unlocks the gate tied to the center post. The sign hanging above the entrance to her ranch is swinging on its chains in the wind. LP stretches up, her fingers trace the words *El Rancho la Tigra* carved into the belly of a wooden jaguar. One of her abuelos had named el rancho *El Tigre* after the Mexican jaguars that crossed into south Texas from Mexico. Neither her brothers nor her mother had wanted to pay the back taxes to hold onto the land. LP had. She changed the ranch's gender to go with hers.

LP opens la puerta de la cerca, gets back in her pick-up, drives through. She stops, turns off the engine, jumps out again and swings the gate shut. Bringing two fingers of the right hand to her straw hat, LP salutes the plastic snake curled around the top of the post. How like Bar-Su to enshrine the gate she calls "LP's altar" with a plastic snake. That was three years ago. They've been novias for four years.

She leans her back against the thick log for a minute and thinks about her crops and how or where she can steal a few hours away from them to give Bar-Su. "Here I am again, mi tigra. Venga por favor, dueña de la tierra, show yourself, madre mía. Once more I call on you. No, I don't want you to send this land rain. Help me figure out what's happening to me. If you could only send me a small sign—anything that would point me in the right direction."

She continues in a sing-song voice for a few minutes, then gets back into the pick-up, pulls into the backyard, backs up to the shed door, unlatches and pulls down the tailgate, and unloads the feed bags. Dropping her boots on the porch she goes in. She pops the Vangelis Papathanassiou tape into the cassette player, and the sounds of "Can You Hear the Dogs Barking?" pulse throughout the house and yard from both the inside and outside speakers.

It's almost dusk, yet the temperature is still in the mid 90s. She walks outside and watches the ruddy blaze in the western horizon and the orange glow on the road and fences.

LP plops down, belly up, onto the grass under el palo verde, sinking into its pungent smell. The ground's coolness soothes her; the tension drops from her shoulders. As the music quickens its tempo, she rises and begins to whirl around, clicking her feet together in the air. She must really be crazy to dance in this heat—and the evening chores to get done. The air seems thick enough to sustain her weight for slow seconds, there between earth and sky. When she was twelve she dreamed of going to Paris to study dance. But of course her legacy was heavy boots, grease, and green growing plants.

She twirls around the graves of el camposanto, weaving in and out among them, startling the sparrows in the dark-green ebony trees. She breathes in the hot evening air fragrant with the smell of dry earth. The sky reels as she dances, the light dims gradually amidst the ear-splitting sound of chicharras and Bo barking in the distance. Distracted by an image from the book, she stumbles and falls as the last orange band finally sinks into the horizon. She lies there, blinking into the darkness, seeing a glowing bed of coals, feeling the light breeze fanning them. She sees herself adding pieces of paper to a fire, sees herself watching the fire consume them. This image slowly fades.

That night, just as sleep begins overtaking her, her knee jerks and she resurfaces, sinks and surfaces. Her hand reaches toward the night table. Reading often puts her to sleep. *Why do I feel this compulsion to read the book again?* Something in it bothers her, but she doesn't know what—and that bothers her more. It takes her even less time than before to read the entire book—an hour and a half. The image of the bed of coals in the book is slightly different from the one she saw that afternoon. In going from the printed word in the book to the words in her mind, the events and people in the book change in subtle ways. Or is it she who subtly changes? Yeah, she thinks, that would make a good topic for the Lit Crit paper: the intrusion of the fiction. Except the intrusion doesn't seem to stop when she closes the book's covers. The book is a trigger of some sort. Suddenly she is afraid again.

"¡Jíjole!" She flings the book across the room, it slides across the floor. She's more awake than ever. Damn. She remembers Mrs. McAlastair, her preschool teacher, reading aloud from a book. She can't remember the book or its topic. Just that every time Mrs. McAlastair read it, something would draw LP to look out the window. She'd stare at the green field bordered by blue bonnet, the wind bending their fragile stems. LP wanted to be out there on the lush grass, but she wanted to take Mrs. McAlastair and the dream her words created with her. The wind whispering the words just beneath Mrs. McAlastair's voice. Then something would shift, like a string snapping, and LP would turn back to Mrs. McAlastair sitting at her desk. And now thirty years later it was happening again.

LP stretches and turns to look out the window, hand reaching for the light and finds herself between two walls. Se halla entre paredes. ¡Epa! Keep calm. Taking deep breaths, she pictures each plane and partition of the house she designed and built with the help of her primas. Click. The light is on and she's back and the house is itself again.

"¡Chingao!" Gotta move the bed away from this wall, it's too close—but she doesn't know what it's too close to. Even now, she feels the book calling. She looks around the room, then shoves and pulls the bed against la otra pared. As she's shifting the night table, she stubs her toes against the book. She grasps her injured foot and topples the floor lamp.

By the time she runs the vacuum over the brighter patches where the bed and table used to be, light is streaking in through the curtains. Five am and morning chores. She straightens the framed snapshots of her mother, brothers, and assorted familiares on top of the dresser. She takes one last glance at the new arrangement, then walks into the kitchen. Wolfing down a tortilla with cheese, beans, and salsa, she walks out into the coral light.

After the morning chores she pulls on her gloves, puts diesel in the gas tank, and rouses the cranky tractor. She backs it to the discs, hooks them up, and drives to the edge of her north forty. Lowering the fluorescent green discs, she begins to turn the sod. Behind the slow-moving tractor a ribbon of the dark plowed ground flattens the weeds, leaving a cleared, smooth surface that will give the harvesters easier access to the crop. She watches the black tierra turn and the birds following the plow seeking the worms exposed by the discs. A tendril from her mind locks into the familiar task. Tierra y sol. Soon the unrelenting sun and tractor roar empty her brain of all thought.

Sometime later she surfaces, dazed. Why has she stopped discing? How long has she has been stopped, shaking with the tractor's idling vibrations? She catches the tail end of a scene, a woman on her hands and knees in the mud, rain pelting her body. Ay diosita, not another scene from the book. Her arms and legs become weak and sweat breaks across her forehead. She shakes her head, trying to shake lose the scene. She may be that woman. It may rain soon, the crops would be ruined. Stop it! She's letting her fear get ahead of herself.

She lurches off the tractor and walks around, trying to find her legs. She pauses, rubs scuffed boots against disced earth, bends, picks up some dirt. Straightening, she rubs it between her fingers testing the texture: Rich, loamy. She sniffs it. Not too much hydrogen. She forces herself back up on the tractor, finishes the discing, then heads back to the house.

At home she pulls off her sweat-stiffened jeans and, in shirt and boots, goes out behind the shed to finish patching la cerca. If she could get away with it she'd never wear clothes. Too confining. But the work is hard on her body, she needs the denim for protection.

She finds herself in the bathroom not knowing how or when she got there. A remnant of memory flashes and disappears like fish in the water. In the mirror she sees red-rimmed eyes and a face darkened with dirt. She removes her cap. Her hair is matted to her head, the white line on her forehead in stark contrast to her red neck. She strips off the shirt sticking to her. Doubled over the sink, she is aware of the compactness of her body, bones, muscles, skin. No, she contains her body. Her body holds her in, her skin protects her from zancudos y mosquitos y el sol. But her skin doesn't keep out. . . . She rinses her face, then stares at the water swirling and gurgling down the drain. She gropes for the nearest towel, pats her face, and digs her thumbs into her ears. What the hell is going on?

She goes into the bedroom for a nap but can't sleep. Pinche libro. She rolls to the edge of the bed, lowers her head to the floor, and peers underneath. Despite her resolution not to get near the book again, she hauls it out and lets it fall open at the beginning. Picking a line at random, she begins to read.

Seventy-five minutes later she reaches the last sentence. She's beginning to realize why she feels a compulsion to read this book over and over. The book is about . . . Gotta hide it. Maybe if it's out of sight the compulsion to read it won't kick in. She glances around the room, picks a place, and hides the book.

Just as she's drifting into sleep she hears a woman's voice saying softly: "When you read fiction you enter its reality. When it's compelling enough it will enter your reality."

¡Chinga tu madre! Where's the voice coming from? She bolts out of bed and, head first, dives under it. El libro, ¿en dónde lo escondió? She crawls out from under la cama and starts rummaging through her chest of drawers. El altar, she thinks—I hid it in the compartment under the altar.

She picks up a writing tablet and, with the book in her hands, goes out to the back porch and sits on the swing. She looks at the sky, hoping not to see the clouds that come before the dark thick clouds of rain. The book opens to page 3: "Yesterday the book fell open when I dropped it onto the kitchen table. . . ." LP rocks and creaks for an hour through the hot afternoon reading the book. With her tongue between her teeth she sits hunched over the writing tablet scratching across the yellow lines.

Afterwards she again decides to hide it. This time in the shed. In the back of the steel shelf, by the calendar of the adelita with a bugle in her hand, the low bodice, the exposed thighs. LP goes outside. The afternoon feels ponderous, oppressive. She looks at the broad flat landscape all around her, then up at the sky. Dark clouds.

Chingao. Suffocating humidity. Sure sign of a big weather change. Looks like it'll rain soon. Rain, rain, por favor go away. The squash and watermelons would rot where they lay. Just last month she'd been praying for rain, hoping not to have to pay $300 an acre to irrigate. No hurricanes, OK? she tells the Jaguar rain god. Not until all the hay is baled.

She empties out the stock tank, cleans it with a broom, hoses it down and refills it. She tosses off her sweat-stiffened canvas gloves, goes to the sink pump outside and dunks her head under the cold gushing water.

Going inside, she makes tuna sandwiches which she downs with big gulps of lemonade straight from the two-quart jar. She's tired. Beyond tired. She sits down on the porch swing for a few minutes and makes a mental list of all the chores yet to do this week.

She wakes up on the porch swing. She's dreamed every scene in the book—all compacted into a few minutes of dream time. But this time it's different—this time she held onto herself, remembered who she was for a few seconds. She wasn't totally lost in . . . whatever/wherever she was. If only she could remember it all! But she'd never had good recall—never could memorize anything, not even the ballads of García Lorca which her former lover Llosi adored so much. Llosi her first heartbreak. Llosi of the slightly dazed look who had married LP's primo. While LP wrote love poems to Llosi, her husband wrote love poems to Prieta. Prieta had been almost tempted when he'd suggested a three-way. Now Prieta realizes why—she'd been as captivated by him as Llosi had been. Now finally she could admit it. But being a part-time student, full-time marimacha, and a sembradora with two hundred acres to farm in the back monte of the southernmost tip of Tejas left her no time to experiment with yet another type of relationship. It was hard enough being una de las otras. She had more than enough in her hands trying to cope with Bar-Su's family, so resistant to queers.

Later she finds herself sitting on an idling tractor listening to the same voice reciting passages from *the book*. . . . When she comes to, she is almost done with the baling. Ese libro desgraciado me va a volver loca. Y este pinche sol. She curses the book, the sun, the cost of the tractor, the baler, water, seed, gasoline, and state land and school taxes. She takes out her taquitos and thermos of decaf con leche.

When she finishes baling she drives the tractor back to the garage. She pulls the long iron pipe attached to the round smooth socket, and unhooks the baler from the tractor all the while praying, *Please don't let it rain, mi tigra.* Weather prone to sudden changes in South Texas.

Bo runs up to her, barking. Exhausted, she stumbles into the kitchen with Bo leaning his shoulder against her leg. She washes up, grabs a container of yogurt and a bag of granola, and plumps down at the kitchen table with a box of papers. She'll do some bookkeeping, write out checks for the farm bills, and if there is time, she'll read up on the new developments with fertilizers in this month's issue of *Farm and Ranch*.

She falls onto her bed, exhausted—just a little nap. But sleep is nudged out again and again. Just as she's about to go under, her hand reaches out for Bar-Su on the other side of the bed, but comes back empty. *Don't, don't you dare reach for that book again. You know what Bar-Su will say, that you're addicted to reading that damn book.* Palms moist, she gets up, goes out to the shed, finds the feed sack, and takes out the book. She comes back and flops down on the living room couch. Before she knows it she's reading the first sentence: "A tall woman enters, 'Hi, what you up to?'"

An hour later: she has re-read todo el pinche libro. Each reading takes less time than the one before. Flinging the book against the wall she hurries outside to feed the animals, milk the cow, and gather the eggs.

Prieta se va de un chore to another, trying to beat the encroaching darkness. But the shadows fatten. She stops, watches the sun sink into the earth leaving smears of orange, amber, and bronze across the horizon. Thin pinpoints of light begin to appear in the sky. The cicadas intensify their shrill cacophony. The more intently she listens to the sounds the louder they grow.

She turns on the shed light and fiddles with the jacked-up Ford. Diosa mía, marooned at the farm with her chariot of the rusting fenders. As she runs the red rag over her greasy hands she mentally tallies her property, which will for sure get repossessed if it rains. The haymaker, sweeper, haycutter, tractor, cotton picker: total worth $100,000. The corn harvester belongs to her cousin. Si se da la cosecha she'll trade in the old tractor for a newer model, one with air conditioning.

She lowers the jack, pulls it out from under, and tosses it into the toolbox in back of the pick-up. She turns the key but the engine won't turn over. ¡Chinpiotes! Now she can't go over to her novia's house. Bar-Su can come to her only on Wednesday afternoons and Saturday nights anyway. Chinga tu madre. What a hypochondriac—she's sick all the time. *Haven't I been understanding? Damn right. I've been a saint not bugging Bar-Su. Una santa. Of course, Bar-Su's right—if she came more often I wouldn't have time for her. Well, así es la vida.*

She raises the pick-up's hood, checks the battery cables, then sits on the ground. She falls back and, supine, slowly wiggles her body under la troca.

Feeling a cramp in her hand, she looks down and finds she's been gripping the wrench too tightly. She must have lain there a long time, immobile, displaced out of herself.

She scuttles out from underneath the truck, stands up and stares at her small calloused hands and the black grease oozing between her fingers. Tiene miedo. Again while under the truck she'd heard a voice. This time it sounded like water racing along a river. Images had appeared, then were swept away by the rushing water. That's all she remembers.

Pero no es nada. Nothing's happened to her. El mal aire le había entrado, es todo. Something had entered her body. Algo le había entrado. Possessed by some spirit. The spirit of the book? Naw, libros don't have spirits. Do they? A curandera could suck whatever it was out of her body. And the fear along with it.

"Jefita, where are you?" Pedro, her hired hand, gets out of his troca and comes toward her. She didn't even hear him drive into the yard.

"Quiúbole jefa, vine a ver si quieres que trabaje mañana. You have work for me tomorrow?"

"No, no te voy a necesitar. I'll be using the tractor so I won't need you until Monday. Quiero que comiences muy de mañanita."

She notices that he's eyeing her bare legs. "¿Qué miras?"

He turns to the side, spits, and scratches his crotch.

"Nada, jefa. ¿Y si llueve?" he says, looking up at the sky.

"If it rains quiero que me ayudes a fix esta pinche pick-up."

"Bueno, jefa. Ojalá que no llueva porque si llueve vas a perder toda la cosecha. ¿Qué tienes, 'tas enferma? You don't look so good."

She shakes her head. "No, I'm not sick. Not exactly. Es que me desvelé anoche."

Inside the house, she turns on the TV in the living room. Any program will do, anything to drown out the images and voice. After a while she discovers that though her eyes are on the TV screen, the scene she's watching is not on TV. A small woman sits cross-legged staring into space. The woman's back is turned toward LP. The image is so strong Prieta smells the tallow from the candles surrounding the woman.

LP leaps up, punches the television's off button, and rushes around the room searching for the book. She snatches it up, along with her cigarettes and lighter, and races out to the backyard.

Caliche stings the soles of her feet and the cooling night air clears her head. She looks up at the moon. It hangs low in the graying sky. Bo trots beside her and pokes his cold nose in her palm, then smells the book and whines. He leans his shoulder against her leg.

"Watch this, Bo. It's going to be fun. We're going to get rid of lo no invitado—it's worn out its welcome."

Her bare foot hits a log, which crumbles to ash under her foot. Soft ceniza oozes through her toes, immersing her feet in the cool powdery ash from an earlier fire. She pitches the half-burned brush she'd cleared from the pastures into the fire bed and feels a fingernail break off. ¡Chin! She examines her calloused hands. Yep, she's got the hands of a marimacha, a real country femme.

She hurries into the shed and searches frantically among tractor implements, mildewed tarp, spools of barbwire, and old saddles suspended from a beam until she finds a can of gasoline and returns to the pile of brush.

As she drenches the branches with gasoline, she stumbles, icy liquid sloshes over her foot. She can't find a rag, so she takes off her panties and wipes her foot with them. Trying not to breathe in the gas fumes, she picks up the book and begins tearing out a leaf. She stops and begins to read. No, don't start, don't start, you'll get sucked in again. She forces herself to stop reading.

The wind ruffles and turns the pages. Like pale gray moths in the moonlight, they flutter softly with each sigh of the wind. She lights a cigarette, takes a few jerky sucks, then tosses it into the heap. It flares up. Explodes. Lights and shadows flicker over her body as she stands motionless watching the flames. When the fire has dwindled to brasas she realizes how odd she would have looked to others—standing there naked, holding a book to her breasts. Pero no hay otra alma for miles.

Wincing at the small rocks under her feet, she walks painstakingly to the house. In the bathroom she bends over the sink. The hot water stings her face and chest but she is at peace. It was getting too scary and she was getting in way over her head.

In bed, at the onslaught of sleep, she strains to hear the shrill whine of a wire stretched to its breaking point. As she stretches out her arms toward the wall on her left, her hands disappear. ¡Ay diosita! She jumps back. Then she sits there with goosebumps all over her body. She looks at her hands. Still the same scarred manos, except they're shaking badly. She thinks she hears a voice.

"Bar-Su?" she calls out. She listens. Silence. Then she remembers that her girlfriend is at her mother's. She hears a sound—a whine. There behind her, growing louder and louder. Sweat breaks out under her armpits. Swiftly she turns to the sound, and is suddenly caught off balance. She grabs the bedpost to right herself, but instead her hand goes straight through. It does not appear at the other side—and the bedpost is only three inches thick.

Slowly her whole body falls forward and follows her arm. She finds herself buffeted by a thick wind that feels like a river of gelatin. There is no bedpost, no wall, no bedroom. She's alone, listening to her breath sawing in and out, almost drowning out the soft whimpering sounds coming from her throat. Alone, in thick blue air.

With trembling hands she touches her face and then the space around her and behind her head. She tucks her face into the crook of her elbow and shields her head with the other arm as she is whirled around and around. In her mind the words from the book—"Tres peras peladas prisoned en la pared. She took a fall. Right through the wall"—repeat over and over.

Suddenly, everything is still and she finds herself lying in a huddle against a stone wall. Her arms reach back and grope for an entrance to the other side, back to her tierra, her tractor, y su ranchito. Her heart is pounding so hard she can't hear her thoughts, can't swallow the knot in her throat.

All of a sudden, she is catapulted once more through the dark mouth of the cave. Someone is screaming—her. She stuffs her fist into her mouth. Immediately, she's bombarded by vibrations of sounds she feels but can't hear. Shadows dive toward her, then fall away before reaching her. Ah! she is about to get it, an inkling of what's going on, of what's really happening, but that too is sucked away by el silencio.

Then all is still. She holds her breath. To her it looks like she's caught in a sticky gauze of carded cotton. She can only move a few inches in one direction. Even if she hacked herself free there might be a wall beyond this one, y otra pared behind it. She's in some kind of tunnel. Or she's inside a serpent—yeah, she's been devoured by the earth serpent. No, this is more like a birth canal. Madness is being caught between worlds, sanity is reaching either side.

Agua.

Huge drops beat her head and back. She lifts her face to the sky, rain buzzard beaks stab at her eyes, feathers flail her face. Senses stifled as if wrapped in sheets of plastic, and she, all fingers and nails, piercing holes in it, but not fast enough. She sits up. Her body makes a sucking sound. She sees herself as others might: a mud-covered scarecrow staggering in the rain, bolts of lightning flickering around her. "Mud-covered scarecrow staggering in the rain" . . . is that a phrase from the book?

Her feet slosh through shifting quicksand.

No not quicksand, only mud.

What is she doing in the middle of a field, pelted by sheets of rain? Well, there goes la cosecha. The cotton is ruined. Thousands of dollars lost to the rain. She can almost see her corn bent double, tassels drooping down to the mud. She tries to total up the damage: it's too much for her to figure out. She'd be lucky if the bank repossesses every piece of junk in the place. ¡Chinga tu madre! Es la noche del tigre, the time of Tláloc, diosito del agua, jaguar face.

She hears someone calling her.

"Prieta linda, what are you doing here? Soaked to the bone?"

"Bar-Su. You? Here in the middle of the night? Is it your mother?"

"No, she's fine, Prieta, and it's mid-afternoon. How did you get here?"

Prieta looks around and finds she's standing in the field behind Bar-Su's mother's house. The sun is shining brightly, there's not a cloud in the sky, and the dirt is bone dry under her buttocks and hands.

"I fell through the bedpost."

"What?!?"

"Jíjole, I thought I was going crazy. It was so real."

"What was so real?" Bar-Su hovers over her, staring intently. "Maybe you *are* going crazy."

LP feels the tug of Bar-Su's hands on her upper arms as Bar-Su pulls her up from the ground and steers her toward her car.

"Hush now. You can tell me all about it when I get you home," says Bar-Su, taking a blanket from the trunk and wrapping it around LP. Then she gently pushes LP into the passenger seat.

When they reach La Tigra, LP opens the car door and waits for Bar-Su to come around the front of the car to her side. She throws herself against Bar-Su's thin body, breathing in her familiar scent. Tremors from the cold and from arousal rise up in waves from the pit of her stomach into her mouth.

They stand arms clasped around each other. Bar-Su tugs LP slowly into the house, helps her shower, and tucks her into bed. Leaving the bedroom, Bar-Su returns about ten minutes later with a cup of orange leaf tea with milk and honey. Then she gets into bed and, cradling Prieta in her arms, gently rocks her.

"OK, baby, ¿qué pasó?"

LP hiccups, "I must have triggered the rain by fooling around in the other place."

"What rain?"

"The rain in en el otro lugar. Gracias a diosita that it didn't rain on this side. I didn't lose the crop. But the bedpost . . ."

"What about the bedpost?"

"Well, I went through it and when I got out the other end I was at your mom's place. Fue bien fácil, Bar-Su. First the sounds, then my hand went through the post, then my head, shoulders, and the rest of me. I slipped right in, smooth as butter. There was only a slight resistance."

She extends her hand toward the wall, then stops short.

"I bet I could do it again. But I'm scared. What if I don't come out the other side? What's happening to me?" She begins to cry.

"Shush, shush," Bar-Su keeps saying as she holds her.

"Listen, I was thinking about you, wanting to be with you when I went through the post. When it started happening, me cagué de miedo. That's where I messed up, I shouldn't have fought it. That's why it took so long."

"I felt you, honey. I sensed you calling me. I thought your hand had gotten caught in one of the machines."

"Chin, it takes me away."

"I'm going to call Joe. I left Mamí all by herself. If I can't find someone to stay with her, I'll have to go back."

"OK."

"What takes you away?"

"The book. It's opened up some kind of passage. And now I don't even need the book to get to the other place. When I'm en ese otro lugar I'm not the same as the me here and now. It's like there's two of me." LP presses her face between Bar-Su's breasts and gradually her taut body softens under Bar-Su's slow strokes.

"Hush now, try to get some sleep. That's it, my Pretty-Quick, just rest. I gotta make the call." A few minutes later Bar-Su returns. "Well, Joe's not home," she says.

After Bar-Su leaves, LP sits up and goes over and over what happened to her. She remembers her body stretching, traveling.

Before going to sleep LP picks up the phone and dials.

"Hello, Bar-Su?"

"How are you feeling, Hon?"

"A little shaky but otherwise fine. Don't want to face it, whatever's happening to me. Don't want to know. And don't know when I'll get my nerve back. I'm trying to psyche myself into trying it again, maybe aim to come out in your bedroom at your mother's."

"Don't you dare! It's too risky. Why are you doing this, LP?"

"I don't know, maybe something is missing in my life. All I do is work from before sunup to after sundown. Maybe what's missing is on the other side."

"What do you mean? What's missing?"

"Pos, I don't know. Maybe I need to learn more about who I am, what I want from life."

"You've got me, honey. Doesn't that count?"

"I don't think this is about you."

They smooch good night and hang up.

Next day they're lying close together on the old mattress on the porch. Prieta sits up and takes a sip from her third cup of té de hojas de naranjal.

"Look, Bar-Su, I went through that pole and I came out ten miles away."

"Sí, yo sé, the book possessed you."

"No, the book was just the trigger. I don't need the book to access the gate or whatever to that other place. It's just a twist of attention, like turning a switch."

"I don't think I want to hear this. Forget the whole thing, LP. It's too dangerous."

"Well, then let's do it together. You're always saying we need to do more stuff together."

"Sure. La gente will really have something to talk about then. Two women who fuck each other now passing into otros mundos. That'll be the absolute limit. We'll get burned alive."

They were quiet for a while.

"Maybe you're right," LP says. "It is dangerous. Unless I can hold on, remember who I am and not get totally sucked in by the other world."

"And how will you do that?"

"I need to be in the two states of mind, here and there, at the same time."

"This is crazy, sweetheart. I'm starting to get really concerned about you. You don't have time to be taking these trips. You barely get any sleep as it is," says Bar-Su.

"I'm not crazy, this is really happening. Time doesn't matter. I mean, I sort of step out of time. At first I was gone for three hours—that's how long it took me to read the book. The second and the third rereadings took me less time. And this fourth rereading, I got ahead of myself."

"What do you mean?"

"It was night when I fell through and I got to your mom's place in the afternoon. Of the same day. See? I didn't lose time, I gained it."

After Bar-Su leaves, LP finishes her cup of té. The nausea is gone. She walks around the house, poking her hands in the air and in the walls, trying to find a spot that feels different. She doesn't have to go through walls. There are veins, streams, currents, or whatever, all around. When she finds one she'll just lean into it and end up near wherever she wants.

She goes outside and walks around in circles for an hour, holding out her hands here and there.

A rock or a leaf will do—if she just . . . really looks at it. Bo runs up to her, barking. Of course. Should she do it? She's afraid. And exhausted. Tomorrow, yes, mañana she'll try. She walks to the tool shed, picks up the hammer and saw and goes back inside the house, the screen door snapping shut behind her.

The dining room doorway frames the door to the living room and the mirror on the opposite wall reflects three more doorways where there should actually only be two. Which wall should she take apart first?

Translations

en el agua: in the water

cagada: shit

la Tigra: the Tiger (the name of LP's ranch)

la tierra: the land

la cara de su casa: the face of her house

las ramas de mesquite: the branches of mesquite

chicharras: cicadas

la pared: the wall

la puerta: the doorway, or door

algo: something

huesos: bones

de cada cuarto: of each room

el espejo: the mirror

de la sala: in the living room

entremados: support beams or spaces between the walls

nervios: nerves

vengo tarde: I'm late

¿Quiúbo corazón?: What's up sweetheart?

¿Tienes hambre?: Are you hungry?

Sí, pero no por comida: Yes, but not for food.

mi Prietita consentida con los ojos soñadores: my beloved Prietita
   with the dreamy eyes

Ay qué fresca.: My but you're fresh.

ruca: pachuco word for girl

pa' no gastar tiempo: so I wouldn't waste any time

la cama: the bed

tetas: tits

pero tu panocha y gusanito están a toda madre: but your pussy
   and clit are hot shit

el trabajo te está matando: the work is killing you

deja eso: leave that

querida: dear, lover

aquí: here

el cabrón: that asshole

y tu familia: and your family

novia: girlfriend, lover

mi pobre madrecita: my poor mama

la siembra: the sowing

dos pinches horas: two fucking hours

la luz de la luna: the moonlight

en el sueño una mujer: in the dream a woman

es el libro: is the book

papas con chorizo: potatoes with chorizo

mamagrande: grandmother

cempazuchitl: a kind of morning glory called "flowers for the dead"

antes de que se de cuenta: before she realizes it

jíjole: shit, damn

ándale: come on

vámanos: let's go

la vaca: the cow

las chichis: tits

abuelos: grandparents

la puerta de la cerca: the gate in the fence

venga por favor, dueña de la tierra: come here please, lady of the land

el palo verde: the palo verde tree

el camposanto: the cemetery

Se halla entre paredes.: She finds herself between walls.

¡Epa!: (exclamation)

primas: cousins (female)

chingao: fucked

la otra pared: the other wall

familiares: family members

tierra y sol: land and sun

zancudos y mosquitos y el sol: mosquitos and flies and the sun

chinga tu madre: literally fuck your mother

¿en dónde lo escondió?: where are you hiding it?

adelita: a Mexican revolutionary woman

por favor: please

primo: cousin (male)

marimacha: tomboy or dyke

sembradora: seeder

monte: woods, thicket, chaparral

una de las otras: one of them

Ese libro desgraciado me va a volver loca.: That no-good book is
    going to drive me nuts.

y este pinche sol: and this goddamn sun

con leche: with milk

todo el: all the

se va de un: moved from one

Diosa mía: my Goddess

si se da la cosecha: if the harvest turns out well

chinpiotes: damn

una santa: a saint

así es la vida: thus is life

la pick-up: pick-up

tiene miedo: is afraid

pero no es nada: but it's nothing

El mal aire le había entrado, es todo.: The bad spirits had entered her, that's all.

Algo le había entrado.: Something had gotten into her.

curandera: healer

jefita: little boss (in the feminine)

Quiúbole jefa, vine a ver si quieres que trabaje mañana.: What's up boss, I came to see if you want me to work tomorrow.

No te voy a necesitar.: I'm not going to need you.

Quiero que comiences muy de mañanita.: I want you to start early in the morning.

¿Qué miras?: What are you looking at?

Nada, jefa. ¿Y si llueve?: Nothing, boss. And if it rains?

quiero que me ayudes a fix esa pinche pick-up: I want you to help me fix that goddamn truck

Bueno, jefa. Ojalá que no llueva porque si llueve vas a perder toda la cosecha. ¿Qué tienes, 'tas enferma?: Alright, boss. Hopefully it won't rain. Hopefully you won't lose your harvest. What's the matter? Are you sick?

Es que me desvelé anoche.: It's just that I stayed up late last night.

caliche: coarse rock used on dirt roads

lo no invitado: not invited

ceniza: ash

chin: damn

brasas: coals

pero no hay otra alma: but there is no other soul

manos: hands

tres peras peladas: three peeled pears

y su ranchito: and her little ranch

el silencio: the silence

y otra pared: and another wall

la cosecha: the harvest

Chinga tu madre: fuck your mother

es la noche del tigre: it's the night of the tiger

Tláloc, diosito del agua: the god of water

linda: pretty

¿qué pasó?: what happened?

en el otro lugar: in the other place

gracias a diosita: thank Goddess

fue bien fácil: it was so easy

me cagué de miedo: I was so scared, I shit my pants

en ese otro lugar: in that other place

té de hojas de naranja: orange leaf tea

sí, yo sé: yes, I know

la gente: the people

otros mundos: other worlds

mañana: tomorrow

16

Like a Crow on the Wing /
Como urraca en vuelo

No cries cuervos porque te sacan los ojos.
Do not raise crows because they may pick out your eyes.

—Mexican saying

I sit on the love seat aquí by the window holding the smashed sculpture on my lap and wait. The moon floats across the sky, slips behind the twisted cypress on top of the cliff whose feathered fingers, black like crow feathers, penetrate the sky. It watches over the fizzing dark waters of the bay. The reflection on the window-pane es mi otra cara.

A knock on the door. Es ella. Es ella que da un toque.

Oh, it's you, comadre. I was expecting . . . no importa. Pásele con confianza, uste' está en su casa. I'm glad you came by. I was beginning to think you didn't want to answer my phone calls.

Sí, I know you've been busy. Come, let's sit by the window. Rearranged the furniture? No, pues, actually I did move the love-seat to the window. Algo pa' tomar, comadre? Or maybe you'd like un taquito?

Here you are, comadre, un cafecito con leche just the way you like it. How long has it been? Months since we've a good chisme session.

Nine months? That long. No te han dicho how I made a fool of myself?

No? I thought I was the talk of the town. You really must have kept to yourself all these months. OK, I'll tell you. Maybe talking about her will help me cope con su engaño y su traición. Sí, traición, comadre, don't look so startled. If I didn't know you better I'd think that you. . . . Never mind, comadre.

What? Oh, thank you, I guess this place does look more like a home now. I tell you, comadre, I wish my nidito was a skylit aerie high up in that cedar tree. Yes, the tall one in my yard. You know how I've always lived in the cerebral zones, en el mundo de la mente. Above it all. But after she came into my life ese lugar alto lost its appeal.

Once she coaxed me back into my body—¡ay, 'manita! el espíritu, alma, y carne se juntaron en ese lugar. What a high that is. Once I learned to live en el cuerpo and attend to its needs I was hooked. The life of the mind is a narrow road, I realized, leading in one direction. Now that she's gone, I want it back—to be alive every second instead of missing it all by being in my head. If I can't have it all—a life of the mind and spirit and not just the flesh—then I'll take nothing.

With Chema . . . What?

Yes, her name is Chema. You're perking up. ¿La conoces? I can't hear you, what did you say?

Oh. Yes, she was a stranger in town, just passing through. We ran into each other. Literally. Bumped into each other at the Queer Delites cafe and bookstore. She was looking at the housing board. Our eyes met. Such fierceness in her eye—the look of a hawk. My instinct for survival told me to belly up—play dumb and uninterested, freeze, play dead. My pride wouldn't let me. I tell you, comadre, esta vanidad y orgullo were my downfall.

I could not look away from esos ojos de caza, her eyes of a hunter. Before I knew it, I was treating her to a double chai. We talked about Chavela Vargas, you know the Mexican dyke singer, and about who was and who wasn't, and some about art. She said she'd been involved with several artists, but none of them had lasted long. We talked until they booted us out. In the end I told her she could crash at my place. Temporarily. Until she found lodgings. She was only going to be in town for two weeks.

Anyway, cómo te estaba diciendo, with Chema me volví una hambrienta. She brought out my hunger. Before, I used to exist just to exist, ate without tasting the food. She woke my appetite for life, for everything. It shames me to admit it but I was just passing time, not living it. But I'm getting ahead of este cuentito.

Where was I? Oh, yes, el cuerpo—what a problem it's always been for me. Until now I thought of it as *the* body and not my body. It was tierra desconocida, where unnamed desires wrestled unceasingly, the mind trying to shut off the feelings, the emotions in full revolt, first pushing back and then retreating. Before Chema el cerebro controlled los hambres. After Chema, I realized que este cuerpo had been tierra abierta all along and that I fooled myself into thinking I had it covered, that I had a place to hide. But all I'd done was shut my eyes. Typical, huh? La urraca playing dead. ¿Qué dices, comadre?

Ah, tienes razón. Será porque soy mexicana—we're not supposed to have sexual feelings, but we can yell at each other and scream over any little slight or put down.

As you told me once when you felt I put distance between us, you said I erect walls between me and my feelings. You're right, comadre, but how else am I going to protect myself? Huh? OK, protective coloration. Blending in with the browns and dull oranges of the autumn foliage.

Yeah, I know. Instead, I stick out like a crow, my voice is different, it cackles. I'm too dark to be overlooked. Skin's too thin, everything comes in. I'm wounded to the bone by the slightest slur. Fea Urraca Prieta, the kids called me. You remember how I'd run from the playground crying, go hide in the library, blow my nose and lose myself in a book and zass—I'd escape my tormentors and their noisy world.

As I got older, I learned to fight back. Como la urraca, I may be stocky, but I have powerful legs. I may not run quickly, but I can claw. Los huercos malos who intruded on my space, forcing me out of the clouds, sure learned that. You were always shocked, comadre. Such fierceness erupting out of a timid little mocosita.

The nickname stuck—Urraca fits me. I was born in the month of the Crow, the season of falling leaves when nature prepares for sleep, when animals anticipate winter and thicken their bodies with fat, when the west wind brings clarity and the dusk brings tranquility.

Yeah, maybe you're right. I should have played with words instead of with clay. But I'm getting sidetracked.

Up until six months ago that was what my life was like—clear and tranquil. The dedicated loner living in a lonely outpost junto al mar trying to push away the business of daily life. I lived on memories of fantasy.

Pero como la urraca, I am not by nature a loner—just been forced into one. For years I managed to elude esas rucas who came sniffing around me. Who looked at me with smoldering eyes. I'd shut down the answering rush and pretend I hadn't seen it.

Oh, I'm sure some saw through my act, even sensed my hiding place. They thought they'd followed me to my nest. I let them think that. But all they had breached was the outer chamber; all they had seen was the mask. Las foolie. The older I got, the less they got of me. I tricked them. I'd expose a secret piece of me, and they thought que me había encuerado.

What is that look for, comadre? Do you strip down to the bare bone?

Those few who got through my first defenses were alike in some ways. They talked commitment and sharing and processing. And forever. Do you know, comadre, what letting someone in that close means? Pain. Noches oscuras del alma. No thanks. I wanted to live in the sun-filled upper reaches forever. If they wanted half of me or less, I'd take them on. But let me tell you, I didn't believe in happily ever after. They didn't have a hope in heaven of taming this mexicanita.

Then came Chema. Listen. What's that sound?

Oh, just the pines rubbing their limbs. Sorry.

Let's see. That first night she spent with me se atrepó allí al árbol. Esa Chema found her way up into my nest, all the way to the innermost cavern, a secret place I hadn't known about or that I pretended I hadn't known. She ripped right through.

I don't know why I let her touch me, comadre. I was terrified. More scared than I'd been the first time with a man. I can retreat under my skin with a man and he can't come near me. Pero esa mujer, she not only knew where to find me deep down en esa cueva—she knew why I hid. She homed in on the pulsing deep in the red slippery cave of my body. Knew exactly how to coax me out.

What attracted her to me? Oh, comadre, if only I knew I could get her back, steal her from that slut that took her from me. Oh, I'm sorry, comadre. My bitterness shocks you.

Let me think. Maybe it was my camouflage that caught her eye. I remember her saying that in concealment I most revealed myself. Her hands and mouth shattered the spell, I slammed my body against the shell I'd built around me until I'd cracked it open myself. Yes, shock must have registered in my eyes and given me away right at the beginning. Or maybe it was the flapping of wings when she flushed me out. She had taken the lid off and now she had vested interests. How? You want all the little details. My, what a voyeur you are, comadre. I'd never noticed this about you. Wait, I'll get to that later.

Chema was in. She'd taken squatter's rights. If she stayed long enough, ownership would automatically become hers. Oh, it wasn't her fault. Being possessive is supposed to show real love. We had a relationship; and we were a couple. Even outlaw queers have a hard time struggling against merger. You know all about that, comadre. I heard your novia left you for another woman, too. I also heard that you have a new sweetie and that you've got her squirreled away. That must be why you've been fidgeting all evening—you're probably anxious to return to her. Listen, comadre, I won't keep you long. I'll try to hurry through the rest of esta historia. You can tell me all about tu amorcito nuevo next time if you need to leave soon.

Yes, comadre, my own motivations are even more a mystery to me. I don't know how I let her in. Maybe because she seemed familiar, like someone I'd known a long time ago. There was not even a creak from the hinges of my cave door to warn me. Ni un rechinito. She moved inside me and my body smoothed her way. No rust in socket joining thigh to hip. Every limb well-oiled, every part animated itself, rose and fell and moved without instruction from me. Something inside me swelled and let her take over. She took care not to spook me until she had slipped in. Then she got more noisy than the cawing crow in the eaves as she banged around among my things.

She stayed, comadre.

Week after week, month after month.

She didn't even ask. My place was warm and tidy. She liked the wooden lizards on my walls, the rubber snakes on my altars, the candles continuously burning, the smell of copal, las tacitas de té limón . . . and me. Bueno, you know my house has always been my stronghold, my sanctuary. I'd barred all the windows, locked all the doors. Let in only a few, like you, comadre. I checked my tendency to expand beyond the boundaries I'd set.

What? Oh, yeah. I guess esta urraca wanted to break out of its self-imposed jaula long before Chema made her appearance. All that time I thought it was freedom and not fear that kept the door locked. You see, I wasn't accountable to anyone, my life was my own. Ran it exactly the way I wanted. Pero lo que era era un infierno. I got lonely in my cage. The sadness would light and roost, I'd examine it from all sides; when the rock entranced me, I'd know which vein to follow with hammer and chisel. Loneliness, comadre, is like that cypress tree bent to the ground and sculpted by the furious breaths of the sea winds rather than of its own volition.[1]

After Chema moved in I barely touched my sketch pad. The chisels gathered dust, the clay dried up. For the first time in my life I didn't have time for my tools. I spent all my time with her or thinking about her. I felt like I was on vacation with no itinerary, no check-out time, no plane to catch.

---

1. Anzaldúa added here "[More Gothic?]."

Of course, comadre, I felt guilty for not working. My art had been my whole life up till then. Una vocecito por dentro nagged me, "You should be with the clay." From the studio my tree stumps and marble blocks reprimanded me in hushed whispers, urged me to take action.

What did they whisper? Comadre, they wanted me free and independent like before; they wanted me to send her away. Every day they would ask when she was leaving.

Once I had given myself over to her, I could see that I too was a speck in that strain, the lowly human species. I'd fallen, comadre, off my high horse. Joined the rest of you mortals. And to my surprise, I rejoiced that now I was part of the whole, no longer a separate cipher flying at the whim of the wind. For the first time in my life I did not feel alien. Being married to this woman is like jumping into a family album. I belonged, albeit in an unconventional family. There was someone to talk to, laugh with, touch. I couldn't keep my hands off of her. I thought I'd said adios to solitude forever. Yes, you see I thought it would last forever. Excuse me for laughing. Ha, ha. I'd bought it all.

OK, enough. Let me get my breath.

Hysterics? Oh, comadre, don't you think I'm entitled. I mean this is the worst fate that can befall a Chicana. Abandonment. Betrayal. That bitch me chingó rete bien.

Si, tú lo sabes.

Oh, comadre, you can't be wanting to go so soon? I haven't finished my cuento. Don't you want to know how it all went down? Here, let me refill your cup and get you some pan dulce. What? Oh, your poor tummy.

Where was I? Oh, yes. It didn't take us long to merge. I was no longer me, and she was not sure we were an "us." I hated the quarrels, the broken windows—this pane here, this is the third replacement. The holes gouged in the walls—over there, comadre. I've left those to remind me of how bad it got. But it doesn't seem to help because I still want her back. Anyway, I, who am usually mild-mannered, became a crazed thing. I spit on her face, I stomped my feet, waved my fists. Amidst the melodrama, I wanted her; I still wanted to please her.

Marriage with this woman was like canoeing down the rapids. I never knew when a rock would gash a hole in the boat or when we'd come to the edge of a precipice and plunge over the edge. Every day was a risk. Exhilarating. Like I told you, I was hooked.

And you know what, comadre? Once she had me in the palm of her hand, she blew me off.

What made her stay that long? Oh, comadre, I do have some redeeming qualities. Or maybe it was the chase that had captivated her. Anyway, once I was caught, the hunter lost interest. Maybe my eagerness to please her drove her away. Or maybe she just didn't like staying in one place. But I'm sure it was the other woman.

Yeah, me volvió loca trying to figure it out. I tried to lose myself in the rings of the tree stump I was cutting. In the piece of driftwood, weathered and tanned, I looked at for weeks until it evoked a figure of a bird. I picked up some crow feathers, drilled tiny holes in the wood and inserted the feathers, and I had a crow on the wing, beak pointing at the sky, dreaming of flight.[2]

Incomplete. Before her, I'd been content. Contained in myself. Encrusted, nearly fossilized. Life passed transparently through me. Then she came, presented it to me. When she left it wouldn't leave. I got to know it quite well, the species of it, its varying shades. Now every night it gnaws un pozo in my heart, refuses to feed on the past, hungers for now and for future. Now life's a blade to be kissed into pieces to keep it from cutting my tongue, a bloodletting.

Mouths opened wide, beaks picking off pulgas out of each other's feathers, nibbling the long cords of each other's necks. I had no antidote. Chema had been bitten so often—I was her twelfth lover—she'd built up an immunity.

¿Qué dices? Yes, she's had twelve lovers. You look doubtful.

---

2. Anzaldúa wrote here "[More landscape specifics?]."

Como quiera, I was heady with this unqualified access to another body—so much power is scary. But she also had unqualified access to my body and that's scarier.

Mesmerized, stumbling over my feet, I fell into sus ojos de halcón. No hay mejor cosa que cazar con halcones.

She licked my armpits, stroked my labia. My hands traced her jutting hipbones, the smooth flesh between belly and breasts. I stared at the abyss between her legs, the furry entrance. Put my nose there and smelled her. Ay comadre, the animal moved inside me. Before Chema I'd induced all my orgasms with the help of a vibrator. Now, she controlled my movements and I was at her mercy.[3]

The shock of it forced me out of my body. From above, I watched the two women on the bed. At first I did not recognize myself. Tremors rocked me as my pelvis breathed in and out. I was hyperventilating. Then, I was back in my body. Boca seca como mazorca, I kept swallowing. But I couldn't put out the fire Chema had lit in the cave where fire originates.

I blossomed; everyone said so. My family was amazed at my jokes and laughter, my new set of clothes, no more mousey colors, reds and purples, turquoises and yellows. I hauled away black crow attire to Goodwill.

We'd been together a few months when one morning she walked out the door, an overnight bag swinging from her shoulder. Not one word from her until three weeks later when she walked back in the door.

An urge to take a trip, she told me. No other reason. No secret motive, no hidden agenda, just that she wanted no marriage, no coupledom.

I didn't believe her, comadre. Would you? No, you don't have to answer that. I can see it's making you uncomfortable. You've

---

3. At the beginning of this paragraph, Anzaldúa wrote "[Should this scene appear earlier? Where?]."

been acting sort of . . . Never mind. Oh, you're wondering about this smashed sculpture. Soon, I'll get to this part.

After that I was afraid she would walk out the door, any second. Leave me for that puta she'd met. Afraid she'd get tired of me, which before had suited me just fine I'd thought until she actually did go away. I know she'd liked that about me: my not clinging.

The second time she let me know the night before. I begged her not to go. I cried, threw a tantrum next morning and clung to her. A child clinging to her mother, comadre, so she dragged me across the room, out the door and down the front steps. I was pitiful.

After she left, I couldn't seem to get enough air in my lungs, she'd taken all the oxygen. I fell on the cement walk and must have passed out. When I came to, I was stiff and sore. I knew she'd gone to her.

Sure, comadre, I'm bitter. Wouldn't you be? If I ever find out who the other woman is, I'll claw her eyes out. Oh, comadre, don't look at me that way.

Fingertips, tongue, nose, belly—all of me needed her. It was like I was suffering from withdrawal. Que brusco arrebato me dio—una patada al corazón que me dejó en rodillas. Rage pulled me down into this animal body, this nagual.

Yeah, that was six months ago. Chema moved out. I became a shadow of the woman who had waltzed around and around my studio. The family took it hard. They had been so happy to see me out in public and in the company of someone, even if that someone was not a man.

Ay, comadre. Why had I not been with a woman for so long? Now, after a long drought, my lover could never attend to me enough to appease my thirst. Pero, tú sabes, thirst increases with drinking, appetite grows fiercer with feeding. The animal appetites overpower their trainer. Ahora yo soy la pájara enjaulada—I am the caged beast. Fíjate como me ha desmadrado.

You know what it feels like, when your lover leaves you? Like the top layer of your skin has been flayed off and the flesh tenderized. If she so much as breathed within a foot of me, I caught flame like dry grass. Even now when I'm out doing errands and I think I see her, arms and hips swaying loosely in that pachuca strut, blood shoots up and sinks and pools on my lower belly. When I realize that it's just some macho, the blood drains down my body, leaving my arms and legs weak. I have to sit or lean against a wall until I recover.

You see, comadre, my desire is so strong it resurrects her image everywhere. Una vez la miré desde una banco del parque. The world stops breathing, all sound fades and my lower belly clenches. My ears hear her footsteps where no sounds ring. Memories flutter around me—Chema laughing, splashing water from the fountain, a film only I can see.

It's been six months and she's not come back to me.

Why did she leave me? She wanted me married to her but didn't want to be married to me.

The things I couldn't bear about her at first, now in her absence I've begun to cherish. She snorted when she didn't like something I did or said. She slurped her coffee.

Desire was the game. And how to satisfy it. Love, as Aleister Crowley said, must be done "under will." But how could I have acted "under will" when I could not discern between passion and principle.

My body had been dead to all the world, no energy had nourished it. I'd lived on weeds, but after you've eaten oats your appetite for weeds is gone for good. Pleasure was a luxury I could not afford. Now, I have no choice, it's become a necessity. Abandoned. Utterly. Felt like I was dying. But once the numbness passed, I raged like a wild beast. You can't do this to me, bitch! I put on a black dress and sat through the nights in vigil over this corpse I called our love. I waited. De rato en rato me asomaba a la ventana. Waited at the window, waited for her. Miraba mi cara desvelada en el vidrio de la ventana. I stared at that face. ¿Qué era lo que quería revelar? I shook my head, "descansa la mente, sonsa," I said to myself. Haz algo, cualquier cosa, lava las vasijas, scrub the walls. Madre Dios, muévete. I kicked the blanket a un lado.

At night es cuando la hecho de menos más. I live with the presence of that animal, desire, constantly moving from my womb to my heart. I feel it peck, peck, pecking my heart. Feel something inside me break. Feel a rupture in the stranglehold. Comadre, every day I look out the window till my eyes swim, see my face reflected in the fogged windowpane. Chema was the mirror where I'd found my other face, la otra cara en el espejo. She'd loosened a hunger to merge that fought my odd self. The hunger won. Nothing but her presence could assuage it. I had driven her away yes, but, then, she was prone to wander.

What, comadre? You don't agree with me? But how would you know? You don't know her.

You do know her.

I can see it in your eyes.

What is it that you're not telling me, comadre? Don't try to protect me. I couldn't hurt any worse.

A numbness settles over my body. I feel like stone. This too will pass. It is a middle ground I seek now, freedom in captivity. Freedom in the wilds is an illusion. A cross between the bird in the cage and the one in the wilds is what I want.

It is a sacrifice I'm working on. A compromise is always a sacrifice. Any way you look at it something gets lost.

Look, comadre. There's a large fire burning en la orilla del pueblo. Voy a abrir la ventana y sacar la cabeza. I see smoke writhing like a serpent. Yes, that's the smell of tires burning. I'll shut the window. Something fell off the sill. Mira, comadre, the obsidian you gave me and that I placed here so I could look at it. When you gave it to me you said it was a stone with a watchful vibration, remember? You said if I gazed into its depths I would find my nature.

No, don't look away, comadre. What's that in your eyes? Oh, why don't you look at me? Why do you say you're sorry? Oh, I get it. You're she—the other woman. You. You stole my love from me, desgraciada. Why am I raising the stone over my head? Why, to hit you with.

You're not the thirteenth lover now; you're just a bloody face on the floor. What right have you to stare at me with reproach in your stark unblinking eyes? It was you, comadre, you betrayed me.

Your blood's all over the stone. A red cactus flower that blooms once a year. I'm not cleaning the blood off, nor putting the rock back on the windowsill. I don't think I'd like the face it might reflect.

Let me think. Yes, I'll bury it with you. Oh, I have a better idea. I'll dig a hole under the cedar. No, not until it's really dark and everyone is asleep. I'll go out now and turn on the sprinkler. Soften the hard soil.

Ah, the moon's disappeared behind the house. Where is that shovel?

At last. Let me rake over it and clean up, wash the dirt off my hands and the red blossom off the obsidian stone. I may need it again.

I sit on the love seat, peer out the window, wait for her.

I put the stone between my legs. Cool. Getting warmer. A heart pulsing. Palpitating between mis piernas.

On the horizon, faint edges of the dawn emerge. Los perros ladran. A woman howls in the night. La llorona aullando.

Algo se desprende de las sombras—someone's emerging from the shadows.

Come in Chema, pásale. I left the door open—I knew you'd come.

Yes, I know why you're here. Yes, I know you're not staying. You're wondering why la comadre didn't come home.

No, she's not here, not anymore. She's run off with la pelona, her new novia. Ha, ha.

Who's la pelona? Don't you know? Here, why don't you sit down? Maybe I'll tell you.

What do I have in my hands? Oh, it's just something mi comadre gave me a long time ago. Would you like a closer look?

I'm fine. I survived.

After you left I missed you so much, missed that delicious sharing of secretos. Ardía por ti como una loca enamorada. My fingers pulsed for you every night, hungering to mold your flesh. Before you came into my life they had throbbed to mold clay. One day I made a bust of your head and prayed you would leave her and come back to me. I prayed for months.

Then one night as I stared at your bust, whispering, "Chema, Chema," I saw spots before my eyes, bright flashes and a slow burning. I'd never been so angry—my eyes throbbed with it. I picked up a hammer and as I hit you again and again, I felt a loosening in all my joints, felt the blood rushing fiercely. I was dead clay coming to life, a dead crow flying. Calm down, baby, it was clay I smashed. What am I going to do now?

After tonight I'll wait till I come back to myself. Like a crow on the wing, I must find my point of balance.

No, for a woman of excesses it won't be easy—yo juego todo aunque lo pierdo.[4]

Branches sway with the wind. Leaves whisper. I know the red sky's loneliness, the peacock's cry, the wind's howl, the pain of parting. I watch the moon drag itself across the sky. The moon is in my mouth and you will never come.

Todo se paga en la vida.

One pays for everything in life, or what goes around comes around.

—Mexican saying

Translations

aquí: here

es mi otra cara: is my other face

Es ella. Es ella que da un toque.: It's her. She's knocking.

---

4. Here Anzaldúa wrote "[End here?]."

no importa: it's not important

Pásele con confianza, uste' está en su casa.: Come in (with trust),
     my house is your house.

sí: yes

pues: well

algo pa' tomar: something to drink

un taquito: tortilla filled with meat or beans or whatever is on hand

un cafecito con leche: coffee with milk

chisme: gossip

no te han dicho: hasn't anyone told you

con su engaño y su traición: with her treachery and her betrayal

nidito: little nest

en el mundo de la mente: in the world of the mind

ese lugar alto: that high region

¡ay, 'manita!: oh, sister!

el espíritu, alma, y carne: the spirit, soul, and flesh

en el cuerpo: in the body

¿La conoces?: Do you know her?

esta vanidad y orgullo: that vanity and pride

esos ojos de caza: those eyes of a hunter

cómo te estaba diciendo: as I was telling you

me volví una hambrienta: I became a starving person

este cuentito: this story

el cuerpo: the body

tierra desconocida: unknown terrain

el cerebro: the mind

los hambres: the hungers

que este cuerpo: that this body

tierra abierta: open land

la urraca: the crow

¿Qué dices?: What are you saying?

tienes razon: you may be right

será porque soy mexicana: maybe because I'm Mexican

Fea Urraca Prieta: ugly black crow

como la urraca: like the crow

los huercos malos: the mean kids

mocosita: little snot nose

junto al mar: by the sea

pero: but

esas rucas: pachuco Spanish for females

las foolie: Spanglish for "I fooled them"

que me había encuerado: that they had stripped me (of clothes)

noches oscuras del alma: dark nights of the soul

se atrepó allí al árbol: she climbed up the tree

pero esa mujer: but this woman

en esa cueva: in that cave

novia: girlfriend

esta historia: this history

tu amorcito nuevo: your new little love

ni un rechinito: not even a little creak

copal: incense

las tacitas de té limón: the cups of lemon tea

bueno: well

esta urraca: this crow

jaula: cage

lo que era era un infierno: what it was was hell

una vocecita por dentro: a small inner voice

adios: good-bye

me chingó rete bien: she fucked me up good

Sí, tú lo sabes.: Yes, you know it.

cuento: story

pan dulce: sweet bread

me volvió loca: I went crazy

un pozo: a well

pulgas: fleas

¿Qué dices?: What are you saying?

como quiera: anyway

sus ojos de halcón: her eyes like a hawk

No hay mejor cosa que cazar con halcones.: There is no better
   thing than hunting with hawks.

boca seca como mazorca: mouth like a dry corn husk

puta: whore

Que brusco arrebato me dió.: What a brutal blow it gave me.

una patada al corazón que me dejó en rodillas: a kick to the heart that felled me to my knees

nagual: animal familiar

pero, tú sabes: but you know

Ahora yo soy la pájara enjaulada.: Now I am the caged bird.

Fíjate como me ha desmadrado.: Look how she's ruined me.

Una vez la miré desde una banco del parque.: Once I saw her from a park bench.

De rato en rato me asomaba a la ventana.: From time to time I would look out the window.

Miraba mi cara desvelada en el vidrio de la ventana.: I saw my sleepless face in the windowpane.

¿Qué era lo que quería revelar?: What was it trying to reveal?

descansa la mente, sonsa: rest your mind, dummy

haz algo, cualquier cosa, lava las vasijas: do something, anything, wash the dishes

Madre Dios, muévete.: Mother God, move.

a un lado: aside

es cuando la hecho de menos más: is when I miss her the most

la otra cara en el espejo: the other face in the mirror

en la orilla del pueblo: on the edge of town

Voy a abrir la ventana y sacar la cabeza.: I'm going to open window and stick my head out.

mira: look

desgraciada: disgraced

mis piernas: my legs

los perros ladran: the dogs bark

la llorona aullando: the wailing woman

Algo se desprende de las sombras: Something comes out of the shadows

pásale: come on in

la pelona: the bald one, vernacular for death

secretos: secrets

Ardía por ti como una loca enamorada.: I burned for you like a crazed woman in love.

yo juego todo aunque lo pierdo: I'll risk everything

17

Ghost Trap / Trampa de espanto

At first Úrsula la Prieta had been devastated by the death of her husband. She had thrown her plump short body into the grave on top of his coffin shrieking, "Ay viejito! ¿por qué me dejaste? Yo te quería tanto. I loved you so much!" Everyone else was dry-eyed. In between sobs she heard someone say, "Hasta que se lo llevo el diablo al miserable." Another said, "Let him burn in hell." She only wept louder. For days she wailed. People felt skeptical, then uneasy at the drama and started referring to her as "la Llorona."

"It's not like he treated you that good," her comadre reminded her.

Often she would wake in the middle de la noche in a sweat, the echo de su grito/llanto still throbbing in her throat and feeling like the atmosphere. Her house was not the same. She would turn to him to be consoled, not that he would soothe her with a calm voice—he had only paid attention to her si quería algo. But she missed cushioning his skinny body and his sharp hip bones and knees. The presence de otro cuerpo had been a source of comfort in the silence of the night. Upon opening her eyes, she would find the bed empty. She would pace from room to room at night think-ing about him and feeling numb and decepcionada. Gradually her loneliness soured and her grief turned into anger. Why, why, why had he deserted her? Actually, his liver had deserted her. Cirrhosis.

One night, two months after his death, a snoring woke her up. Se despertó to find him, or rather his ghost, in bed with her.

"¡Viejo!" she cried out, astounded. She smiled for the first time since his death. She reached for him, then suddenly drew back her hand and clutched her corazón.

Durante el día he would follow her around the house, but only her steps creaked the floorboards. She was amazed at just how small her house had gotten. He dogged her steps or hovered nearby while she hoed up and down the rows and rows of corn, squash, and beans of her immense jardín. Still, he would never go beyond the front gate when she left to do her mandados. She began to spend more time in the homes of her comadres o se iba a pasear con ellas.

"Ay, Doña Úrsula, you never used to spend time chismiando with us," said one of her comadres.

"Sí, comadrita y a hora tú eres la alcahuete."

After a couple of weeks, as they were in the living room watching TV, she asked him, "Viejo, why do you keep coming back every night? Did you forget something? Did you leave something unfinished? Is there some business you want to complete? Tell me y yo te ayudo a hacerlo. If only you'd tell me what you want."

"Vieja, prietita linda, bring me clean clothes." His voice was thin as a trail of smoke.

"Ba, estás muerto, you're dead ¿pa' qué necesitas ropa?" she whispered back. He repeated his request, his voice getting louder and louder, finally driving her to the closet. Of course his clothes were missing, she'd given them away. Now she would have to go into the shop to buy men's things and face the look of censure on the shopkeeper's face at how fast she had replaced her marido con otro pelado.

"Vieja, vieja, fix me some dinner," he said in a harsh mutter. Le guisó carnitas, his favorite dish, and set it on the table. But a ghost can't eat so the comida sat on the table gathering moscas. "Vieja, viejita linda, traime una cerveza." Off she would go to la tiendita de la esquina to get the beer. La gente de la colonia began to talk about how her grief had driven her to drink. She would pull the tab and place the can of beer en la mesa by "his" chair. "You know I only drink Tecate," he growled. But a ghost can't drink.

The beer would go flat. She was tempted to drink his cerveza to alleviate her increasing irritation.

Instead she thought of all the cositas she would make with popsicle sticks. She would give them away as gifts or sell during fiesta days. She would make altar pieces, frames to hold photos of dead ancestors. She would paint them with bright colors.

Tending to his ghost seemed to take all her time. She began to resent the time she had spent washing and cooking and trimming his hair and toenails when el pelado had been alive. She realized that she missed her solitude. Hadn't he made her feel wanted and protected? Well, now his constant presence stifled her. Just when she thought herself free, el pendejo was back and even more trouble than when he was alive. Her only consolation was that she didn't have to wash his smelly calcetines and dirty underwear. She had been two months without him. Pero su nueva vida de dos semanas sin él ya no era suya. She wanted her new life back. Yes, now that she was free of taking care of others, now that she lived alone, now that she had time to get together with las comadres things were different. Now, how was she going to stop her marido muerto from returning?

One day inspiration brought a smile to her face. She made a little model of her house with popsicle sticks and glue and placed it in a safe spot half-way between his grave in the nearby camposanto and her home. One of her comadres had told her that ghosts have no sense of perspective. Her chair creaked on the porch as she waited and rocked, hoping el espanto would enter the model house thinking it was hers.

That night nothing woke her. In the morning cuando despertó she turned toward the side where su viejo had been sleeping the past thirty years. His ghost was not there, nor was it there the following night. While she didn't want it to return, she had a feeling it would come back and waited all nerviosa for it to appear. But suppose someone found la casita and accidentally opened the door and let the ghost out. Some element of nature—a strong wind or a fire—could destroy the flimsy cage and her dead husband would get out. The tiny house was too fragile to be buried—the earth would crush it and the ghost would escape. She went to where she had left la casita and barred the door with a popsicle stick. Now she had to put it somewhere safe and out of the reach of others.

After several days of deliberation, she carefully carried the ghost trap into her house and placed it under the bed where mischievous nietos would not find it.

That night a voice woke her. It called out, no longer at a whisper, "Vieja, vieja todavía estás buenísima. Ándale, déjame probar ese cuerpazo. Let me touch ese cuerpo exquisito." El pelado chiflado was back. She thought she felt his body stirring under the bedcovers. Half dreaming, half awake, she pushed him away, saying "Vete viejo aguado." But he kept climbing on top of her.

"I wish you were alive so I could wring your neck." Both were surprised by the sharpness in her voice.

"You shouldn't talk to me like that."

"Why not? You've always said mean things to me."

All night she refused to open her legs to him.

The next morning she woke with deep grooves down the corners of her mouth and bruises on her breasts, arms, and inner thighs. She peered under la cama and saw that the mattress had squished the cage forcing the door to crack open. She walked from room to room looking for el pinche desgraciado and muttering to herself. "¡Ya me voy a deshacer de ese cabrón!" She considered going to the local curandera and asking her to drive his soul into el pozo, better yet, al infierno. Huh, or she could look through the yellow pages to find an hechicera.

Ah, no, if my loneliness has summoned him, my anger will drive him away. I'll do it myself, she said to herself. "Afuera desgraciado. Get out of here. Be gone you ghost. If you don't leave te voy a maldecir."

Just in case her words failed, she plugged in the vacuum cleaner and put it by her bed. To make it harder for his hands to reach her body, she tugged on two of her sturdiest corsets, several pairs of pants and three shirts, turned off the lights, and got into bed. Almost immediately she jumped out of bed to fetch her heavy sartén just in case he'd taken on more substance than the vacuum could handle. But if the suction wouldn't get him maybe the noise would drive him back to the cemetery and into the other world. She hid it under las cobijas. "Come on cabrón, hijo de la chingada, vente pendejo," she said under her breath. "Viejito, viejito lindo, come into my bed. I'm waiting for you," dijo con voz de sirenita.

She saw his ghostly body edge cautiously into the room. "¿No estás enojada, viejita?" he asked softly.

"¡Apúrate viejo! Que te quiero dar algo."

Translations

Ay viejito ¿por qué me dejaste? Yo te quería tanto.: Why did you leave me old man? I loved you so much.

Hasta que se lo llevo el diablo al miserable: Until the devil took the miserable old man

la Llorona: the weeping woman

comadre: co-mother, close female friend

de la noche: at night

de su grito/llanto: of her cries

si quería algo: if he wanted something

de otro cuerpo: from another body

decepcionada: disillusioned, disenchanted, disappointed

se despertó: she woke up

viejo: old man

corazón: heart

durante el día: during the day

jardín: garden

mandados: errands

o se iba a pasear con ellas: or she'd go for a ride with them

chismiando: gossiping

Sí, comadrita y a hora tú eres la alcahuete.: Yes, friend, and now you're the instigator.

y yo te ayudo a hacerlo: and I'll help you do it

Ba, estás muerto: Agh, you're dead

¿pa' que necesitas ropa?: what do you need clothes for?

marido con otro pelado: husband with another good-for-nothing man

Le guisó carnitas: She cooked him beef seasoned with spices

comida: food

moscas: flies

traime una cerveza: bring me a beer

la tiendita de la esquina: the little corner store

la gente de la colonia: the townspeople

en la mesa: on the table

cositas: small things

el pelado: the good-for-nothing

el pendejo: the stupid asshole

calcetines: socks

Pero su nueva vida de dos semanas sin él ya no era suya.: But her new two-week-old life without him was not hers anymore.

marido muerto: dead husband

camposanto: graveyard

el espanto: ghost

cuando despertó: when she woke up

nerviosa: nervous

casita: the little house

nietos: grandchildren

Todavía estás buenísima. Ándale, déjame probar ese cuerpazo.: You're still really hot. Come on, let me have a taste of that big, beautiful body.

ese cuerpo esquisito: that exquisite body

el pelado chiflado: the scoundrel

Vete viejo aguado.: Go, get away from me you flabby old man. (one with flabby genitals, i.e., who is sexually wasted or worn out)

la cama: the bed

el pinche desgraciado: that no-good son of a bitch

¡Ya me voy a deshacer de ese cabrón!: I'm going to rid myself of that stubborn man!

curandera: healer, medicine woman

el pozo: the hole

al infierno: to hell

hechicera: female sorcerer/witch

afuera desgraciado: get out you damned man

te voy a maldecir: I'm going to curse you

sartén: iron skillet

las cobijas: the bedcovers

cabrón, hijo de la chingada, vente pendejo: you old goat, son of a bitch, come here stupid

viejito lindo: sweet old man

dijo con voz de sirenita: she said with a siren's voice

¿No estás enojada, viejita?: You aren't angry, are you, old lady?

¡Apúrate viejo! que te quiero dar algo.: Hurry up, old man, I want
to give you something.

18

La Werejaguar
in the Woods of the Dream*

Prieta stands near the half-opened window. A beam of light zigzags over the nearby woods. Night air sweeps into the room bringing a rash of goose bumps to her arms and ruffling the gauzy curtains around her as she stares into the woods. Something is moving along the edge of el monte leaving shrubs and grass rustling in its wake. A sound like a deep cough brings her to the edge of remembering. She steps to the window, and, bracing her hands on the sill, she bends down and sticks her head out. The smell of wet dirt and vegetation teases her memory, bringing a whisper of another age, a sound so elusive it's gone before her ears capture it.

Prieta scans the edge of the woods. The moon illuminates a patch of ground, casting mottled patches of light on a feline body stretched out on its belly. ¿Un gato montez? No, a bigger feline, with golden reddish buff. Ears pricked, it lifts its head, nostrils flaring. It smells her, the jaguar of her dreams.

The jaguar rises, then crouches down again. It flattens its ears and opens its jaws. Its deep-chested rattle, followed by a throaty cough, resonates through Prieta's body. "Oh no, not again." She jerks her head back. Eyes fixed on the jaguar, she presses her fingers against her lips. The big feline tenses, poises to spring, and,

---

*Anzaldúa labeled this the ninth version.

313

with tawny, rippling muscles, sprints across the meadow toward her in slow loping leaps.

De volada, the animal crosses her backyard. Hurtling through the air, it scrambles up onto the window box scattering clods of dirt and trampling the zempasuchitl and the morning glories. The weight of the huge cat partly unhinges the plant box, but the posts keep it from collapsing.

Quick, shut the window. Lock it. Step back out of sight. Frozen in place, se queda parada. From two feet away the jaguar stares at her, its yellow eyes burning like coals. Its face looks human. Ay, diosa, tiene cara de mujer, the face in her dreams. She'd know those feverish eyes anywhere, and that musty cat smell. Its penetrating gaze breaks Prieta's paralysis.

Reaching up, she pulls the window down with a bang. She backs away, only to move forward and press her nose against el vidrio. Lightning darts over el monte. She searches the darkness, but the animal is gone. Ni un rugido del jaguar, only the wind keening through the trees, riffling the dead leaves in her backyard.

Wake up, she tells herself, anticipating flinging the down comforter to one side, sliding out of bed, going to the bathroom, running the shower until it steams, then getting in and letting the water pummel her awake. Arching her body and stretching, Prieta tries to get up, but she's not in bed and she's not sleeping. She's out in her patio, the early morning sun is shining, and her imagination is conjuring images that are much too real. What the hell is happening? Is she dreaming a dream while wide awake? She swallows; her mouth is dry as a corn husk.

The lingering yearning throbs in the hollow pit of her stomach. But a yearning for what, for whom? She wants to stuff the yearning, wants to stuff the nagging feeling that maybe she's slowly going out of her mind. Just another Chicana loca slowly becoming more loca. Barefoot, she walks on the cold tile floor, enters her study, concentrating on the soft carpet, the slap of her feet on the hardwood in the living room, and the cool tile in the kitchen.

Minutes later she's still peering blankly into the refrigerator, images of the jaguar running through her head. She turns on the gas burner and holds her hands palm down over the flame to warm them. She puts the comal over the burner, takes a container of leftover salad and the makings for a quesadilla out of the fridge. When el comal is hot she drops a whole wheat tortilla on it. She sprinkles soy cheese and vegetarian chicken over it, tops it with salsa, folds the tortilla, and puts a lid over it. She turns it over and, when the cheese begins to bubble and ooze out, she slips it onto a plate. She grabs the salad and takes the food to the kitchen nook.

A subdued sun slants through the window. She watches how light strikes the gossamer wings of a dragonfly, the light fracturing into overlapping dimensions. Prying open her laptop, she hits the start key, listens to the whirl as it boots up. She begins pecking the keys, stopping at intervals to eat. Her mind wanders away from the grant she's writing. Images of the jaguar flash in her inner eye and she's caught up in the puzzle of why the jaguar keeps appearing in her dreams. Didn't Jung discuss this?

An hour later she hears the click of the key turning, the squeak of the front door as it opens, then slams shut. Teté saunters in. He takes one look at her, strips off his black leather jacket and, flinging it onto the back of a chair, asks, "What's wrong, Prieta?"

"Quiúbole to you too," she says, clicking the moon icon to put the computer on sleep mode.

Teté looks fit and lithe in shocking pink suspenders. His hair is tied back in a queue leaving his ears sticking out. Six small silver hoops shine in one ear. He pulls out a chair and straddles it. Eyes locked with hers, he cocks up one brow and waits.

Prieta takes a deep breath and says, "Teté, la jaguar came to me again. In broad daylight. I was just going about my day when zas, there she was. It felt real, familiar—like it happened before, but I'd forgotten."

"¿A poco?" Teté smiles, his lips canting to one side. "Maybe you fell into one of your deep daydreams."

"It sure didn't feel like a daydream."

"Maybe 'tas encantada. Maybe one of those brujas you pal around with put a spell on you, sent a south-of-the-border jaguar to stalk you."

"Uh-uh, cousin, I don't think so."

"Too easy, huh. Why do you always have to make things hard?" He raises both eyebrows twice saying, "Wink, wink."

"None of that 'hard' stuff. I'm serious, Teté. In the beginning, yeah I daydreamed it like I imagine scenes in a story I'm writing. Then I started dreaming about it. Now the jaguar's out of my inner world and in the real one."

"Are you saying that the jaguar is like a character coming to life?" He winks at her with one of his ojos flojos.

"Uh-uh, she's not a character."

"Yeah, well, imagining is not the same as sensing, mi prietita. Dreams have no objective reality in the waking world. Babita, can't you tell the difference between reality and imagination?" He goes to the fridge and takes out a Tecate.

Though he's trying to be patient with her she hears the exasperation in his voice. "Yeah, I can. After years of meditating, I know whether I'm thinking, feeling, remembering, or fantasizing. Créeme, I know when my attention shifts to something in the 'real' world," Prieta tells him.

"OK, so what you were experiencing was real when it shouldn't have been. Is that what you're saying?"

She watches him raise the beer to his lips, watches his throat swallow. "Yeah, it depends on how you define 'real.' Even if it's my own hallucination, that doesn't mean it isn't real. What goes on in the inner world is as real as what happens in the outer. But I do distinguish between the two. They're both realities, just different intensities, different layers. It's all a matter of how aware you are. Some people are prisoners of their conditioning and only see what their tribe tells them is real."

"OK," he says, staring at her through half-closed eyes. "I'm with you there."

"Good. What I'm worried about is when what I imagine or dream jumps its boundaries and ends up here." She thumps the table. "First it just roamed in my daydreams, then it was stalking me in my dreams at night, and now it's stalking me here, in my own house. How did it leap out of my dream and into this world, and bring the wild with it, the woods and everything?"

"Ya ni la chingues, Prieta. It can't be in both. They're separate realities—one you make up out of images in your head and the one that's made de carne, hueso, y uñas that you can touch with your hands."

She frowns. "What about powerful simulations like virtual reality. Aren't those a little bit of both?"

"Chale, esa. For those you need electronic machines. It's controlled. And you don't confuse the VR with the real one. Not unless you're crazy; only the crazy confuse the two."

Virtual realities: being in two places at once. "Yeah, carnal, but what if some of us border gente don't need electronic equipment to access virtual realities? Why couldn't I have been in both realities at once? Sort of like what happens in a lucid dream." Is that pleading she hears in her voice?

Teté stares at her with his mesmerizing gaze and says, "Most people need the machine and the goggles, Prieta. Are you saying you're some kind of mutant?"

She continues. "No, I'm not saying that. Maybe it's an ability that lies dormant. Anyway, the two realities cross, and maybe they intersect and mix. People are always walking between the real world and the imaginary one, you know, in a nepantla of some kind. You and I, queer freaks like us, know the cracks between the worlds and are able to see both sides of the crack. Some of us are forced into the cracks between the worlds, and some of us choose to live in them."

"You got my number, cracks are my favorite places to bridge." He leers.

"Come on, Teté, I'm trying to have a serious conversation. You know ghosts and spirits inhabit both worlds. Remember when la Llorona appeared to us by the irrigation ditch?"

"Ay mi prietita, something bothers me about this. You're making too much fuss over a make-believe cat. Wasn't she in your bed the last time you dreamed about her?"

"Yeah," she says, looking away.

"I told you, baby, if you want a dream lover look no further." He growls and moves his ears up and down by flexing his jaw. "Aquí está tu mero mero." He thumps his chest with one fist.

"Menso, cochino eres ¿un poco? primo," she says, swatting him on the arm.

He smiled. "Kissing cousins and getting closer by the second. Besides, the horse done already entered the chute, mi'ja."

"¿N'ombre?" She tosses her hair back, then leans over and pops him a kiss. "You think I want to dream de ese animal noche y día?"

"Yeah, I do. Or at least some part of you does or that jaguar wouldn't be tearing through your dreams."

"Well, I can't dream to order." She gets up and paces along the edge of tile and carpet, staying just within the tile line. "Besides, what if I'm not the one making it up, not the one directing the dream? When I encounter the jaguar I feel kind of empty, empty of myself; what if I'm not there, and the dream just shows up? When it happens I feel so out of control."

"I think you like dreaming about it even though it scares the caca out of you. Fess up, Prieta. You like dreaming, period. I know you don't want to be confined to just this pinche mundo. Your imagination breaks you out of it."

"Yep, I know. I've always known there's more to reality than just this," she waves her hand in the air. "I want to find the stuff that's missing. We have the right to the whole enchilada, to mix and make it up and not be made to swallow the ready-made realities society foists on us."

"Holy tortilla, so now you want to fight for the right to other realities when many of la raza don't even have basic human rights in this reality. Yeah, that's smart. You know what's causing this? You spend too much time alone. No, listen, carnalita. I know you don't want to be in this world all the time. But this is the terrain we are given. We need to live in this world. What I'm saying is you need to socialize more, spend time with la camarada instead of with an imaginary cat."

"What I need is a flesh and blood wife, alguien que hace la casa, who'll keep me company while I write."

"Don't you think I'd make a good little wifa?" He takes the kitchen towel, spits into it and wipes the table. "Zenobio sure thinks so."

"Ha, I'm not sure you are flesh and blood." She tweaks the skin of his forearm. "Now that Zenobio's transitioning, who knows what she will want. En serio, Teté, what do you think this sueño or ensueño is all about? It's got to mean something."

He sticks his head inside the refrigerator and plunks out a carton of eggs, salsa de nopalitos, corn tortillas, and a package of soy chorizo. "Where's the real chorizo? Yeah, yeah, I know, it's bad for you. It tastes too gringo when you leave the Mex out of the Tex." He stops dicing a potato to glance at Prieta. "Oh yeah, tus sueños. Doesn't the jaguar symbolize rain, fertility? Isn't that what it meant to los abuelos? Maybe it means you need to revitalize your writing. You've been complaining of how stale it's gotten and how stuck you are. I think it's called writer's block." He throws the potato into el sartén with the chorizo.

"Maybe, but I think it's more a symbol of connecting to el otro mundo. I think the jaguar represents a disruptive force beyond human control," she says.

"Esa gata is a disruptive force alright." He stirs the pan. "I think that in your case tu tigra de la noche represents some kind of fear, a real deep fear, I'd say. One of your bigger monsters. But one that you're probably ready to face. Otherwise, you wouldn't be dreaming about it."

"I thought you despised that kind of depth psychology," Prieta tells him. "Besides, don't you think I'd know if I was exploring some fear?"

"Simón, the aware part of you would, but what if it's another part of you that's orchestrating the whole thing? In just a few days it's invaded your life and gotten under your skin," he says, sitting down by her and running his fingers up her arm.

She shivers, reaches for his other hand. "What do you think I'm afraid of?"

Hands clasped, they stare at one another. For once Teté has nothing to say. Prieta leaves Teté to his soy chorizo con papas y huevo and walks past her study to the glassed-in patio. Rain begins to fall, gently at first then faster and faster. Soon rain is pinging against the glass. The drone of the rain almost drowns out the heartbeat of the crashing waves. The wind howls, rattling the window. The chill edge of the wind crawls under her shirt, making her pesones tighten. She shuts the window and paces.

She stops, places her palm against the cold windowpane. Through the water-streaked glass she watches the rain beat the plants and darken the gray gnarled branches of the big tree. It pummels the woman of stone in the grotto. Beyond the backyard, gusts of wind and rain flatten the stalks of her small patch of corn until the stalks lie green against the black earth. Another gust sweeps through her milpa like a swell, undulating the flattened stalks in its wake as though trying to raise them upright once more.

Beyond the corn the emerald meadow shimmers, and, beyond that, the wall of woods cupped by the purple matte of the sky. The indigo mass of mountains edging the east looks like a rain-drenched watercolor painting. To the left, over a wind-tossed sea, the moon floats in a sodden sky.

Sky, sea, mountains, woods, meadow, milpa, and yard are like countries with varying transitions and increasing degrees of distance, and the patio is the midway portal between the outside and the inside.

Lightning flashes to the north and, a few seconds later, the thunder is so loud it rattles the glass under her palm. Like a wild thing trying to get in, rain beats insistently against the panes and walls of her house. Water gurgles down the eaves and gutter spouts, a counter sound to the drum of the rain. The wind wrestles with the big tree, whipping its branches from side to side. With a loud pop una rama splits off and falls to the ground like an amputated wing.

She senses she's being watched, and not by the watcher within. "It's just your imagination," says her mama in her head. "Que soñadora eres, always living in your head." Behind her mama stands her grandmother beaming at Prieta and saying, "Ándale mi'ja."

Stop dawdling and get to work, she admonishes herself in her mother's voice. But she remains by the window moving her palm on the pane where, on the other side, a branch rubs against it. Scratch tap scratch tap. Let me in, let me in. The familiar chant in "la Vieja Inés," a childhood game, repeats over and over in her head: "¡Tan tan! ¿quién es? La vieja Inés." Another voice in her head says, "Only it's not the something that wants in that's troubling you, it's the something that wants out."

Palm against the cold glass, she pushes away and walks across the patio into her study. Why can't she get the jaguar out of her head? The details were so clear. It couldn't have been a dream. Ya párale, stop with the jaguar and concentrate on the paper. Finish it, turn it in, get the rest of the grant money.

She strikes a match; it flares and she touches it to la Virgen de Guadalupe candle that she's placed on the floor. Cross-legged, she sits before it and stares at the flame with unfocused eyes. She follows her breath, in and out, in and out, until her awareness dwells in the cave and she is alone with nothingness, just empty space and the indwelling watcher.

Thirty minutes later she rises and stretches, cracking her spine. She sits in her armchair, pulls the powerbook onto her lap, and wakes it from its sleep. As she bends over the computer, something moves in her peripheral vision. She snaps her head around. No one there, nothing out of place. Probably just a reflection of lightning on the walls.

She pecks the keyboard. Again, out of the corner of her eye she sees something move. She looks around the room. Nothing. She fidgets.

Bright light bursts into the room and vanishes in a second. Sitting quietly in the closed room she holds her breath waiting for its promise. The rumble that follows disappoints her.

She sees herself sitting in a closed room, imagining the jaguar moving through the woods. Then suddenly she imagines the jaguar itself. And then, just as suddenly, she's physically out in the wet woods.

"Oh, no, you don't." She jerks herself back.

She goes to her bookshelf, searches for, and plucks out a book on el nagualismo indígena. She flips through the pages until she gets to the section on the jaguar. The jaguar is a symbol of the forces of earth and night, also deity of earth and death. The Olmecs believed the jaguar devoured the misdeeds of humans. It appeared as a warning of lapses of behavior. They also believed that the jaguar was a nagual, a spirit animal counterpart of the shaman. Her gaze rests on a sculpture of a werejaguar with both feline and human features.

Snapping the book closed, she stares into space. She remembers the jaguar she encountered in the dense brush of el monte when she was seven or eight. Had it been a dream or an actual happening?

The persistence of the dream troubles her, not so much because of what's in it but because it makes the claim of solid reality. Teté's words replay in her head: "Waking life continues day after day, dream life does not continue night after night. If you continue dream life every night it would rival concrete reality."

Chingao, maybe Teté's right and some unknown part of her is producing them—you have to have intent and put forth some effort in order to make up images. A deep, hidden part of herself must have willed what she's imagining. But these images aren't faint or two-dimensional or short in duration like those that are imagined. The jaguar arrives the way sensations do. It's vivid and solid and lasts a while. OK, there are three things that could be happening. One, it's a projection and it comes from her. Two, it doesn't come from her and the jaguar slips through some crack from whatever world it's from and enters her world, first her inner world and then the world of the senses. Which means the jaguar and its world enter in and displace hers. Or three, she slips through the crack and goes into the realm of the jaguar, again, first in her dreams, then in actuality.

She wanders around the house, pacing from room to room. Maybe she can control its comings and goings. Again she sits, unfocusing her attention. Come on, dream. Nothing. After half an hour she gives up and begins vacuuming the house.

De repente, the dream enters. After a few seconds she jerks herself out of the dream by concentrating on her surroundings: the table by the window, the vase of flowers on the table, the sound of rain against the roof. She runs the vacuum again. Again the jaguar is suddenly there at the window, again she shifts her attention to the sound of the Hoover. Como una nepantlera entre duerme y vela, she travels back and forth between the worlds as she cleans her house. Well, that didn't work. She can't control the dreaming. The knot in her mid-section tightens.

She finds herself staring out the window at el monte oscuro. A tendril of her waking dream floats across her consciousness. She lets it reel her into el ensueño. The Prieta in the dream hears the deep, hoarse cry of the jaguar and knows it's a mating call. She watches herself as the call pulls her out of the patio and tugs her toward the line of trees edging the woods.

At the edge of the woods she hesitates. The jaguar calls again, drawing her into the woods. She passes under the arched canopy of branches aware that she is crossing some kind of portal. Now she is no longer observing the dream but in it. It is dawn, the fog, chilly and sepulchral, clings to her body. Under the trees' canopy the air is dank and heavy with the smell of musk and wet vegetation. The path is slippery with wet leaves, and her sneakers are soon soaked. A mushroom under her feet bursts. A bird cries from deep in the forest. Wisps of mist float like ghosts along the path. Skirting branches darkened with moisture and shoving away wet fronds, she moves slowly through the undergrowth deeper into the woods. Leaves thick and lush shimmer with beads of water that drip on her arms and back. Her hair catches in a branch. An animal squeals and she jerks her head around. The shadows cast by trees and bushes look menacing.

A sudden gust of wind rattles the leaves, making her jump. She feels pursued by the woods, senses the woods with their ancient presence waiting quietly, straining toward her. The moist dark earth seems to harbor an intelligence. When she was a child she felt comforted by the woods. Now she distrusts them and the wild things in there. She's afraid something in the woods will absorb her into itself and she will forever be lost in the dream of the woods, lost in the woods of her dream.

Hearing the jaguar's growl, she looks up in the direction of the sound. The jaguar crouches on a limb of a nearby tree staring down at her out of golden eyes. It jumps down, lands on padded feet and walks away, disappearing in the gossamer trails of mist that float down the path. Prieta follows its spoor trail through el monte. Leaves in various stages of decay give under her feet como un piso hueco.

She glances back. The stark gray bones of the forest loom behind and ahead, their solid weight pressing against her. She is alone in the middle of the dark, tangled, impenetrable forest. But the woods protect her from the chilled wind. Through a gap in the branches she sees the moon, Coyolxauhqui. A shaft of light illuminates a spot in front of her. The hoarse cry of the jaguar startles her and she jerks. And finds herself back in the patio. She touches her sleeves; they are bone dry. Heart thumping in her chest and hair crawling on the back of her neck, she jumps away from the window.

Throughout the day, at odd times she hears the throaty purr of the jaguar and looks up to see her walking across the room toward her, three-dimensional and holographic, claws clicking on the hardwood floor. After the fourth appearance her nerves stop jumping. Again she becomes aware of an insatiable yearning that sweeps over her, feels the dull hollow of something missing in her life. She flashes back to her childhood, to the secret friend who played with her in her private place by the lagoon in the woods.

A shadow or reflection draws Prieta to the window. Allí on the edge of the corn field, sunlight speckles amber-brown patches on the ground. Could it be the blurred outline of a crouching animal? "Hey, Teté, come look at this," she shouts. "Ándale."

"Can't it wait? I'm online."

"Come on, cyber-vato, you can look for digital love later."

He gets up and joins her at the window. Resting his right arm over her shoulder, he stoops to peer out.

"Qué, I don't see anything."

"Allá en la huerta, doesn't that look like un tigre?"

"Frigorific, Prieta," he says, putting his hands on his hips. "Now you've not only got your mythic beast popping out in daylight but you want me to see it too. Well," he raps the wall with his fist, "in this world there is no jaguar. If you went out there now you wouldn't find any paw prints. Only in the woods of tu fantasía are you ass deep in jaguars. Prietita linda, it's dangerous to walk in two realities. I guess that's what abstinence does to you."

Prieta pushes him. "Want to hear of an even scarier notion? That what I'm 'imagining' is contagious and you're going to catch it."

"Chale. You know I'm not a cat person."

"Seriously, Teté, there must be dozens of realities, dozens of worlds, not just two. Maybe reality is a continuum made up of connecting and superimposed layers."

Teté cants up an eyebrow. "So what you're saying is that physical reality is at one end and the reality of spirit and myth is at the other end?"

"Simón," says Prieta, "or maybe it consists of layers like an onion. I think reality is whatever channel you're tuned to."

"That must be some channel you tune to. I know you have la facultad to focus somewhere between the inner eye and the outer eye. And that you can switch from one to the other—everyone can. In theory it doesn't matter which one it is, they're all made up, they're all fabrications, they're all just sueños. And I believe but. . . ."

"No, I know it does matter because we have to live by the fictions of this reality, and these fictions need to be consensual," says Prieta. "It's not enough for me to believe in other realities, I need others to believe it too."

"Chingao, 'at's deep, prima. But you're missing the point. We have flesh and bone bodies that live in a physical world, and that's the reality we have to live in. But not you. You're seeing with your outer eye what you should only be seeing with your inner." He shakes his head and puts the back of his hand over her forehead and says, "Uh oh, a tad warm. Must be all that world shifting."

"Anda vete. ¡No seas gacho!" She slaps his hand away. "Let's go have a look."

He follows her out to the backyard. The flagstones leading from the patio door glisten with moss and lichen so alive they look chartreuse. The stone goddess with arms upraised is still standing in the grotto, rose petals strewn at her feet. The big tree is split right down the middle; the other trees are intact though wind-combed. Leaving the backyard, they weave through the corn field. The stalks cant to one side where wind and rain bent them almost to the ground.

Finding no sign of the jaguar, they return to the yard and poke through the debris left by the storm. Prieta retrieves a small saw, an ax, pruning shears, and trash bags from the shed. After pulling on canvas gloves, she saws, chops, and cuts up the smaller broken branches while Teté rakes up debris.

Though Prieta turns her back on the woods, she feels the pull—like a ripple in the air currents, a sensation passing through her chest. It calls to something deep within. Prieta leans against the stone goddess, gaining comfort from its solidity. Her eyes lock on the dark line of woods, black now with nightfall. She senses Teté's eyes on her occasionally. The phone rings and she hears him trotting into the house to answer it.

Something shifts as though trying to realign in a new pattern. Prieta closes her eyes and lets her spine move down the stone until she's sitting on the wet ground. She lies on her side pulling her knees up to her chest and cradling her head on her folded arm.

Sometime later she hears the door slam and, opening her eyes, sees Teté walking toward her. It's nearly dark and he stumbles on one of the round cement slabs that dot the path. Seeing her on the ground he rushes to her.

"What the fuck are you doing down there?" He pulls her up. She struggles, then slumps into his embrace.

"Chinpiotes, Prieta, don't scare me like that. I thought maybe that jaguar was for real and had attacked you."

Prieta focuses on his troubled face. "But you say she's not real just a projection of my own mind, so how could she attack me?"

"If you believe she's real, she could hurt you. You know, like the chupacabra in the *X-Files*. Now a goat I could handle. You know I'm not a cat person."

Prieta smiles.

When he reaches to turn on the outdoor light she says, "No, leave it off. The moon is so bright it might be day."

"Maybe for you, mi prietita, but the rest of us mortals can't see in the dark." He searches her faces. "I think you're part gata. I wouldn't be surprised if your eyes shine when light hits them."

She growls.

He lifts her into his arms and carries her into her bedroom. She tells him, "¿Sabes qué? I don't know about la tigra entering this world, but I have definitely entered hers."

"I don't know what to believe anymore. You've always had such a vivid imagination," he says. "Remember when we were kids and you saw that big coyote en el monte you thought was a nagual?"

"Yeah, it was a jaguar not a coyote. And I remember how terrified you were of it. I've got your number. You act all cynical, but deep down you're a believer."

"No way, José."

Prieta finds comfort in the familiar crooked smile, sus ojos flojos, and the way half his eyebrow rises like a drawbridge.

"You want to hear what my mind conjured up today while I was cleaning the house and when I was trying to get some writing done?"

He grunts. "OK. ¿Qué?"

"OK, fragments, entire scenes with sounds and smells and everything, they flash out of nowhere. In the blink of an eye the jaguar's there in the room. I can smell her. Once the images come, I can't stop them. How do you suppose she comes into this reality?

"In one of these 'dreamings' she swam across a river—there's no river near here. Then she ran through the woods toward me. Then we both went deeper into el monte. Y de repente I'm back in the study as though I'd never left, only there's dirt on my slippers."

Teté drops his wounded hero act. "Jíjole, baby, you're spit-shit scaring me. You passing through some hole into her world is scarier than her coming into ours," he says, putting his arms around her.

She snuggles against his chest breathing in his familiar smell. "I don't know what time or place she comes from. Maybe you're right and it all comes from un paisaje interior, from some deeper part of myself I never knew was there."

"If it does come from inside your head is there someone else inside who's doing the imagining? Like you're possessed by some thing? Like in *The Exorcist*," Teté asks. "Te apoesto que 'tas embrujada."

"What? No, I don't think I'm taken over by some spirit but by something that's me. A mind under my conscious mind, one that's waking up and intruding into the conscious one. Whatever it is, I can feel it waiting to claim space here, to become part of this." She waves her hands through the air.

"Waiting how?"

"It's sort of just waiting, waiting like the woods do. It's waiting until it can enter this one. Chingao, I wish I could be sure that she's a spirit and not a part of me. What if I'm part of her? What if I'm the one invading her world?"

"Shi-it, Prieta, that's too otro-worldly. It's creeping me out. I think we need help. There's a therapist that Zenobio goes to, a curandera, though some claim she's a bruja. Let's call her up and ask if she'll see you."

"Thanks a lot primo." She tries to look wounded.

"Want to know what I think? That you suffered some kind of susto. You lost part of your soul. It's under a spell and it's wandering somewhere out there where it encounters the jaguar. Or maybe your curandera can figure it out. She'll give you una limpia and call back your soul."

"I've already considered susto. I don't think I'm suffering from it. Teté, I can't go to la curandera until I figure out what's going on first. Mamagrande told me that when an animal appears to you four times in your dreams it means it's your animal companion. The jaguar could be my naguala come here to help me with my problems, to give me strength, whatever."

"Help you how?" asks Teté.

"I don't know. According to the Medicine Cards the jaguar means focus and drive, power and steadiness. Endurance. These are lacking in my life right now. I've been feeling out of focus, like I've lost my direction, I jump from one project to another, and complete none of them."

"If you ask me, prima, she's shaking you up, distracting you, instead of steadying you," he says.

"But don't you see, if animals represent instincts, then maybe I'm supposed to reconnect to the kind of instinct that I'm repressing, instincts that the jaguar represents."

"Újale." He blinks his thick-lashed eyes. "Get with the program, you're supposed to slay the beast, not get seduced by her."

"What's happening to me could be right out of Cortázar's stories. Remember 'La noche boca arriba'? This guy's in an accident and is taken to the hospital. While he's lying there he goes in and out of consciousness. Sometimes he's in the past, centuries in the past, and he's running from Aztec warriors who are trying to capture him and make him a human sacrifice. What do you call that? A reality from the past bleeding into the present?"

"Yeah, I remember. Here, let me see your hand." He takes her hand, raising it up and staring at it and rubbing the top. "Yeah, I can almost see esa civilización antigua, el otro mundo that sleeps under your skin." He raises her hand and kisses it.

"Quítate, chiflado." She jerks her hand away.

"So what you're saying is that the jaguar is from the past?"

"No, more like from out of time, an ahistorical time. Or maybe a parallel time."

"Well, whatever it is and wherever it's from, it's surfacing in this reality."

Prieta goes to the living room couch and lies down.

She stirs, turns on her side, the jaguar purrs, sniffs Prieta's hand. She jerks up, heart racing, every nerve strumming, her nipples tight and hard. The rank musk of the animal is overpowering. She blinks and the animal and its smell disappear.

"Teté, did you see her? She was here in this room sniffing my hand."

Teté looks up from the window seat at the other side of the room. Putting down his book, he gets up and comes to her. He peers into her eyes and puts the backs of his fingers to her forehead. "¿Pos, qué te pasa? You're sweating and your skin is cold and clammy. Why don't I make you some té de yerba buena. Fresh from the garden. Would you like that, mi prietita?" he says looking worried.

A few minutes later he's back. "Here you are gatita," he growls, handing her a cup of tea. She sips from it, then blows into the cup. Teté stretches down beside her and puts his face in her hair. Her fingers comb through his side wings of deep black hair. They curl and uncurl in light massage strokes, her fingernails gently scrape his scalp. He squirms closer, snuggles his face into her neck. She feels the brush of his eyelashes open and close like butterfly wings. When his hand starts to wander she shoves him off the couch. He falls on the carpet, rolls to his feet.

"Ay tú, well excuse me," he fake pouts. "I can take a hint." He goes back to the window nook with his critical race theory text and highlighter. She's glad he's gone back to school to finish his degree, glad to have her study buddy back.

She drains the cup, gets up and stretches, then goes outside to the garden, slamming the door behind her. She sits in her garden. No noise, just the soft rustle of the wind in the leaves. In the indigo sky la luna looks more swollen than it did last night.

Prieta stares at the wash of dead leaves piled against the stone figure nestled inside the shallow cavity of the grotto. She greets the ancient goddess. "Coyolxauhqui, mujer en pedazos, you who mirror my face, diosa de la noche, shine tu luz de conocimiento down on me," she whispers, laying a marigold flower at the stone feet.

She sinks down to the ground, closes her eyes and quiets her breathing. The clouds drift, unveiling la luna, and she feels herself shifting. She's in a small village. Men and women gather around her. Copal smoke spirals up. She sinks to the ground and sits cross-legged. She closes her eyes. Something in her shifts. It is night and it is thundering. Un aguazal is flooding the land. A jaguar takes to the trees and travels noiselessly from branch to branch. It is large, three feet tall and nine feet long and weighing about 300 pounds. It bounds out of the trees y anda disquieta por el monte.

Prieta follows her until she gets tangled up in some low-lying branches. The jaguar paces restlessly, waiting for her. Prieta feels her body expanding until it is as big as the tree. Prieta and the tree merge. The limbs of the tree become the nerves in her body. She keeps expanding until the woods become her nerves. La tigra watches her. Her jaguar eyes swim in the rivers of night, eating up the night. La tigra opens her mouth, tongues of fire shoot out, prendiendo fuegos en el monte, setting fires to Prieta's nerves. La tigra swims across the flash-flooding waters of an arroyo. When Prieta comes out of her trance she tells la gente gathered around her that it is time to plant.

Slowly surfacing Prieta opens her eyes, stares at the stone goddess, for a few seconds unsure of which world she's in. She takes one last look at her jardín and goes inside.

She follows the sounds of pots rattling. Teté is washing the dishes. "Why are you cleaning up? I know que lo haces a puro huevo."

"Tío would say I'm making like a vieja."

"I say you can't ever be too in touch with your feminine side," Prieta says.

He stares at her, then starts to wipe the counter. "You want a wife, don't you? That jaguar dream lover of yours is not going to mop the floor. Eso es lo que te pasa por imaginar la vida en vez de vivirla."

"¿A poco? La vida se hace al contarla, you make life as you recount it, you make it out of your thoughts. You make it from images que saltan de la memoria. You make it de lo imaginado. Todo está en los modos de contar: it's all in the mode of telling."

"You know what I both loathe and love about you, carnala?"

"Yeah, I do. But you'll tell me comoquiera."

"Your independence. The rich life you live in your head. Unfortunately, you use it to keep people from getting too close. Your land of dreams has 'Keep Out' signs posted around it," Teté says, trying to look put upon.

"Eso, chiquito, is because I'll never get any work done if I don't."

"Uh uh. I don't buy that," Teté tells her. "What's a friend for if not to slay any and all tigers for you?" He puts up his fists and shadow boxes.

"What if algo o alguien, the soul maybe, is imagining us, imagining this. What if we're being dreamed. What if you, me, the jaguar are all dreamworks. Something Neelix said in last week's *Star Trek: Voyager* episode stuck with me. He said 'The dream frames the dreamer.'"

"Huáchate, you're beginning to sound like Borges."

That night her dream is so intense it wakes her, but not fully. She's in nepantla, that in-between space. Prieta listens, ears cocked inwardly, eyes on the window trying to peer through la noche. She senses the jaguar's presence, senses its intelligence. La jaguar bufa, it calls her. The longing pulses through Prieta like a live thing.

She sits up and grabs her laptop. She feels an urgency to record the scene, to describe how the images are reorienting her mind, rearranging the cells of her body, remapping the nerves and synapses. She stares at the blank screen for a second. Her fingers begin clicking over the keyboard. They click faster and faster, keeping time to the drumming of the rain. A great peace gradually settles over her. Hours later her eyes glazing over, she scrolls to the beginning and reads:

In my dream   window nightsky and jaguar   are a still shot.   Then the jaguar leaps onto the floor of my bedroom footpads on the floor and boards   I hear her muffled growl coming closer   La tigra is padding   across my bedroom   In the dark I hear the soft thump   of her tail against my dresser she's gathering to spring   she springs   the bed quakes   then stills   the mattress shakes   I cower against the headboard she crawls toward me   advancing   an exhalation   a rustling   a ripple over my belly   a cold nose   she's nuzzling my neck   gently pushing with her head   her whiskers brush my lips   from deep in her chest   a purr rattles   I feel the vibrations on my chest   her tiger breath hot on my face   she stretches out   the movement rocks the bed   "nice pussycat" outside the wind is howling   she nudges me over   on my knees   burrowing my face into the pillow   the fine hairs from her underbelly   rub my buttocks   an earthy heaviness

settles in   back and forth   I clutch the mattress with   both
hands   jaguar haunches over my thighs   the heat is   streaming   into me in waves   her saliva drips on my hot skin   the
moon-faced sea in squall   an inhalation   an arching   the
rough tongue   The weight on my body lifts   the shadow of
a woman   it's gone   my body is suddenly cold   footpads
on the floorboards   retreating   growing fainter   a smooth
silent spring   jaguar   window and nightsky a stillshot   then
just window and nightsky

Prieta puts her laptop to sleep and goes to the kitchen where
she hears Teté rattling pots and pans.

"What do you feel like eating?" Teté asks.

"Nothing. Do you think that some people can really convert
themselves into animals, en sus nagualas, or do you think they just
imagine they can?" Prieta asks him.

"I think it's just a mind trip. I mean, it would have to be a
fucking miracle for human flesh to all of a sudden sprout fur and
fangs."

"I think my dream jaguar is a nagual who used to be a woman."

He bursts out laughing. "Yeah, sure. What have you been
watching? *Cat People*? You're getting carried away with this nostalgia
for mythical Indigenous origins?"

"Hmph." Prieta thumps him a wallop. "Teté baby, it's not
nostalgia that's got a hold of me, it's the origins."

"Maybe you should stop watching *X-Files* and *Outer Limits*,"
Teté suggests.

"Maybe you should stop being such a worry wart."

"Maybe you're just pre-menstrual?" Teté asks.

La Prieta throws a spoon at him.

"¡Épale!" It glances off his back and skids across the floor.

"Well, don't you sort of slip into some kind of weird state,
just before your period? You get as prickly as a nopal. You know
you do."

"You're pissing me off. You guys can't blame whatever you
don't like about women on PMS. And you want to know something else?"

"No, but you'll tell me anyway."

"Damn right, primito. I do my most creative work when I'm in this state. That's when it all clicks and I know stuff; it's like I can see beneath the surface of things."

"Shit. Tell me you're not saying that bleeding once a month gives you women an edge when it comes to creativity or spirituality or whatever special abilities esas facultades tuyas give you? That's a bunch of essentialist crap. How could you fall for that?"

"Just because I'm a woman and I have hormonal changes doesn't mean I'm saying that you or other men don't have similar shifts. If you want to claim you have them then you go and track your own damn states."

"God, I love aggressive bitch-macha-patlache. What you need is some progesterone."

"To make me less aggressive? Yeah, right. You're implying I'm not in full possession of my faculties. But primo, mi amor, this is when I'm most in full possession," says Prieta, putting her face so close to Teté's that their noses almost touch.

"Well, what if you are a victim of your own biology? Is that so bad?" he says.

"Yes it is. No te hagas pendejo, Teté."

She smiles, leans against the counter, and shaking her head, mutters, "I don't know why I put up with you. You're a real thorn in my side."

"Admit it, you love it when my thorn is inside you. You love me, corazón de mi vida, come on, admit it." When he sees La Prieta reach for a plate he ducks behind the other side of the counter.

"That was entirely too much on the wild side for me," Teté tells her, smacking a kiss on her mouth and jogging out of the room.

From her bed Prieta looks out at the stars scattered like luminescent pearls across the night sky. Wrapped up in her white down comforter she listens to the rain patter on the roof in a hypnotic drone. The wind gusts against the window screens y alluvia por los rincones del cuarto. La jaguar calls to her from the edge of the wood, its song opening all the empty spaces in her body and filling them. Su vientre se hincha.

She waits.

Pulling the other pillow into the curve of her naked body, she breathes in its fresh laundered smell. Turning on her side, she watches the white curtains stirring slightly. The candle flutters on her nightstand, its flare casting long dancing shadows on the walls. In her mind's eye she sees the huge drops of water plopping into the earth making small craters and then filling them with water. Each tiny drop of water that falls into the small pools makes undulations resembling squiggling snakes. Serpents, rain, jaguars—all forces that humans can't control.

The jaguar is coming. Camina por el techo de los árboles, her sinewy body rippling. Holding her breath, Prieta stares through the window at the moon.

This time when the air ripples around her and the jaguar beckons something deep in her belly loosens. She lets go and abandons herself.

Window, night sky with moon and jaguar a still shot.

La tigra jumps through the window and pads across her bedroom. She springs onto the bed, stares at Prieta unblinkingly with fierce amber eyes. Her tawny coat is dotted with black rosettes. Thick tail twitching, la mujer jaguar exhales, her breath a musty hot wind. Whiskers and a cold nose nuzzle Prieta's neck, the brush of fur against her skin sends heat pulsing along Prieta's body like a wash. Her mouth opens, a deep rough cough shows her upper and lower bicuspids are sharp, slightly longer than her other teeth. She sinks her teeth into Prieta's flesh, breaking the skin. Fear mixed with passion raises the hair on Prieta's nape. Her nipples peak and a trembling flushes through her. A toenail brushes Prieta's thigh and she shudders. The woman moves smoothly, lithely, like her nagual counterpart. Her eyes gleam jaguar not human. Prieta notices a faint tremble in the woman's muscles.

Le lambe, lavando su cuerpo con an incredibly long tongue hasta que Prieta está mojada por donde quiera. She licks the tattoo around Prieta's ankle. Prieta shivers, her whole body is wet and she says, "You want to feed on me, don't you?" Gruñiedo la arrulla del lado.

La mujer tigra la acaricia con sus labios. She runs her tongue from neck to chest and sucks Prieta's nipple until it's hard. Then she licks her way down to Prieta's navel, and on to her triangle of hair. With each lick, she goes lower. Prieta spreads her legs wider and wider. La tigra puts her face to her wet crevasse and licks until Prieta is mewling.

El rumor de ranas wakes Prieta. Se fija al reloj. It's four o'clock in the morning, the hour of the tiger. It is still night and there's a woman sleeping in her bed. A lithe woman with tiger breath, hot and fetid, smelling of damp mulch, forest, and cat. Prieta switches on the bedside lamp and watches the woman's fingernails flex on the down comforter. They are long and sharp. The woman opens her eyes, stretches languorously, elongating her spine, her body is tanned a rich gold. She stares at Prieta with sleepy amber eyes.

Prieta knuckles her eyes whispering, "What are you, who are you? You remind me of a girl I knew a long time ago."

The jaguar woman smiles, places her palm on Prieta's thigh, strokes Prieta's leg and runs her foot up her other leg. She rubs her soft breasts against Prieta's. She yawns and her mouth opens widely, her long pink tongue snakes out and licks Prieta's eyelashes. Then she kisses Prieta on the mouth, pushing in her long tongue. Prieta's nipples pucker.

"¡Ay gatita! Are you bilingual, ¿Hablas Tex-Mex, o qué?" Prieta asks.

"Growl." Ronronea.

"Guess you aren't one for pillow talk," Prieta murmurs.

While rain pounds on the roof, Prieta lightly scratches her belly. Her fingers rub and pull her nipples, first one then the other. The woman purrs with pleasure.

Prieta smiles. "You may be la bestia, but I am not beauty."

The woman's fierce amber eyes shine and she growls, "Let's both be the beast."

Prieta strokes the pale gold breasts, traces the whorls of her ears. Rubs her finger down the woman's nose and across her upper lip. She runs her fingers down the arch of her spine. Scars from very old injuries, Prieta thinks. A feeling of tenderness unexpectedly enters Prieta. She embraces her, rocks her tenderly in her arms, and breathes in her clean cat smell.

A short quick push with her hand and the cat woman flips Prieta over on her knees. She places her palm over Prieta's snatch and flexes her fingers gently. She nuzzles Prieta between her legs, nibbles the hardened nub, then laves it with her tongue, lapping up the juices.

She mounts Prieta and presses into her. Pounds her haunches until Prieta is slippery with sweat. Prieta feels her hot panting breath sweeping across her neck as she throws her head back to rest on the woman's shoulder. She feels the tug, the pull, and her muscles contract, tighten. Panting, the woman hovers over Prieta, muscles bulging, shadows between the muscles, her bones protruding.

The woman is still for a second. Then Prieta feels the rhythmic inner squeezing, fierce clenches that shake her. The pulsations force air out of her lungs in a great rush. Prieta shudders, sobs, and struggles for breath. Languid, she sinks, back into the mattress, and gradually the shimmering quiets. Head resting on Prieta's pubic mound, la mujer tigra watches her.

Next morning Prieta awakens to find tears on the comforter and goose down rising up from the covers. Pelos anaranjados stick to her pillows and mattress. "¡Jijo de su!"

She leaps up, a cloud of white feathers floating around her. She rushes down the hall and into Teté's room. She catches a glimpse of herself in the mirror. Her cry of surprise sounds like a growl. Yes, definitely whisker burns on her face and are those whiskers at the edges of her mouth?

Teté lies sprawled on his stomach fast asleep. She shakes him. He turns over. When he refuses to open his eyes, she tweaks the black hair curling up and out of his groin.

"Ouch, that hurts." He says, sitting up and wiping his face with one hand. "Well, did you score with la jaguar ruca of your dreams? Huh, did you get lucky?"

She nods, her face heating.

"Jíjole, a naguala lover," he says, heavy-lidded gaze on her. He strokes her face and arms. "Your skin is luminous and you look soft, not at all like the tough Chicana patlache I know and love. Just how did you get her off? I hope you remembered to wear latex gloves. Don't tell me you forgot the dental dam or the saran wrap, hon. You can't be too careful nowadays."

"Tonto."

"OK, give me a blow by blow. Was she a tiger en la cama or what? Just what do two gatas do in bed?"

"That's for me to know and for you to wonder."

"It's a substitute for the real world," he teases, a skeptical gleam in his eyes. "Are you that lonely and hard up and horny that you have to resort to bestiality?"

"She may not be entirely human nor entirely animal, but she's woman enough. Now, doesn't that make you envious?"

"Wrong object-choice, mi Prieta. What would Freud say about this perversion?"

"You're a fine one to talk. What you do with your herenga. . . ."

"Well, there's holes and there's holes. You sure it wasn't just a dream?"

"Do dream jaguars rip the bedding and leave fur on the bed? For sure I didn't sprout fur and fangs. No, Teté, some boundaries definitely got crossed last night."

"Yeah, like the one between your imagination and your needs," he says.

"When I was a kid, I could pass from one world to the other as easily as stepping through a doorway or changing channels. You all thought it was too weird, too scary, dangerous, even. So I closed the door to it all. Well, the door's open now and I'm going to explore that terra incognita all I want."

"Mi'ja," says Teté. "Cuando esa luz que tienes por dentro sale de tu piel, I know you've stepped into the wild. It scares me. I don't want to lose you. Wait till Zenobio hears that the other woman es un animal. No not even an animal, but a spirit animal. The word bi-sexual can't begin to cover this."

"You're not going to lose me. I'll still be here. And you'll be here. The only difference is that there'll be a third addition to our happy home," Prieta tells him.

"Oh, and pray tell, how does your spirit wife feel about sharing you with me? And what about me? You know I'm not a cat person. I'd be more tempted to be the third of your menage a trois if the jaguar had cojones. Ask her if she knows any shapeshifting maricones."

"Be serious, Teté. We'll work it out. I'm sure she'll take to you," Prieta says.

"There must be something you can do to free yourself from that were-woman, some ritual that'll release you from her claws. But no, estás enamorada. You don't want to get rid of her, do you? You like the cat in your bed. A menage a trois, and she and I have never had the pleasure."

"¡Cállate el hocico!"

"You know what I think? Maybe she's your captive instead of you hers," Teté says. He kicks the pillow, looking bereft. He flounces into the bathroom, a mutinous pinch around his mouth.

Prieta goes to the kitchen to fix a snack. She'll bake some biscochitos, a peace offering. Teté loves biscochitos. She places butter, sugar, anise seed, and an egg and beats them together, adds flour, baking powder and some brandy. She rolls it out, cuts it in pieces, sprinkles the tops with sugar and cinnamon and sticks the pan in the oven for fifteen minutes.

The smell soon draws Teté into the kitchen. He puts water in the pot and gets the Cafix out of the cupboard. The timer beeps and Prieta takes the cookie sheet out of the oven. They sit down and scarf up the biscochitos.

"Get real, Prieta. The problem is not which reality to live in. No way can you live in hers. Oh, I get it. You're enamored of the dream, of being star-crossed lovers in a post-millennial version of the West Side Story of interspecies love. A tear jerker of a story."

"Menso." Prieta pushes him over. "You jerk, she's real. There's even a word for her kind, therianthrope, a being that is part animal and part human."

"¿Que qué? Now that's giving hybridity a new spin. I wonder how Chicana high theorists would theorize that." Teté dips his biscochito in the cup of coffee. "¿Qué piensas hacer?"

"It feels like I'm standing between the worlds. I think everyone has an animal companion, a nagual who can exist in two planes. I listened for and saw this animal companion when I was a child. But I think most people don't listen or look for it. I think she's always been in my life, out of sight in the shadows. I'm sure it was her that appeared to me en el monte when I was little."

"What good does it do you to have a wife in the woods? Will she help you keep house, be here when you need her?"

"Well, I've changed. I don't think I could tolerate a full-time lover; you know I need my space. A lover in the woods. And you here," Prieta says. "Now that would work."

"Why can't I be enough for you? It's one thing to compete with those wild lesbians always coming on to you, but it's another thing to compete with an imaginary lover." Teté slumps. "And a damn cat at that."

Prieta strokes his bent back.

"Hey, I know what it's like to be so damn lonely that you have to resort to a fantasy lover, but Prieta it's not like there aren't flesh and blood bodies out there who would jump for the chance. But no, what do you do? You shut yourself up in this place."

They stare at each other.

"Frigorific." Teté nestles up close by her on the couch. "I guess if I have to share you, I'd rather do it with a part time lover who's a spirit cat from a mythic time. Can't get queerer than that. Maybe we'll set a precedent for the new alternative family."

La Prieta dreams. Something is trying to come out of her body, pushing against las paredes de su cuerpo. She gives birth. Teté lays the baby in her arms. They hover over the baby marveling at the cleft forehead, the tiny incisor teeth. "Ay, criatura fiera de la lluvia, you will bring the rains down from the spirit world," Prieta croons to her. The baby's eyes gleam jaguar not human.

Prieta walks through the meadow toward el monte, swells of grass cresting and falling around her. The woods open to her and let her in. The trees' branches enter her body, become her bones.

Awareness of the woods, the sounds of the rustle of leaves and of the scurrying of animalitos flow through her, like a river leaves her open.

Teté follows holding the werejaguar child in his arms. The light shining through the misty rain polarizes into hundreds of tiny rainbows. Prieta llama al jaguar. As the three pass under the arc of tree branches, they step out of time.

Translations

el monte: the mountain (el monte also refers more broadly to her homeland in South Texas)

¿Un gato montez?: A mountain lion?

de volada: in flight

zempasuchitl: marigolds

se queda parada: she stands still

Ay, diosa, tiene cara de mujer: Oh, goddess, you have a woman's face

el vidrio: the window

ni un rugido de jaguar: no jaguar roar

loca: crazy

comal: frying pan

Quiúbole: What's up

¿A poco?: Huh?

'tas encantada: you're enchanted

brujas: witches

ojos flojos: lazy eyes

créeme: believe me

ya ni la chingues: don't mix it up

de carne, hueso, y, uñas: of flesh, bones, and nails (fingernails)

chale, esa: take it easy, woman

carnal: brother

gente: people

nepantla: between ways

Aquí está tu mero mero.: Here is your real man.

menso, cochino eres, ¿un poco? primo: stupid, you're a pig, cousin

mi'ja: my daughter

¿N'ombre?: No way!

de ese animal noche y día: of this animal night and day

caca: shit

pinche mundo: lousy world

la raza: the race

carnalita: sister

la camarada: comrade

alguien que hace la casa: someone who will clean/make the house

wifa: wife

en serio: seriously

sueño: dream

ensueño: enchantment

salsa de nopalitos: sauce with shredded cactus

tus sueños: your dreams

los abuelos: the grandparents

el sartén: the frying pan

el otro mundo: another world

esa gata: this cat

tu tigra de la noche: your tiger of the night

Simón: yes

con papas y huevo: with potatoes and egg

pesones: nipples

milpa: plot of land for farming

una rama: a branch

Que soñadora eres: What a dreamer you are

ándale mi'ja: come on

la vieja Inés: a color guessing game for children

¡Tan tan! ¿quién es?: Who is it?

ya párale: stop now

la Virgen de Guadalupe: the Virgin of Guadalupe

el nagualismo indígena: Indigenous (Mesoamerican) shapeshifting

chingao: fuck (exclamation)

de repente: suddenly

como una nepantlera entre duerme y vela: like a bordercrosser in between sleep and wakefulness

el monte oscuro: the dark (or shaded) mountain

como un piso hueco: like a crumbling floor

Coyolxauhqui: lunar goddess

allá en la huerta: there in the garden

tu fantasía: your fantasy

linda: pretty

la facultad: the power of acute awareness

prima: cousin (female)

Anda vete. ¡No seas gacho!: Go away. Don't be nasty!

chinpiotes: geez

¿Sabes qué?: You know what?

nagual: spirit animal

y: and

jíjole: wow

un paisaje interior: an interior passage

Te apoesto que 'tas embrujada.: I bet you're under a spell.

otro: other

susto: fear

una limpia: a (spiritual) cleansing

mamagrande: grandmother

La noche boca arriba: a movie

esa civilización antigua: this ancient civilization

quítate, chiflado: stop that, you spoiled man

¿Pos, qué te pasa?: Well, what happened to you?

té de yerba buena: mint tea

gatita: little cat

ay tú: oh, you

la luna: the moon

mujer en pedazos: woman in pieces

diosa de la noche: goddess of the night

tu luz de conocimiento: your light of knowledge

copal: incense

un aguazal: a puddle or swamp

y anda disquieta por el monte: and walks disquietly through the mountain

prendiendo fuegos en el monte: starting fires in the mountain

que lo haces a puro huevo: that you're doing it unwillingly

tío: uncle

vieja: old lady

Eso es lo que te pasa por imaginar la vida en vez de vivirla.: This is what happens to you when you imagine life rather than living it

La vida se hace al contarla: You make life as you recount it

que saltan de la memoria: that leap from your memory

de lo imaginado: of the imagination

Todo está en los modos de contar.: It's all in the mode of telling.

comoquiera: anyway

eso, chiquito: that, little dear

algo o alguien: something or someone

huáchate: watch out (slang)

la noche: the night

la jaguar bufa: the jaguar snorts

en sus nagualas: into their sacred animal bodies

¡Épale!: Hey!

nopal: cactus

primito: little cousin, an endearment

esas facultades tuyas: these faculties of yours

macha-patlache: queer butch woman

mi amor: my love

no te hagas pendejo: don't make yourself a fool

corazón de mi vida: heart (or love) of my life

y alluvia por los rincones del cuarto: and it rained from the corners of the room

su vientre se hincha: her abdomen contracts

camina por el techo de los árboles: walks over the roof of the trees

la mujer jaguar: the jaguar woman

le lambe: licks her

lavando su cuerpo: washing her body

hasta que Prieta está mojada por donde quiera: until Prieta is wet all over (in unnamable places)

Gruñiedo la arrulla del lado.: Growling and cooing at her side.

La mujer tigra la acaricia con sus labios.: The tiger woman caresses her with her lips.

el rumor de ranas: the sound of frogs

Se fija al reloj.: She focuses on the clock.

¿Hablas Tex-Mex, o qué?: Do you speak Tex-Mex, or what?

Ronronea: Purr

la bestia: the beast

pelos anaranjados: orange hairs

¡Jijo de su!: Son of a . . . !

la jaguar ruca: the female jaguar

tonto: dummy

en la cama: in the bed

herenga: penis

cuando esa luz que tienes por dentro sale de tu piel: when that
   light inside of you comes out from your skin

cojones: balls

maricones: queers

estás enamorada: you are in love

¡Cállate el hocico!: Shut your mouth!

biscochitos: cookies with cinnamon

¿Que qué?: What what?

¿Qué piensas hacer?: What are you thinking of doing?

las paredes de su cuerpo: the walls around her body

criatura fiera de la lluvia: fierce creature of the rain

animalitos: little animals

llama al jaguar: calls out to the jaguar

19

Song of the Rattlesnake / Canción de cascabel

Pero la muerte, desde dentro, ve.
pero la muerte, desde dentro, vela.
pero la muerte, desde dentro, mata.
    But death, from the inside, sees.
    But death, from the inside, keeps vigil.
    But death, from the inside, kills.

                —Blas de Otero, "La Tierra"

La Prieta stood before the glass door of St. Luke's clutching her stomach. Her reflection startled her. She looked thin, almost skeletal, like a small version of la pelona. She walked through, the door shut behind her dimming the roar of the San Francisco afternoon traffic. Rattle, rattle, slither—sound stopped her in her tracks. She looked around. Couldn't anyone else hear it? She held up her left hand and stared at her rattlesnake ring. Pain jabbed through her lower body. When it eased, she shuffled her way to Admissions. From there she was escorted down a white corridor to a room where a plastic bracelet with her name was put on her left wrist.

Did she want a TV? No, she said. Did she have any valuables she wanted locked up? No, she wanted her books and her journal with her. Her vocation? Poet and teacher. Next of kin? Mother. Contact in San Francisco? Teté. Teté? Yes, just Teté.

A male orderly escorted Prieta to the elevator and up to the tenth floor. He led her down a hallway smelling of alcohol, chlorine, and pine cleaner. The orderly left her before the door to 1014, a private room at the end of the hall. Private? In the isolation ward? Was her infection that dangerous? She totaled up the number. Numerologically, it added up to six. Six was her destiny.

The door swished shut behind her. The bed had rails. It reminded her of prison bars, and she wondered if she'd escape this place alive. She dropped her backpack on the narrow bed and walked to the window. Through the venetian blinds she saw the hills of Bernal Heights to the east. Below, traffic snarled at the intersection of Valencia and Army. Teté was somewhere out there in Noe Valley or the Castro. She could picture him with notebook and pen in hand, books stacked on the table, as he enthusiastically aired his political views with the radical flamboyant queer boys that hung out at Cafe Flor downing tall glasses of lattes.

Swish. Squish, suck. Suede soles on tile. A slender blond nurse wearing bright red lipstick said, "Let's get you settled in." From her slight accent Prieta realized she was Latina, a light-skinned Latina. Prieta wondered if she looked down on Chicanas as did a lot of the Latinas she had met. Prieta locked eyes with her, thought she saw compassion in her eyes. Ve algo en mis ojos, Prieta guessed, hugging her stomach. You'd think she'd get used to wan, anemic-looking people in a hospital.

The nurse reached to help Prieta get out of her shirt and jeans.

"No gracias, I can do it," Prieta said. She stripped and slipped her arms into the sleeves of the gown with the tiny blue flowers and the split down the back.

"Here, honey, let me," said the nurse, tying the ends into bows at neck and waist, then gently smoothing her back. She put away Prieta's things, chatting all the while, "There's this singles club I go to, been going for years. Every Saturday when I get off work. You don't think it's too late for me to find the right man, do you?"

Prieta's hair flowed down to her waist, and straights assumed she was like them and talked about their husbands or boyfriends.

"No," Prieta said, "it's never too late to find a mate." Prieta knew the nurse lied about her age.

"Have you been here before?"

"A couple of times as an outpatient for lab work," Prieta told her, feeling that at least there was one other person she had something in common with even if it was only Spanish.

The door swished. Alone. Glad for the respite, Prieta opened the drawer of her bedside table and, taking out the Guadalupe candle and photos of her father and grandmothers, created a tiny altar on top. She took off her snake ring, a birthday gift from Teté, and placed it in the drawer with her pen and black journal. Then she eased onto the high bed, drawing the thin cotton sheet up to her chin. The venetian blind slats cut the sunlight into vertical strips down her lower body.

Swish. Squeak. A second nurse came in pushing a cart. Needles in yellow packets, long catheters, and packets of alcohol sponges lay on the tray in neat order. The nurse placed a thick rubber string about Prieta's left arm, tightened it, then raised her left wrist. Prieta watched as she plunged the needle in a vein, pulled it out, jabbed it into another vein. Pulled. Jabbed. Prieta looked up into the nurse's eyes, saw apology in them.

"Tough hide," the nurse said under her breath. Thud, the nurse had tossed the bent needle into the wastebasket. Plop. The alcohol-sodden puff followed the needle. Prieta took a deep breath. Blood, alcohol. Over the last three months she'd gotten used to the smell.

The nurse leaned toward the headrest, brushing against Prieta. Buzz. She spoke into the intercom over the bed.

Swish. Another nurse came in and, moving Prieta's arm this way and that, tried to find a vein big enough for the IV needle. "Your veins aren't prominent enough and your skin is very resistant to the needle."

Prieta examined her own pale lavender veins, feathery and broken. Another metallic clink, another plop. The nurse leaned into the intercom. Buzz. A minute later the Latina nurse swished in.

"No, I can't do it. I've never liked pricking people," the Latina told the other two nurses, winking at Prieta.

"But you like getting pricked, don't you?"

"Oh, and what were you doing with the doctor in the linen closet?" said the Latina.

"How'd you ever make it to an RN?" said one.

"How'd you ever make it with the doctor?" the Latina kidded her.

Except for the Latina the other two nurses ignored her; she might as well be a piece of furniture, better yet a pin cushion.

Swish. The fourth nurse, a thin wiry woman with a no-nonsense manner, found a thin bluish vein along the inside left wrist. She hung the intravenous bottle on the pole. All eyes monitored its slow dripping. Tears, Prieta thought, beading down the plastic tube and into her vein. The Latina pulled up the bed's side rails. Swish. Prieta, wrapped in a frayed bed sheet, felt like a baby abandoned in a barred crib.

She was alone at last. But before she could relax, swish, "I'm your dietitian and I'd like to discuss your meal selection." The thin white woman hid her face behind a clipboard. Chicken and fish but no red meat, no caffeine, yes, Sanka, said Prieta. She closed her eyes. Swish, squeak-squeak, slither. Another nurse entered—or was it one who had attended her before—all their faces were beginning to look alike. A Black orderly pushing an empty wheelchair followed her.

Squeak, swish. The orderly pushed Prieta onto the white corridor, the nurse rolled the IV pole on its tripod wheels alongside her. The rubber shish, the inseams of the orderly's starched white pants rubbed together. Tinkle, the elevator doors opened. Schup. The swift descent to the fourth floor. They parked her before the X-ray lab door.

A small Asian American woman with a mobile mouth, one that quirked at the corners, wheeled her inside. It was the same woman who had been nice to her weeks ago on her two previous visits as an outpatient. "What do you like most about your work?" Prieta asked her.

As they talked, Prieta relaxed, body sinking into the wheelchair. She saw the sign again, orange letters on a black background: "Si hay posibilidad de estar en cinta, por favor notificar el Doctor Técnico que está en servicio antes de tomar un examen de rayo-x." She ran her hands down her swollen belly. The writer in her put in the missing accent mark on Técnico and noted the incorrect verb form.

Two white male technicians came in. The tall heavy-set one injected dye into her kidneys. She stared at the needle piercing her vein, syringe taped along her right forearm. It was filled with a chemical ready to be pumped into her blood stream if she should have a bad reaction to the kidney injection. The other, thin and balding, took x-rays before and after. Soon her crotch got hot and her skin began to itch.

Prieta asked, pointing at the apparatus. One answered, "An IVP."

The technicians did three blood tests. One of them pulled her gown up. Prieta forced her hands to lay still and not jerk her gown down again. She felt open to their male gaze with her belly exposed. She wouldn't have minded as much had they been women. She willed herself not to flinch when his gloved hand rubbed something cool and gelatinous on the mound. He placed the metal scanner, which looked like a cup lined with rubber, on her belly. She didn't let herself jerk from the touch nor at the prying eye of the ultra-sonogram looking through the walls of her abdomen and uterus. It bombarded her insides with a beam of high-frequency sound waves inaudible to the human ear. As the three pairs of eyes watched, the echoes of the waves bounced off the insides of her stomach and appeared as dark masses on the monitor. The tech slid the mouth of the camera up and down and around Prieta's belly and she realized there was nowhere to hide, no longer any refuge inside the body, the last frontier transgressed.

"I can't find her bladder. There, that's her bladder." A mass the size of a grapefruit appeared on the screen.

"Nah, that's her uterus."

They spoke softly, but Prieta heard them. She looked from one to the other, shivered and clenched her stomach trying to contain the nausea. In the eyes of all white-cloaked beings, she was just a collection of body parts, not a whole. Voyeurs all, including her. They took x-rays again, to compare with those taken before.

Back in her room the Latina nurse helped Prieta out of the wheelchair and Prieta lurched toward the bathroom, the nurse following. Prieta grasped the rim of the sink with one hand to steady herself, and, with the other hand, swept the mass of long black hair to one side. She bent down until her forehead touched the cool porcelain. The heaves turned dry then stopped. Prieta rinsed out her mouth, looked around for the toilet paper and, not trusting her legs to reach it, she blew her nose with her fingers and let the water wash it all down.

"You've got a bit more color in your cheeks now," the nurse said. Prieta looked up and stared at the ghost face in the mirror.

"I've been sick for months and they haven't got a clue. I'm tired all the time; my whole body aches," Prieta said.

"Let's get you into bed, dear." The nurse gently pushed her toward the bed. "The doctor will fix everything."

"Maybe I throw up because there're things I can't stomach," Prieta said.

"I'll send the dietitian in."

"I'm not talking about food. You know—feelings, stuff I don't want to face. My body takes it on."

"Yeah, that's hospital food for you, but actually the food here isn't so bad." Swish.

She might as well be invisible. But she couldn't really fault the nurses, they were overworked and under paid. And here she was in this sterile place without her eagle feather. They'd taken it away and now she'd lost her way. Swish. The nurse helped her onto the bed and gave her a painkiller and two sleeping pills though it was not Prieta's bedtime. Prieta never went to sleep before three in the morning, nor before smoking her two cigarettes. She'd be OK as long as she stayed awake. She lit her candle; the slow-burning brasa in her belly was flaring into a small conflagration—the virus feeding on her flesh, her blood, growing. Her uterus, the site of infection, had to be conquered along with the virus. After months of antibiotics and weekly visits to Valencia Clinic in the Mission her doctor still did not know what kind of virus it was. And now ¡ay diosita! they were going to cut her open.

Thu-dud, thu-dud, thu-dud, her heart beat faster and faster. She took deep breaths. El soplo del miedo chilled the sweat beading every pore. Sintió la frialdad de la brasa, the iciness of a burning coal.

Las sombras crept closer. She reached for the small cabinet beside her bed, pulled the drawer out, groped for pen and black bound journal. A cramp in her uterus froze her. When it eased, she felt a strange sensation in her womb—ovulation signaling with a pin prick? Or the seaweed the doctor had shot into her cervix in order to dilate it and make the pain go away? Estaba acalambrada. Le entró asco, se iba a vomitar. She clamped down on the nausea before it could rise up her throat. Pero dejó un sabor ácido en su boca. Swallowing, she clutched her pen and her journal and concentrated on relaxing her body muscle by muscle. She stopped resisting.

She was very quiet, bien quietita estaba Prieta. Only her eagle eyes moved, searching the room . . . for what? She looked at the long slats of the venetian blinds, tucked into each other like scales on a snake. She looked through the window searching for la diosa de la luna Coyolxauhqui. La luna le había tocado. Her period had started. She didn't want the masked strangers in the operating room staring at the Kotex between her naked thighs. It probably wouldn't make any difference to the doctor cutting her open—what was a little more blood. When the nurse came in Prieta asked her for a sanitary pad.

She remembered the last time she had seen her grandmother: Mamagrande lay broken under the hospital sheets straining to breathe. Her breath, a storm raging in her chest, driving out through her nostrils a fine mist that sprinkled the pillow with tiny red dots. Again, Prieta heard her moaning. She remembered the last time she had seen her papi: he lay bleeding and broken under the red truck, under the white bales of cotton, his blood coagulating on the hot pavement. Again, Prieta heard him moaning.

The nurse brought her a large sanitary napkin.

Clutching her fountain pen she fell asleep. In her dreams she was lying in bed naked. A red river flowed along the edge of her bed. La Llorona floated near the foot of the bed, crying, "Ay mijita." La Llorona turns into "la pelona," la muerte.

Swish, the sound of the breakfast cart woke her. She got up, brushed her teeth and peed. Dark red blood clots lined the center of her sanitary napkin. Tenía too much asco to eat. She pushed away the scrambled eggs that resembled dry dog vomit. She was finishing her grapefruit juice when her doctor from the Valencia Clinic walked in. He was a handsome man with intense blue eyes, a shock of blonde hair over a receding hairline. Two days ago, he'd called her at home, told her that the latest lab report had just come in, and ordered her to go immediately to the hospital, to have her friends take her, or take a cab if she had to. She'd told him that none of her friends own cars, that she was too weak to take the bus, that she didn't have money for a cab, and that she'd go on Monday. He told her that he was not going to be responsible if anything happened to her, anger and fear rising in his voice. Was he afraid for her or afraid that she'd slap a malpractice suit on him.

"Why didn't you check in when I told you?" He placed his hand briefly over her small hand cupping her swollen belly. "This thing could have exploded in your belly. You could be dead right now. You must have been in excruciating pain for months. Why didn't you say something?"

¿Cómo quería que se quejara? How could she speak with the gag in her mouth. The gag had been there since before kindergarten. Mexican girls, muchachas buenas, did not speak of their private parts, their nalgas and verijas, except when snickering in private. As for the menstrual cramps, she was too young to have them. The doctors said it was all in her mind. She'd gotten used to the pain. Given enough time you can get used to anything.

After three months of probing her vagina, of prescribing antibiotics of one type after the other, of blood and urine tests, he hadn't been able to bring her fever down, nor get rid of the viral infection, nor determine exactly what were esos animalitos, los

viros, colonizing her insides. Estaba empreñada. She'd had a dream
before coming to the hospital. Her eyes had crawled underneath the
skin down to her swollen stomach and watched the thing moving,
gnawing her tender core, prodding the walls. It was trying to find
a way out. She was pregnant with death. She was the host; death
was the fetus with a giant snake's head.

But now the white walls of the hospital were eating up all
her dreams. She hadn't remembered one in days. And the doctor
still didn't know what it was, didn't know what had caused the
fibroids in her uterus to turn into tumors. Had no idea. ¡Chingao!
Western medicine!

Again her eyeballs turned and sank down into her belly.
Down the slick red visceral tunnels to her belly. The tumors were
covered with blisters, pulsating mouths, hot and thirsty with tiny
teeth all speaking at once. How could she have known whom to
believe? Hadn't her body betrayed her from the very beginning?
La había traicionado. Aquí estaba ella, her body driven by pain.
Había preferido, había buscado los altos fuera del cuerpo, but pain
had pulled her back into her body. She was unable to escape the
body nor the bronze earth in the Valley of South Texas that held
her deepest roots.

Piedra. Quería volverse piedra. She wanted to turn into stone,
but the drug was beginning to loosen her limbs. She was falling.
Slither. Rattle, rattle, rattle. Entre sueños oía el ruido seco de
víbora. Between consciousness and sleep, entre suspiros roncos,
en una vocecita lejanísima alguien le hablaba from the other side
of the wall. Esa serpiente negra, desde las sombras la miraba con
reptile eyes con ojos sin pestañas. With her thousand lidless eyes
the snake stared at Prieta. Rattle. Lo único seguro en ésta vida era
la muertecita. Sooner or later Death would lay her hand on her.
At night she sensed it hiding in the darkened corners of her room.

When she woke up from her nap, a man in a white jacket
was sitting at her bed side. She smelled the smoke on him. He
coughed into his hands and told her he was to be her surgeon.
She took out her journal and pen and began to record what he
was saying. She had large masses in her stomach, he said. Cough.

They'd become infected. Cough. The kidney x-ray showed that she was anemic. Her blood sugar was 65, below the lowest normal level. She was suffering from malnutrition. Why hadn't she been eating, he asked her. The white count was 3300, 10.9 hemoglobin. Her urine was concentrated—she wasn't getting enough fluids. It was necessary that he take out the tumors and the abscesses in the tubes. Cough. He would try to save the ovarian tissue, but he might have to make a clean sweep of everything: tubes, ovaries, uterus, appendix. He wanted carte blanche from her. Cough, cough.

"What will happen to my body if you take my ovaries out?" she asked him. The function of the uterus was to have babies, he said, and to have periods. The ovaries were what made a woman feminine. If she lost her ovaries what would that make her? Unfeminine, barren. She and Teté had considered having a child, but she'd vetoed the idea. Though medically it would have been OK, they were cousins.

The doctor stood up; said she would go through artificial premature menopause. But, they would give her hormone shots. Cough, cough. Swish.

After he left, she wrote in her journal. Menopause. Chingao, she'd go through menopause before her mother. At lunch she nibbled half-heartedly on the tuna on white bread. Swish, the surgeon walked in like a tour guide with her Valencia Clinic doctor trailing behind. Today they would do an EKG cough, cough and try the sonogram again and tomorrow or the next day, when she was stronger, they would operate. They would do a pre-op on her, and empty her bowels, the surgeon said.

When they stepped out, she began meditating on the unlit Guadalupe candle—they had prohibited her from lighting it. "What an amazing story," she heard the surgeon tell her doctor, their voices barely audible on the other side of the door.

"Bleeding at such an early age."

"Imagine," said the other, "she was three months old when she started menstruating."

"The over-production of hormones must have slowed her growth," said the surgeon.

"Yes, she stopped growing at 12." He had a term for it.

"And you say when she first came to you, she'd been ill for months and hadn't even known it?"

"Yes, for a couple of months, maybe more. The only reason she came in was that one of her housemates had hepatitis and everyone there had to get checked out. Otherwise, it would have gone undetected until it was too late."

Then voices faded down the hall. She wanted to write the word for the defect she was born with in her journal along with what the doctors had said, but she couldn't remember what they'd called it. Her fingers were trembling, and her writing looked large and ungainly, like that of a child.

Later just when she thought she'd have some time to herself, swish, the surgeon entered with another lab report. He had looked at the sonogram photos, he said. Masses of new tissue were growing in her uterus. Something was amiss with the E. coli, an intestinal tract bacterium. Yes, the infection had seeped into her uterus and the microorganisms were multiplying at an alarming rate and they were spawning tumors where her fibroids used to be. Ten of them. One was bigger than a grapefruit and growing fast. If it burst, well. . . .

"We can't wait another day like we'd planned. You know, to fatten you up," he said, cough, as he put the metal disc over her chest. Breathe deeply. Hold. He put the stethoscope into the side pocket of his white jacket. Mañana, he said, they'd have to operate. Mañana. Anglos always used the word when speaking to a Mexican.

"As it is, that may be leaving it too. . . . Well, cough, we couldn't operate today."

Swish. He left before she could ask the question she'd been wanting to ask since her first day in the hospital.

She pressed her fingers into her belly and reached for the glass of water with the other. The monster in her womb had gotten bigger. She could feel it crowding the other organs. She could feel it pressing against the ceiling of the diaphragm. Embarazada. In utero. But with nothing human, a virus that wouldn't die. No antibiotic could kill it. None could bring the fever down. The fibroids inside the lining of her uterus, outside the uterus, on her ovaries and the tubes were growing—ten sets of tentacles with sucking mouths feeding on her. Incubi. She'd been wrestling with these parasites for months. If the abnormal fetuses came to term they would kill her. Sweat pooled in her armpits and between her breasts. Fever was burning her up.

And her mami knew nothing about it. Prieta hadn't wanted to worry her. Now in her loneliness she needed su mami. Pero su mami estaba allá lejos en el rancho. Her mother had no money to fly here from Texas and Prieta had none to send her. Besides, Prieta couldn't imagine her dealing with airplanes, she who had never been on a train, bus, nor taxi. The big city would swallow her while Prieta lay hooked up to the drip drip, listening to the dry scaly rattle coming closer, her stomach swelling and swelling. Where was Teté when she needed him? Nothing but to go through her ordeal alone.

Swish. The nurse was back. Had she passed gas? Had she moved her bowels?

"No, I can't fart, and I can't shit," Prieta told her.

The nurse's lips thinned. Swish, the door shut. Swish, the nurse returned, held out a tiny pleated paper cup with four tablets in it—to help her move her bowels.

Swish. Had she moved her bowels yet? No, Prieta told her, the train hadn't moved. The nurse held out a pack of Fleet suppositories, saying, you know the drill, right? No, Prieta said, but I can read instructions, you go on. But the nurse stayed. Swish. Another nurse saying, "Nothing yet? Give her an enema." Swish. A rubber bag with a clear nozzle. Prieta felt them part her cheeks, felt the fingers and the cool lubricant. And though she wanted to escape those fingers Prieta stood perfectly still. She felt the rectal tip pressing against her anus, and then warm liquid entering her. She felt a fullness, then a fierce churning and a bittersweet pressure in her bowels. She spread both palms on her belly, felt it expanding. She had to hold it in, had to squeeze her buttocks together. Rushing to the bathroom, her feet caught on the IV tubing, the pole swayed, she righted it, hands hitting the bathroom door.

She just barely made it, whoosh whoosh water and a great wind erupting into the john. Olió la pestilencia de la bacteria colonizing her female organs. Fucked twice, three, four, five times—by the microscopic snake-like bacteria, the doctors' fingers, the speculum, the suppository, and now the enema. ¡Que chingen a sus padres!

Her friends called, even her landlord called. Teish, a practicing Santería priestess, phoned, offering to do a healing ritual to Yemayá by the ocean. Sus amigas trooped in in twos and threes. One walked in, the subtle aroma of roses wafting from the bunch she held in her arms lifted Prieta's spirits. Another handed her a small jar of lip balm in her favorite flavor, banana, and a third gave her a marijuana cigarette. Swish. They left.

Swish. Her house mates, Teté and Zenobio, came in. Her primo Teté brought in the sun with a painting of Seal Rock in bold colors and his lopsided smile. When he saw her, he looked so panic stricken she almost giggled. She knew he was thinking, "how dare she be sick?" She the strong one was flat on her back and oh so pale. Guilt in his eyes and behind it fear.

"You're looking better," he lied, hugged her hard.

Sensing Zenobio's eyes on them, she released his embrace though she wanted nothing more than to feel his solid body. Teté handed her a pack of peacock ink cartridges for her fountain pen. Prieta unscrewed the pen and replaced the spent cartridge, her hand trembling so much she almost dropped the cap.

Zenobio gave her a small hug, saying, "I brought you some incense though I wasn't sure they'd let you light it. I can't stay long; I've got to go back to work."

Prieta asked him, "How are you liking your new job at the frame shop? Is it allowing you enough time to do your collages?" Teté's personality was so vibrant that others paled when in the same room, and she didn't want Zenobio to feel slighted by her, or jealous of her relationship with Teté. You had to tread gingerly when you lived with two lovers and one of them was your best friend.

Zenobio left. She and Teté stared at each other. "¿Y cómo está la malita?" he asked.

She wanted to tell him how sick she was, but the look on his face made her say, "Me van a desmadrar."

"Yeah sure," he snorted. "You always hang tough."

"Yeah well, if I didn't, you'd fall apart," she said. "Te hecho de menos, cabrón," she told him. "¿Apesto a perra muerta o qué?"

She scrambled out of bed and into the bathroom, barely making it to the sink. As she retched noiselessly Teté held a wet washcloth to her brow. In the mirror, she watched their two faces, saw fear in both sets of eyes, saw guilt. She saw the sheen of tenderness in their eyes.

Holding his eyes she told him, "I will survive this. Haven't I always survived everything?" She coaxed her lips into a smile saying, "Besides, now that my stomach is empty the doctors can have one more shot with their tests."

He helped her back to the bed and sat on the edge of the bed clasping her hand tightly. This somber serious face was so unlike him. Where were his mad antics, off-color jokes, and irreverence toward the world?

"I hate it when you're ill. I can't beat up on you when you're too sick to fight back."

She stroked his arm trying to comfort him. Tomorrow was the Vernal Equinox, she told him, the time to get rid of all the shit you no longer needed. Ni modo, certain pieces of her body just had to go. And you know something else, she told him, numerologically March 20 adds up to two, the vibration missing in her name. Yes, two was her karma. The sun was in her fourth house. She'd timed it just right, hadn't she?

Teté had read her cards last week and she'd drawn the Tower Card, number 16. Lightning had struck her house and her foundations were crumbling. No, don't. She didn't want him to call 'Amá. There was nothing her mother could do, she'd just worry. No te ahuites. Que será será, she said, knowing that cliche bugged the shit out of him. Pura macha mi prieta, he said, bending down and kissing her head.

Ten minutes later Teté left. Despair settled on her body like lead. Even the thin hospital blanket was an intolerable weight pressing against her swollen belly. She clasped her hands under the sheet and raised them to form a tent over her body. Pinche buey, he could have stayed a little longer, probably thought Zenobio would mind if he spent too much time with her.

Her eagle eyes searched. It wasn't in the closet, or behind the shower stall on the other side of the walls or windows. Where? Her visitors had distracted her from her vigil, and now it had gotten inside. Was it hiding or in the bottle dripping fluid into her veins?

Swish. Cough. The man in white. She waited for words of power to ward off fear and the other demons. She waited for the magical word, for the spell that would repel the thing under her bed. Instead, the white-frocked surgeon gave her a piece of paper. The consent form. He wanted carte blanche, "may need to take out the appendix, before we sew you up quick, ha, ha. It'll be easy once you're wide open." She told him she wanted to think about it. He stopped talking. Quick—she might not have another chance to get a word in. She asked her question: "will this operation kill me doctor?" Sir? They were dealing with an unknown virus, he said, not meeting her eye. Swish.

As she fell back into the bed she saw the slasher wielding his scalpel, saw the knife sliding down her belly, the belly of the deer. Back en el rancho she was the one gutting the deer her brother had killed. She and her mother skinned it, decapitated it, quartered it, dismembered it, cut it into strips, hung the strips on the clothesline to dry.

She reached for the lever, turned it. Metal grated on metal, the head of the bed quaked, and rose. Should she embrace esa callada amenaza del cuchillo or not? The Mexican in her lay still, an impenetrable rock, after thousands of years of being kicked around. She knew there was no longer any refuge inside the body. Cuchillo o ningún cuchillo, iba al encuentro de su destino, even if she had to crawl. Pero amachada iba Prieta. Stubborn as always, balking, her mother would say if she knew. To her mother the doctor was god.

Where was la diosa de la basura, Tlazolteotl and her priest, to hear her confession? She pulled out her journal, propped it on her chest. From a small pouch she emptied out the three Chinese coins, rubbed her fingers over them feeling the raised squares within the circles. The smooth side was yang, the side with letters was yin.

She sat legs tucked under her, feet against her buttocks, Indian style. Swish. Time for your medication, the nurse told her, lowering the top of the bed and removing the journal and I Ching coins. But Prieta had her answer, the spirit of the oracle had spoken. If she did not give the doctor carte blanche, The Darkening of the Light hexagram, with 9 in the third and 6 in the fifth, going into Difficulty at the Beginning would be her lot. If she did give him carte blanche her situation would be The Clinging, the hexagram of fire over fire, with 9 in the third place and 9 in the sixth. Its future hexagram was Chen, The Arousing, her birth hexagram, thunder over thunder.

She closed her eyes, breathed deeply and thought of the two double sevens in her name. 7, the number associated with initiation; 7, the number of steps of the inner journey; 7, the number of stages in the alchemical process. Both her inner and her total self were double sevens.

Submit, submit. In ire, "to enter into." Carte blanche, blank letter.

She picked up her pen, signed the form, and blew on her signature.

The nurse told her they would shave her pubic hair in the morning. The next invasion.

In the morning, an orderly showed up with the food tray. Prieta told him that she wasn't supposed to eat but he fed her—hasta le trajo vino. Híjole, alcohol and downers! The nurse returned later and told Prieta they had fed her by mistake. Down this, she told her, handing her a bottle of castor oil. She would have to wait another day for the operation, wait for the Spring Equinox, the time ridding yourself of unwanted stuff. She tore out a blank page from the journal, then tore half a dozen strips from it. On separate pieces of paper she listed the things she wanted to get rid of: fifteen pounds, insomnia, her obsessive need to control everything, and her impossible love for her queer cousin. She couldn't burn the strips of paper—hospital safety rules—so she tore them into tiny pieces and flushed them down the toilet.

Next morning Prieta waited, eyes turned to the window staring at the orange haze slowly rising over the city. Swish. No food, no water, the nurse told her, enforced fast so she wouldn't vomit during the anesthesia. Immediately Prieta was thirsty.

Prieta waited. Las sombras se movían en las esquinas. Swish. The nurse returned and turned her on her side. The smell of alcohol, the cool dab on her buttocks, and then the needle's sting. Slowly the live coal inside was extinguished. Bien quieta estaba Prietita. She was about to fall, she was falling headfirst into the shadows.

When she woke up, she held onto the fragment of a dream by a thin strand. Slowly she reeled in the rest of the dream. She was standing by a freshly dug grave. Her brother Nune stood twenty-five feet away, his piercing eyes holding hers. He pointed a rifle at her. The shot rang out and she fell into the grave and was buried. She rose up beside another freshly dug grave and again he shot her, and she fell into the grave and was buried. She was standing by a third grave. Again, she saw the flash of the gun and heard the spat of the bullet, and again she fell. She rose up again, he shot her, she fell, until the air was gray and reeked of gunpowder. La tierra estaba vestida con zempazuchitl flowers. They shrouded the long line of graves all bearing her name. The drug had been charitable; it had at least left her this dream.

Sentío una presencia in the shadows. She heard the dry slithering sound of the serpent, saw su luz negra. Vío su hocico open. She wanted to swallow Prieta por entero y por fin, to possess her once and for all. And closer still oía el ruido seco de las víboritas inside her entrails. Estaba embarazada—de la muerte, con la muerta.

The scrub nurse stripped her, shaved her abdomen, and her pubic hair, washed her lower body. Bautismo, ritual bath, Prieta said under her breath. Another priestess in regulation white drew blue lines on her belly, dressed her in a wrinkled gown, then stretched her flat across the gurney.

They rolled her into the elevator. It was March 20th, the Spring Equinox. She descended to OR-B on the second floor. The letter b equaled two. In the Tarot the second trump card was the Priestess. In the Crowley deck she sat at the entrance with arms raised, full moon on top of her head. She kept watch at the threshold, the portal of the soul. A transparent veil of light emanating from her covered the scroll with truths which cannot be conveyed to the outer world. They wheeled her into the room with white ceramic tile walls and white vinyl floor. The anesthesiologist brought her ether. Ese seco sonido de las víboras, couldn't the nurses hear it?

She was about to cross the threshold.

She was falling into the arms of darkness, her mother.

Prieta is asleep. But los muchos ojos que son Prieta watch the anesthesiologist inject a drug through the valve of the IV line, paralyzing her skeletal muscles, paralyzing the muscles of the throat—she can't breathe. He pushes an endotracheal tube past her stilled tongue. He compresses the ventilation bag, it breathes for her. He adjusts the flow meters on the ether bottle, checks the gauge pressure of the compressed air cylinder. He rubs jelly on her lower chest and attaches the electrodes. He monitors her heart rate and rhythm, temperature and blood pressure.

Doctors in scrub suits enter the white room. The nurse washes her belly with antibacterial soap. Large rectangular-shaped lamps shine bright. Covered heads and masks converge on the still figure lying on the table. The surgeon holds the scalpel over the belly, makes a vertical incision through the skin from an inch above the belly button down to below the line of shaven pubic hair. He cuts through the subcutaneous tissue, turning up the flaps of the fascia.

"Clamps," the word loud in stark lights. The assistant clamps hemostats on the ends of the bleeding blood vessels, then ties them shut.

"Scalpel." Slap. The knife flashes, cuts the peritoneum, baring the contents of the abdomen. The gloved hands plunge in, come out glistening. Slap of the knife against palm. The blade catches the light; he frees the uterus from the other organs, then pitches the red shining mass into a plastic bag. Plop. Fallopian tubes and ovaries follow, then other bits of flesh. He drains the abscesses. A tie on an artery slips off. Her abdominal cavity fills with blood.

"It's taking too long," he mutters.

"Suture." The slap of needle holder against open palm. The hands move faster, sews up the peritoneum with catgut that will dissolve in two or three weeks. With sutures of silk that will never dissolve, he pulls the stomach muscles together. "Close up, 6-0 silk skin sutures." The slap against open palm, he sews up the hole. The watcher with the many eyes waits.

Like the blow of an ax   de repente   I hear the wind start howling.   the humming gets louder   and louder   a thunder   coming from inside her head.   Swoosh   a stream of white light   a   pulsing and a convulsing stretching the membrane   the portal   like birthing   I gasp   I rest the last wrenching   I crown and push out   through Where-the-Vagina-Is   a luminous thing   quivering in the arctic ice thumping on the ceiling   I huddle in a corner   watch red flowers bloom   on the body below   white-robed priests with blood on their hands hover over her   I flutter against the ceiling feel myself getting   thinner   longer   oigo el machetazo del viente   someone is diving feet first through me (who is this me?) through Where-the-Vagina-Is   diving through a red glisten-ing   tunnel of whorls contracting   pulsing   propelled faster and faster   moving sideways   pushing its way out   No, I am standing still   and it is the luminous thing   inside me rushing through the vagina   turning   spiraling   slithering free still veiled in its casing   a popping sound   then it's free of the cave   light   fills the corridor

I, we are that light floating above the moon. I, we have no body. From above the bright lights I, we watch the body huddling in the corner ceiling and then I, we watch the other body, the lump under the white sheet, watch the belly through the wide slit. Watch He-who-recovers-the-stone slide a shiny obsidian knife over the slit, turning up flaps of pink flesh, see the blood welling up, her life blood sucked by a hose. Her chest rises and falls and then does not rise again. Someone whispers, "Oh, Jesus, she's going into arrest." I, we watch the dreaming body flying from corner to corner, then look down at the white-clad figures. They watch the squiggly line flatten across the blue monitor. The cure-doctor intones the magic word "adrenaline." Into the fourth interspace between the ribs he plunges a three-and-a-half-inch needle to the hilt. They place a round paddle over her left nipple. Place a second one between her breasts. A current of light flows from one paddle to the other. Her body jerks. Again it jerks up, then again. "It's no use. We lost her," he says. I see shadows at the edge. (I, me, we, the body, the other body, her—how many layers are there?)

Prieta is alone with Her, the watcher, the indweller. But where is Teté, her hummingbird, her Hermes, her Ninshubur, the one who will help her mediate between this world and the other? La estira the siren song de cascabel. Its current bears her along a river of black light y la desemboca en el hogar de la muerte. Prieta cae como cuerpo tendido, su cuerpo es el terreno death dances on. Allí canta su canción de cascabel. There at the in-between place, Prieta walks back and forth, desbalagada como huérfana. La mujer serpiente opens her jaws and Prieta slides into her cave mouth. She lands in the Place of No Return, the cave womb of la madre.

She crawls on hands and knees into the abode of darkness. It is pitch black in Tlillan. There is not one ray of light. She comes before a great stone image of la mujer serpiente, Cihuacóatl, la Llorona, the night walker who weeps. Her lower face is bone, stark and naked. Her jaw wide, large mouth open, teeth bared. A slithering sound and the familiar rattle. She gazes at Prieta with her thousand lidless eyes.

Something jerks Prieta out of the mother's arms. No, Prieta cries, I don't want to leave. But the walls contract, forcing Prieta out. Desde su mundo de sueño she feels the serpent slide along her body. The sound of its hollow eternity shakes her, chicotea su cuerpo hasta que la desborda. Como mar chubascozo Death la arrebata into life. A ball of black light la revolca, la tumba. As Prieta descends tiny hummingbird wings brush her face.

I came back   without the help of the cure-doctor   sin
su ayuda volví   I knew the way   conocía el camino   I

had walked this road before   but Prieta does not remember
only I remember   they were trial runs   her near drowning
the assault   her failed suicide   and this   the next will be
her last   dying is an act everyone performs   several times
a lifetime   only nobody remembers

The anesthesiologist stops the ether, removes the endotracheal tube from her mouth. She is wheeled to the recovery room. Nurses monitor her vital signs. She wakes to find a Foley catheter in her urethra. Fucked again; she isn't hija de la chingada for nothing, she laughs. The vulture, pain, jabs her. What a fucking mess it's made of her body. They want her to sit up, to move about, to talk to them. She wants to be left alone.

Waking again to the smell of antiseptics, she floats in time and time keeps no hours. Falling into sleep. Waking, the feel of the thin hospital blanket on her neck. The slow dribble of the purplish blood of strangers slides down the transparent tube into her veins. She has become a vampire. La luz le da golpes. Someone is talking. Is it her dreamself? Talking with the spirits of her dead?

In between sleeping and waking, in the liminal zone of nepantla. Noche, she writes in her journal, me quiero esconder en tus pétalos. Like Schrodinger's cat, both dead and alive simultaneously. She hears the murmurings of other worlds.

She listens to my disemboweled voice
speaking from the depths:
She follows my voice down into this black cave
She and I are together. But her "visits"
become briefer and farther between.
She can not bring me up to her surface,
can no longer bring what she has learned in the cave
up to the light of day. She floats in between
where I am
where I am the source. Down here
she is oblivious to the white-robed inhabitants
of the upper region, her ear and eye spin
in the vortex of my pulse.
Here in this way-station she lacks nothing.

Her severed womb and other pieces join each other
like the separate parts of Coyolxauhqui,
the one dismembered by her brother.
Now she lacks nothing.

Prieta was sleeping, dreaming she was six years old. She felt
the thirst of the parched earth, heard the wings of the hummingbird, saw it hover over the red flower. Now she is fourteen; there
was a hoe in her hands. The fierce heat of the sun fell on her back
like the blow of an ax. Now she was much older and sitting in a
room surrounded by white kids, her head buried in a book, hoping the Anglo teacher would not call on her. Prieta was bending
over her papi's coffin; then she is an adult putting flowers on her
grandmother's grave; now in Elmwood Park on a swing, kicking
her legs into the air and laughing at Teté's jokes. Prieta looked into
the eyes of her best friend, her primo. Suddenly she knew. Knew
the answer to a question she had never dared ask. In Teté's eyes
she saw her own eyes reflected. And in the sound of one chord of
her rattlesnake song she knew something else. A fierce tenderness
filled her. She had fallen in love with Death, too, and had lost her.

And waking she remembered. Drifting, she was drifting away.
She touched her tongue to the sides of her mouth and palate; they
were as dry as ojas de maíz.

Olor de alcohol, the coolness of her exposed buttocks, the
prick of the needle. Riddled with marks. Her buttocks would be
dimpled in dozens of places forever. "What day is it?" she asked
the nurse. Her thick tongue filled her mouth slurring her words.
She couldn't swallow.

At first, the nurses helped her to the bathroom. Soon she was
walking her turtle pace on her own, listening to the shuffle shuffle
of her Birkenstocks, the squeak of the IV on wheels. She toddled
to the bathroom on her own. Shhh. Water showered down on her
naked body. A treat. Joy entered her; no more bed sponge baths.
This door she could lock, here she could be sick and helpless,
for a few minutes she could surrender to the tubes and catheters.
Her hospital room was the most public place she had ever lived

in, and about one hundred times more expensive than any hotel room. Without Medi-Cal they would have let her die.

Puh-thud puh-thud. The scaffold-looking walker ate one foot of the long white hall, then another and another. It slowly swallowed the curve of the U-shaped corridor, slowly creeping up the hall to the other side, then back into her room where she carefully edged herself onto her bed. Every few hours a nurse came and uncurled her from her burrow. Holding the syringe up to the light, flushing out the air bubbles, she would pierce her buttocks with pain killers and estrogen shots. Better to bear the indignity and feel the prick than the invisible invasion through the IV tube. Su sangre espesa como piedra se hizo un mar hirviendo, then caught fire.

Puh-thud shuffle puh-thud shuffle, the song of sacrifice and healing. "Otomy is to cut into, scalp, to make incisions, extomy to remove, suture to stitch. To love myself is to die, to love myself is to live." She chanted the words to the rhythm of: puh-thud, shuffle shuffle.

> Prieta's eyes are dull, she no longer sees me
> no longer hears el ruido de mis alas de víbora
> no longer feels el chicoteo entre su cuerpo
> ni mi beso desperatador
> No light shines under her skin and
> her breath is shallow
> Prieta has forgotten that she knows me

Swish. A nurse stood over her, rubbed lotion on the purple welts riddling her arms, combed her long hair, alive as any snake, brillísimo como si fuera vivo. She had lost 50 pounds, the nurse told her. In her mind's eye Prieta saw the strip of paper with the words 15 lbs. torn to pieces and flushed down the toilet.

"You know what's strange? That I'm going through menopause before my mother," Prieta told her. "Do you know what they call a castrated woman?"

The surgeon came in. He checked her stitches, told her that the infection still lived, the fever persisted, but that both would go away in a week or so. Prieta opened her journal and counted the days. It was the seventh day of the ninth week since the doctor had noticed the virus. Diosa-dios only knew how long it had lived inside her.

Hadn't he scraped it all out, she asked him. Yes, he said. What was left her body's immune system would kill. But would it kill her other "infection," she wondered.

Snip, snip. As he snipped the stitches, intermittent fits of trembling would overtake the hand holding the scissors over her belly. No wonder her scar was so crooked and jagged. She took the tweezers out of his hand and pulled out the stitches. They would have to burn everything even though it was sterile, he said. So if she wanted this stuff—scissors, tweezers, gauze, surgical tape, the sheets and blankets—she should take them, he told her.

"Can I have my uterus?" she said. "Did you save it for me like I asked you?"

"I forgot."

Prieta's breath hitched. "Oh, but I wanted to do a ritual." She and Teish had planned to walk to the edge of the sea and offer Yemayá a watermelon.

"Do you want a memento?" he asked.

"No, I've got one," she said running her finger down the livid snake-like scar that undulated from waist to clit. When she'd first looked in the mirror the scar looked like the seam of her labia, a grotesque pussy extending to her waist.

She exercised and exercised. Shuffle, shuffle thump, went her cane. Every evening after Teté or one of her other visitors left she would shuffle shuffle thump alone past the U-shaped counter of the nurse's station. She would pass the familiar row of trays, the patients' charts in their steel gray jackets. She would lurch along the long hall, turn left, then walk back down the hall. Another left and she would find herself back at the nurses' station.

A white gay male nurse started offering his arm, inviting her for a "promenade" every evening. Limp-wrist, he'd swing his hips and exaggerate his "oh honeys," as he walked her up and down the hall. Soon he had her laughing. His antics reminded her of Teté's.

When the robed inhabitants looked at him sashaying amongst their midst, Prieta saw disgust, outrage, and pity in their eyes. When she was with him, she no longer felt so isolated. In an Arctic land two queers is a community. Soon she could walk without clinging to his arm.

One night, her ninth night in the hospital, she walked past the nurses' outpost. No nurse stood vigil. The patients snored in their rooms. She found herself in front of the stack of charts. Hers was the first one. She plucked it up, opened it, and leafed through it hurriedly: history and physical; chief complaint and history of present illness; physical exam, labs and x-rays; summary, assessment and treatment plan; physician's progress notes—OPERATION: pre-operative diagnosis, labs, B-Scan, operation plan, operation as performed, complications, anesthesia notes, estimated blood loss, post-operative diagnosis.

The tick of the big clock on the wall above her sounded inordinately loud in the empty hall. Rustle, rustle. The dry rustle of pages sounded como el ruido de ojas de maíz or the soft hiss of serpents. Her eyes were drawn back to "complications." Her breath snarled in her chest. There it was. Cessation of heartbeat. Her heart had stopped beating.

The squish suck of suede soles on linoleum. Snap. She shoved the chart back on its rack and started hobbling back to her room, thump-thump thump-thump, as fast as she could. Put her in a private room away from the other patients. Don't talk about it. Cover death up, cover its death rattle. Cover it up. Tell her she dreamed it. Or better still, don't tell her anything. Knowing would just upset her. Besides, while she's here we own her body.

Prieta fell on the bed, felt the tremors coursing through her body, felt the sweat pooling under her armpits.

They had not told her.

They had kept her own death from her.

That couldn't be. She must have dreamed the whole thing—the walk, the chart, the words. Or hallucinated it, a hallucination caused by the ether, or the flash of residual LSD or the remnants of the mushrooms, los niñitos, she'd ingested years before. Maybe all she'd had was susto, and the fright had driven her soul out of her body. And her soul had crossed over, plunging down into el otro mundo. Had she actually talked to the spirits of her dead? Had she really embraced her sister self, her other self, su doble—that exiled female self relegated to the shadows?

She really had entered that infernal region, stripped bare, stood utterly exposed, unprotected, alone. And when she returned, she'd left behind her veils and illusions, her false identities, and like shimmering water from the well or gold from the earth's core, her exiled self had risen up through the center of her body. She had become one of those who crosses thresholds. Was she a messenger now? And here she was, once more stripped bare, utterly exposed, unprotected, alone.

Fingers trembling, Prieta picked up her pen. Death, she wrote in her journal, is a woman and she wears a red dress. Death is a black hole. I hadn't intended to reach the land of night, but once there, standing before antigua mi diosa, I knew I had found my beloved. In her embrace I wanted to travel the inner routes of her tierra de noche. In her land I felt no pain, no crampness. No quería volver; I didn't want to leave.

Prieta closed the journal. She picked up the gift Teté had dropped off earlier and tore off the wrapper. She clasped the cassette to her heart, Silvio Rodríguez' album *Mujeres*, and put it in the tape player. She hummed along with the song, "¿Qué hago ahora?"

¿Qué le digo a la muerte
tantas veces llamada a mi lado
que al cabo se ha vuelto mi hermana?

[What can I tell death
so many times called to my side
that finally she has become my sister?]

She got out of bed and swayed to the music, and, despite the pain at the pull of the stitches, began to dance slowly. She looked out the window. The full moon was quartered by the window panes, Coyolxauhqui dismembered once more. Prieta's arms rose, stretched toward the moon. She opened her mouth, took the moon between her teeth, and swallowed it. Una nueva canción entered her body, an echo of the rattlesnake song. The song was life. Energy surged through her. She fell back onto the mattress. She stroked her breasts, ran her hands down the scar on her pubis, probed the velveteen entrance, wanting only to strum the new song. But when her fingers touched the plastic tubing, she let her hands fall to her side.

She called on the spirits of her dead to heal her, she called on Coyolxauhqui to knit her severed parts together. She opened the drawer, took out her snake ring and placed it on the altar saying, "Cihuacóatl, Snake Woman, I can no longer deny you. You tended my difficult birth. You showed me that life is a passage to death and death is a passage to life—there is no end." She opened herself, made room for the flesh, touched the flame to her new passion, igniting it. She glanced at la luna. The bright orb was framed by a single pane, fractured no longer. On the pane a snake face with a cleft forehead, drooping mouth, flat nose and lidless eyes stared back at her. And superimposed over the snake face she saw her own face reflected.

The nurse came in and asked Prieta what she was writing. She nudged Prieta onto her side, pulled up her gown above her buttocks, and plunged in the syringe.

Translations

la pelona: the bald one

Ve algo en mis ojos: She sees something in my eyes

gracias: thank you

Si hay posibilidad de estar en cinta, por favor notificar el Doctor Técnico que está en servicio antes de tomar un examen de rayo-x.: If there is any possibility that you are pregnant, please notify the technician on duty before having an x-ray.

la brasa: a burning coal

¡ay diosita!: ay goddess!

el soplo del miedo: the breath of fear

sintió la frialdad de la brasa: she felt the iciness of a burning coal

las sombras: the shadows

Estaba acalambrada.: She was cramped all over.

Le entró asco, se iba a vomitar.: Disgust invaded her, she was
   going to vomit.

Pero dejó un sabor ácido en su boca: But there was an acid taste
   in her mouth

bien quietita estaba Prieta: Prieta was good and quiet/calm

la diosa de la luna Coyolxauhqui: the goddess of the moon,
   Coyolxauhqui

La luna le había tocado.: Her period had started.

mamagrande: grandmother

ay mijita: my little daughter (endearment)

la muerte: death

tenía: had

¿Cómo quería que se quejara?: How could she complain about it?

muchachas buenas: good girls

nalgas: buttocks

verijas: penises

esos animalitos, los viros: those tiny animals, the virus

Estaba empreñada.: She was impregnated. (with the virus)

chingao: fuck

La había traicionado: It (her body) betrayed her

aquí estaba ella: here she was

Había preferido, había buscado los altos fuera del cuerpo: She had preferred and looked toward the skies

Piedra. Quería volverse Piedra.: Stone. She wanted to turn into stone.

Entre sueños oía el ruido seco de víbora.: Between her napping she heard the dry sound of snakes.

entre suspiros roncos, en una vocecita lejanísima, alguien le hablaba: between hoarse sighs a distant voice speaks to her

Esa serpiente negra, desde las sombras la miraba con ojos sin pestañas.: With her lidless eyes, the black serpent watched her from the shadows.

Lo único seguro en ésta vida era la muertecita.: The only sure thing in this life was death.

mañana: tomorrow

embarazada: pregnant

pero su mami estaba allá lejos en el rancho: but her mami was far away in the ranch

olió la pestilencia de la bacteria: I smelled the pestilence of the bacteria

¡Que chingen a sus padres!: They should fuck their own parents!

sus amigas: her friends (female)

primo: cousin

¿Y cómo está la malita?: And how is the sick one?

Me van a desmadrar.: I'm going to go mad.

Te hecho de menos, cabrón.: I miss you, man.

¿Apesto a perra muerta o qué?: Do I stink like a dead dog or what?

ni modo: doesn't matter

No te ahuites. Que será será.: Don't be scared. What will be will be.

pura macha mi prieta: mi prieta is a true macho

pinche buey: damned idiot

esa callada amenaza del cuchillo: this quiet menace of the knife

Cuchillo o ningún cuchillo, iba al encuentro de su destino: Knife or no knife, it was to be an encounter with her destiny.

Pero amachada iba Prieta.: But Prieta resisted.

hasta le trajo vino: he even gave her a drink of wine

se movían en las esquinas: moved in the corners

Bien quieta estaba Prietita.: Prietita was very quiet.

la tierra estaba vestida con zempasuchitl: the ground was dressed with zempasuchitl (flowers to honor the dead)

Sentío una presencia: She sensed a presence

su luz negra: her black light

vío su hocico: she saw her muzzle

por entero y por fin: entirely and at last

oía el ruido seco de las víboritas: she heard the dry sound of the snakes

Estaba embarazada—de la muerte, con la muerta.: She was pregnant from and with death.

bautismo: baptism

ese seco sonido de las víboras: this dry sound of the snakes

los muchos ojos que son: the many eyes that are

de repente: all of a sudden

oigo el machetazo del viente: I hear the blow of the wind

la estira: the buzz

de cascabel: of the rattlesnake

la desemboca en el hogar de la muerte: and leads her to the mouth/home of death

Prieta cae como cuerpo tendido, su cuerpo es el terreno: Prieta fell like a stretched-out body, her body is the land/dirt

Allí canta su canción de cascabel.: There she sings her rattlesnake song.

desbalagada como huérfana: wandering like an orphan

la mujer serpiente: the snake woman

la madre: the mother

desde su mundo de sueño: from the world of her dream

chicotea su cuerpo hasta que la desborda: whips her from side to side until she loses her boundaries

como mar chubascozo: like a hurricane sea

la arrebata: grabs her

la revolca, la tumba: rolls her over, tumbles her

sin su ayuda volví: without his help I returned

conocía el camino: I knew the way

La luz le da golpes.: The light beats her.

Noche, . . . me quiero esconder en tus pétalos: Night, I want to hide in your folds, petals

ojas de maíz: corn husks

olor de alcohol: odor of alcohol

su sangre espesa como piedra se hizo un mar hirviendo: her blood thick as stone then became a boiling sea el ruido de mis alas de víbora: the sound of my snake wings

el chicoteo entre su cuerpo: whiplash in her body

ni mi beso desperatador: nor my wakening kiss

brillísimo como si fuera vivo: brilliant as though it were alive

como el ruido de ojas de maíz: like the noise of the corn husks

los niñitos: the little kids

susto: fear

el otro mundo: the other world

su doble: her double

antigua mi diosa: my ancient goddess

tierra de noche: the night land

No quería volver: I didn't want to leave

"¿Qué hago ahora?": "What do I do now?"

una nueva canción: a new song

la luna: the moon

Acknowledgments / Reconocimientos

Anzaldúa's acknowledgments exist only in partially completed draft form; had she lived to bring this project to completion, she would have added others to her list. However, it's important to note that she thanked the following people:

Carolyn Woodward, Randy Conner, and Kit Quan ("the wo/men who feed my spirit, mind, body, and soul"); Irene Reti, Carmen Morones, AnaLouise Keating, and Elana Dykewoman ("mis writing comadres"); Magdalena Zschokke, Carmen Morones, Edna Escamill, Lynda Mar'n, and Megan Boler ("las escritoras del grupo Quelite fiction-writing group"); Rachel Steiner, Melissa Moreno, Carmel Atkinson, Dianna Williamson, Molly Nixon, María Elena Jauregui, Vicki Alcoset, Rosalinda Rodriguez, Jamie Lee Evans, Claire Ricardi, Audrey Berlowitz, Michelle Euland, and Cynthia Taines ("my interns/literary assistants"); Vita Islanker, Fabienne, and Joan Pinkvoss ("the dedicated staff at Aunt Lute Press"); and Roz Spafford, Donna Haraway, and Francisco X. Alarcón ("Teachers at UCSC").

Editors' Appreciation

First and foremost, we are grateful to Gloria Evangelina Anzaldúa for creating Prieta and these stories, for working so diligently (and for so many years) to bring Prieta's adventures to life. Thank you, Gloria, for your meticulous work, for your bold imagination, for your willingness to risk vulnerability. Your stories open new worlds.

Thank you for saving all your drafts and for putting dates on most of them. We are grateful to Hilda Anzaldúa for her steadfast support of Gloria and her work over the years

Thanks to Stuart Bernstein for immediately recognizing the value in these stories and facilitating their publication. Thanks to Rebecca Colesworthy and the team at SUNY Press for responding so enthusiastically to *Prieta*. Thanks to Sara Ramírez for assisting us with the translations, for keeping our language embedded in Gloria's South Texas regionalisms. The drawing of Prieta on the cover was made by Gloria's good friend, Randy Conner. Thanks to David Hatfield Sparks for permission to use the image. Thanks to Carla O. Alvarez at the Benson Latin American Collection for assistance with archival materials. And thanks to our ancestors, spirits, and guides for untold support.

Appendix 1

Instrucciones a la autora /
Instructions to the Author

As indicated below in "Instrucciones," Anzaldúa planned to include this short piece at the end of *Prieta*. She began drafting it in 1990–91 and briefly returned to it in 2000. Unfortunately, financial and health matters prevented her from completing it. Although it is not in polished form, we include portions of it here because it offers invaluable insights into Anzaldúa's writing process, Prieta's psyche, and more. The draft suggests that she was also working to include additional ideas such as a "transhistorical party" in which people like Pancho Villa, la Llorona, and Prieta meet; her experiences as a nightwriter who focuses on the dark; encounters on alien planets as depicted in television shows like *Star Trek* and *Twilight Zone*; and "the convergence of two ontological structures, the overlap or interpretation between the fictional world, heterocosm, and the real." (Drafts are located in the Gloria Evangelina Anzaldúa Papers, at the Benson Latin American Collection at the University of Texas, Austin, in box 66, folder 13 and box 72, folder 16.)

Instrucciones a la autora / Instructions to the Author

Prieta is writing a collection of short stories. Or is it a novel? She started it in 1974. Seventeen years later she is about to finish it. Some of the autohistorias are about her development as a writer. She looks at the genesis of each story/chapter of her book and decides to put her reflections at the end of the book in a Notes and Glossary section. Also at the end will be this essay/cuento that's about what Prieta thinks the book *Prieta* is about. She keeps in mind that sometimes the author is the last person to find out what her own book is about.

Prieta does not question the need to memorialize herself (and me). It just feels strange to see herself as an invented character. She hardly recognizes herself now that she's put herself into words. She feels herself, the middle-aged writer, so removed from her early self. Time has blurred the border between internal and external reality. Can she know what was real and what was not? Oh, yes, I know what you will say: that these are species of reality.

How can you make up stuff like this when you can only remember a few particulars of an event, the overall feeling? And how can you stand to have a memory so vivid that for a moment it erases the present moment? It's so arbitrary—on a whim you decide which memory to recreate, on another whim you decide what other memory to connect the first to, the second to, and so on.

Here's a memory that often comes to me: mamagrande Ramona cutting her corns with a razor blade.

The first part of *Prieta* deals with recollections and memories. The book consists of an autobiographical series of stories trying to become a "novel." She documents her growth through autohistorias full of representations of conscious self-formation. It is a sort of a mestiza ethnic künstlerroman depicting Prieta's struggle to become a creative artist, especially how she overcame the difficulties that beset a writer of color, how she strategized to decenter patriarchal traditions of narrative authority by rewriting her life and world, by producing her identity. This "novel" interweaves several realities together: the surreal—a surface, rational, and unconscious subreality, the world of everyday life, the inner world of thought, fantasy, and dreams, the fictive world of a literary or nonliterary text, the world of the spirit, and the nepantla, in-between space, interface between the different worlds. The interpenetration of the several worlds makes it a type of fantastic, with shadings of realismo mágico, a mythical realism. Plurality as available ontological orders.

Prieta inhabits nepantla, the in-between spaces, lugares entre medio, a postmodernist landscape of worlds in the plural. With it comes an attendant meta-discourse reflecting on its process—making it a work of meta-realism. She tries to show the fusion of the physical and emotional and their symbiosis, their inseparability. The author uses "Prieta" as a character's name in each story to disprove the modernists' conception of individual identity; she uses "Prieta" to conflate the autobiographical with the fictional, to show that representations of the lived life are constructions—are fictional—and that fiction is lived fantasy and as real as lived experience. What Prieta is trying to do is come up with a better definition of "realism." This book is about interior realities, about the spaces between marginal, imaginal, and lived reality, between the spiritual world and the external world. These in-between spaces, "para" spaces, are nepantla spaces.

Some of the stories explore the connection between the physical world and literary reality. They explore the relationship between the fictional and the real and the discontinuity between the two.

Many autohistorias use the ontological structure of the fantastic—a confrontation between two worlds whose physical norms are mutually incompatible. Convergence at the liminal meeting point, "the point of ontological transition between the supernatural world and the world of men" (D. Carrasco), is the central theme of the book.[1]

Some stories explore the relationship between language, myth, symbols, and the unconscious. One section of *Prieta* focuses on narrators'/protagonists' experiences of sexuality and search for female eroticism. Another section focuses on death, dying, and healing. The book focuses on moments (imagined and real) which have been turning points in the development of the narrators'/protagonists' life history from childhood to the present. A depiction of ethnic female development interrupted with poetry,

---

1. David Carrasco, *Quetzalcoatl and the Irony of Empire* (University Press of Colorado, 2000), 122.

dreams, theoretical discussions, or commentaries from the author results not in linear chronology but in montage. The organizing principle of the book is poetic associations of the author, one that foregrounds the consciousness of the writing self. She attempts to deviate from the historical narrative by reducing patterning and organization of experiences.

In this Bildungsroman she tries to write against the idea of a coherent and one-dimensional self incapable of changes that patriarchy wants women to maintain. By giving Prieta muchas caras, many roles and slightly different names and multiple identities, she tries to collapse the boundary between the categories of la mujer mala, la buena, la puta, y la inocente, between generations and historical periods and thus attempt to subvert the distinctions between past, present, and future.

She struggles to create a form broad and deep enough to accommodate all the different genres, points-of-view, languages, literary and stylistic devices, voices, image patterns, and thematic concerns. Genre-bending, crossing genres of short stories, novel, autobiography, and essays, ranging from lived experience to pure fantasy. This book does not contain a chronological continuum but a series of events of coming-to-consciousness in which a radical shift in the ways of seeing in the world occurs and therefore a change in identity develops. Prieta, the protagonist, is preoccupied with the problems of self-knowledge.

A testimonial stance is evidenced in many of the "autohistorias" in this collection. If G doesn't give testimony to these events her past will be lost. If her past is lost she will not know how to make sense of her present—my present—and she will not know how to get to her future. Ella es un carácter imaginario en el que los hecho historias están deformados por la invención poética. Su vida es una invención fabulosa.

A communal sense of the past in which the autobiographer inserts (insinuates) herself into a common past which "is frequently a mirage, a poetic construct on the part of the author" (Molloy, 130), though not devoid of a factual base. Her-myselves create a (theory) system of interrogation, multi-tiered, autosubjective and intersubjective communication. This book is about derealization, which means not being sure the world is real, and depersonalization, not quite feeling herself, not knowing who she is, not feeling her body was her own. She experiences jamais vu when a place she knew well suddenly seems unfamiliar.

The alter ego multiplied, the doppelgänger doubled. Prieta journeys in time; in the journey dream interpenetrates reality to produce a work within a work.

The ancient past is as personal as any individual past. Her individual anecdotes and personal memorias are historically significant. The autohistoria signifies its own *importance*. Prieta wants what every writer wants—to garner, to sweep up more and diverse audiences to her feet, to bring them all around her. Thus she shows and conceals, reveals and hides pieces of herself, pieces that are the bait to lure the reader into following, gobbling, and being pulled into text.

The autohistoria returns to the idea of literature as function, of service to ideology after the last phase of literature as autonomous. Here it returns to the idea of art as practice not just as product.

Doubling the Doubled "I"

Prieta makes the reader distrust her discourse with its unreliable narrators. Instead of the expected singular I, she doubles the "I" and doubles the doubled "I." And through this distancing the reader recognizes something of herself. And that is how Prieta lures her into the discourse. Once in, hopefully the reader will be hooked until the last page.

Aventuras narratives: short shorts, short stories, "historias," folkstories, short novel, journalistic news story, case history, mythological tale, essay-narrative. Zazanilli, the Nahuatl word for "fable," and tlamachiliztlalolzazanilli, means wisdom-word fables.

The author tries to create a kind of literary borderlands where the marginal and outlaw experience and other subworlds overlap. In this terrain all the world's architectural styles are fused, all its races and cultures mingle—el barrio, la colonia, the red-light districts are juxtaposed with the fictional worlds of the mass media—the movies, TV. In this place metaphors become literal, the actual and the imaginary intermingle, physical reality is confronted by the "other" world, el más allá, it is confronted by fantasies. Books thrust themselves into this reality; historical reality (the past) invades the present physical reality at an interface, the meeting surface for two or more worlds, an ambiguous and liminal space which is constantly being constructed and deconstructed at the same time—a postmodernist topos, un nepantla. It is a space capable of accommodating worlds of incompatible structure—mutually exclusive worlds, discontinuous and inconsistent worlds.

ON METHOD AND MADNESS

What Prieta is attempting to do is join forces with writers who are trying to reinvent narrative forms. Concerned with the aesthetic possibilities of narratives but also with a glaring awareness of social realities. A narrative where imagination, fantasy, and myth cross into social/political realities of our times and the fabricated realities of art and literature. She uses jarring disruptive technical moves, such as interrupting the text with the framing meta-communication, like, "This is work/text of fiction, poetry."

Some of the autohistorical stories involve a violation of boundaries, and the making of a mestiza identity between the characters in her projected worlds and the real-world historical figures emphasizes the contradictions between Prieta's version, for example, of Pancho Villa and the known facts of his life . . .

How do we come up with innovative writing practices to agitate gender and racial inscriptions both white and ethnic to parody, to halt, to interrupt a person gendered as female? "We resist," Prieta is telling a friend, "by throwing in a monkey wrench and bringing the machinery of genre law and order to a screeching halt. Or at least intervene, to do the same with language." To challenge cultural assumptions about women and men with a racialized narrative. To interrupt the traditional racial narrative by inserting markers that will breach the smooth flow of the reader's loss of consciousness and her seduction into the world of text and jerk her back from the reality of the text to her own physical reality. "Entramado de PQ" [an early version of "Reading LP"] attempts to do this.

Writing is a temporal site/space of power though one of seismic instability. Prieta's writing projects may be accused of being too difficult to read, to decipher, that her writing may be inaccessible, unreadable. But the text itself tells you how to read it. Writing teaches reading strategies, educates the reader.

Appendix 2

A History of the Stories

This appendix offers brief summaries of each chapter's origins and development. Given the amorphous, dynamic, shapeshifting nature of Anzaldúa's archives, as well as the intricacies of her process, our summaries are incomplete and open to revision and expansion as further discoveries are made. Our goal is not to offer an exhaustive history of each manuscript (which would be impossible) but rather to underscore the enormous amount of time, energy, and thought Anzaldúa poured into *Prieta*.

In many ways, *Prieta* was Anzaldúa's passion project. She began developing her protagonist's stories in the late 1970s and continued working on them until shortly before her death. This appendix contains brief histories of each story, charting origins and development, as well as key alterations and revisions. As mentioned in the editors' introduction, Anzaldúa lived with and worked on *Prieta* for most of her literary career. Her writing process was recursive and so intense that at times it bordered on obsessive: She did not sit down and produce Prieta's stories in one sitting—nor even in one year (and in most cases, not even in one decade). She brainstormed, jotted down notes, drafted passages, typed them up, inserted them into new drafts, made handwritten edits, shared drafts with writing comadres and other readers, and incorporated their feedback into new drafts, which she then edited, revised, and so on. Anzaldúa was thoughtful and painstakingly meticulous during every stage of her process. Look, for instance, at her frequent use of reader feedback.

Anzaldúa generally sought feedback on her drafts—always from her writing comadres and often from additional readers (students in her classes and workshops, for instance). Moreover, she did not simply give drafts to readers and ask for general comments, but instead she typically included specific questions for each story. (For an example of the questions, see the summary of "She Ate Horses" below.)

Fortunately, Anzaldúa meticulously saved her many drafts, which are now located in the Gloria Evangelina Anzaldúa Papers at the Nettie Lee Benson Latin American Collection, University of Texas, Austin. We relied primarily on this material to investigate and document each chapter's genesis and development—their historias, as it were. At the end of each historia, we've included references to specific archival boxes and folders containing the various drafts. We hope this information will assist with future discoveries.

1. The Second Heart / El segundo corazón

This story has its source at least partially in Anzaldúa's experiences as a young child. The earliest versions can be found in her early autohistorias, "Esperando la serpiente con plumas (Waiting for the Feathered Serpent)" (1981–82) and "La serpiente que se come su cola: The Death Rites of Passage of a Chicana Lesbian" (1982–83), in sections titled "El Segundo Corazón," "El Segundo Corazon Y La Llama Inicial," and "El Caballo Negro." Anzaldúa continued working on the story in the 1980s. She included a version, also titled "El Caballo Negro," in an academic paper, "Noche y su nidada / Night and Her Nest," that she wrote for a 1989 University of California, Santa Cruz course taught by Teresa de Lauretis, and another version in "Autohistoria of the artista as a young girl" (1991), her unpublished künstlerroman. In the early 1990s, she explored the possibility of converting the story into a children's book, tentatively titled "El Caballo Negro," but by 1994 had decided not to do so. In 1995, she further revised the story and changed the title from "El segundo corazón" to "The Second Heart / El segundo corazón." Anzaldúa continued editing and revising the story in 1996–97 and last saved it in March 2001. (Papers, 68.1, 78.8–9, 94.12–13)

2. Out of the Corner of the Eye / De reojo

This story had its genesis in one of Anzaldúa's most memorable childhood experiences. The earliest versions can be found in her early autohistorias: Anzaldúa included a version titled "Second Initiation" and "The Devil Appeared to Her" in a 1981 draft of "Esperando la serpiente con plumas"; the following year she revised the story, titling it "My Nagual," and included it in "La serpiente que se come su cola." Throughout the 1980s she continued revising this story, titling it "Her Nagual" and "The Devil Appeared to Her." In 1991 she included a version, "EL DIABLO SE LE APARECIO / THE DEVIL APPEARED TO HER," in her "Auto-historia de la artista as a Young Girl." In 1994 she reimagined the story as a children's book, "Prietita y el ánimal nagual," and drafted the following statement, which she envisioned functioning as a preface or an afterword: "This experience happened to me when I was a little girl. Years later in the midst of painting this episode with my oils, I realized that this animal, half-wolf, half-dog, was my nagual, what the Aztecs call the animal-companion that each person has and whose destiny she is closely alligned [*sic*]. It was this closeness that was so frightening, this total merger with an animal. The nagual is an ally." She continued working on the story in the mid-1990s, titling it "El ánimal en el monte / The Animal in the Woods" (1995) and "De reojo / Out of the Corner of the eye" (1996). In 2001, she returned to it as she finalized *Prieta*, making minor edits and soliciting feedback from writing comadres. (Papers, 57.12, 69.9, 73.11, 76.1, 77.5, 78.9–10)

3. In the Mouth of the Sea / En el hocico del mar

Anzaldúa based this story on what, in her journals and conversations, she viewed as her second encounter with death. In the early 1980s she drafted versions titled "Drowning" and "Padre Island" and in 1982–83 included a version titled "En El Hocico de la Muerte" in "La serpiente que se come su cola" (1982–83). She continued revising and editing it in the 1980s, expanding it for "Autohistoria of the artista as a young girl" (1991), where she titled it "EN EL HOCIO DEL MAR / THE MOUTH OF THE SEA." She worked extensively on the story from 1994 through 1998, titling it "Hocico del mar," "Entre dos aguas / Between Two Waters," "Entre los dientes del Mar," "In the arms of the sea / En los brazos del mar," "En el hocico del mar / In the muzzle of the sea," "Señas en la arena / Imprints (signs, marks) in the sand," and "Huellas en la arena / Tracks (traces) in the Sand." These many titles attest to the large number of drafts and amount of time she spent on this story. She returned to it in 2001 as she worked to finalize *Prieta*. (Papers, 70.3–5, 78.10)

4. People Should Not Die in June in South Texas

Anzaldúa based this story on the death of her father, who died in June 1957. She included a brief version, titled "Third Initiation," in "Esperando la serpiente con plumas" (1981–82) and expanded it into "People Should Not Die in June in South Texas," in "La serpiente que se come su cola." Several years later, in 1985, she published a revised version in *My Story's On: Ordinary Women, Extraordinary Lives* (ed. Paula Ross, Common Differences Press). In 1989, she returned to the story, soliciting feedback from friends and extensively editing and revising it. In 1993, she published a version in *Growing Up Latino: Memoirs and Stories; Reflections of Life in the United States* (ed. Harold Augenbraum and Ilan Stavans, Houghton Mifflin). During the 1990s, Anzaldúa also considered including it in two larger manuscripts, "Entreguerras, entremundos," to be published by Spinster/Aunt Lute, and "Nightrider, Noches de insomnia." She continued editing and revising the story in 1997 and made minor edits in 2001. (Papers, 66.28, 75.1, 75.3–4, 75.6, 77.16, 78.9–10)

5. Como Quelite

The histories of "Como Quelite" and the following two stories are perhaps the most intertwined in this volume and possibly began as a single story. Throughout the various drafts, Anzaldúa experiments with terminology for expressing queer identities, moving between frameworks like "lesbian," "una de las otras," "butch," and "half and half." Anzaldúa began working on this story in the early 1980s, writing out the first version by hand. In August 1984, she typed up this handwritten draft, titling it "Mita' y Mita' (Half and Half)" but also considering other titles: "Making la movida" and "Movidas Chuecas," as indicated by handwritten edits. Throughout the early 1990s she worked on the story, renaming the protagonist Quelite and emphasizing "her spiritual connection to nature." By 1995 she was exploring alternative titles like "Palabras como quelites" and "Como Quelite / Weed." In 1996, she noted that "quelite is a wild weed like nettles"; also around that time, she jotted down notes for "Quelite" in which she discusses eating and cooking quelite (with garlic, onion, chorizo, and eggs), and considered titles like "Quelites en la comida," "Cooking quelites," and "Como Quelite / Like a Weed." By 1997 she had decided to split "Como Quelite" and "Movidas" into two stories, at the encouragement of a writing comadre, and in 1998 she arrived at her final title, "Como Quelite." (Papers, 66.26, 74.15, 77.15–17)

6. Mita' y mita'

Anzaldúa developed the outlines of this story in spring 1984 while living in Brooklyn, jotting down notes and typing up early drafts that she variously titled "Half and Half," "Mita' y mita'," "Movidas Chuecas," and "Mita' y mita' (Half and Half)." She continued working through ideas for the story in late 1984 and 1985. She returned to the story in the 1990s, receiving feedback from writing comadres and others. By 1997 she settled on "Mita' y mita'" for the title and considered including it in a story collection tentatively titled "Patlaches." She last saved this piece in March 1998. (Papers, 66.26, 73.8, 74.15, 77.15–16)

7. Movidas of a Baby Butch

As stated above, "Movidas" grew out of "Como Quelite," and so part of its history is explained above. Anzaldúa drafted ideas for the "Movidas" protagonist in 1984, in handwritten notes. Later that year she developed these notes into a draft titled "Making La Movida." During the 1980s and early 1990s, she generally viewed this material as part of "Como Quelite" as she revised and edited Quelite's story. By 1997 she made "Movidas" its own story and planned to include it in an edited collection tentatively titled "Patlaches." Although she last worked on "Movidas" in 1998, she was still considering possible edits and revisions, as indicated by these comments at the end of the draft: "Maybe use 3rd person present tense? Quelite of the Green Hands. Story takes place a couple of years later. Prieta is exploring, trying to locate her personal identity (that of a smaller group) within the greater queer identity. She plays with different costumes. She is clear about being a dyke, but is not clear where in queer model she fits. She recognized the plus and down sides." (Papers, 66.26, 74.15, 77.15–16)

8. Eating the Fruit / Comiendo del árbol
como Xochiquetzal

Anzaldúa began drafting this story in the 1980s and viewed it as a continuation of "Movidas." She titled the earliest drafts "La hurta / The Orchard," "El naranjal / The Orange Grove," and "La prueba / The Test." She worked more extensively on it in the 1990s, soliciting feedback from writing comadres and exploring a variety of potential titles: "En el naranjal / In the Orange Grove," "The Bet or La puesta," "A las scondidas," and "Come Here / Ven aquí." She also changed the protagonist's name several times: from Úrsula to Prieta to Analise and back to Prieta. She finalized the story in 2001 and gave it its current title, "Eating the Fruit / Comiendo del árbol como Xochiquetzal." (Papers, 66.27, 70.7–9, 77.16)

9. El Paisano Is a Bird of Good Omen

Originally titled "La Boda" ("The Wedding"), this story is one of Anzaldúa's earliest and most extensively revised. Anzaldúa began working on "La Boda," which she conceptualized as a story "about a wedding of the 1940's or '50's," in September 1974 when she was enrolled in the comparative literature doctoral program at the University of Texas, Austin. Inspired by Gustave Flaubert's *Madame Bovary*, her goal was to "fuse the objective and subjective more tightly together than Flaubert did." In 1982 she published a version in *Conditions* and a year later in *Cuentos: Stories by Latinas*, edited by Alma Gómez, Cherríe Moraga, and Mariana Romo-Carmona. Throughout the 1980s and early 1990s, Anzaldúa conceived this story as the opening chapter in her novel in progress, which she referred to as "Andrea," named after the protagonist, Andrea de la Cruz. The protagonist enacts Anzaldúa's holistic epistemology and her definition of queer, a definition that includes but goes far beyond sexual identity. In 1995, she considered including the story in a collection titled "Nightrider, Noches de insomnia." In 1998, she renamed the protagonist Prieta and explored several alternative titles: "La Naguala," "El Paisano Is a Bird of Good Omen," "Reading Signs," or "Looking for Signs." In 2000 she settled on "El Paisano Is a Bird of Good Omen" and in 2001 she finalized the story. (Papers, 73.19–20, 73.22–28, 74.1–9, 224.4)

10. In the Shadow of la Chingada (or Smoking Mirror)

Anzaldúa created this piece by combining two earlier autobiographical narratives, "Her First Fuck" and "Seguin 15," both based on her first sexual relationship with a man. She included short versions of

"Her First Fuck" in "Esperando la serpiente con plumas" (1981–82) and "La serpiente que se come su cola: The Death Rites of Passage of a Chicana Lesbian" (1982–83) and then expanded them into a more fictionalized story, "Her First Fuck," which she drafted in 1983 while living in Brooklyn, New York. She considered using it for her contribution to *Cuentos* but ultimately decided not to do so. She edited and revised "Her First Fuck" throughout the 1980s, expanding the title to "Her First Fuck or La clit es un especie de puente." By February 1988, she had drafted "Seguin 15," a first-person, self-reflective account of her drive home from college on December 22, 1974, to spend the holidays with her family. By 1992, at the suggestion of a writing comadre, she combined "Her First Fuck" with "Seguin 15," keeping the latter title. She worked on it from 1994 through 1996, renaming the protagonist Urraca. In 1998 she explored other titles, including "Signposts," "Enre [*sic*] guerras," "Smoking Mirror," "Smoke and Mirrors," "In the Shadow of la Chingada [or Smoking Mirror]," "Entre guerras / Civil Wars," and "Ghost Riding on My Shoulder." In 1997, she considered including it in a story collection tentatively titled "Nightrider, Noches de insomnia" or "Patlaches." In 2001, she returned to the story, now titled "In the Shadow of la Chingada [or Smoking Mirror]," as she finalized *Prieta*. (Papers, 66.20, 74.15, 77.16, 78.6, 78.9–10, 81.7)

11. The Crack Between the Worlds

On November 4, 1974, while in graduate school for her doctoral degree in comparative literature at the University of Texas, Austin, Anzaldúa was mugged as she walked home from class. She viewed this experience as one of the most formative events in her adult life, processing its traumatic aftereffects for years. Indeed, the event was so overwhelming that she refused to write about it until 1979, when she explored it both in poetry—creating drafts titled "Mugged," "La barranca," and "Every Three Seconds"—and in her early autohistoria, "La serpiente que se come su cola" (1982–83), in a section titled "El Asaltador." (See Appendix 3 for the poem.) In 1984, she extracted this section and began converting it into a short story, also titled "El Asaltador"; in 1990, she changed the title to "La Barranca," named her protagonist "Paloma Prieta," and included a version of the earlier poem, now titled "Every Three Seconds A Woman Is Battered." She worked on the story during the early 1990s, removing the poem from it in 1992; in 1995, she considered including "La Barranca" in an edited collection titled "Nightrider, Noches de insomnia." In 2001, she returned to the story, retitling it "The Crack Between the Worlds," as she finalized *Prieta*. See Appendix 4 for sample drafts documenting this extensive drafting and revision process. (Papers, 66.25, 67.12–13, 78.9)

12. Becoming luciérnaga / Swallowing fireflies / Tragando luciérnagas

This story is loosely based on Anzaldúa's experience when she attended the University of Texas, Austin, in the summer of 1971 and 1972, to obtain her master's degree in English and education. Anzaldúa included a short, four-paragraph version in her early autohistoria, "La serpiente que se come su cola" (1982–83); in 1989, she published a slightly longer version, titled "Lifeline," in Irene Zavaha's *Lesbian Love Stories* (Crossing Press) and described it as part of her "forthcoming book *Entreguerras entremundos / Civil Wars Among the Worlds*." She expanded and in other ways revised "Lifeline" throughout the 1990s, changing the protagonist's name to "La Prieta" (1991, 1994), "La Piedra Prieta" (1992), and "Kika la Prieta" (1995). In 1998, she further expanded the draft, revising the protagonist's name back to Prieta, and explored several other possible titles: "The Spark," "Lifeline," "Luciérnaga or the spark/ripples," "Face in the Water," and "Reflection on Water." From 2000 to 2003, she continued editing and revising the story and published a version in Lynda Hall's 2003 edited collection, *Telling Moments: Autobiographical Lesbian Short Stories* (University of Wisconsin Press). She continued exploring possible titles: "Luzecita de luciérnaga / light of the firefly / firefly light," "tragaluz or luzecita de luciérnaga / light of the firefly," "luzecita de luciérnaga / flight of the firefly," and "Becoming luciérnaga / Swallowing fireflies / tragando luciérnagas." (Papers, 73.1–5, 76.2)

13. Night of the Lizard / Noche de la lagartija

Although Anzaldúa drafted this story in 1991 and published a short version of it as "Puddles" in 1992 in *New Chicana/Chicano Writing*, volume 1, edited by Charles Tatum (University of Arizona Press), she continued developing "Puddles" throughout the 1990s, revising it and soliciting feedback from her comadres. In 1998, she began exploring other options for the title, landing on "La Velada de una largartija." In 2001, as she continued editing, she considered various titles, including "Vigil of the Lizard / Velada de la lagartija" and "Noche de una largartija / Night of the Iguana," before finalizing the manuscript. From its earliest versions, the story is dedicated to Rodrigo Reyes and Jaye Miller, who in the final draft Anzaldúa identified as "victims of AIDS." (Papers, 73.14, 77.11–14)

14. She Ate Horses

Anzaldúa began drafting this story in March 1984 while teaching at Vermont College. Initially a fictional, first-person narrative titled "A Sacrifice of Masks," this version featured protagonist Pajara and explored Pajara's fear of desire and search for self. This same year, Anzaldúa combined "A Sacrifice of Masks" with a second, overlapping piece titled "She Ate Horses." Although Anzaldúa kept the same title over nearly two decades of revisions, she explored a variety of options both for the protagonist's name (Pajara, Prieta, Pescada la Prieta, Monse la Prieta) and for the name of her girl-friend (first Andrea, then Osi, and finally Llosi). After spending six years on the initial version, Anzaldúa published it in 1990 as "She

Ate Horses" in Jeffner Allen's edited collection, *Lesbian Philosophies and Cultures* (SUNY Press). Throughout the 1990s, Anzaldúa continued developing the story, titling her 1990 (post-publication) draft "She Ate Horses II" and seeking input from writing comadres with questions like these: "Where do I overdevelop, over write? Especially horse metaphor?"; "Does connection between horse, sexuality/desire, island/isolation/autonomy come through?"; "Am I too heavy handed?"; "Areas where you lose interest/use of Spanish?" In 1995, she considered including it in a volume tentatively titled "Nightrider, Noches de insomnia," and in 1997, she considered including it in "Patlaches." She continued editing and revising "She Ate Horses" in 1999, determining that it would be the fourteenth story in *Prieta*, and she last saved it in 2001. (Papers, 74.13, 74.15, 77.16, 80.5–6, 80.8–16, 81.2–4, 88.13, 88.15)

15. Reading LP

Anzaldúa began working on this story, originally titled "The Book, the Wall and J.P.," in December 1974, when she lived in Austin, Texas, and revised it the following month (January 1975). This early draft featured a male protagonist, Jorge Pullido, reading a mysterious book authored by "G. Anzaldúa." Anzaldúa returned to the manuscript in 1983, when she changed the protagonist to a woman named "J.Q." Although she planned to include this piece in an edited collection titled "El Mundo Zurdo and Other Stories," her work on the manuscript that eventually became *Borderlands / La Frontera* took up much of her time, and she didn't return to this piece until 1992. Anzaldúa worked on it from 1992 through 1995 and returned to it again in 2001, making extensive edits, expansions, and other revisions. She cycled through numerous possible titles: "La Paredas de PQ / PQ's Walls," "Entremados de PQ," "Dreaming PQ," "Dreaming La Prieta or Reading LP or Noche del tigre / Night of the Jaguar," and "La tigra, dueña de la tierra." Posthumously published in *The Gloria Anzaldúa Reader*, edited by AnaLouise Keating (Duke University Press, 2009), this story is the only one in *Prieta Is Dreaming* that is identical to its previously published version. (Papers, 70.13–14, 71.1–5)

16. Like a Crow on the Wing / Como urraca en vuelo

"Como Urraca" had its genesis in a poem, titled "Obsession," that Anzaldúa drafted in 1984 and revised in 1987–88. Using third-person voice and depicting a conventional heterosexual relationship, Anzaldúa explored themes of obsessive desire. In 1991, she drafted "Urraca Prieta" to continue this exploration and included portions of the poem in the draft. As she continued revising and drafting this piece throughout the early 1990s, she integrated portions of the poem into the piece as prose. In 1995, she changed the title to "Como una urraca en vuelo / Like a Crow on the Wing" and then "Like a Crow on the Wing / Como una urraca en vuelo." During the late 1990s, she continued working on the story, soliciting feedback from writing comadres and other readers. She last edited it in 2001. (Papers, 72.24–25, 73.15)

17. Ghost Trap / Trampa de espanto

Anzaldúa began writing this story, by hand, in October 1984 but did not type it up until 1990, when she drafted a very short version. From 1991 to 1992, she revised the manuscript, titled "Ghost Trap," and published it in Charles Tatum's edited collection, *New Chicana/Chicano Writing*, vol. 1 (University of Arizona Press, 1992). But publication did not signal completion, and Anzaldúa continued revising and expanding it throughout much of the 1990s. In 1992, she changed the title to "Ghost Trap / Trampa de Espanto" and gave the nameless protagonist a name, Úrsula. In 1993, she solicited feedback from writing comadres and others; and in 1997 she renamed her protagonist Úrsula, la Prieta, thus signaling her decision to include this piece in her *Prieta* volume. She finalized the story in 2002. A version called "Ghost Trap" is published posthumously in *The Gloria Anzaldúa Reader*. (Papers, 71.19–23)

18. La Werejaguar in the Woods of the Dream

In March 1980, while in the hospital after her hysterectomy, Anzaldúa had a dream in which she encountered a woman with golden eyes in the woods, a dream so memorable she recounted it two years later in a draft of her unpublished memoir, "La serpiente que se come su cola," in a section titled "How She Re-encounters the Devil." Around 1990, Anzaldúa used this section to create the first draft of her "very early version Were-Jaguar Story." In 1991, she titled the piece "The Were-Jaguar Mouth," and named the protagonist Gata Prieta. Over the next decade, Anzaldúa's steady revising included multiple title changes, research notes, and musings on ontology, reality, shapeshifting, and nagualismo. In the late 1990s, as the story expanded, she considered dividing it into two but ultimately decided not to do so. Draft titles included "The Were-Jaguar," "La Prieta Tiene Animal," "La Prieta and the Dream of the Were-Jaguar," and, finally "The Were-Jaguar in the Woods of the Dream," demonstrating that Anzaldúa grappled with Prieta's permeable subjectivity. As Prieta becomes one with her surroundings, she partially merges with the were-jaguar. Prieta's cousin, Teté, is also prominently featured here, offering a glimpse into Anzaldúa's skill for dialogue and her sense of humor. Anzaldúa continued working on this story in the final years of her life, receiving feedback from writing comadres in 2002; in 2004, the year of her death, she had planned to include it in *Bearing Witness*, an anthology to be coedited with AnaLouise Keating. Anzaldúa considered "La Werejaguar in the Woods of the Dream" to be the ninth version. (Papers, 76.6, 78.11, 82.1–4, 82.6)

19. Song of the Rattlesnake / Canción de cascabel

This story originated in Anzaldúa's March 30, 1980 hysterectomy and near-death experience. (A brief account of this event is included in "La Prieta," published in 1981 in *This Bridge Called My Back*.) Anzaldúa included a short version in "Esperando la serpiente" (1981–82) and expanded it further, titling the section "How She Finds 'Where The Vagina Is'" for "La serpiente que se come su cola" (1982–83), her "autocanción" (or autohistoria). In 1984, she took this section from "La serpiente" and expanded it into a stand-alone piece, also titled "How She Finds 'Where the Vagina Is.'" During 1984, she created multiple drafts of this story, simplifying the title to "Where the Vagina Is" and envisioning it as part of a book-length project, "Prieta: Journeys into Death and Other Terrains" (Papers, 68.3). She worked on the story intermittently throughout the 1990s, heavily editing and revising, creating multiple drafts, in 1991 retitling it "Canción de cascabel," and in 1995 considering it for inclusion in the tentatively titled story collection "Nightrider, Noches de insomnia." Anzaldúa worked on the story extensively in 2000 and made her final edits in 2001; she explored various titles, including "Canción de cascabel / Song of the Rattlesnake," "Canción de cascabel / Rattlesnake Song," and "Song of the Rattlesnake." (Papers, 68.3, 68.5–6, 77.16)

Appendix 3

Anzaldúa's Writing Process:
"The Crack Between the Worlds"

As explained in the editors' introduction, Gloria E. Anzaldúa's writing process was recursive, dialogic, and painstakingly detailed. This appendix draws from Anzaldúa's many drafts of "The Crack Between the Worlds" to illustrate her process. The story's origins, Anzaldúa's mugging, occurred in November 1974. She was so traumatized by this experience that she did not begin working through it until 1979, when she drafted a poem about the encounter. These excerpts, drawn from two of her many archival drafts, offer a small glimpse into her recursive, dialogic process:

- Her 1979 poem about the mugging, as well as hand-written notes from 1985 (Papers, 66.25)

- The version Anzaldúa included in her 1982 autohistoria, "La Serpiente que se come su cola" (Papers, 78.10)

Key in

~~Courting Death~~

~~Death~~ ← Every Three Seconds in the U.S.

In autobio [?]

You don't understand.
He tried to kill me.
I was taking the short cut home,
the one I always take from school.
It was 4:30, a ~~sunny~~ day,
~~with a tranquil~~ sky, tranquil and wide as only Texas skies are.
I was coming down the ~~steep~~ ravine. It was steep
At the bottom stood ~~a blood man~~
~~with~~ a white pullover,
He was tall, young with ~~crew~~ cut hair, blond
~~Can I help you, he said,~~ holding out his hand awkwardly
~~offering me his hand.~~ like a bird balanced on one foot
~~I say something strange~~ he said, can I help you
~~in his eye.~~ No thanks, I said seeing a sign, a strangeness
~~walking on past.~~ The next No thanks in his blue eyes
thing I know his hands are Ihurrying past him leaning
around my throat, he's grabbling shutting wide as you
for my purse. would a rattlesnake ready
to strike.

Later, they told me I should
not have fought him,
that I should not have scratched
his face nor screamed,
nor kicked. They said, I should
have been passive. To fight back
is to die they said.
He slugged me in the face
dragged me across rock,
gravel onto a wooden bridge.
Twenty feet below, a thin creek
with huge jagged rocks.
He pushed me against the rail,
picked me up by my shirt front,
shoved. Below me the rocks
grew bigger. The thought 'but
my shoes will get wet, kept
running through my head
and all the while I screamed.
What saved me was the strap
of my purse breaking.
He took off.
I picked myself up,
found a rock twice as big
as my fist and chased him
across the streets.
We nearly got run over.

There was something funny about him
hair too short in hippie university
He seemed to be waiting for someone
She'd already started down
could turn back thought him suspect
He'd [?] she thought him suspect
No I don't need your help
I learned to be wary of men

El asalto
El Ataque
Violación
El asaltador   La barranca

lo que puede ser
asaltado

A las cinco de la tarde.
Eran las cinco en punto de la tarde.

Ya luchan la paloma y el leopardo
a las cinco de la tarde.

La estaba ahorcando.
He was strangling her. His hands on her throat pressing, pressing. She couldn't breathe. With her nails he scratched at his
eyes, his beautiful blue eyes. Nice looking young blonde,
he was not supposed to be the enemy. The mexican, the Black--
those were the dangerous ones. Not this young blond male with
baby blue eyes.

She had taken a short cut, through/in down the side of
a ravine, through the wooded area, at where she would reach
the bridge over Waller Creek and cross San La_____, a four lane
thoroughfare where five streets crossed.

When she spotted him she sensed something, became uneasy
but overrode her instincts. He looked so innocent with his
cross/ close cropped hair, so different in a university of long-
haired bearded men. Just as she'd passed him, he arm locks
her from behind, the fold of his elbow hooking onto her neck, the breath
knocked out of her. She held on to her purse and somehow screaming
managed to twist around and face him, and screamed in his face. This
scared him, he tried to shut her up with his hand over her
mouth but she bit it so he started choking her and she started could
kicking but her suede soles the thuds of her suede soles
against his shins and sthey were pulling away from each other
but he was 100 pounds heavier and so she is dragged her across
the rocks on her knees scraping against the rocks and the
sting on her knees their knees dragging across the planks she
they were on the bridge he was trying to pick her up, ett
to raise her, was pushing her, the rail against her waist,
the her back digging against the iron rail she looked down
the meager stream, at the huge rocks, her shoes would get wet,
but clothes would tear on the rocks. She would fall fall
head over heals would tumble to her death. the strap of her

                leather purse broke and he was running down
the bridge across ~~Stopping only to pick up two~~ St. and she was running after
him, ~~big rocks in her hands she did not remember picking it~~
~~up~~ She chased him across the street the cars

      It was five in the afternoon, she told the cops.
screeching to a halt almost running over them.
A ~~state~~ woman in one of the cars asked could
she help. ~~I told~~ Paula told her to call the cops & send
~~them to me,~~ gave the woman her address and
started running again. She'd seen him disappear
into an alley. In the alley she ~~saw two asked~~
two hippy looking guys if they'd seen a man in
a white sweat shirt and quickly told them what
had happened. The three started running in the
direction they'd seen him disappear. But they couldn't
find him. All three returned to her apartment to
find two cops waiting for her

                    It's true   was
      Evil existed, ~~or a better~~ name is ignorance. All crime
was a result of ignorance, of the self as other, of the self
of the flesh as held in common with others with the very victims
that fell under the knife or gun or hand. An ignoring of the
humanity of others.
      For her, the universe was no longer a safe place
and evil (or ignorance) walked on two legs and he was male.

      She took to sleeping with a knife in her bed.

Works by Gloria E. Anzaldúa
(Editors' References)

Borderlands / La Frontera: The New Mestiza. Aunt Lute, 1987.

"Doing Gigs: Speaking, Writing, and Change; An Interview with Debbie Blake and Carmen Abrego" (1994). In Keating, *Interviews / Entrevistas*.

"El Paisano Is a Bird of Good Omen." *Conditions* 8 (1982): 28–47.

"El Paisano Is a Bird of Good Omen." In *Cuentos: Stories by Latinas*, edited by Alma Gómez, Cherríe Moraga, and Mariana Romo-Carmona. Kitchen Table/Women of Color Press, 1983.

"El Paisano Is a Bird of Good Omen." In Keating, *The Gloria Anzaldúa Reader*.

"Esperando la serpiente con plumas (Waiting for the Feathered Serpent)" (1981–82), Box 78, Folder 9. In Gloria Evangelina Anzaldúa Papers, 1942–2004.

Friends from the Other Side / Amigos del otro lado. Children's Book Press, 1997.

"Ghost Trap." In *New Chicana/Chicano Writing*, vol. 1, edited by Charles M. Tatum. University of Arizona Press, 1992.

Gloria Evangelina Anzaldúa Papers, 1942–2004. Nettie Lee Benson Latin American Collection, University of Texas at Austin.

The Gloria Anzaldúa Reader. Edited by AnaLouise Keating. Duke University Press, 2009.

Interviews / Entrevistas. Edited by AnaLouise Keating. Routledge, 2000.

"La Prieta." In Moraga and Anzaldúa, *This Bridge Called My Back*.

"La serpiente que se come su cola: The Death Rites of Passage of a Chicana Lesbian" (1982–83), Box 78, Folders 10–11. In Gloria Evangelina Anzaldúa Papers, 1942–2004.

"Lifeline." In *Lesbian Love Stories*, edited by Irene Zavah. Crossing Press, 1991.

Light in the Dark / Luz en lo Oscuro: Rewriting Identity, Spirituality, Reality. Edited by AnaLouise Keating. Duke University Press, 2015.

Making Face, Making Soul / Haciendo Caras: Creative and Critical Perspectives by Women of Color. Edited by Gloria E. Anzaldúa. Aunt Lute Foundation, 1990.

"People Should Not Die in June in South Texas." In *Growing Up Latino: Memoirs and Stories, Reflections of Life in the United States,* edited by Ilan Stavans and Harold Augenbraum. Houghton Mifflin Harcourt, 1993.

"People Should Not Die in June in South Texas." In *My Story's On: Ordinary Women, Extraordinary Lives,* edited by Paula Ross. Common Differences Press, 1989.

"Puddles." In *New Chicana/Chicano Writing,* vol. 1, edited by Charles M. Tatum. University of Arizona Press, 1992.

Prietita and the Ghost Woman / Prietita y la Llorona. Children's Book Press, 2001.

"Reading LP." In Keating, *The Gloria Anzaldúa Reader.*

This Bridge Called My Back: Writings by Radical Women of Color. Edited by Cherríe Moraga and Gloria E. Anzaldúa. Kitchen Table / Women of Color Press, 1983.

this bridge we call home: radical vision for transformation. Edited by Gloria Anzaldúa and AnaLouise Keating. Routledge, 2002.

"Tlilli, Tlapalli / The Path of Red and Black Ink." In *Borderlands / La Frontera.*

"She Ate Horses." In *Lesbian Philosophies and Cultures,* edited by Jeffner Allen. SUNY Press, 1990.

"Swallowing Fireflies / Tragando Luciérnagas." In *Telling Moments: Autobiographical Lesbian Short Stories,* edited by Lynda Hall. University of Wisconsin Press, 2023.

"Within the Crossroads: Lesbian/Feminist/Spiritual Development; An Interview with Christine Weiland" (1983). In Keating, *Interviews / Entrevistas,* edited by AnaLouise Keating. Routledge, 2000.

"Writing Notas." Box 107, Folder 8. In Gloria Evangelina Anzaldúa Papers, 1942–2004.

Editors

Suzanne Bost is a professor of English at Loyola University Chicago. Her work focuses on the intersections of gender/queer studies and Latinx literature. She has published numerous essays on disability studies, posthumanism, decoloniality, and *The Gloria Anzaldúa Papers*, with a particular focus on ethics and futurity. In the past five years, her writing and teaching have become increasingly experimental, moving away from traditional literary arguments and toward more speculative, embodied, and cross-genre practices. Her most recent book is *Quiet Methodologies: Humility in the Humanities* (2025).

AnaLouise Keating is a professor of multicultural women's and gender studies at Texas Woman's University. Her work primarily focuses on transformation studies, spiritual activism, Gloria Evangelina Anzaldúa, and pedagogy. Keating is the author of a number of books, most recently *The Anzaldúan Theory Handbook*. She is the editor of Anzaldúa's *Interviews/Entrevistas*, *The Gloria Anzaldúa Reader*, and *Light in the Dark / Luz en lo oscuro: Rewriting Identity, Spirituality, Reality*; and coeditor, with Anzaldúa, of *this bridge we call home: radical visions for transformation*. Keating has also published articles on Latina authors, African American literature, queer studies, eighteenth- and nineteenth-century American writers, feminist theory, and pedagogy.

Kelli D. Zaytoun is professor of English language and literatures at Wright State University, where she has also served in numerous administrative roles including most recently the director of inter-disciplinary curricular development for the College of Liberal Arts. Her research and teaching focus on identity and narrative, con-temporary American literatures, particularly Arab American, Latinx, and Native American fiction, and the works of Gloria Anzaldúa, María Lugones, and Clarice Lispector. Her book *Shapeshifting Subjects: Gloria Anzaldúa's Naguala and Border Arte* is published in the University of Illinois Press series Transformations: Womanist, Feminist, and Indigenous Studies (2022).

About the Author

A key figure in the creation of academic border studies, **Gloria Evangelina Anzaldúa** (1942–2004) was an internationally acclaimed independent scholar, cultural theorist, creative writer, and social justice activist who has made lasting contributions to numerous academic fields, including Chican@ studies, composition studies, feminism and feminist theory, literary studies, queer theory, and women's studies. Anzaldúa's work spans multiple genres, including poetry, theoretical and philosophical essays, short stories, innovative autobiographical narratives, edited collections, and children's books. As the author of *Borderlands / La Frontera: The New Mestiza*, Anzaldúa has played a major role in shaping contemporary Chicanx and lesbian/queer identities. And as editor or coeditor of three multicultural anthologies, she has played an equally vital role in developing an inclusionary, multicultural feminist movement. Anzaldúa's writings have been included in over one hundred anthologies to date. Her published works include *This Bridge Called My Back: Writings by Radical Women of Color* (1981, coedited with Cherríe Moraga), a groundbreaking collection of essays and poems widely recognized by scholars in women's studies as the premiere multicultural feminist text; *Borderlands / La Frontera* (1987), a founding text of Chicano/a studies and border studies, as well as a classic of twentieth-century American literature; *Making Face, Making Soul / Haciendo Caras: Creative and Critical Perspectives by Feminists of Color* (1990), a multigenre collection used in many university classrooms; two bilingual children's books—*Friends from the Other Side / Amigos del otro lado* and *Prietita and the*

Ghost Woman / Prietita y la Llorona; *Interviews/Entrevistas* (2000), a memoir-like collection of interviews; *this bridge we call home: radical visions for transformation* (2002, coedited with AnaLouise Keating), a multigenre collection that examines the current status of feminist/womanist theorizing; *The Gloria Anzaldúa Reader* (2010), a multigenre collection of previously unpublished and published works; and additional stories and essays.

Anzaldúa and her works won numerous awards, including an award from the National Endowment of the Arts, the Before Columbus Foundation American Book Award, the Lamda Lesbian Small Book Press Award, the Susan Koppelman Award, the Smithsonian Notable Book Award, and the Américas Honor Award. *Borderlands / La Frontera* was selected as one of the 100 Best Books of the Century both by Hungry Mind Review and by Utne Reader. Anzaldúa was born in the Rio Grande Valley of South Texas in 1942, the eldest child of Urbano and Amalia Anzaldúa. She received her BA from Pan American University, her MA from University of Texas, Austin, and her PhD (awarded posthumously) from the University of California, Santa Cruz.